# WINGS

KARL FRIEDRICH

# WINGS

## A NOVEL OF WORLD WAR II FlyGirls

McBooks Press, Inc.
www.mcbooks.com
ITHACA, NEW YORK

Published by McBooks Press 2011
Copyright © 2011 by Karl Friedrich

Cover illustration and design by Panda Musgrove.
Author photo © 2010 Rhonda J. Friedrich

Library of Congress Cataloging-in-Publication Data

Friedrich, Karl, 1946-
 Wings : a novel of World War II flygirls / Karl Friedrich.
    p. cm.
 ISBN 978-1-59013-570-9 (alk. paper)
 1. Women air pilots--Fiction. 2. World War, 1939-1945--Aerial operations, American. 3. World War, 1939-1945--United States--Fiction. 4. Women Airforce Service Pilots (U.S.)--Fiction. I. Title.
 PS3606.R5555W56 2011
 813'.6--dc22
                        2010045066

Visit the McBooks Press website at www.mcbooks.com.

Printed in the United States of America
9 8 7 6 5 4 3 2 1

*This book is dedicated to every woman who
defies convention in order to live her dream.*

# PREFACE

As losses of men and aircraft skyrocketed in the early years of World War II, the shortage of trained pilots to handle flying duties back home became acute. The War Department, after months of badgering by a handful of visionaries of both sexes, finally agreed to launch an experimental program, under the control of the United States Army, to train women to carry out domestic flying chores for the military. The army was the natural choice because its flying program was the largest, a separate air force not yet having been created. The result was as much a testimonial to the women's ability to fly whatever was strapped to them, as it was an exhibition of ignorance by men who set out to prove them "silly, incompetent females."

More than 25,000 young women volunteered for training as Women Airforce Service Pilots (WASP). Of the 1,830 who were accepted, 1,074 graduated. Almost all went on to fly many types of aircraft, from the smallest and slowest trainers to giant bombers and hot fighters. Missions ranged from ferrying aircraft to dispersal points for shipment overseas, to towing targets for student gunners firing live ammunition. Flights occurred in all kinds of weather, sometimes in worn-out aircraft returned from combat, or in machines fresh from the factory and making their first hop. These missions were often as dangerous as combat, and in fact thirty-eight WASP died. By war's end, Women Airforce Service Pilots had flown sixty million miles in seventy-eight different types of aircraft.

This piece of fiction is based on their accounts.

# WINGS

# ONE

Sally Ketchum peered over the edge of the cockpit.

They were over Oklahoma by now. Or maybe it was still Texas down there. There was no way to tell, really . . . the pitifully dried-out browns of one were pretty much identical to the other. But the truth was that she didn't care where they were, exactly. And she was pretty sure that Tex didn't, either. Texas was behind them, or soon would be. Oklahoma was beneath them, or soon would be. And soon up ahead was sure to be a town that was near a field of adequate width and flatness and emptiness to set the Jenny down safely.

Once the wings and tail were staked and the big cloth sign hung beside the nearest road to announce their intentions, they'd make a fire to heat their beans and water for coffee, and break out what was left of the makings for sandwiches. Then they'd crawl beneath the Jenny's wide old cloth wings and into each other's arms and drift off to sleep beneath a blanket of a billion stars. Come sunrise, word would have spread like wildfire that an airplane had landed in so-and-so's field, its two occupants intending to sell rides to whomever was adequately rich in spirit and free with dollars for a once-in-a-lifetime, bird's-eye view of the world.

She leaned back. The hurricane force of the propeller and the blast of gases from the engine's exhaust instantly lessened, thanks to the little cocoon of relative protection provided by the wooden cockpit and the small windscreen that jutted from the fuselage a few inches forward of her head. Farther forward, just behind the howl of the engine and even more directly in the path of the sheen of engine oil that accompanied the howl, was an identical cockpit and within it, Tex. She could plainly see the top of his shoulders and neck, and the canvas flying helmet and goggles on his head that were like her own. She couldn't see his face, but she knew from experience that it would be even grittier than hers. Despite a hard and not-so-profitable day of giving rides in Texas, he had insisted that she take the more comfortable rear cockpit, the one from which the Jenny typically was flown. She'd had a twinge of guilt but still had jumped at the chance. Next to Tex, flying had become the most important thing in her life.

It had been six months since Tex introduced her to the good things that lay beyond the huge East Texas piney woods that circled her daddy's poor dirt farm. The farm and her daddy's drinking and ranting had been her suffocating hell for eighteen years. Then Tex had dropped out of the sky one morning on his way to nowhere in particular, and after they'd talked for a while like two people who'd known each other all their lives, she'd climbed aboard the Jenny and flown off with him. Just like that, she'd gone from breathing but being dead, to loving life as much as rock candy. Tex had even insisted she get her pilot's license so she could share equally in the flying from one county fair to the next and to the hick towns in between. He'd become the only person she'd ever loved, the only person she'd ever felt completely at ease with, the only one who'd ever understood her, and her only try at completely trusting someone other than herself. The experiment had paid off bigger than the electric light bulb.

She pushed her foot against the left rudder pedal and shoved the control stick in the same direction. A slight crosswind was causing the Jenny to drift off course. Or more probably, the rigging—the wires and pulleys that allowed the plane to climb and to turn and dive—needed adjusting again. Or maybe the old plane's guts were just exhausted from a quarter-century of impolite flying. This Jenny and a thousand more like it had been built more than twenty years earlier to train pilots for the First World War. Those not reduced to kindling in the hands of bad students or by bad luck had eventually been sold to everyone from former military pilots to farmer wanna-be pilots. The fact that this one still was in one piece was a near-miracle. But in Tex's hands, and increasingly in her own, the ancient relic performed like a ballerina, albeit one of advanced years and with more than a touch of arthritis.

The browns two thousand feet below were darkening. It would be nighttime soon. They would need to land while there was still enough light to see what they were doing.

Tex had reached the same decision. They could almost read each other's minds now, which was handy as noise from the engine and the distance between the cockpits made conversation impossible. He lifted his hand to his forehead as if shading his eyes and moved his head from side to side in an exaggerated movement, and then looked back to see if she understood.

She nodded quickly. She was already looking for a town, or at least a clump of civilization. Without instruments to guide them, they navigated by railroad tracks that inevitably lead to a town. Or when they could get them, they used automobile road maps. But this evening there were no steel rails, nor any maps. All that she could see in all directions were miles and miles of brown, broken occasionally by the glint of a solitary farmhouse. The unfurling of their sign would have to wait. They would be spending tonight alone, with nothing but the stars and maybe the distant howl of a coyote for company. She smiled greedily. She doubted that even the angels were in for such happiness.

She again moved the rudder and control stick. This time she used considerable force. The Jenny's engine was underpowered even on the rare days when it was running at its full potential. Huge amounts of stick and rudder were necessary for just a little change in direction. Finally she let the old plane lazily right itself. A flat spot of ground lay directly ahead. She began working the throttle toward her. The sound of the engine instantly dipped. Tex extended his thumb above his head, signaling his approval. Her grin deepened, and she didn't even notice her chapped lips.

The air around them was unnaturally calm, as if some invisible hand were protecting them from the ordinary turbulence that so often lingered during the blistering days of August.

She played the landing in her mind's eye: The big wire-spoke wheels brushing spots of burnt grass. The tires kissing the brown underneath, raising little trails of dust. The wheels, unfettered by any brakes, rolling roughly for a few moments and then coming to a stop.

Her feet and hands continuously adjusted the Jenny's path through the air. Her smile exploded. She was born for this, just as she was born to be with Tex. She had become more than herself. She and the Jenny and Tex and the world had become one.

Suddenly something fluttered in the gloom ahead. Two enormous black shapes rose from the ground, their wings flapping mightily in the listless air. As if intent on murder and then suicide, they hung in the very spot where the Jenny was pointed.

Her left hand slammed the throttle forward. Her right pulled back on the stick as much as she dared while her brain fought to sense the stall that would send them crashing like a brick into the ground. But just then Tex wrestled the controls from her. In a dangerously calculated move, he was turning the plane to the right and lowering the nose to gain airspeed.

She felt the plane teeter. She held her breath.

But it wasn't enough. One turkey buzzard hit the prop dead-on. The engine screamed and the old airframe started shaking itself to pieces as the propeller shattered. The second bird struck the upper wing on the right side. She sensed more than heard the ancient wood and fabric splinter and rip apart. Even Tex couldn't save them then.

The Jenny met the ground head-on. The hot engine drove backward into the fragile gas tank; the impact threw her clear of the fireball.

She lay on the ground and watched the flames consume the cockpits. And she screamed and screamed, as all that she loved vanished forever from the universe.

# TWO

Say, hon . . . have ya got your feet planted across this whole seat because you're afraid somethin's gonna skitter up your skirt? Or are you hoggin' more than your fair share of the room just to be ornery?"

Sally opened her eyes. At first she was confused over where she was; then she recognized the railroad car. She had boarded late in the afternoon and finally had fallen asleep. Now a slash of hard morning light streamed through the windows. Nicks and scrapes left by the passing of countless riders, invisible before, stood out on the seat back in front of her.

The seat padding did nothing to stop the jolts and jars of the wheels, and there really wasn't enough room to get comfortable, anyway. She worked herself into a sitting position, being careful of the crick in her neck.

The stranger staring down at her from the aisle was five-foot-eight, maybe even five-nine, and voluptuous. Not a wrinkle marred her tailored yellow suit or a speck of dirt her matching heels. Her thick black hair was so well combed, her lips so perfectly painted, that she might have stepped out of a magazine. Without waiting for an invitation, and with a grace that seemed impossible, she slid onto the seat and stuck out her hand. Her grin was an ear-to-ear thing, her voice a bit too powerful for the earliness of the hour.

"Dixie Ray Beaumont." All of the parts of her face moved when she spoke, as if each was vying to out-express the other. The result was an intoxicating brew of novelty and beauty.

"Sally Ketchum." She met the hand with her own.

"Happy to meet ya, honey."

Some flaw sensed only by Dixie's tongue set off a warning, and she reached into her purse to retrieve a lipstick and mirror. She banished the defect with a single stroke, then went on to check her hair with a pat and a shove.

Sally felt self-conscious. A fever blister was sprouting on her lip. She pressed her mouth together to conceal the spot. She started to check her hair but stopped. Compared to Dixie's, her own shag was too short and shapeless, her hands too rough, too cracked, too swollen from farm chores to be put on display, and she slipped them into the folds of her dress. The dress was the best one she owned, but it had been washed so many times that the sleeves were coming apart.

Dixie returned her tools to her purse and snapped the sides closed with a click and smiled. "Where you headed?"

"Sweetwater." Sally locked her arms against her sides to hide her arm pits.

"Sweetwater?" Dixie's expressions scampered. "Why . . . that's where I'm goin'! I'm gonna be a WASP. That's short for Women Airforce Service Pilots. What's your business there?"

Sally felt a rush of elation. "Me, too! That's why I'm going, too!"

A look of disbelief came over Dixie.

Sally felt her excitement vanish over meeting this fellow pilot, the first she'd ever known who was a woman. Not that she could blame Dixie. But for the letter of invitation in her pocket from the War Department, she wouldn't have believed that the army wanted her to fly their airplanes, either.

Tex had been dead for three years now. She'd had no place to go to but back to the farm and her daddy. His drinking had worsened, as had his prophesies about her eternal doom, delivered more frequently with the broadside of his belt; he'd never let her forget what she'd done with Tex, and he'd belittled her right up until he'd died. That had been two days ago. She'd gone into the kitchen and found him where he'd fallen down drunk and hit his head. Soon thereafter, she'd discovered the War Department's response to her while sorting through what little he'd left that didn't belong to the bank. He'd kept it hidden from her for a month, even though he knew she'd slaved for days over her letter to the army asking to join the WASP. He'd hated her for running off with Tex. But he'd hated her even more after seeing that the army wanted her, because he would be losing control of her for good.

Dixie was studying her. The nightmare that Sally had told herself wouldn't happen already had. WASP were sure to be rich and look like Dixie, something she had conveniently ignored in her fantasies about flying for the army. Only the rich could afford pilot training and all the costs that went with flying. Tex had liked to say that a rich man could learn real quick how the other half lived just by taking up aviation for a week. If she hadn't met him, she never would have gotten close to an airplane, much less gotten her pilot's license. Learning to fly had been a fluke, just like her invitation from the army. Dixie was what the WASP were looking for. Dixie had the looks that sold newspapers.

Dixie cleared her throat, as if she were an adult about to correct a child for doing something embarrassing in public. "You do know, don't you, honey, that you have to already be a pilot for 'em to take you? You can't just show up. You have to be invited, which means you have to already have your license."

"I have my license!" Sally did her best to control her voice.

"I mean your pilot's license," Dixie insisted. "You have to already be a qualified, licensed pilot before you can get into the WASP. It's not like bein' a man. They won't go to the bother of trainin' you unless you already know how to fly and have all the paperwork to prove it." Dixie's eyes were the color of the sky on a spring morning when the clouds don't show up, the kind of eyes that look through lead; and just then they were looking through Sally and over her. She might as well have been a plate glass window, for all the secrets she was hiding from Dixie.

Dixie's voice dropped a notch. "How much air time do ya have, honey?" Sally sensed that Dixie was trying hard to be kindly.

Her humiliation was complete. She already looked like a rag-a-muffin, and now Dixie was about to know that she was little more than a student pilot. The War Department had made a cruel mistake; certainly she had no right trying out for the WASP. She might as well get off the train at the next station.

"Two or three hundred hours," she said softly.

Dixie's eyes narrowed. "I don't mean how long it feels like you've been ridin' on this-here train! What I meant was, how many flyin' hours do you have, with you bein' the pilot of the airplane?"

A knot of anger gripped Sally. She was allowing herself to become a victim. That was something she'd promised herself she would never be again. Her father had been a victim. She'd been a victim, too, until she met Tex. Pretty much everyone she'd known growing up had been a victim, if not of ignorance then of isolation and poverty. Men killed themselves plowing and picking cotton for what amounted to a bare living. Women grew old early by working the house and often the fields, too—all the while punching out child after child—until those women became worn as trampled hay. Tex had shown her that she could rise above her beginnings, but first she had to learn not to be swayed by those around her into remaining like them. She had to believe in herself, too. And she had to be tough. That part had come easily, thanks to her daddy. He'd taught her strength and tenacity. His suffocating domination and narrow-mindedness would otherwise have crushed her years ago.

She looked Dixie squarely in the eye. "I told you . . . I have two or three hundred hours."

The last trace of fun tightened out of Dixie's face. "I hope you'll forgive me, hon, but you wouldn't be my first pick from a crowd of strangers to be a pilot."

She didn't care if Dixie had a thousand hours of flying time, and money to burn. She wasn't going to let anyone call her a liar. "And you wouldn't be my first, nor for that matter my last, pick as someone to go barnstorming with," she snarled. "I doubt you'd last one night in a cornfield with no plumbing and a breakfast of cold beans, while you hoped and prayed for enough paying passengers before sundown to eat as well again the next morning."

All the parts of Dixie's face snapped to a dead stop. "You're a barnstormer? You made money flyin'? Is that what you're sayin'?" Her eyes bulged.

"Texas!" Sally said. "Oklahoma! Arkansas! For six months, for about three hundred hours. Yes, that's what I'm saying. I don't know how many hours exactly because we were too busy flying to keep count." Her nose always ran when she lost her temper. She reached into the pocket of her dress for a handkerchief but came up empty.

An expensive piece of embroidered cloth appeared in Dixie's hand.

Sally took the handkerchief and blew her nose, then carefully refolded the cloth.

Dixie stuffed the piece back into her bag without so much as a glance. "Are you married, honey?"

Sally turned away to the window. She wanted to be alone.

"Gum?" In the reflection of the glass, Dixie was holding out two small balls of the stuff, a rare commodity for a civilian in wartime rationing. Sally wondered where she'd gotten it.

She shook her head.

Dixie nudged, "The gum or being married?"

"No, to both." She stared out the window.

Dixie grunted and pressed one of the things into her mouth and began to chew with great, luxurious bites that brought a look of sugary satisfaction to her face. "Who's the other part of the 'we'?"

"My boyfriend." The scenery passed without Sally seeing it.

"Where's he at?"

Sally wondered if Dixie had any secrets of her own, or if she relied entirely on others for her supply. "He's dead."

"From what?"

"A crash."

"Were you flyin' with him?"

"Yes."

"Then how come you're not dead?"

"Luck," Sally answered gruffly.

Dixie persisted. "Why?"

"Why, what?"

"Why'd you crash?"

"Two turkey buzzards. We hit 'em while we were landing."

"What kind of plane?"

Her exhaustion from her daddy's funeral, her excitement and surprise over the letter, and now the resurrection of fears and self-doubts . . . they all came together in an explosion. "A Jenny! It was a Jenny! Maybe you'd like to know what the fire felt like? Or what he looked like burnt up? You wanna hear about my boots smoking while I was trying to pull 'em off?" Every head in the car had turned around. She didn't care.

Dixie leaned close, making it impossible to ignore her. "Hon, I'm sorry about your boyfriend, and I'm sorry for you. But I'm gonna be real honest: I've seen spider webs thicker than that dress you're wearin'; the barnstormin' business must be mighty poor. On the other hand, you do know a thing or two about airplanes—I'll give you that—so maybe you are the real McCoy. If you are, I apologize." She hesitated before continuing. "You gotta admit, hon, you do look a whole lot more like somethin' that just crawled off a farm than out of a cockpit."

"That's a rotten thing to say," Sally gasped, ". . . just because you're rich."

"Rich?" Dixie's face did an amused jitterbug. She pointed to her feet. "See those shoes? Those toes walked many a mile in mud before they ever walked in fancy high heels, and I don't mean just when I was little; not that I was ever hungry, but only because my daddy could sell ice to Eskimos. My daddy was the best damn salesman in Texas. He was a go-getter, and he brought me up to be a go-getter, too. You got it all wrong, honey. I'm not rich. In fact, I stay broke most of the time ever since I started flyin'. But like I always say, what's the good of money if you don't spend it?"

Sally bit her lip. Tex had been fond of saying something similar. Each of their rare quarrels had been over money. She had wanted to hoard every penny, while he had argued that he could always make another dollar to replace the one that he intended to spend. That philosophy was common among barnstormers, who usually stayed one engine overhaul away from bankruptcy. The hardness of the life eventually ruined all but the toughest and most dedicated, which was why, she'd assumed, she had never met any other woman flyers. But Dixie wouldn't have to be rich to fly. She was beautiful, charming, and confident. In a world of men, those qualities were even better than money.

She pushed her jealously of Dixie aside. She was what she was: not homely, but not pretty. She was too thin by her own judgment, her breasts a little too small and her hips a little too narrow, and she was only of average height. But she was clean and honest, and she'd been told more than once that her skin and her coloring were good. Of course, that had been by farm boys who had more experience judging corn than women. But if life had taught her anything, it was to take what you get when you get it.

She leaned her head against the window, but the track was laid out straight as an arrow and she was unable to see any sign of a town. What she could see was a vast dry emptiness that stretched to the horizon—the only signs of life, clumps of scrawny grass and scrawny trees. She'd once heard an old cowboy say about West Texas, "If thar is anythang of a gentle nature livin' out thar, it's 'cause it's got itself locked up inta protective custody." She had to agree.

Growing restless with the silence, Dixie prodded, "So, you got three hundred hours? I've got thirty-six."

Sally whipped around. "You have thirty-six hundred flight hours?"

Dixie snickered. "No! Thirty-six!" She retrieved two pieces of paper from her handbag. Sally immediately recognized one like her own. It had come from Jacqueline Cochran, director of the Women Airforce Service Pilots, and invited Dixie to train at a flying school in Sweetwater for a period of six months to qualify as a WASP ferry pilot to deliver airplanes to bases all over the United States. The director hadn't pulled any punches. Trainees had to pay their own travel expenses to Sweetwater and, presumably, to leave should they wash out. Sally remembered the initial fear as she realized she'd have to come up with more money than she'd seen since her barnstorming days with Tex. It'd taken every penny she could find—she'd had to sell everything she could get her hands on—to buy the one-way ticket. Now she didn't even have enough left for a cup of coffee.

Dixie was pointing to the other sheet. "Lookee right there. What does that say?"

Sally read, "Minimum flying hours required for WASP training: thirty-five."

Dixie nodded. "Until you came along, I never heard of any woman havin' three hundred hours, unless she was Amelia Earhart or that gal who runs the WASP, Jackie Cochran. And I sure never heard of any woman barnstormin'."

Sally snatched the sheet from Dixie's fingers. Typed boldly across the top were the words, "An Overview Of Facts For Personnel Considering Entering WASP Training." Her mouth turned dry. By mid-page, her tongue had become cotton.

"... train in military aircraft ... the same number of training hours as male pilots ... learn navigation and instrument flying ... station at a military airfield following graduation ... fly bombers and/or pursuit aircraft to wherever ordered within the contiguous United States ... base pay of one hundred and fifty dollars per month during training ... "

Dixie grabbed the papers back. "Didn't you get one like this?" She stuffed the papers protectively into her purse.

Sally shook her head. "I guess they forgot to put it in the envelope."

"And you just up and quit whatever you were doin' to climb aboard this train, without knowin' anything about the job or how much it paid?" The insinuation was that at least one of Sally's birth parents must have been a half-wit.

But she didn't care what Dixie thought. She had almost ten times more flying experience than this beautiful woman. The government must be desperate if it was accepting such inexperienced pilots for training. Suddenly all of her conclusions about not being good enough to become a WASP seemed crazy, the idea of getting off the train absurd. For the first time since she lost Tex, she had a real chance to be somewhere other than on the bottom looking up. Maybe she even could be on top looking down. With an opportunity like this, she didn't care how she was dressed or how unattractive she looked. She'd show up in Sweetwater covered in tar and wearing a barrel, if she had to. The military was bound to give them uniforms, and then everyone would look alike. Dixie could be the most beautiful woman in the world, but it wouldn't make any difference. The playing field would be leveled. The army would see to that.

She did some quick mental arithmetic. One hundred and fifty dollars a month was a king's ransom. But more important than the money was what she would learn: mastery of the art of real instrument flying, which used sophisticated instruments like a radio. Once she knew that, she truly could fly anywhere, day or night, in virtually any kind of weather, just like the airline pilots. Not that she expected to become an airline pilot—that world belonged to men—but she was sure that with the proper training she could somehow realize her dream of staying in aviation once the war was over.

Clearly not satisfied with this new lag in the conversation, Dixie declared, "I'm from Dallas, myself. Where you from?"

The openness of West Texas, so different from the thick forest that covered East Texas, pulled at Sally from the window. She and Tex had flown over this land, in fact followed this same railroad track. She answered absently, "A farm in East Texas."

Dixie took this as encouragement. "I was over in New Orleans enjoyin' a little workin' vacation when I got my letter," she said. "My landlady was supposed to send me my mail, but I guess she didn't think it was important or she forgot about it until the last minute. Anyway, I let out a whoop when I opened that envelope that I bet they heard all the way to Atlanta. Then I nearly died when I saw I hadta get to Sweetwater by today if I was gonna join up. Let me tell you, I did some serious packin'. That cabdriver damn near ran over two little old ladies and a blind man's dog to get me to the station on time. And I still almost didn't make it. If that letter had come an hour later, you and I wouldn't be havin' this conversation, and right now I'd be gettin' ready to squeeze my butt into a Lady Swan girdle for Pierre Valois."

Sally's surprise that a total stranger would share such an intimate detail must have shown, for Dixie laughed. The sound was more than a little naughty. "I'm a model, honey. It's my job to walk around in my underwear. Pierre's a famous photographer. He's in all the magazines. He invited me over to vacation, and when we wasn't busy doin' other things, we did a little work." She grinned slyly.

"What do you know about the WASP?" Sally asked abruptly. She didn't want to hear any more about Pierre Valois, nor about Dixie's personal life.

Dixie eyed her coolly. "Just what I read in the papers and what this gal I met who'd been a WASP told me." But her annoyance quickly disappeared, and she warmed to her new subject.

"It was Jackie Cochran that sold the army on startin' the WASP. She's that gal that won all those air races. The army went along with the idea because it wanted to free up more men for combat by usin' women to fly planes to wherever the army needs 'em. Except for overseas . . . men do the ferryin' if a plane's gotta go overseas.

"This gal I knew—her name was Betty Lane Striplin'—said the army flew her butt off, and not just in the new stuff, either. She flew a lot of old worn-out junk that'd been in combat and was gonna be melted down. Her job was to get it to the scrap yard. And she flew target tugs. She said that was the worst. They'd make her fly back and forth over the same spot of ground down in Florida for six or seven hours at a stretch, while a bunch of trainees practiced firin' live ammo up at this target she was pullin' behind her on a cable. She said she kept waitin' for a round to go through a gas tank and blow her up, but I guess it never did because she was about as alive as you can get when I knew her. By the way, the army doesn't bother puttin' any kind of female relief tube in its planes. I guess they expect you to either pee in your pants or stand up in the seat and hang your butt over the side of the cockpit."

Despite Dixie's frankness, Sally found herself hanging on her every word.

Dixie was fully wound up now, and talking a-mile-a-minute about Betty Lane Stripling. "She never knew where she'd be goin' to next, and they only paid her half of what men get for doin' the same kind of flyin', and some of the men treated her like dirt. But she got to fly just about everything the army and the navy has and she had a ball doing it, in spite of a few men who tried to keep her out of the cockpit. She even got to bump a senator off a train once because she had to get somewhere in a hurry to pick up a plane."

"Oh, come on!" Sally was sure now that Dixie was making this up.

A look of mortal hurt crossed Dixie's face, and she held up her hand. "I swear! That's what she said! The army needs planes so badly that a WASP can bump anybody but the president off any plane, train, ship or bus, so long as she has orders to get somewhere in a hurry."

"The day a politician jumps off a train because I tell him to is the day I hope somebody's got a camera handy," Sally said dryly, "'cause that's the day cows are gonna fly."

Dixie wasn't going to be stopped a second time from finishing a story, and she continued quickly: "I don't know anything about any flyin' cows. All I know is what this gal, Betty Lane Striplin', told me. After a while, she said she got so tired of never havin' a day off and all the rest of it, she just quit. She'd met an officer and they got married and she settled down to have babies. That's when I knew her. This department store I was modelin' for sent me out with all these celebrities to help sell war bonds, and her husband was there. He'd shot down a bunch of German planes. She was pregnant as a blimp, and her feet was swoll up like pontoons. But she was holdin' up to it and havin' a swell time."

"Soldiers can't quit anytime they feel like it," Sally said. "They'd be shot!"

Dixie studied her closely, as if she were seeing Sally for the first time. Her face tightened with concern. "You really are jumpin' in with both feet without lookin' first to see what you're landin' in, aren't you? Honey, the WASP aren't soldiers. They're civilian workers. They can quit anytime they want. And accordin' to that gal, they do. The army has a terrible time keepin' WASP."

Sally didn't care whether the WASP were civilians or soldiers. Nor was she really concerned about the condition of the planes they flew. WASP got advanced training and were paid to fly; that put being a WASP head and shoulders above anything she'd done so far except barnstorm with Tex. "Not me!" she said. "I won't quit! Any kind of flying beats anything else, any day of the week."

Dixie assumed a knowing look. "I could have sworn a minute ago that you were mighty close to quittin'."

How could Dixie have read her mind? "I was not!"

Dixie gave her a long look. "OK. Just so long as your mind's made up one way or the other. 'Cause you're gonna look mighty strange jumpin' off and on this train while it's goin' down the track."

Sally stifled a smile. "My mind's made up. I'm going to Sweetwater."

"Well, so long as you're sure." Dixie blew a bubble. The thing grew and grew until it seemed ready to burst all over her face. But at the last minute she successfully sucked it back into her mouth.

"If I say I'm sure, then I'm sure," Sally said stiffly.

Another bubble emerged from Dixie's mouth, this one even grander and more dangerous; she had to tilt her head to keep the thing away from her hair. She deflated it with an expert punch of her tongue. "OK. That's fine by me."

The silence grew. Finally Dixie added, "I knew the truth about you the minute I saw you. It's plain as a whump upside the head with a baseball bat."

"What is?" Sally snapped.

Dixie looked self-satisfied. "That you're an even worse liar than you are a dresser, which is why I know you've got every bit of three hundred hours. You've probably got a lot more, but you're so scared of takin' somethin' that doesn't belong to you that you won't claim what's rightfully yours."

"You've got a lot of nerve!"

Dixie wiggled her rump unconcernedly. The effect was similar to a large bird settling onto a nest. She made a loud smacking sound with her gum. "Your momma or your daddy used to wallop you for fibbin', didn't they? And ever since then you've been livin' like you're still six years old and they're hidin' around the corner listenin' to everything you say— which is the reason you're in the predicament you're in."

"What predicament?"

"Bein' broke and down on your luck and lonely as a soul in a grave," Dixie answered easily.

"That's none of your business!"

Dixie patted her hair. "You asked me. I was just answerin'. My guess is that you were brought up livin' by a bunch of rules instead of common sense, which don't do you a bit of good unless everybody is playin' by the same rules, and in my experience, they never do. The world's full of opportunities, honey. You ought'a take a look around to see what's where and how to put it to work for you. You gotta learn to be an Indian fighter, hon. Otherwise, you're gonna get scalped."

Trying to keep her voice low so the other passengers wouldn't hear, Sally hissed, "My father went crazy on religion; he was a drunk, too; he died this week; I found him in the kitchen where he fell and hit his head. My mother died when I was born. I went to a poor country school. I've had one boyfriend and if he'd lived, I'd be his wife; but he didn't, and I'm not gonna grow old and die on a dirt farm like everybody I grew up with; I'm going to make something of myself, with or without the army's help, and nothing is going to stop me. Now you know everything about me that's worth knowing. So you can stop your prying and your prodding and you can put away your crystal ball. I want to be left alone!"

Dixie rested her head against the seat and closed her eyes. A knowing smile tugged at her lips. She muttered, "Okee-dokee."

Sally returned to the window. Talking about herself had brought back the nightmares. Her guilt: if her mother hadn't died giving her life, maybe her daddy wouldn't have gone hog-wild. And her fear: she was to blame somehow for her daddy's failures and her mother's death. Her parents had met when he'd joined the army and gone back east during the First World War. She knew her momma's first name had been Jane and that her maiden name was Mason. Almost everything else about her was a mystery. She'd never even seen her picture.

She remembered as a little girl when her daddy had decided that the Devil lived in pictures, and in a rage had gone around the house gathering up and burning what few photos they owned. The memory was especially bitter now that she was gone from the farm, for she'd always hoped to stumble across something of her mother's. She'd tried a thousand times to imagine her face and hands, and her smell as she snuggled deep into her arms. But each question about her mother had been met with her daddy's curt rebuff. She'd accepted that when she was little. But as she grew older, she came to guess the truth. He'd left for overseas a weeks-old husband and come back to the farm a soon-to-be father. That explained his anger. He'd been ill-suited for both, and he'd blamed her for each.

Those who had known him had confided that he'd been a good man when he was young. But the war had given him the Thirst. That's when the weakness in his character had grown. He took up religion when her mother died, but not just to trot out on Sundays or to hold close for personal comfort; he'd wrapped himself in the Word. He'd slathered himself in it. And he'd done everything he could to give Sally a full dose, too. Eventually every other word out of his mouth became "God" or "Jesus" or "sinner" or "hell " or "fire" or "brimstone," more often than not strung together with a prophesy of doom more terrible than the human mind could possibly contemplate. He hadn't been an educated man, but he'd learned to scare her to death with his tongue just as well as any preacher. Still, she'd tried to love him, and so desperately tried to get him to love her back. But he'd only gotten worse and worse, and finally she'd grown ashamed of him.

She remembered her constant fear when she was little. She waited for the Devil to jump out at her, or for the ground to rip open and belch sulfur and hellfire in the final, evil moments of life on Earth, as her daddy predicted. She spent many an afternoon watching the sky for angel sign. She made up her mind that she was going to hitch a ride to heaven before the rickety old house and barn, and what there was of the rest of the farm, went straight down to hell. She worked her little fingers to the bone to make sure her spot between their comforting feathers was reserved. But no matter how hard she tried, he always found something to condemn her for. And one day when she was a young teenager, she realized that every day of her life in East Texas had pretty much been like the day before: no Devil sightings, no angel sign, just monotony and hard work and poverty and superstition. Everything changed for her on that day. She and her daddy parted paths. She started to think for herself. Books became her constant companion in a world that was lonely and stifling but for the occasional teacher who took an interest in her.

When she was eighteen, she reached the opinion that religion gave the clever and the unscrupulous power over the desperate and the naïve; and in a moment of anger and great misjudgment, she had expressed that belief to her daddy. He'd slapped her so hard she nearly went unconscious. Then he'd fallen into a praying frenzy that had lasted the rest of the night.

Tex appeared out of nowhere the next morning. And finally, her life had begun.

The rest of the train was waking up. The sounds brought her back to the present. Almost every seat was occupied by a soldier sporting a night's stubble and a wrinkled uniform, on his way, she suspected, to fight in the Pacific. The nation was at war and the entire population seemed to be on the move. Traveling, never easy, had become nearly impossible for anyone not in the military.

A deeply Southern male voice boomed suddenly, "Dixie! We been lookin' all over this train for you!"

A second voice added, "Yeah! For you and for our money!"

The two soldiers hovered overhead. Neither could have been older than nineteen. The one grinning boyishly was taller and slimmer and blond, and by far the handsomer of the two. The other one, who looked ready to fight the whole car, was short and squat, with the build of a boxer and the face of a not-very-good one. Both wore haircuts that were little more than fuzz, suggesting that they were fresh from boot camp.

Dixie reached for their hands as if they were long-lost family. "Bobby Ray! Milton! I was prayin' I'd run into you boys again!" Something told Sally she wasn't nearly as happy to see them as she let on.

"Sally, honey, I want you to meet two boys I met right here on this train last night," Dixie said. "This is Bobby Ray and this is Milton. Bobby Ray's the friendly one who's just cute as he can be. And Milton's the one who looks like he's gonna eat us both alive."

Milton grimly jerked his hand away, but Bobby Ray showed no sign of letting go, and Dixie had to almost pry herself away from him.

"Boys, this is Sally Ketchum. She's on her way to Sweetwater with me to join up with the WASP."

Sally nodded.

Milton was too busy glaring at Dixie to nod back. But Bobby Ray nodded quickly and then got back to admiring Dixie. Sally thought he looked exactly like what he almost certainly was, a sweet but simple farm boy who was making a fool of himself over the most beautiful woman he'd probably ever seen.

"What you boys been up to since I saw you last?" Dixie dipped into her handbag for her compact. When she pursed her lips at her reflection, Bobby Ray turned so red Sally thought steam would come out his ears.

"Lookin' for our money by way of lookin' for you!" Milton blurted. His accent was thicker than Bobby Ray's, his neck and arms and upper body all muscle, probably from growing up on a farm in Alabama or maybe Mississippi, Sally decided. When he said the word "money," his mouth tightened, and his eyes got cold and hard. She knew she wouldn't want to get into an argument with him. She was sure the outcome would be settled with his fists.

Bobby Ray shifted uncomfortably. Clearly, he would have forgiven and forgotten the theft of his firstborn, so long as the thief was Dixie. "Now don't be that way, Milton," he said. "We been through this last night, and we already agreed that Dixie won that money fair and square. Why don't you go on back to the chow car? I'll catch up to you just as soon as I finish talking with Dixie."

Milton brushed him away. "You say. I say those cards was marked, and she's a thief!" He motioned at Dixie. "I had me ten dollars when I climbed aboard this-here train in Tuscaloosa three days ago. But as of right now, I ain't got the price of a spit! I'm warnin' you: I ain't gettin' off this train without that money. And you ain't gettin' off *with* it."

Dixie stood up. She towered over Milton and very nearly over Bobby Ray. If she were scared, she didn't show it. She said sweetly, "Milton honey, Bobby Ray's right: we settled this last night. And what was right then's still right this mornin'. Neither of you boys has any luck with cards. I already told you that. If you're in financial difficulty this mornin', it's your all-encompassin' bad luck that's to blame, not me."

Milton's eyes narrowed. "You got big city ways. And you got big city talk. But a thief's a thief, no matter if she wears fine dresses or calico."

"Now don't you go talkin' to Dixie that way, Milton," Bobby Ray said.

"She got all your money, too, Bobby Ray! Or have you forgot already, now that she's practically rubbin' off your sleeve?"

Sally saw that Dixie's breasts were nearly touching Bobby Ray's arm. But by some miracle of premonition, every time he leaned toward her, she leaned away an instant sooner, so the space between them remained unchanged.

Bobby Ray turned violently red. Whatever amount of money he'd lost to Dixie obviously wasn't as painful as being humiliated in front of her.

The commotion was attracting attention. Soldiers were getting up to see what was going on. Others craned their necks.

Dixie's voice rose to a commanding level. "Now wait a minute, boys. There's an easy way of settlin' this. Milton, Bobby Ray . . . here's what I'm gonna do." She reached into her purse. "I'm gonna prove to you fair and square that you're so lackin' in natural luck that you couldn't pick a winner if your momma and your daddy was Gypsies and the family crystal ball was the genuine article." She opened her hand, revealing a quarter. "I'm gonna flip this quarter two times. If tails comes up even once, I'm gonna give you back every cent of your money. And if it don't, you're gonna have to promise me you'll never gamble again for the rest of your natural lives and that we'll part company friends. Is that fair?"

"Hell, no, it ain't!" Milton exploded. "That's a trick quarter!"

Bobby Ray stared at the quarter. His face clearly showed he wanted with all his soul for Dixie's quarter to be just like all the other quarters in the world.

Sorrow pulled at the corners of Dixie's mouth. "Milton, honey, I hate to say this, but you got a mean streak in you wide as Texas." She dipped the hand with the quarter back into her purse and closed the massive yellow satchel with a snap. "But because I'm one to forgive and to forget, and because I sympathize with your financial difficulties, I'm not gonna get angry at you and I'm still gonna let you take me up on my offer—and we'll use your quarter. Now what do you think about that?"

Milton's face said he clearly was unclear what to think. Bobby Ray's face clearly showed he thought Dixie was an honest woman and he was sick in love with her.

The crowd pushed forward, vying for a better view. Sally felt her throat tighten. She hated crowds. She detested the closed-in feeling, and her inability to get away if she had to. She slid lower in her seat, and wished she were somewhere else.

Milton demanded, "Why tails? Why's it so important that we get tails and you get heads?"

A look of near-fatal pain crossed Dixie's face. "Milton . . . I swear, you really are somethin' else. If, by a miracle, come judgment day you do somehow get invited inside the Pearly Gates, I expect before takin' a single step into eternal bliss, you're gonna wanna know the price of beer. Which is another way of sayin' you wouldn't know a good thing if it up and bit you in the butt."

The crowd, grown now to the entire car, roared. Milton glared at them.

"Heads is my lucky side of the coin, Milton," Dixie said. "I can't lose if I'm callin' heads."

The crowd pressed closer. Sally judged the distance to each end of the car. She was about in the middle—and trapped. The palms of her hands felt sticky-hot. She couldn't lie to herself. She was worried.

"And we'll use my quarter?" Milton demanded. "And if we win, we'll get all our money back?"

"Sure, honey." Dixie smiled at him.

Milton nodded.

The men cheered. So many faces had crowded around now that Sally no longer could see either end of the car.

Dixie held out her hand. "Well, where's your quarter?"

Milton fumbled in his pockets, but he couldn't come up with that kind of cash, and he turned to Bobby Ray, who also proved destitute.

A quarter appeared from the audience.

Milton grabbed for the silver. "I'll do the flippin'!" But he was an instant too late.

"Be my guest, Milton." Dixie held out her hand, a shiny quarter waiting in her palm.

He eyed the quarter suspiciously but accepted the piece and, with no fanfare, flipped it into the air. The tension in the crowd skyrocketed. Sally felt a growing sense of dread as she watched the piece tumble end-over-end in a near-vertical rise before coming to a slamming stop between the back of Milton's hand and his palm.

All eyes fixed on the spot.

"Heads," Dixie announced with an umpire's finality.

A hundred throats roared. Even Bobby Ray looked happy, though he had just lost half his chance to get his money back.

Milton eyed the quarter as if all his prior eying had only been a warm-up.

"What are you waiting for? Toss it!" someone yelled.

"Maybe he's waiting for it to grow another tail!" someone else hollered.

"Hey, Milton honey, everybody would like to get back to gettin' ready to go to war," Dixie said. "So if you don't mind, stop lookin' at that poor defenseless quarter like you're gonna snap its head off and give it a toss so the rest of us can get on with winnin' what's left of the war."

Sally gritted her teeth. If only Dixie had never opened her mouth. If only she'd minded her own business, instead of robbing who-knew-how-much of the train of every penny she could get her hands on, no one would be minding them now—and an entire car of young soldiers wouldn't be on meat hooks and excited out of their minds to do who knew what! She wished that she'd never met Dixie!

Milton gave Dixie a look of pure malevolence. But he tossed the quarter skyward with a quick jerk of his hand.

"Heads again!" Dixie bellowed and snatched the piece away. "Milton . . . Bobby Ray honey, it's been fun knowin' ya. You-all see you don't get hurt overseas. And whatever you do, don't gamble. It don't pay off for ya." She turned to sit down and paused to plant a quick kiss on Bobby Ray's cheek and to give Milton's shoulder a squeeze.

"Hey!" Milton demanded. "I wanna see that quarter!"

She held the piece out to him.

He eyed it closely. "This ain't the same quarter, is it? You switched 'em, didn't you?"

"Now hold it, Milton." Dixie's voice grew icy, and she straightened to her full height.

He reached for her. "You lemme see your hands. What you hidin' in yor hands?"

"Milton, stop!" She tried to back up, but the crowd was in the way.

In the ensuing shuffle, a soldier's elbow thunked Sally in the head. She started to get up but changed her mind. The seats offered at least some protection, and she had a rising fear she would need it. She'd never seen a bunch so dangerous, so spoiling for a fight.

She and Tex had been in plenty of crowds. But those had been men and women and children enthralled by flight. This bunch was different. This crowd was tightly packed. And it was full of wild eyes, and faces blood-red and boiling with need for something to happen. She examined the window. If things got really rough, she probably could get through it. But the train was going full tilt. She was sure to get sucked under the wheels, or at the very least, break every bone in her body when she hit the roadbed.

Her fear became anger. She'd wanted to ride to Sweetwater to join the WASP. But Dixie had popped up like a bad dream and insulted her and read everything about her as if she were just a bunch of tea leaves. And now, thanks to Dixie, there was a very real and growing possibility she was going to get stomped like an old turnip!

"Show me them hands." Milton pulled at Dixie's fingers.

"Milton!"

Charged by the urgency in her voice, the crowd somehow surged forward.

Suddenly Dixie screamed. The effect was like throwing gasoline on fire, and in an instant, the crowd turned into a mob.

A fist, big as a plate and toughened by the best training the United States Army could provide, crashed into Milton's jaw. He flinched, but his grip on Dixie's hands held fast. Then a second fist, and a third and a fourth, found their mark. Suddenly the whole car seemed to be swinging. Torn between releasing Dixie's hands and defending himself, Milton chose to cling to whatever chance he had of regaining his money, even as he was being driven to the floor.

Dixie let out another scream.

Sally spotted a hand. It had snaked through the bedlam and found Dixie's rump. The hand clamped down hard, causing Dixie to yell again—only this time, it was a full-blown bellow.

Sally jumped to her feet and onto the soldier's back, surprising herself almost as much as him, and they both toppled to the floor. Suddenly she found herself trapped by a swirl of feet and falling bodies. The toe of a heavy combat boot brushed her forehead. Another barely missed her eye.

She raised her arms to protect herself. But boots were coming at her from all directions. It was all she could do to avoid being trampled.

After what seemed like forever, she heard an enraged voice bellow, "Attention!"

Those who could do so stood up. Others, fallen across the floor and the seats and each other, complied as best as their individual situations allowed.

"What's going on here?" The young lieutenant who had pushed his way into the car was boiling mad, the two MPs with him obviously poised to perform whatever mayhem he desired.

Milton scrambled to his feet. His left eye was swollen and his nose looked broken, but only the threat of the lieutenant's glare caused him to finally free Dixie's hand.

Sally pulled herself from beneath a soldier whose eyes had rolled back in his head. He looked no more than sixteen. After satisfying herself that he was breathing, she climbed to her feet.

"Well?" The lieutenant was tall and thin, and his ears stuck out like buckets. He reminded her of a boy she'd known from church who'd gone off to the Pacific to proselytize and had so annoyed the locals that they'd eaten him.

Dixie took her time rearranging her dress and the items underneath before answering. "We were havin' a discussion and it kinda got out of hand."

"A discussion?" The lieutenant glared. "How did you women get aboard this car? You know better, I'm sure; I imagine you've been arrested before." He slapped his hand against his leg in a subtle act of punishment. "Well, I can assure you it won't go lightly for you this time. Perhaps six months in a cell in one of these West Texas jails will convince you to find another line of work."

"Jail?" Dixie dropped all pretense of preening. "What for?"

"Prostitution!" The word cracked like a rifle shot.

Sally stared at him in disbelief.

"The hell you say!" Dixie's chin thrust forward.

"You will not curse! Do you hear me? You will not curse!" His face turned a redder shade of red.

"Sergeant!" The lieutenant nearly screamed the order.

One of the MPs stepped forward. "Yes, sir."

"Place these women under arrest. When we reach Sweetwater, turn them over to the sheriff."

"Now you hold it right there, Lieutenant," Dixie said. "And you, too, cowboy." She stuck a finger into the surprised MPs chest, causing him to stop and back up. "Nobody's arrestin' nobody! We have as much right to be in this car as any of these boys." She indicated the wide-eyed soldiers who were watching the unlikely drama unfold. She dug into her purse and shoved the papers from the War Department into the lieutenant's face. "I'd think long and hard about what I was doin' before I started doin' any arrestin'. 'Cause you're about to get yourself into a heap of hot water for keepin' two pilots from reportin' to the army for duty."

"Pilots?" He snorted. "Are you suggesting you're flyers . . . that you're going to fly for the army?" The buckets on the sides of his head wiggled menacingly. "I would have thought you could concoct a better story than that. You must take me for a fool."

Dixie looked like she was deciding which side of her mouth to spit him out of. "The only place I'd take you is out behind the barn, Lieutenant. And you can bet I'd have my leather strap with me when I did."

They glared at each other until the lure of the papers became too strong, and he snatched them from her hand. His expression quickly changed to doubt.

"I never heard of the WASP." He looked at her.

"Well, that's OK, Lieutenant, 'cause I think all of us are pretty sure Eisenhower's never heard of you." She snatched back her documents. "But you might make it a point to remember the name in the future, just so you don't make the same bone-headed mistake twice."

"I am an officer!" he bellowed. "You will not speak impertinently to me!" His cheeks bulged. His buckets wiggled.

Dixie didn't flinch. "And I am a civilian traveling on orders from the War Department. You will not piddle on me!" She returned the papers to her purse.

"Sergeant!" He almost choked from the effort of yelling.

"Yes, sir."

"Return the men to their seats and then report to me in the mess car. And bring the perpetrators of this melee with you. I'm going to get to the bottom of this."

"Yes, sir. And what should I do about them?" He indicated Dixie and Sally.

"Do as you're told, Sergeant."

"Yes, sir."

The lieutenant spun on his heel and marched out of the car.

The sergeant swung into action with the practiced ease of someone who travels the same road daily. "At ease! Shut up! Get back into those seats and stay put! You'll get your bellies full of fighting soon enough. The next man who causes trouble is gonna cross the Pacific doing the dog paddle—and I mean double-time, with full backpack and ammo!"

Two-hundred feet scrambled to obey.

"You and you . . ." He indicated Milton and Bobby Ray, whose ragged appearance suggested they had been at the center of the fighting and therefore must be guilty of whatever offense needed a culprit. "Come with me."

Milton glared at Dixie, but one look from the big MP kept him from arguing. Bobby Ray looked longingly at Dixie, his will to live lost.

The sergeant turned smartly and, with a final appreciative look at Dixie and barely a glance at Sally, he and the other MP ushered Bobby Ray and Milton from the car.

Sally collapsed into her seat. She wished the lieutenant were still in front of her. She would have punched him in the face.

Dixie retrieved a fresh handkerchief from her purse. She leaned sideways, and Sally felt her dab at her face. When Dixie pulled away, there was a smudge of blood on the cloth, and Dixie's hands were shaking.

Dixie took a deep breath. "I wanna thank you, honey, for helpin' me out. I was startin' to feel like Custer after he got himself surrounded by those Indians. If that numbskull lieutenant hadn't showed up when he did, those boys would have had my virtue in another minute."

She leaned forward again to press the handkerchief against Sally's forehead. "On the other hand, I'm not gonna blame these boys too much. I bet most of 'em haven't even had a real girlfriend yet, and now they're goin' off to war. They just saw a chance to see what a real woman feels like and they took it. I may be the last thing some of 'em ever touch that feels real good. If that brings any comfort when they need it, then more power to 'em." Despite her bravado, a quiver still lingered in her voice.

Sally shoved her away. "Quit pretending that you weren't scared! And you may not care who touches your body, but I'm mighty particular who touches mine!" Too late, she realized she was shouting. Every head in the car had swung around.

Dixie put her finger to her lips. "Honey, I'd appreciate you lowerin' your voice. Soldiers stay in heat pretty much all the time, from my experience. I'd hate for 'em to get the wrong idea about me. If you think back to what I said, hon, I didn't say anything about warmin' any sheets with anybody. I just said I'd look the other way while they got a little feel to remember home by. As to bein' scared: maybe I was, but I didn't back down. And neither did you!"

Sally wondered if it was even possible for a soldier to get the wrong idea about Dixie. She still was shaking. The terror of the last few minutes was only now getting its full grip on her. She hadn't thought before jumping on the soldier's back. Dixie had been in trouble and she'd just acted. It had been the right thing to do, and she knew she'd do it again— even for Dixie, who, she reminded herself, was responsible for getting her into this mess. She hissed, "I didn't know when I climbed aboard this train that I was going into hand-to-hand combat, thanks to you! Thanks to you, I nearly got killed!" She started to get up.

Dixie grabbed her arm. Her voice dropped so no one could overhear. "Most of 'em are barely eighteen, Sally. They're going to die, a lot of them. It's got nothin' to do with preachers or with fancy books or with whatever high and mighty morals and rules somebody fed ya so you wouldn't have to think for yourself. It's just a fact and it's goin' to happen, just as sure as the sun is comin' up tomorrow—and they don't have anything to say about it. Though they know it, deep down, some of 'em. They're going to die in a thousand horrible ways so what's good and right about the world can go on bein' good and right. So it's OK by me if they get a little worked up. Just like it's OK by me for 'em to get a little feel of a soft fanny; it seems like a small price to pay. Wouldn't you say so?" Her face, normally so much in a hurry to go its dozens of different ways, was rock-still.

Sally bit her lip. She wondered what Tex would have thought of this beautiful woman who talked like a typical Texan, but who handled wild soldiers with the same skill and confidence that she dealt cards and challenged authority, and who had a way of making sin sound no more wrong than offering a hand to a drowning man. He would have liked her, she was sure.

With that firmly in mind, and in spite of her father's preaching, she had to admit she liked Dixie, too. Being with her was like riding a cannonball. Everything speeded up. Every moment became exciting. She was sure Dixie would never be cold or hungry, or down-and-out-poor. Dixie would never get into a jam she couldn't get out of, nor fall in love only to have her heart broken. She was going to learn plenty from Dixie, though she wasn't ready yet to forgive her.

Dixie apparently had decided that a peace agreement had been struck between them, for she gave the handkerchief a final swipe and, as if nothing at all had happened, leaned back and inspected her work. "You know, hon, you're really not that bad lookin'. I suspect the army'll put some meat on ya. Then if you wear some makeup and do somethin' with that hair and start dressin' in somethin' other than an old wore-out flour sack, you'll turn a head or two." She returned the handkerchief to her purse.

Sally felt her forehead. The wound was small. It would heal quickly and leave no evidence behind. She asked, "You don't think this is the way the army is going to treat us, do you?"

Dixie had been inspecting her own damage in the mirror of her compact. Miraculously, her makeup had mostly survived, as had her hairdo. She patted back a raven-black tuft. "Hon, in the words of Betty Lane Striplin', 'You'll meet some who'll try to paw ya and you'll meet some who'll try to keep ya from doin' your job. But mostly, you'll meet some of the greatest guys in the world, and some of them will become your friends and you'll wind up havin' more fun than any good girl ought to.'"

She finished herding her hair and making repairs to her face, and she returned the compact to her purse. "Just remember that we've got the president on our side. He's kicked the Germans' butts and the Japs' butts, and I'm confident he'll kick American butts if anybody gets in the way of us becomin' WASP."

Sally nodded. But in her limited experience with men, she'd learned enough to know that even a president wasn't likely to change ways of thinking that had started at the beginning of time.

Dixie leaned forward again. Sally felt the graze of her hand against her ear. Dixie opened her fingers, revealing a quarter. "What you wanna bet that you're not the only one whose lucky side is heads?" She sent the piece soaring and captured it with an expert snatch, and then opened her hand to reveal that it had landed head-up. Dixie grinned. "See, you've got nothin' to worry about. Your luck's changed already."

"You stole those soldiers' money! If you'd left them alone, none of this would have happened!" She remembered this time to keep her voice low.

Dixie grew serious. "No, I didn't. Those two couldn't have won at poker if they'd been playin' a nun, and I told 'em so. Honey, soldiers and poker go together just as naturally as people and breathin'. You can't separate the two for very long, any more than you can hold your breath."

Her grin reappeared. "But what I didn't tell 'em about was me. My daddy was a great salesman; I told you that. Well, he learned from the carnies. I knew the taste of cotton candy almost before I knew the taste of my momma's milk. He was a short-changer. Do you know what that is?" She didn't wait for an answer. "He's the fellow who sells you your ticket. You give him a dollar for a nickel ticket, and he gives you back fifty cents in nickels and pennies. A good short-changer can make more money than Rockefeller, and my daddy was one of the best. He could look at a man once and know whether he hid his money in the backyard or under the mattress. That's the biggest part of bein' a great salesman, bein' able to read people." Her hand made an ever-so-slight movement, and the quarter disappeared. Her smile broadened, sending the parts of her face racing. "Just like an open book."

The squeal of brakes on hot steel announced that the train was slowing down. Sally looked out the window. Ahead was the unmistakable outline of a station.

Dixie stood up. "Well, you better start gettin' goin', if you're still plannin' to get off at Sweetwater, 'cause this is it."

Sweetwater looked exactly as Sally remembered it from the air: a little town in the middle of nowhere, its residents mostly merchants who brought civilization to West Texas's far-flung ranchers.

Dixie busied herself with the adjustment of some garment beneath her dress. "Hon, you never did tell me the name of that boyfriend of yours who got himself killed."

Sally remained fixed on the town emerging outside the window. "His name was Tex Jones."

Dixie popped a bubble from a fresh wad of gum. "Oh, a Yankee."

Sally looked at her. "What do you mean?"

Dixie gave her gum a half-dozen chomps.

"I wouldn't have guessed he would have been a Yankee, is all. I would have thought you'd have fallen for a Texan. That's all I meant." Seeing Sally's confusion, she added, "Oh, come on, honey. Nobody from Texas calls himself Tex. That's strictly for Easterners. Your boyfriend was a Yankee. That's nothin' to be ashamed of, so long as you liked him. I'm sure he was nice enough."

"Sweetwater. Next stop Sweetwater." An elderly conductor strolled down the aisle. He slowed to admire Dixie's derriere before disappearing through the door at the end of the car.

The train slowed to a creep.

Dixie gave her hair a final pat, Tex apparently forgotten.

But Sally was still thinking about what Dixie had said. Tex hadn't talked like a Yankee. In fact, he'd had no accent, which she'd noticed when they met, but it had become so unimportant that she'd forgotten about it until now. Over the course of their months together, she had assumed he was as much a Texan as herself, but somehow had escaped the twang and drawl that were so characteristic of the state. She'd even consciously emulated him, to the point that she'd lost most of her own accent. Now to have an entirely different possibility thrust upon her after all this time was dizzying.

The train stopped.

Dixie pointed out the window. "Uh, oh. Look what's waitin' for us."

Standing on the ramp adjacent to the track, and looking annoyed to be doing so, was a sergeant. He held a clipboard in his hand and there was a stub of yellow pencil wedged behind his right ear. Sally guessed him to be in his mid-forties, judging by his thinning gray hair and belly. His face, which was burnt deep red by the sun, was set in the downcast and forlorn look of a basset hound.

Dixie straightened.

"I do believe we're about to meet the army."

# THREE

You Ketchum? You Beaumont?"

He was from someplace back east, someplace big, Sally thought. He was a Yankee. His accent gave him away.

They nodded.

"You're late! You were supposed to be here an hour ago."

Dixie piped up, "Sorry, Sergeant. But nobody on the train wanted to help us push."

He obviously hadn't wanted a reply and he ignored hers. "Get your gear and get in the trailer on the double. The colonel and Mrs. Teetle are gonna welcome you. They won't like you missing it." He pointed to a large enclosed trailer parked at the end of the ramp. Despite its olive green paint and the wide windows that someone had cut into its boarded-up sides, Sally could see that its original purpose had been to haul cows. The rear of the trailer was enclosed and equipped with Dutch doors.

But Dixie wasn't finished. "What's your name, Sergeant?" she asked.

He eyed her the way a weary mother looks at a neighbor child who's asked itself to dinner. "Sergeant Crawford." He turned and walked toward the trailer.

They followed.

A small audience of old men had gathered to watch the comings and goings of the station from a bench. Their worn coveralls and weathered faces spoke of lifetimes spent wrenching a livelihood from the land. Sally felt uncomfortable before their stares, but Dixie handled the attention with the same ease as her luggage, which was nearly a sea trunk. Smiling at the ancient gaggle, she chirped, "Mornin', boys." They responded with toothless grins—and one giggled.

They climbed aboard the trailer with only moments to spare. Sergeant Crawford started the engine with a roar and the old truck lurched forward.

Sweetwater up close was only negligibly more interesting than Sweetwater from the air, Sally decided. Downtown had the usual smattering of Texans going about their business inside the usual mixture of typical small town businesses. As with everywhere in America, male civilians of fighting age were a rarity, leaving Sweetwater heavy with women and children and the old and the infirm. The children watched their passing with curiosity. The women, when they looked at all, seemed strangely hostile.

And then downtown was behind them and the scenery became rural. The road narrowed and climbed steeply. The truck lost headway, and Sergeant Crawford had great difficulty downshifting. Finally, after much grinding of gears, he succeeded, and they proceeded slowly with the engine howling.

"He's not much of a truck driver, is he?" Dixie sprawled on one of the rough wooden benches that ran the length of each of the trailer's sides. A gentle breeze, kicked up by the truck's laconic progress up the grade, barely ruffled her hair.

Sally tried to imagine the airplane she would fly first. One thing was certain: Army Wings would be nothing like the Jenny. The Jenny had been made of wood and cloth, an artifact of another era, a dinosaur relative to modern aviation. Whatever the army was using to train WASP would be as different from the old Jenny as a battleship was to a rowboat.

The road leveled. They were on a wide plateau. Ahead lay a large clump of buildings surrounded by a broad expanse of dusty fields, the architecture of a modern airport. Suddenly from behind the farthest row of buildings appeared a small blue-and-yellow open-cockpit airplane. Another appeared then, and another and another, all rising gracefully, one behind the other.

Dixie joined Sally on the bench. "PT-19's."

Two other types also appeared above the buildings. These were somewhat larger, with long canopies over their cockpits, and were silver in color.

"BT-13's and AT-6's," Dixie volunteered.

Sally looked at her in awe.

"Airplane magazines, hon," Dixie explained. "You oughta try readin' sometime. You'd be surprised at what you'd learn." She moved back to her place on the other side of the trailer.

Sally bit her lip. She could think of no reason to explain to Dixie that the library in her country high school was better stocked with shelves than with books, and that a person was likely to go a long, long time before finding any airplane magazines there.

Sergeant Crawford held the accelerator to the floor to make up for time lost on the hill, and the old truck and lumbering trailer finally picked up speed. They held on to keep from being bounced to the floor. Sally stuck her head out the window. The sky was filling with silver, and blue-and-yellow specks. She could taste the grit kicked up by the truck's tires, but she refused to pull her head inside or to erase the grin on her face. This was the beginning of her new life, and she wasn't going to miss a single moment of whatever was going to happen.

A lonely elevated wooden beam straddled the road ahead, its sole function apparently to provide a place to mount the sign that announced the entrance to Avenger Field. A crude guardhouse at the foot of one of the beam's legs provided shade for a disinterested sentry. Accompanying the sign on the overhead beam was a large painting of an impish female cartoon character diving feet-first through the sky, her costume a whimsical collection of tall boots, short skirt, long gloves, leather helmet and goggles.

"That's Fifinella," Dixie hollered. "The Walt Disney people out in California thought her up. She's supposed to keep bad gremlins away from the airplanes."

The cartoon blurred in the dust devils of their passing.

"Damn," Dixie added. "I sure hope this thing has brakes. Otherwise, we're gonna wind up in El Paso for sure." She held onto the bench with both hands.

Sally squinted against the dust. At the speed they were traveling, they were sure to plow into one of the buildings.

But as if reading her mind, Sergeant Crawford slammed on the air brakes, and their runaway came to a halt amid much hissing and a cloud of dirt. The air inside the trailer filled with the smells of burnt brakes and Texas soil.

"Lordy. Lordy. Lordy." Dixie stood up. Her luggage had upended in a pile in the front of the trailer.

Sergeant Crawford's face appeared above the lower half of the door at the rear of the trailer. "Get your stuff and get a move on. The colonel's probably already started talking."

Sally scrambled to her feet.

Dixie, close behind, wedged her trunk through the narrow door. "I hope whoever's teaching you gives you another drivin' lesson real soon, Sergeant."

He ignored her and pointed to the building, where a small pyramid of suitcases and other paraphernalia were piled on the dirt near the door. "You flygirls put your stuff there and get inside. They don't like anybody missing their talk."

They slipped inside the building as quietly as they could and found seats on one of the backless benches that faced a giant blackboard at the front of the room, where a powerfully built, square-jawed officer was addressing the audience of forty or so young women. Sally guessed him to be in his early forties, suggesting that he was a career officer. Many men had escaped the hard times of the nation's recent depression by making the military their home.

"Ladies . . . on behalf of the President of the United States and the United States Army, I would like to welcome you to the 319th Army Air Forces Flying Training Detachment, which is home to the Women Airforce Service Pilots program, more familiarly known as the WASP. My name is Colonel Buck Bowen. I'm the commanding officer here at Avenger Field." He smiled. Sally didn't know what a commanding officer should look like, but this one looked friendly enough.

"You are following in the footsteps of some very brave and talented pilots. Since the WASP were formed in 1942, over one thousand young women have graduated from this field. Today, WASP are delivering everything from little open cockpit PT-19's like you'll soon be taking your first lessons in, to the hottest fighters and the largest bombers that America can build. The work you will be doing is as essential to the winning of the war as bombs and bullets, for every aircraft that you deliver frees a man for combat. In some ways, you are even more important than combat pilots, for without you, they would have nothing to fly."

Sally felt a swell of pride. The crowd murmured its approval. Colonel Bowen's smile widened. His hair was showing the first traces of gray. He made a commanding presence in his sharply pressed brown uniform.

"You may have noticed a number of civilian workers on the base. In fact, it may seem to you at times that we have more civilians working here than military personnel. The reason is that the army has contracted with a civilian school, Air Services, Inc., to run both our flying and ground schools. So while our operations are being conducted under the auspices of the army, due to wartime shortages of instructor personnel, civilian instructors will be providing you with the bulk of your training, though certain highly specialized phases will be taught by military personnel."

He fiddled with the podium.

"One other thing I want to mention before I turn you over to Mrs. Teetle." He glanced to the edge of the room where a short, tough-looking little dark-haired woman dressed in civilian clothes waited. "This class is going to be a little different from those that preceded it." His mouth tightened. The moment came and passed quickly, but his distaste was unmistakable. "Congress has sent an observer to see how we do things. He's not an elected official, nor is he military. He just arrived, so he hasn't briefed us yet on how he will go about executing his mission, but suffice to say that should you have direct contact with him—and I think the chances of that are slim—you will show him every courtesy and respect."

He looked again to the corner of the room and the little bulldog of a woman, and an unspoken agreement passed between them. "Now I would like to introduce you to Mrs. Teetle, who will be your civilian supervisor during the approximately five-and-a-half months that you will train here. Any questions or problems of a non-flying nature that you have should be directed to Mrs. Teetle. Questions regarding the various regimes of flight should, of course, be directed to your instructors. Thank you for your attention and good morning.

"Mrs. Teetle."

He abandoned the podium.

The little woman walked briskly to the front of the room. Sally guessed her to be in her late forties.

"Thank you, Colonel Bowen. Good morning, girls. On behalf of Jacqueline Cochran, director of Women Pilots in training and of the Women Airforce Service Pilots, I would like to welcome you. My name is Mrs. Teetle, and as Colonel Bowen has said, I am your senior civilian liaison to the military."

"I heard about her," Dixie whispered. "She's a royal pain in the ass if you get on her bad side."

Sally motioned Dixie to be quiet before she made her miss something. But Mrs. Teetle was only getting started: "First I am going to get the subject of tennis rackets and golf clubs out of the way. I noticed that some of you brought each. You won't be needing them. The sergeant will show you how to ship them back to your homes. Keep nothing that doesn't fit inside a three-by-six-foot locker.

"You are here to work and certainly we expect that of you, though at some time in the future you will be issued weekend passes. There are a number of churches in Sweetwater and they've been quite generous in extending hospitality to Avenger's trainees. But for now there will be no passes, no tennis, and no golf."

She consulted a paper that she had retrieved from her pocket. "Supper will be served at 1800 hours. That's at six. Lights will be turned off promptly at 2200 hours. The time after you are finished with supper until lights out will be your own, but I strongly suggest that you use it to study. To help you accomplish this, you will be required to spend a minimum of one-and-a-half hours per night in study hall, Monday through Thursday.

"Reveille will be at 0615 and breakfast formation and roll call at 0645. Calisthenics will be conducted every day, weather and schedules permitting. As with all classes, attendance is mandatory.

"You will be responsible for your room and board. That is, it will be deducted automatically from your salary. You will pay for your own laundry and clothing. Civil Service will retain five percent of your income for Social Security. You will purchase war bonds. Also, you will need to set aside an adequate amount of money for your transportation home, should you wash out."

She paused for a breath.

"You will wear slacks and blouses when not on the flight line. While on the flight line, coveralls will be worn. Coveralls may also be worn while in class, but at no other time. Nail polish may not be worn at any time.

"Regulation wear will additionally include your blue dress uniform, which will be issued to you and which you will be required to purchase. Blouses will be white. Slacks, socks and low-heeled shoes will be brown or tan. For those of you not owning appropriate blouses, slacks, socks, and shoes, you will be taken to Sweetwater this morning to purchase them. Should any of you be unable to pay for your purchases, the cost will be deducted from your wages."

She looked up as if suddenly remembering some unhappy memory.

"A word of warning to those of you going to Sweetwater. Fraternization between WASP trainees and civilians and military personnel on and off the base is forbidden. Any breach of this rule will result in your immediate dismissal."

Someone groaned.

Mrs. Teetle's voice assumed the quality of icicles. "This rule is inviolable, and there will be no exceptions to it. I hope I make myself clear."

The groaner had the good sense to keep quiet.

Mrs. Teetle studied her audience like a warden sizing up a shipment of cutthroats. Her face took on the ferociousness of a pit bull, and her voice summoned the power of a bullhorn. "One final thing. There will be no liquor on the base. That means none brought in and none brewed. Anyone caught with liquor in her possession will be immediately sent home. Does everyone understand that?"

A sea of heads nodded.

She returned the paper to her pocket. Doing so seemed to drive her to a new low of grimness. "I want to re-emphasize what Colonel Bowen told you. And I want to add something of my own. Should any of you at any time come in contact with our visitor, you will treat him, or anyone with him, with the utmost respect. Should he ask you a question, you will courteously refer him to a civilian or military supervisor. You will not—I repeat, will not—engage him in conversation, nor allow yourself to be engaged. He is here to do a job, and so are you." She glared. "Shooting off your mouths or otherwise giving your opinion, be it about the training or the weather, is not your job. Remember—what you say, what you do, how you conduct yourselves in public and perhaps even in private, might very well find its way to Congress in the form of an official report." She added darkly, "And it is Congress that will decide the future of the WASP."

A foot scraped the floor. The sound was deafening.

"Now I hope each and every one of you understand this. Because violations will be dealt with swiftly and, I can assure you, harshly, by me. Does everyone understand?"

Every head nodded.

Mrs. Teetle stepped away from the podium. "Very well. Assemble outside beside your baggage. You have a lot to do and not much time in which to do it. The sergeant will march you to sick bay for your physicals, and then to your quarters. Those who are rejected will be returned to the train station. Be sure to keep your pilot's licenses and logbooks with you, as you will need to answer a few questions. As outlined in your letters of invitation, no one with children will be accepted. If you have children, let the sergeant know and you will be returned to the station with those who fail to pass their physical and/or interview. Those of you in need of brown slacks, etc., will be taken to Sweetwater. The truck leaves in one-and-a-half hours. I suggest you not waste even a minute. You are dismissed." She turned on her heel and strutted from the room.

Her shocked audience rose, their whispers growing to loud chatter.

"Oh, Lord." Dixie got wearily to her feet. "Napoleon in a girdle, that's what Betty Lane Striplin' called Teetle."

Sally no longer was thinking about Mrs. Teetle. What did worry her—and mightily—was the obvious concern over this visitor from

Washington. Especially troubling was Mrs. Teetle's veiled threat about Congress deciding the future of the WASP. She had assumed the only decision anyone was making about the WASP was how to find more qualified women pilots who would join up. But now it suddenly sounded like the program might be less than assured.

The crowd was milling toward the door. She grabbed Dixie's arm. "What did she mean about Congress deciding the future of the WASP?"

The girl in front of them turned around. "Don't you read the papers?" She spotted the worn spots in Sally's dress and her scowl deepened. "Or don't you know how?" She had an upturned nose and pale skin and red hair, but her beauty was distorted by her contempt and arrogance.

Sally clamped her arms to her side. She'd been so fixed on Colonel Bowen and Mrs. Teetle that she'd completely forgotten how ragged she looked. She already knew that she was, by far, the worst dressed in the room. Five or six girls obviously had no interest in fashion, several were dressed more like men than women, but the majority plainly were used to dressing well.

"Sure, we read," Dixie piped up. "How 'bout you? Or do you stay too busy runnin' your mouth?"

They were through the door now and outside. The gaggle of bodies thinned, and the mob drifted to a stop.

The girl glared up at Dixie, who towered over her by a good four inches. "What do you mean by that crack?"

Sally appreciated for the first time how wonderfully dressed the stranger was. She wore an expensive gray skirt with a matching blouse that looked like pure silk. Her hair and makeup were perfect. She could easily have stepped out of one of Dixie's modeling magazines. A flicker of realization hit her. Dixie wasn't coming to her defense just because of their new friendship.

"What did you mean by that readin'-the-newspapers crack?" Dixie glared back.

Sensing a brawl in the making, Sally pointed at the road. "Look! A general!"

Everyone turned.

A huge black Packard was approaching. They glimpsed a gaunt figure sitting alone and erect in the rear seat. But instead of a uniform adorned with stars, he wore a business suit and a straw hat.

The girl snorted. "That's no general! That's Ira Waterman."

"Who?" Dixie watched the quickly disappearing car.

"Ira Waterman! He's who Bowen and Teetle were talking about. That's his Packard. He goes everywhere in the thing; he probably had it shipped out here with him on the train. He's the lawyer that Congress hired to find an excuse to shut down the WASP. They don't come any smarter, or any dirtier, even in Washington. My father knows him. He came to our house once for dinner. I managed to be out." She returned to glaring at Dixie. She had to elevate her chin to an unnatural angle to do so.

"What do you mean, 'shut down the WASP'?" Sally demanded.

"You don't know . . . really?" The girl's bewilderment, feigned or otherwise, caused her eyes to widen dramatically.

Dixie straightened to her full height, giving the girl the choice of looking away or looking up her nose. "The news has a hard time catchin' us, we stay so busy barnstormin'." She nodded toward Sally to indicate the other part of the "we."

"You're barnstormers?" A crack of uncertainty appeared in that wall of superiority.

Dixie nodded grimly. "I'm Dixie Ray Beaumont. This is Sally Ketchum."

"Geri Delaney." She gave out the information reluctantly, as if concerned about getting it soiled. Then she added, "If you're barnstormers, you must not be very good at it." She indicated Sally's dress.

"Someone stole my clothes from our hotel room in Dallas last night," Sally answered before Dixie had a chance to. "This was the best I could come up with on short notice."

"So you shopped at a tramp?" Geri's tone got nastier.

"It was a secondhand store," Sally lied. "It was all that was open, and we had a train to catch. Now what's this about the WASP shutting down?" Out of the corner of her eye, she saw Dixie wink approvingly.

Geri threw her head back. Doing so caused the folds of her beautiful red hair to rise into the air and collapse gently about her shoulders. "It's been in the papers. Some congressmen and a big part of the Pentagon don't want women flying military planes, so Congress formed a committee to find a reason to cut off WASP funding. Officially, it's an investigation, but everybody knows it's really a witch hunt. It's been going on for about a year. The committee's come up with a few things, but nothing important that I've heard about. That's why they hired Waterman. Not that it matters. Everyone in the know thinks this will be the last class that graduates. That's why Bowen and Teetle are so worried. The whole base will be out of a job. The army would transfer Bowen, of course, but Teetle would have no place to go, and she likes the power that the army's given her. Avenger is a cushy deal, and everybody stands to lose if it closes."

Sally fought down a wave of panic. "Why would a lawyer in Washington hate the WASP so much?"

Geri chuckled. The sound was mirthless. "Oh, I'm sure Ira doesn't hate the WASP. I doubt that he cares one way or the other. He's strictly a hired gun. He'd just as soon cut a deal with the Devil as drive a stake through his heart. Some say Ira's whole life is working to make other people's lives miserable. All he cares about is power and money. And winning, of course. Probably that's the biggest thing. There's a rumor that he's so in love with himself he never got married. He just never found anyone ruthless enough to meet his standards—or willing to let him be right all the time. When he makes a mistake, you can bet that somebody else's head rolls, because his ego is so big he thinks he's incapable of being wrong. He treats people like dirt, and acts like he's doing them a favor." She paused to let her audience absorb all this before continuing.

"There's the religious thing, too. Ira's views on religion make the Spanish Inquisition look tame, though no one's ever caught him inside a church. He probably considers himself to *be* the Church: women in the kitchen, men telling them what to do, that kind of thing. Come to think of it, maybe his interest in the WASP is personal.

"He doesn't have any relatives, at least none that will claim him. He lives alone in a big townhouse in Washington. My father met him there once. He's convinced Congress couldn't have picked a better man to find a reason to get rid of the WASP." Geri pulled a cigarette from an engraved gold case. She tapped the end and caught a flame from a matching lighter. She crossed her arms and blew smoke in their direction.

"Personally, I don't care one way or the other what Ira does. I'm just here to teach Daddy a lesson. He wouldn't let me have my own apartment, so I moved out on him." She rolled her eyes. "It's not like he couldn't afford it—he owns plenty—on Park Avenue." She addressed Sally: "That's in Manhattan, New York City."

Sally held her tongue. It was true that she had never been to New York City. But that world—home to this nasty rich girl and to so many of the country's powerful—was no more important to her than the comings and goings of a Chinese farmer. That Geri thought otherwise was as telling about her as her perpetual sneer.

Dixie quickly challenged, "How much flyin' time do you have?"

Geri's importance inflated. "Fifty, mostly in Daddy's Beech Staggerwing."

"Would those be actual flyin' hours," Dixie snapped, "or sittin'-in-the-hangar-makin'-airplane-noises-with-your-lips, hours?"

Geri flushed. "Are you calling me a liar?"

Dixie leered. "Now what do you think?"

Geri snuffed the cigarette out beneath her shoe. She'd only taken one drag. Either it wasn't her regular brand or she'd only recently taken up the habit. Turning her back on Dixie, she continued, "A lot of people think Congress is going to shut down the WASP. But even if they don't, Jackie Cochran and the army are in a big fight over who's gonna run the program. She wants the army to take us, with her in charge, but the army doesn't see it that way; she's stepped on too many generals' toes. But I wouldn't bet against Jackie. She has pull in high places. General Arnold's a good friend of hers, and I hear she's visited with Mrs. Roosevelt in the White House."

Sally clenched her fists. It was all she could do to listen to this rich girl drone on as if she were talking about an upcoming baseball game. Geri would obviously be OK, regardless of what Congress did, while she was just one step away from realizing dreams that those same men could take away forever. That had been the story of her life: the haves and the have-nots—she always had been one of the "nots."

"All that was in the papers?" Dixie asked maliciously.

Geri spun around defiantly. "Not all of it."

"Where'd the part that didn't come from the papers come from?"

Geri glared. "Daddy and his friends."

Dixie was relentless. "What's he do?"

"He's in steel."

"Delivering it or riveting it?"

Geri's nose rose. "We own Manhattan Steel!"

"Never heard of it."

"It's the fourth largest steel company in the world!"

"Ah, that would explain it. I only keep up with the majors."

Geri's eyes turned to cold fury. "I don't think I like you."

Dixie smiled insincerely. "You be sure and let me know when you're sure, honey; you hear?"

A girl who had been standing nearby stepped forward. She was tall and slender with short, thick black hair and large brown eyes. Though boyish in appearance, she was extremely pretty, even exotic looking, Sally thought, and she was one of the few trainees wearing pants. The girl extended her hand to each of them. "Twila Tschudi."

They shook.

"I'd feel a lot better knowing I made the right decision to drop out of college if it weren't for all these rumors about the WASP being disbanded," Twila said.

Sally examined Twila curiously. She suspected that Tex had been to college, though he'd always changed the subject when she'd asked. To the best of her knowledge, no one else that she had ever met had even been near a real college, much less attended one, and certainly no woman had.

"A college girl?" Dixie looked at her oddly.

"I was," Twila answered. "I was studying aeronautical engineering."

"You wanna design airplanes?" Dixie's mouth fell open.

Twila nodded. "There's going to be an explosion of growth across all segments of industry after the war, especially in aviation. A lot of women aren't going to want to stay at home like they've always done and raise babies. Ten years from now, there'll be women flying for the airlines."

Sally could scarcely believe what she was hearing. She had dreamed about earning a grand salary while watching the world three-thousand feet below go by from the cockpit of a great airliner. And now Twila was confidently predicting that it would be possible.

"Women airline pilots?" Dixie hooted. "Maybe in the next life, where everybody's got their own set of wings, so it don't matter. But if you're talkin' about right down here on earth in the here and the now, I'm gonna have to disagree with you, hon. 'Cause a whole bunch of men had rather fight bears barehanded than see a skirt in a cockpit. The nature of the male isn't gonna change in my lifetime nor in yours."

Twila clearly was enjoying Dixie. She shrugged. "Maybe not. But circumstances will change things. Circumstances always bring about change."

Dixie grunted. "Yeah, well, the only kind of circumstances that's gonna bring about the kinds of changes you're talkin' about will be a change in the male anatomy. And I can speak with authority when I tell you they won't agree to that."

"It'll never happen," Geri interrupted loudly. "Look at the way the army's treating us. We make half the money of men who're doing the same job. We're as expendable to the army as bullets."

Twila answered, "Yes. We are expendable. If someone's got to die delivering an airplane, the army had rather it be one of us than a man. The army is saving them for combat. A man dying in combat is far more beneficial to winning the war than if he dies here at home because hopefully he'll die killing some of the enemy.

"You're also right about the army treating us differently. We don't even get the benefits that a private gets, like life insurance and a burial. That's wrong, in my opinion. Someday that will change. Just like someday I think the Air Corps will get out from under the thumb of the army and become its own branch of the military, probably as the air force. That will mean more money for airplanes and research and training—and pay, too. But right now it's the way it is, and we have to put up with it because there's nothing we can do about it and because winning the war is more important." She smiled at Geri.

In what seemed like an unnatural act, Sally thought, Geri smiled back.

There was a surprised childishness about the way she did it, as if she wasn't used to being agreed with.

"How long have you been flying, Twila?" Sally was sure that Twila was older than she, though by how much, she couldn't tell. Something about Twila suggested a quiet confidence, a maturity beyond her years.

Her face lit up. "For my whole life. My parents have had airplanes since before I was born. My father says I took the controls at one, when I sat in his lap. I made my first takeoff and landing at six, when I sat beside him. And I soloed at ten, when no one but him was looking." She laughed.

Even Geri looked impressed.

"How many hours do you have?" Sally was trying hard to keep the envy out of her voice.

"Around two thousand."

"God-a-mighty! How old are ya?" Dixie clearly was impressed.

"Twenty-eight. But I've done a lot of flying for Eastern Aviation. That's a big maintenance and charter outfit. I did post-maintenance test flights on single-engines and flew some of their charters."

"How did you get a job like that?" Geri was hanging on Twila's every word.

Twila grinned. "My father is a close pal of Jack Malone. Jack owns Eastern."

"Would Mr. Malone need another pilot once the war's over?" The words sprang from Sally's mouth.

Geri piped up, "Or two?"

"How 'bout three?" Dixie added.

Twila shrugged. "Maybe. You'll have to wait and see. Right now, the government's taken over everything of Eastern's that'll fly. They've done that with all the outfits. That's why I signed up for college. But I just missed flying too much."

A blast of light stopped the conversation. Sally spun around in time to see a man eject a spent flashbulb from a camera and squeeze in a fresh replacement.

A new explosion caught her again, this time full in the face. His thumb sent the fried, blackened orb arcing toward the ground, and another was jabbed into its place. The camera looked big as a Buick, but he hefted it easily.

He stepped closer. "Smile!" He spat the order in a thick Yankee accent.

Sally instinctively reached out to shield herself. He was so close that this time the camera's heat hung in the air around her. Another glass carcass struck the ground.

He knocked her hand away. "Do not interfere!"

He was tall and hard. He wore a sharply pressed suit that had no color and a tie that matched. He had small beady eyes and a face that looked like it never changed expression.

The next blast bounced harmlessly off her back. This time Dixie, Geri, and Twila had also turned away.

"Turn around!"

*Pow.*

Sally saw red spots. She'd stupidly obeyed.

*Pow.*

*Pow.*

She gritted her teeth. Was he *trying* to make them mad? If so, he was succeeding. Dixie's fist was clenched. Her teeth were bared. The narrow tip of a raised yellow high heel was aimed at his shin. Geri and Twila looked equally dangerous.

"Stop!" Mrs. Teetle charged out of the headquarters building.

Geri made a snatch for his camera, but he lifted it, and her, until her feet dangled in the air. She went sprawling onto her butt.

*Pow.*

Geri's rage was preserved forever.

*Pow.*

*Pow.*

*Pow.*

"Stop! Stop!" Mrs. Teetle arrived in a huff and a puff. "What are you doing, Mr. Offner?" She stuck herself between his camera and her charges.

"Taking pictures." He had closely clipped blond hair that showed his scalp. Sally guessed that he was in his mid-thirties. She wondered why he wasn't in the military.

"Why?" Anyone could see that Mrs. Teetle wanted to sink her teeth into his throat.

"Mr. Waterman told me to."

The name caused her to wither.

The whole class had stopped whatever it had been doing and was watching.

Geri got to her feet and brushed herself off. Her eyes were on fire. She started to say something, but Mrs. Teetle hissed her into silence and in the same motion addressed the photographer. "I'm sure you've fulfilled Mr. Waterman's needs, Mr. Offner. Now we must get on with processing these girls. Sergeant!"

Sergeant Crawford had been slouching in the shade of the old trailer. His name apparently was code for a slew of instructions that previously had been programmed into him. He unwrapped himself and stepped forward, addressing the class as he did. "Listen up! Grab your bags and line up two abreast. Drop your things outside the barracks and fall out for your physicals. Those that don't flunk go to town, if you need to go to town. This is gonna be your only chance, so take it if you need it. Everybody else goes to the library. Two abreast. Two abreast in front of me." He swung his arm over his head as if directing traffic.

Mrs. Teetle busily steered Mr. Offner inside, presumably where she could keep an eye on him.

Sally fell into step beside Dixie and her sea trunk. "What do you think that was all about?"

Geri and Twila were one step ahead. Geri snarled, "Can't you two figure out anything for yourselves?" A golf bag was slung over one shoulder and a heavy purse over the other, and she grasped a suitcase with each hand. Particles of dust fell from the seat of her fashionable gray skirt as she moved. "Ira Waterman's lining up his ducks."

"What do you mean?" Dixie asked.

Geri's face found a new savagery. "His job's to make the WASP look bad. What better way than pictures that just happen to show us looking like we're insane? That's why he hired that Nazi! He was supposed to make us angry. A week from now, those pictures will be on the desk of every congressman in Washington who Waterman thinks he can sway, as well as in the hands of every important newspaper and magazine editor who might fall for his line. It's plain as the nose on your face. It's classic Waterman. And we gave him just what he wanted!"

"You mean, you gave him just what he wanted!" Dixie corrected. "You're the one who was swingin' like Tarzan from that gorilla's camera!"

"Shut up!" Geri bounded ahead, her golf clubs banging noisily inside their expensive leather case. For some reason, Twila sped up to catch her.

Dixie sighed. "Welcome to the women's part of the army, honey, where they humiliate ya and mistreat ya and make ya pay for everything your-self but your bullets—and they'd probably make ya pay for those, too, if they were sendin' ya into combat. But then they'd have to give ya a medal when ya got shot, and they can't figure out a way to make ya pay for it when you're dead." She chuckled mirthlessly.

Sally had to agree. The number of things they were expected to pay for themselves was shocking. She wasn't certain, but she felt pretty sure the army didn't make men buy their own food, much less pay rent. But she was willing to endure anything—buying her own bullets, even—if in re-turn the army would just keep the WASP long enough for her to get her career in aviation.

The old trailer rattled to a stop. Everyone had passed her physical and interview, only to discover something from Mrs. Teetle's list that they had left unpacked, and so they had all been forced to go shopping. The chatter of forty excited girls—which during the ride to Sweetwater had focused on airplanes and Mrs. Teetle and Colonel Bowen and Ira Waterman and the bizarre behavior of his photographer—silenced, and every eye peered through the windows in the trailer's side at the weather-beaten sign that hung over a storefront.

HAY, FEED, DRY GOODS
HARDWARE, HOUSEHOLD GOODS
WORK CLOTHES & DRESS

## SOLOMON's

*Maurice Solomon, Proprietor*

Dixie offered gloomily, "I'm sure happy to know where this place is at. It'll come in real handy next time I need to overhaul that plow that I keep in the middle of my livin' room."

"It looks fine to me," Sally chided.

"Oh, I'm sure there's everything a person needs in there," Dixie said. "Especially if she's a horse."

Twila pointed to the street. "Look."

Traffic along Sweetwater's main thoroughfare had pulled to the curb, and it seemed like every face was staring wide-eyed at the girls from Avenger.

"What's wrong with them, do you think?" Twila asked.

"Maybe it's the heat," Geri suggested.

Dixie stuck her hand out the window. She shook her head. "Naw, can't be the heat. It's too early in the day. Not even a hundred yet."

Sergeant Crawford exited the cab and walked toward the rear of the trailer. He moved with the deliberate pace of a man who knows exactly how long a task should take and will tolerate no abridgment, Sally thought. Watching him reminded her of a milk cow that's given all it has and is being badgered for more. She wondered if the sergeant had come into life in the usual way, or from some collection of machines whose task it was to spit out cogs and gears and cotter pins by the millions. She tried to picture what he had been like before the army, or if—going back to her earlier thought—someone in a warehouse somewhere had simply opened him from a can one morning and set him free upon the base.

His face appeared above the lower half of the door. "You got the store to yourselves for fifteen minutes. Get a move on."

"Yeah, let's get in there before all the diamonds and rubies and silk stockin's are taken," Dixie grumbled.

The inside of Solomon's was murky. Bare bulbs hung from the high ceiling on long cords, their glare soaking into the darkness like water into a sponge. From the cracked masonry walls to the long tables of merchandise that ran like a spine through the length of the store, all was cast in gloom.

"I bet you could find a dinosaur in here if you dug deeply enough," Twila marveled.

"I bet you wouldn't have to dig all that deeply," Geri said.

Two years had passed since Sally had owned anything new, and that had been the hand-me-down dress she was wearing. She moved forward eagerly.

Sergeant Crawford took up guard duty at the door. His job, apparently, was to keep out the locals.

Standing atop a platform that supported an old office chair and a huge rolltop desk, and keeping an accountant's eye on everything, was a large, white-haired humorless man dressed in overalls and a long-sleeved work shirt. Sally guessed that this was Mr. Solomon.

Racks of white blouses and brown slacks had been set up in the center of the store. With only minutes to find what they needed, a frenzy of young women had already surrounded each. Sally tried to elbow her way into the throng, only to get a painful shove in the ribs for her trouble, and she quickly retreated.

Dixie thrust something into her arms. "Here. You can thank me later. I almost got a black eye gettin' these for ya." Sally saw that she was holding two pairs of pants and two white blouses. Dixie continued, "It's a good thing I did, too. Those gals have elbows like steel punches. They'd have poked a hole right through you." She rubbed her arm.

Sally examined the garments. "Thanks, but aren't you getting anything for yourself?"

Dixie shook her head. "I've got plenty of white blouses and brown slacks. Besides, getting wounded once today is enough. And anyway, all that stuff's rough as a cob. I wouldn't put my worst enemy in any of it."

Sally saw that neither pair of pants had a label, nor did the blouses, and her instincts told her that both were at least a size too large. She wondered what Solomon's was charging for these garments, which though sturdy, were obviously roughly made. She hated to go into debt any further than she had to. On the other hand, she had no choice.

"I think I'd better try them on," she said.

Dixie pointed to the front of the store. "Lookee over there."

A crude dressing room had been erected in a front corner by hanging curtains from a wire. Twelve girls were trying to use the thing all at once, much to the delight of the spectators on the street who were being treated to a rare show of partially exposed breasts and buttocks. Sally watched a portly woman in a sunbonnet give the man standing beside her, probably her husband, a solid whack to the back of the head. The look of bliss that had been on his face evaporated into somber piousness.

"I wouldn't pull my pants off near that mob," Dixie advised. "There's no tellin' where you'd get a toe."

"I guess I can take these pants in," Sally said. "And maybe I can shrink these blouses by soaking them in hot water."

"Better than gettin' a football injury, in my opinion." Dixie had started to drift toward the tables. "I'm gonna look for some soap. Betty Lane Striplin' warned me about the army stuff. She said it'd take the hide off a cow."

Sally decided to find shoes and socks as quickly as she could and go wait in the truck. Leaving Solomon's couldn't come a moment too soon. Not only was the place depressing, but Mr. Solomon made her uneasy. He hadn't lifted a finger to help his customers, nor the harried clerk who was trying to crank the giant register and fill out sales receipts and bag purchases. In fact, now that she thought about it, he hadn't moved a muscle since they had come into the store, except for his eyes—and they seemed never to rest. Mr. Solomon's feet might have been welded to the floor, but his eyes kept track of every pair of hands and the merchandise they touched.

The crowd outside was continuing to grow. Faces, mostly ancient, crowded the big window. But one in particular—a tall, slender drink of water, who obviously had once been a cowboy—looked embarrassed by the spectacle inside Solomon's. His eyes darted nervously from one group of young women to the next as if looking for someone. Sally wondered if he knew someone in the class. An aging town constable, dressed typically in western garb, was trying to control the mob, but he, too, seemed more interested in the goings-on inside than out.

"What a bunch of yokels, huh?"

"What?" Sally turned. She had everything she needed and was anxious to pay. She tried to remember the girl's name. They'd spoken on the truck.

The girl eyed the bunch on the sidewalk contemptuously. "I said, what a bunch of yokels. You know about the rumor, don't you? Why they're so interested in us? They think we're the new whores."

"The what?" Sally was sure she had misunderstood.

The girl nodded. "That's right. The army's supposed to be secretly running a bunch of brothels for GIs, and Avenger's supposed to be where they're training the whores to put in 'em. My sister's a WASP, and she told me all about it when she was here."

Surely she was making a tasteless joke, Sally thought. But then she saw that the girl was serious and she demanded, "Why would anyone in their right mind think something like that?"

The girl chuckled condescendingly. "Because this is about as far out in the sticks as you can get without falling off the edge of the earth, and these bozos, though friendly, are as sophisticated as rocks. I guess it's easier for them to imagine women prostitutes than women pilots."

"That's crazy!" Sally no longer tried to control her anger.

The girl shrugged. "Yeah. But they're gonna believe what they're gonna believe. Anyway, Avenger's been here so long now that I don't think most of 'em still believe that. I think they act this way just because they don't have anything else to do." She returned to shopping.

Sally studied the faces. They were little different from the ones she'd grown up with: simple God-fearing folk who, for the most part, followed whoever stepped forward with a Bible and a promise of knowing more than they. She thought—had hoped—that she'd left that behind when she left East Texas.

Sergeant Crawford announced, "Shopping's over. Line up in front of the cash register. Line up. Line up. Line up." He waved his hand over his head.

Dixie tugged her arm. "Come on, honey; let's get in line and watch him lasso himself."

Sally fell into step. For the first time, she was beginning to understand the real problem that faced her. If everyone in America—from the Congress right down to people in little towns like Sweetwater—found it easier to imagine women prostitutes than women pilots, how could the WASP ever hope to succeed?

# FOUR

"Alright. These are PT-19's, the Army's primary trainer. They're what we're gonna use to try to teach you girlees to fly the Army Way. Take a good look at 'em—a good, long look. Memorize every nut and bolt; they're there for a reason. Loosen, lose, or otherwise cause to disfigure any nut or bolt on any PT-19 and you can consider yourself washed out of this here training program. Do I make myself clear?"

Sally guessed he was in his sixties, with a pronounced paunch and a face that was swollen like a ripe tomato—red from too much exposure to the sun, and probably from high blood pressure caused by too much shouting and too much drinking, judging by the condition of his nose, which was also red and pockmarked and swollen. He had introduced himself as Mr. Skinner, senior flight instructor. Immediately thereafter, he had started yelling and pacing back and forth along the flight line like a caged lion.

The subject of his tirade, the PT-19's, sat behind him in a wingtip-to-wingtip row: pretty little blue and yellow low-wing airplanes, with two open cockpits situated one behind the other, and big fat round tires. Slouched comfortably in or against each PT-19 and looking universally bored—except for several who looked lecherous—was an assortment of men of all ages, including many who seemed plenty young enough to be in the military and a handful who looked old enough to be someone's grandfather. These were the civilian flight instructors who would have total and absolute control over everyone's flying in the months ahead, and ultimately over who would graduate. She sensed that several were nursing hangovers.

"We don't care who you are. Who you know. What kind of flying you've done. Or what you think you know. Because as of right now, you don't know crap until you know how to fly the Army Way." A blood vessel stood out above Mr. Skinner's right eye, making Sally wonder if he was going to have a stroke. "You will fly the way we tell you to fly: stalls, spins, inverted flight, and anything else that we decide to throw at you. Your fair-weather civilian training don't mean crap here. Because the day is gonna come when some big bad black storm cloud is gonna try to eat you. And a lousy engine is gonna try to make you crash. And you're gonna get lost in the middle of the night with a dead radio and wish to God you'd stayed at home with your momma. It's my job to see that you live to deliver airplanes another day, so you will learn to fly our way. And God help you if you try giving us any lip." His eyes narrowed.

Sally's knees were shaking. She'd tried squeezing them together, and stiffening her legs, and standing as straight as she could, but nothing had stopped the feeling that she was about to fall down. She hadn't even taken off, and already she was crashing! But she sensed that the other girls standing at attention with her were just as scared. They had barely gotten out of the truck after returning from Sweetwater before Sergeant Crawford rushed everyone to the quartermaster to get their leather helmets and dark green flight coveralls. As the latter were only available in size 42-44 extra large, the whole class soon resembled amputees. Only after much hasty folding and pinning did the sounds of flapping cloth disappear and hands and feet reappear—though no amount of alteration could eliminate the feeling of having enough room to play football inside one's pants. The sergeant had then ordered Sally and eleven others to the flight line and everyone else to the classrooms. This apparently was to be the routine: fly when aircraft were available; study every minute of the rest of the time.

Mr. Skinner's voice, a bruised, tortured instrument, was growing hoarse. "Now here's what we're gonna do. Each of you is gonna go up with an instructor so you can see the landing pattern, the airplane, and the Army Way Of Flying. This is gonna be a freebie, the only one you're gonna get, so keep your eyes open and your mouths shut and your hands off the controls unless you're invited.

"Abrams."

"Here, sir," a frightened voice answered.

"Thirty-Nine. Get over there. Your instructor's waiting."

A tiny blonde started forward, her giant fanny parachute pack bobbing left and right. A balding, middle-aged instructor who had been leaning against Thirty-Nine's wing straightened listlessly.

"Archer."

The names cracked like rifle shots, each time setting a body into motion.

"Beaumont."

"Here, sir."

Dixie's instructor, a swarthy character with a pencil moustache and slick black hair, snapped to attention when he saw her step forward. No doubt Dixie would be doing as much or as little flying as she wanted this morning, perhaps with a quick stopover in El Paso for a little personal shopping, Sally thought. She once again was becoming resentful of her new friend, despite her efforts not to. Everything just seemed to fall into place for Dixie. Of all the girls in the class, only she actually looked good in the ugly coveralls that prior classes had dubbed "zoot suits," after the baggy dresswear that had been popular with men before the war. The name so fitted the ungainly uniforms that even the people at the quartermaster's had called them that. She watched Dixie stalk across the tarmac in her new zoot suit toward her new plane and new instructor with the same ease that she did everything else. Every male eye followed every sway and bounce of her progress, including those too bloodshot to focus.

"Ketchum."

"Here, sir." Her heart was beating against her chest.

"Eighty-One."

She started forward. Rivers of sweat ran down her back and chest and legs. The cumbersome parachute pack felt like a lead weight. In her mind's eye, she saw a waddling Donald Duck.

Eighty-One squatted in the sun, a marvelously sleek jewel waiting to leap into the air. She had been right: compared to the Jenny, Army Wings were a rocket ship to the moon. She felt a jolt of cold apprehension. This was no stick and cloth relic of World War I. What if she wasn't smart enough to fly Army Wings the Army Way? She would grow old without ever seeing her new friends again, or wearing the smart new leather helmet she hadn't even broken in yet, or the stupid zoot suit which was so big she hadn't even gotten it wet with her own sweat. And she would never again look down upon the earth like a bird. The threat of so much going so wrong on this first flight pulled her stomach into such a knot she feared she would be sick right there on the tarmac.

"Ketchum?"

She was struck the moment he stepped from the other side of the fuselage. He had a sensitive face and keenly intelligent eyes. He was several years older than she, she guessed, and barely taller—short for a man. His brown hair had a cowlick and needed a trim, and his flight suit was wrinkled as if he'd slept in it. He wasn't handsome, yet he certainly wasn't unattractive. He had a boyish face and a deep dimple in each cheek. He simply was positively cute.

"Yes, sir." She came to attention.

He smiled and those dimples winked at her. In addition to intelligence, dimples had always been her weakness. And he was a flyer! For a brief, horrible moment, her yearning for Tex was nearly unbearable.

"My name's Bayard. Pronounced Bay-Yard. Beau Bayard. I am a civilian, so you don't need to salute me."

"Yes, sir."

His smile widened and his dimples deepened. "I'm not Skinner. We can bid adieu to the formalities." He held a clipboard in his hand. He used the thing to pat himself on the butt.

He rested the hand that wasn't busy with the clipboard against the front of Eighty-One's propeller. "Now the important criteria to remember this morning are that this is nothing but an introductory flight. Not aerobatics. Not a cross country. Not a flight of mercy. And not air-to-air

WINGS: A NOVEL OF WORLD WAR II FLYGIRLS 61

combat. It's just a little ascent." He illustrated with his hand. "And a little descent. With a little interlude in between in which you get to either validate or dissuade me from championing your aptitude for flight." He gave himself another pat, and he smiled some more and his dimples winked at her. He knew that he was cute, she thought. And he certainly was proud of his big words.

She felt let down. She had assumed her instructor would be all spit and polish and by the book. But he was none of that. He was, she was beginning to suspect, a jerk who was either trying to impress or to intimidate her. She thought about what Geri had said about Waterman's attitude toward women and his goal to find cause to shut down the WASP. Could the instructors be part of that plan? She discarded the idea. She doubted even Waterman would salt Avenger's cockpits with his own people. That would be too difficult, considering the scarcity of pilots, and probably too easily discovered. No, jerk or not, Mr. Bayard obviously was a better pilot than she; otherwise the army wouldn't have hired him. But the fact that he knew a bunch of big words didn't impress her one bit, and her initial attraction to him was already gone. In fact, the more she listened to him, the more she disliked him. She decided that unless he was an exceptionally good pilot, that opinion was only going to worsen.

He leaned against the propeller as if posing for a camera. Sally nearly asked if his regular job was in the movies. "Can I conclude that you fully comprehend the mantra by which we will attend each other this morning?" He patted his behind again.

She was clueless as to what he'd said, but she nodded anyway. Suddenly she had a terrible thought. She wondered if he was talking like a college professor because that was part of flying the Army Way. If so, she might as well catch the next train.

He started for the engine but stopped. "One more thing. Once we're up there"—he pointed to the sky as if she didn't know where it was—"don't touch the controls until I tell you to. Got it?"

She nodded solemnly.

He opened the cowling. "I'm going to lead you through a walk-around. As I elucidate, I want you to pay close attention. The next time you go up in a PT-19, you will be expected to know its manual by heart."

She promised herself that should she get the chance to meet a PT-19 again, she would know its likes and dislikes as well as she knew her own—unless he was the one who wrote its flight manual. And in that case she was sure that she might as well try reading Comanche.

"Oil." He rubbed a little from the engine between his fingers as if suspicious that it might be something else. He held his fingers to his nose and scowled.

Sally couldn't imagine what was wrong. The oil looked fine to her, and she was an expert. The Jenny had leaked like a sieve.

"Leaks." He stuck his face right down on the engine. He poked and peered and pried. He got down onto his hands and knees and crawled under the fuselage.

He went on and on, leading her around and under and atop the airplane in search of everything from loose bolts to bald tires. She listened carefully and made mental notes, though she already knew how to preflight an airplane, or at least how to preflight the Jenny. No good pilot ever took off without thoroughly checking certain items on his airplane, even if he'd just landed. And the more she saw of the PT-19, the more she realized that its simplicity made it not so unlike the old Jenny. But never in her life had she seen any pilot preflight an airplane so thoroughly. All the other instructors already had their students buckled in and were warming up their engines. Some had even taxied out to take off. Yet he continued to poke into the PT-19's most private parts, and the more he looked, the more he seemed to want to keep looking. She had suspected all along that something was wrong. Now she was certain of it. She just hadn't figured out yet what it was.

Finally, after investigating every fluid and seemingly every single piece of metal, rubber and wood on the little plane, he ordered, "Get in," and pointed to the rear cockpit.

She eagerly swung her leg over the fuselage and settled into the rear seat. There was no radio, and few other items to contend with. The seat, oversized to accommodate the bulky parachute, had a familiar and comfortable feel, and her feet automatically started for the rudder pedals and her hand for the stick. Then she remembered his warning not to touch the controls, and she stopped herself.

He ordered over his shoulder, "Plug in the gosport."

She found the hollow tube that would allow him to talk to her while they were flying and connected it to the earpieces in her helmet. She was unable to find anything that would let her speak back. Their conversations would continue to be one-way.

He called off the appropriate settings of switches and controls for the preparation of flight. Finally he yelled, "Clear prop!"

The little engine started with a chug and a puff of smoke, and settled down to a pulsating vibration. Sally broke into a smile.

All the other PT-19's had already pulled from their parking spaces and, like piglets eagerly following a mother sow, were lined up nose-to-tail as they taxied to the takeoff area. Now, finally, they, too, took their place in line.

"The tower's got a light gun. Steady green, OK to take off or land. Flashing green, OK to take off or land but with caution. Flashing red, stop. Or if you're landing, don't. Steady red, make a go-around." The gosport gave Bayard's voice a tinny quality.

Sally mentally nodded. She already knew what the color codes meant. Since small airplanes usually weren't equipped with radios, light signals were the only way for the tower to communicate with a pilot.

The PT at the head of the line began to roll and moments later its wheels lifted from the Earth. The rest followed. Blue-and-yellow dots quickly littered the sky.

He urged the throttle forward. They moved faster and faster. Suddenly she felt the familiar lift in the seat of her pants that told her they were flying. Avenger's buildings and parked aircraft disappeared behind them, and Texas's familiar sprawl appeared beneath their nose, stretched out in all directions like a giant skillet brushed by a rainbow of green and brown hues, just as she remembered it. She fought back the lump in her throat. This was where she belonged. All thoughts of returning to anything else were a lie that she had fed herself. She no longer felt angry or tired or old. Those emotions, so much a part of her life since Tex's death, were replaced by a happy calm. For the first time in three years, she felt content.

"I want to get away from this Avenger traffic. We're going to a practice field about twenty miles from here."

He could fly to the moon, for all she cared—to the moon and beyond, and never turn back. The instinct to take the controls was so powerful. Sally made herself wedge her hands under her legs. All the things that Tex had taught her were coming back, things about how to judge an airplane. The PT had long, plump wings and a long fuselage with a large, sturdy tail. One look told her the plane should practically fly itself, asking only that the pilot not get too much in the way. But to her surprise, the ship acted jittery and hard to fly, rather than friendly as a new puppy. She quickly figured out why. His use of the stick and rudder was rough and uncoordinated, his throttle work harsh. Rather than soaring through the air, she felt like they were crashing through invisible potholes in the sky.

"OK, you've got the airplane." His voice sounded sweaty. "Stay between three and four thousand feet. Give me a right turn. And watch out for traffic!"

Her hands and feet sprang to the controls as if propelled by springs. She couldn't have wiped the grin off her face if she'd tried. Her head automatically went on a swivel as she scanned the sky for other airplanes, just as Tex had taught her. She saw plenty, but none close. She moved the stick to the right and slightly back, at the same time gently pressing against the right rudder pedal with her foot. The airplane, which had behaved like a sick whale for Bayard, instantly became the obedient companion she had imagined in her mind's eye, and they floated effortlessly to the right, the nose neither dipping nor rising but remaining rock steady against the horizon. Her suspicion was true. He wasn't a very good pilot.

"OK, that's enough! Level off and give me a stall."

She leveled the wings. Glancing at the altimeter, she noted with satisfaction that the instrument showed they hadn't dropped so much as a foot during her turn. She eased the control stick back into her lap. The PT obediently lifted its nose higher and higher, until the little airplane teetered on its tail. Then, just as she had expected, the nose dropped, and they fell into a dive. She grinned so hard her ears hurt. No surprises here: this airplane was gentle as a baby and honest as a Boy Scout. She felt sure that, with some practice, she could fly it through a needle's eye and leave a bow tied behind her.

"I've got it! I've got it! Give me the controls!" Bayard sounded panicky.

Wondering what she had done wrong, she took her hand off the stick and was surprised to see him yank the nose up so sharply that the horizon again disappeared. In an instant, the feeling of teetering returned, and she knew they were about to enter another stall. She glanced at the altimeter. The instrument showed thirty-four hundred feet. They had lost six hundred feet. If he wanted to stay above three thousand feet, why would he enter a secondary stall at this altitude?

**BANG.** The nose dropped like an anvil and they fell sharply onto the right wing. The cockpits were identically outfitted with rudders and stick and throttle. She could see whatever he did in his because it was duplicated in hers. His right foot was pushing on the rudder pedal. They were in a spin. A friend of Tex's who did aerobatics had taken her up in his ship once and let her practice the maneuver, which she had enjoyed enormously, though it was violent and potentially dangerous. Different airplanes reacted differently to spins. Pilots routinely died by accidentally entering a spin near the ground where there wasn't enough altitude to recover.

A patch of Texas brown was turning around and around beneath the PT's nose, proof that they were going straight down. The air was becoming a howling demon, the altimeter a spinning top. She shifted uneasily, and not entirely because of the growing forces on her body. They had dropped past two thousand feet. She didn't know how long a PT-19 took to recover from a spin, but her intuition told her that now would be a good time to start the process. But there was no sign of activity in the front cockpit. The stick remained pulled all the way back, and the right rudder pedal was still partially depressed. His shoulders were hunched and frozen. The unbelievable truth hit her: he was paralyzed with fear!

"Give me the controls!" The demon wind whipped her words away. Even if she'd been able to talk through the gosport, she realized that he probably wouldn't have heard her. Instinct took over. She closed the throttle. At the same time, she pushed against the stick and the left rudder pedal. But nothing happened.

*"Turn loose of the controls!"*

She might as well have screamed into a hurricane. Texas, big as a planet and unforgiving as forged steel, was rushing up at them at the speed of a bullet. In a moment, they would die.

She put her full weight on the left rudder and shoved against the stick with all her might.

*Push or die! Push or die! Push or die!* The phrase repeated itself in her head like a silly radio jingle.

In the front cockpit, something gave way, and the controls suddenly moved freely in her hands. She jammed the stick forward with such force that her knuckles left skin on the underside of the instrument column. At the same moment, she shoved in the left rudder.

The spinning stopped.

She centered the rudder and pulled back on the stick. The nose came up. She added power. And they leveled off with one hundred feet to spare.

She was aware of her heart beating and of being unusually alert, but mostly she felt an unnatural, satisfying calm. The thought of how close they'd come to dying seemed neither real nor important, for she had known somehow that she would fly the plane to safety; any other outcome was unimaginable. The certainty surprised her. She had always known that she was a good pilot, but capturing the controls and pulling out of the spin had been the most natural thing that she had ever done. She hadn't thought about what to do; she simply had known. She was so taken by the revelation that she let the plane fly itself for a moment while she adjusted to this new way of looking at herself.

The engine backfired.

The sound snapped her back to the chores of flying. Her first thought was water in the gasoline, probably churned up by the spin. She and Tex always siphoned their gasoline through a chamois when filling the Jenny's tank. That the Army Air Corps wouldn't be as conscientious surprised her.

Another backfire and a steady roughness replaced what had been a smooth purr. Sally nursed the throttle, adding gasoline carefully to gain altitude. Experience told her that if there was water in the gas, it likely would settle back to the bottom of the tanks, or the engine would simply quit. The other possibility was a mechanical problem. On a hunch, she flipped the switch that selected either or both of the magnetos, devices that made the electricity that fired the spark plugs, but the roughness continued. She scanned the huge slab of Texas below in case she had to land. She wasn't afraid. They were headed in the direction of Avenger and gaining altitude. Besides, if worse came to worst and she had to put down, she was confident she would know what to do. She'd survived plenty of forced landings in the Jenny. Anyway, everything was flat as a pancake for as far as the eye could see. She could have landed a bomber down there without so much as scratching its paint.

Almost as an afterthought, she glanced at the figure slumped in the forward cockpit. She wondered if Bayard was actually dead from fear. Never in her life had she heard of an instructor so scaring himself that his student had to save him. She wondered how he'd ever gotten this job. She knew that instructors were scarce, especially in a place in the middle of nowhere like West Texas, but she was almost willing to bet that someone who had never flown an airplane before would have performed as well.

She put him out of her mind. Her only concern was landing safely. Not that she wished him any harm, but with any luck he'd step in a ground-hog hole getting out of the cockpit and break his leg. That would keep him out of airplanes for a while, which would make Avenger a safer place.

The engine quit. The sudden silence was almost as deafening as the engine's roar had been.

That was that. The PT's engine couldn't be restarted in flight. Sally picked a clearing a short distance ahead and dropped the nose ever so slightly to maintain airspeed. She looked around happily. They were altitude rich. She'd managed to nurse them up to twelve hundred feet. The morning was glorious, with no wind to speak of, and she was flying. What more could she ask?

Something happened to the controls. The stick jumped out of her hand, and the rudder pedals danced up and down as if trying to run away. The throttle, the mixture control, every lever in the cockpit, suddenly came alive.

"I've got it!" His command to surrender the controls rode the rushing wind and slapped her in the face.

The nose jerked up. A frenzy of wing dips and twisting tail skids followed. A quarter of her hard-gained altitude vanished in an instant, along with the glide angle that she had so carefully set up to conserve altitude. Bayard was squandering the two things a pilot values most: altitude and airspeed.

"What are you doing?" She slammed her fist against the fuselage.

His answer was a flurry of new aerobatics that cost two hundred more feet.

The whistle of air dropped suddenly. She felt a slight buffeting. He was putting them into another stall without realizing it. This time, from this low altitude, there would be no recovery. They would crash. Suddenly for the second time in her life, she felt afraid in an airplane.

She grabbed the stick and planted her feet on the rudder pedals just in time to regain airspeed. No sooner had she solved that problem than she saw he'd put them on a collision course with a pond—probably the only one within fifty miles. She immediately banked toward dry land.

"I said, I've got the airplane! Let go!" Bayard jerked the controls away from her.

She wrapped both fists around the stick but he was stronger, and she watched helplessly as the nose rose dangerously and the wings dipped crazily and another hundred feet were lost while he floundered about and water once again appeared in front of the lifeless propeller.

"This isn't a seaplane, you idiot!" she screamed. "You'll kill us!"

But he didn't respond. She wondered if he even saw the pond. His shoulders were stiff and hunched, his flying desperate. They'd be in the water in a moment. Only a hundred feet of altitude remained. There was no excuse in the world for what was about to happen. A bowling ball could have rolled a hundred miles in any direction and not bumped into more than an anthill. She felt sorry for the little plane that had flown so wonderfully for her, seeming to come alive in her hands. Very soon, it would be mangled and broken, probably never to fly again.

Sally pulled her seatbelt and shoulder straps as tight as she could. She figured they'd hit the water about in the center of the pond. She wasn't afraid of drowning. The pond wasn't large and she was a good swimmer. Unless he dropped a wing and they cartwheeled or they bellied in hard and she was injured, she was certain of making the shore. What scared her were snakes. West Texas was famous for its snakes, some long as a man and thick as a forearm. And like the land they lived on, they'd turn on you and kill you before you knew what had happened. She imagined herself trying to get free of her seat harness while hundreds of enraged water moccasins slithered, open-mouthed, into the cockpit.

Something black and round suddenly poked its head up from the water ahead. Whether snake or stick, she couldn't tell, and it made no difference anyway, because just then they hit. She was slammed forward with tremendous violence. Water filled the air. Seeing . . . breathing . . . thinking became impossible. Her instincts told her that she had to get out; the plane, with their bodies strapped inside, might never be found. But her shocked brain held her prisoner.

Something brushed her hand.

"Snake!"

She clawed at the releases on her seat belts and parachute.

"Snake!"

The metal tore at her flesh but she didn't care. No pain could compete with the thought of razor sharp fangs.

"Snake!"

The clasps parted and she struggled to her feet. Water poured in over the open sides of the cockpit. Her cushion floated off the seat. The PT was sinking in a torrent of bubbles, each probably providing air for a hungry snake. Her terror of being bitten in the cockpit met her terror of being bitten in the water, and she screamed at the top of her lungs until she lost her balance and tumbled headfirst overboard.

She popped up for air. "Help!"

She popped up again after her foot slipped. "Help!"

She finally managed to stand. The water reached her chin. "Help!

"Help! Help!"

"Stay where you are! I'll save you!" Bayard dove in from the cockpit, swamping her nose. His fingers found her arm and dug deep into her flesh, knocking her off balance and once again beneath the surface of the pond of death. She popped up, spitting brown water and gasping for air.

"Help! Help!" She tried to pull free.

"It's OK! I've got you!" He nearly broke her arm.

The bank wasn't more than twenty feet away. She could get there easily if she could get away from him. Her knee found the tender spot between his legs.

Her zoot suit, full of water and weighing seemingly a ton, threatened to pull her under, but she carefully worked her way toward the shore, alternately swimming and walking on her toes. She collapsed at the brown water's edge. She lay on her back and sucked in great lungfuls of sweet air.

He came from the water slowly, like a bowlegged duck, his face gray with pain. The little PT sat behind him, nearly submerged and clearly done for. A film of gasoline and oil had already spread over the surface of the water.

She struggled to her feet. "Are you crazy?" Her fists were balled and dangerous.

He whispered, "I was about to ask you that." Still holding himself, he sank gently to his knees, which promptly disappeared into the mud.

"Waterman paid you to crash, didn't he? Just like he paid that photographer!" Bayard no longer held power over her to end her dreams. He had killed an airplane, and nearly both of them. He was the most loathsome creature on Earth.

"I don't know what you're talking about," he groaned.

She wanted to drag him back into the water and drown him. But she realized she probably was wrong about any connection to Waterman. Paying someone to crash was a big step from paying a gorilla to enrage some girls by shooting off flashbulbs in their faces. But Waterman would use the accident to his advantage. Sally was sure of that.

"How long have you been flying?" She was shaking with rage.

"A day." His face was still gray.

"And they made you a flight instructor? Why didn't they just send me up with someone who's never seen an airplane before! Or better yet, make me your instructor! I've got over three hundred hours barnstorming. I'd have washed you out before you ever got off the ground, for being a bully and talking crazy so no one can understand you. And the army would still have an airplane, instead of pieces of an airplane sitting on the bottom of a lake!" She didn't bother wiping the foam off her lips. Maybe she could drown him right there on the bank.

"Look at that airplane!" she screamed. She pointed to the PT. Only the tail and propeller tip were visible. "Look at what you've done to that beautiful airplane!"

He struggled to his feet, being careful not to squeeze his legs together. "I had control until you grabbed the stick." They both knew it was a lie, and a lame one at that; he looked embarrassed the moment he said it.

Sally crossed the distance between them in two steps. "You couldn't control that airplane if it was cemented to the floor!"

Bayard jerked off his helmet. "You can't talk like that to me!"

She nearly bent double from the effort of yelling. "You crashed my *airplane!* You nearly drowned me! You almost broke my arm! I can talk to you any way I *want!*"

"You kneed me!"

"You were drowning me!"

"I was *saving* you!"

They eyed each other.

She pointed to the pond. "A blind man could have missed that water-hole. It's the only one in West Texas, and you landed right in the middle of it! Which side are you on in this war, anyway?"

She jabbed her finger into his chest. "You've got no business teaching flying! I've given rides to farmers' wives who did a better job of flying than you!"

He caved in. The change happened so quickly that Sally was taken by surprise. "What I meant was, this is my first day as an instructor. You're my first student."

She recoiled. All she cared about was making clear to everyone at

Avenger, from Colonel Bowen and Mrs. Teetle right down to whoever took out the garbage, that she wasn't responsible for this crash, and who was. But at the same time, she felt a need—a *patriotic* need—to see that Bayard didn't get his hands on another student.

Not that she cared, but she snorted, "How did you ever get to be an instructor?"

The mud made sucking sounds as he trudged up the bank. When he got to high ground, he turned and looked down at her and she realized that she foolishly was the only one still getting wet, and she quickly moved to dry land, too.

"Every branch of the military needs experienced flight instructors," he said. "But there aren't any because everyone who knows anything about aviation is already in the military. That leaves a civilian outfit like the WASP out in the cold. The only flight instructors that Avenger gets are civilians who've fallen through the cracks."

"What crack did you fall through?" she demanded.

"I've been in South America," he said.

"Hiding out from the relatives of everybody who's flown with you?"

"I was a reporter for an American news service," he said. "Flying was the easiest way to get around, but the local pilots stayed drunk most of the time so I took lessons in self-defense."

"You're a reporter?" She didn't believe it for a minute.

"More of a novelist, really." He suddenly glowed so grandly that she would have hit him over the head with a stick, if any had grown in that part of Texas.

Novels had been her escape from the farm. She had imagined novelists to be the most interesting people alive. Having him destroy that fantasy only made her angrier.

Sally looked at him hard. "Do you have any books in the library?"

A cloud passed between him and the glory he'd been sunning himself under, and he shifted uncomfortably. "No. But there will be! In every library and every bookstore from New York to Los Angeles."

So he was lying. She had known all along that he wasn't a real writer. She wondered if he even knew the meanings of those big words he liked to throw around. Or if he'd made them up, like he obviously had made up a story to convince the army that he was a pilot.

"I bet you don't write any better than you fly!" she said. "I think you're scared!"

"Anyone with any sense would be," he said. "Flying's dangerous."

She was speechless. Bayard had admitted he had no business instructing! No one, not even Waterman, could pin the crash on her now. But instead of jumping for joy, she found herself rooted to the heat-cracked soil beside the pond. He held her prisoner with his unapologetic eyes.

A library of things that she hadn't known she knew suddenly fell into place. She knew everything about him. Or at least, she knew all about the parts that were like Tex. He'd go his own way and burn in hell before he'd take the ordinary path like everyone else. That had been one of the things that had drawn her to Tex. And he didn't care what anybody thought. Until Tex dropped into her life, she'd never met anyone with either of those qualities. Now she had again, and she didn't like the revelation. "Why didn't you join the infantry and stay on the ground, if you hate flying so much?" she demanded. "Or are you scared of rifles, too?"

"Somebody's always wanting to shoot you when you carry a rifle," he answered easily.

"You're a coward!" The slur felt so good, spitting off her tongue.

"I'm serving my country."

The truth hit her. It was so terrible that she barely could speak. "The instructors—the ones young enough to be in the army—you're all avoiding the draft!"

She expected him to look guilty or self-righteous or simply to lie, but he just nodded. "That and the money. We make a lot more money than army pilots."

She couldn't control her revulsion. "Millions of brave men are risking their lives fighting for freedom, and all of you are hiding and getting rich. You should all be arrested! You're disgusting!"

"I'm alive!"

They glared at each other. She had hoped to set him on fire, but he didn't catch.

An airplane swooped low over their heads. It was a trainer from the base. The pilot wiggled her wings. Rescue would come soon. They both understood what that would mean.

"The army's going to want to know what happened this morning." There was a hint of dread in his voice. "What are you going to tell them?"

"You crashed!" The words felt better than sex, leaving her mouth.

"They'll fire me."

"They should!" she said. "You're a terrible pilot!"

"They'll send me into combat."

"You'll have plenty of company, you coward!"

He squared off with his chin. "I'm too good a writer—I'm too valuable a writer—to die before I've published anything. Plenty of guys want to fly and are good at it; put them in a cockpit. Let me fly a classroom."

"Too valuable!" Suddenly she understood how fistfights started.

The little airplane made another pass overhead. Whoever was in the cockpit was showing great skill. She was flying so slowly that the plane was teetering on the edge of a stall.

Sally poked Bayard with her fist. "I'd be first in line to fly combat, if they'd let me. And do you know who I'd shoot first? You!"

# FIVE

Dixie had finished brushing her teeth. Sally heard her spit into the sink in the latrine that joined their bedroom—known as a "bay" in army lingo—to the one occupied by Geri and Twila. The latrines were equipped with two showers, two sinks and two privies. The bays were obviously intended to offer only the most basic comforts and protection from the elements. Each was bare-bones furnished, with six metal cots and a similar number of freestanding closets, six chairs, two tables, and one window. The walls were bare, the floors hard and unadorned. And though every surface looked clean, Sally could still smell the dirt that was as much a part of the West Texas winds as clouds and the ever-present circling buzzards.

Dixie stuck her head through the doorway. She had already put on her pajamas—fashionable blue ones made of silk. Her face was uncharacteristically free of makeup and her hair was securely protected by a net. "Well I can tell ya right now that before this is over, we're gonna turn into a couple of gophers. I swear, I don't believe I've ever tasted so much dirt! The wind's not even blowing—for a change—but I bet I could still write my name in this air!" Dixie paused to apply cream to her hands. She had already moved her cot outside, where practically the entire barracks had fled to escape the fiery heat that still lingered hours after sunset. Only Sally and a handful of others, whose fear of snakes even exceeded their misery from the heat, had chosen to remain inside.

The pores of her skin finally cleaned and lubricated to her satisfaction, Dixie continued. "Well, honey, you've had quite a day for yourself. I bet nobody else can say she ever got into the middle of a fistfight on her way to join the army, crashed an airplane, nearly punched out her instructor and started an investigation, all on her very first day of service to her country."

Sally carefully rolled onto her back. She ached all over from the crash and was in no mood to satisfy Dixie's insatiable appetite for conversation. She had stripped naked in the hope that the rough military sheets would soak up some of the perspiration that flowed from her body.

She and Dixie were the sole occupants of the bay, Avenger apparently having more rooms than trainees. She wondered if that meant that Congress really did plan to eliminate the program. The first WASP had graduated in 1942. In the two years since then, more than one thousand girls had followed. How many licensed female civilian pilots could there be in America? What would the army do when the last one showed up at Avenger? Would women who had no flying experience be accepted for training, as men now were? Or would Ira Waterman and the congressmen who paid him use that as another excuse to do away completely with a program that was delivering desperately needed aircraft to the army and the navy?

She could hear either Twila or Geri rattling around in the bay on the other side of the latrine. She felt sorry for Twila. She couldn't imagine herself facing the next six months and having to live with Geri, too. Either Twila was the nicest person in the world or the most naïve.

Dixie again interrupted her preparations for bed. "Say, listen, hon . . . are you sure you don't want to drag that torture rack you're lyin' on outside? You're gonna be dryer'n old cow bones come mornin'. Any snake with any brains is gonna have the good sense to go somewhere else just to get away from that bunch outside. They make as much racket as geese, and some of 'em look downright scary with all the stuff they put on their faces to go to bed."

"No, thanks, Dixie," she said. "I think I'd rather take my chances with heat stroke."

"Suit yourself. But don't blame me if come mornin' a truck from the renderin' plant rolls up to collect your bones." She headed outside but paused. "By the way, good luck with that review board tomorrow, honey."

"Thanks, Dixie. Good night."

"Night, hon."

The overhead light flicked off, and the near searchlight strength of a full Texas moon instantly turned the bay into a stark contrast of bright colorless things and deep shadows. Sally rolled onto her side. Every muscle in her body hurt. Her shoulders and thighs were black and blue where the force of the crash had thrown her against the seatbelts. Looking back, she realized how lucky she was to have walked away, though the wreck hadn't been nearly as violent as the one that killed Tex. She forced those images from her mind. They'd been the stuff of her nightmares once, but she'd long ago made herself confront them and they no longer had the power to make her cry until she was parched. Now they just made her sad and lonely.

She rolled onto her stomach. The last few days seemed like a dream: her father's death, her letter from the WASP, the train ride, the crash and swirl of questions by angry military men and civilians, and now the order to appear before a review board tomorrow morning. Nothing good in her life ever seemed to stick around. Every two steps ended in a half-mile slide backward.

She rolled onto her back again. She was too exhausted to sleep, but she had to get some sleep before she confronted the board and Bayard tomorrow.

One thing was for sure: he was going to lie to try to save his hide. He'd been scared to death when the army showed up to rescue them, though he hadn't said much before they whisked him away. He hadn't actually accused her of anything. But that would come.

Why were men always wanting to ruin her? Why couldn't at least a few of them be honest and kind and loving and loyal, like Tex had been? Why was he the only one who was good, while all the rest were hell-bent on telling her what to think and how to act? Even when she tried to obey, they wanted to crush her will and to break her spirit.

Tex had once said something that she would never forget. They had set down outside of a little town in Louisiana to sell rides. The propeller had barely stopped turning before some hick sheriff had showed up demanding they buy a half-dozen different licenses he'd obviously invented, and threatening them with jail if they didn't. Tex had put up with him for a while. But when he'd had enough, he'd told her to get in the cockpit. Then he'd coolly turned his back on the man, and they'd flown away. It happened so quickly that the sheriff, a great, sweating, cigar-chewing pig of a man, had to jump for his life.

They'd flown on to the next town and had a profitable day without further incident. But Tex had stayed mad in a way that Sally had never seen before. When she asked him about it, he'd told her that he'd had enough of being controlled and pushed around and bullied, and that he was never going to put up with it again. Then out of the clear blue he'd added that he'd rather be a dead man than a slave, and had walked away from her and kept to himself the rest of the afternoon. It was the only time she'd seen him act like that, and one of the few times he'd let her glimpse his past. Tomorrow, before the review board, she intended to stand tall and straight and to tell the truth, no matter the consequences, just like Tex would have done.

Someone was playing a radio. The sounds of the Glenn Miller Orchestra slipped easily through the open window. Ray Eberle's honey voice sang,

> At last . . . my love has come along.
> My lonely days are over,
> and life is like a song.

Miller's saxophones became a thousand voices in crescendo. Eberle sang again:

> At last, my love has come along . . .

Miller's trombones spun silk.

> And here we are in heaven . . .
> For you are mine at last.

Somewhere too far away to threaten, a coyote howled. Its mournful wail blended with Eberle's voice and Miller's trombones and the saxophones. Sally decided they were the loneliest sounds in the world. Once again, as she had every night since that terrible evening, she missed Tex. The years had worn away some of the yearning, but what was left was still so powerful that her stomach felt like she was being poked by knives.

As sleep's heavy blanket descended, she promised herself that, come hell or high water, she wasn't going to let Mr. Beau Bayard pin his crash on her.

# SIX

Sally had woken up stiff and in pain. And now her first morning in the army had just become even worse.

She stared down at the brown and yellow lumps on her plate. The plate wasn't of the ordinary kind but of metal, with variously shaped indentations to hold different foods plus one round indentation for securely holding a cup or a glass. The lumps had been hot when the cook dished them from the steam table; she'd assumed that he was serving her French toast and eggs. She wondered how she could ever have made such a mistake. The browns were now cold and tasted like sweet cardboard. The yellows were even colder and tasted more like something from a chemical factory than a chicken.

She looked around at the one hundred or so inhabitants of the mess hall. They were seated shoulder-to-shoulder on long benches that ran the length of wooden tables. Many were trainees, but there were also civilians and military types. Her class, easily identifiable by their new zoot suits and grouchy expressions, mostly fiddled with their browns and their yellows. The rest, girls who soon would be graduating, downed the contents of their plates with the apathetic determination of battle-weary soldiers who no longer remember any breakfast that doesn't come powdered from a tin.

Everyone looked exactly like what they were: refugees from semi-comfortable bunks, thrust into the day at too-early an hour. As far as she could see, none had bothered with the usual routines of getting dressed, beyond doing just that. Geri's red hair was pulled into a tight ponytail. Twila's and her own, cut short for practicality, showed evidence of a fast comb. While Dixie—who had enough hair for any two heads, and who probably could have parachuted into combat and still managed to look better than any MGM starlet—had tamed the morning bird's nest with a rolled-up silk scarf the color of a fire engine. The contrast to her jet-black hair made her stand out from the rest of the mess hall like a double ice cream sundae amongst a pile of old baloney sandwiches, a fact which she was sure to have calculated, Sally thought. Dixie talked a lot, appeared to have no sense of anyone else's privacy, and really did seem to read minds as easily as newspapers. But she was genuine and likeable and certainly unique. Sally was surprised that she was feeling more and more at ease around her new roommate.

She'd discovered two other surprises in her first twenty-four hours as a WASP trainee: the number of women who loved flying as much as she did was surprising, and the variety of their personalities and backgrounds amazing. Unlike her earlier assumption, every trainee wasn't rich. While many obviously were—and a few like Geri went out of their way to make sure everyone knew it—a great many apparently came from modest roots yet somehow had found the money to fly. That was the one thing that made everyone alike. To a person, her classmates walked a different path than other women.

No matter what happened in the future, by being here at least she had the satisfaction of knowing that she had done what she knew was right for herself, instead of what her daddy and their neighbors insisted was right. And if she died some day because of bad weather or a bad airplane or just plain bad luck, at least she would die on her own terms, doing what she loved. She wouldn't be a slave to another person or to some bank. That was more than she could say about most of the people she had known, be they men or women.

But before worrying about bad weather or her luck, she had to worry about getting through the next few hours. She had been ordered to re-port right after breakfast to a review board, which would decide whether she shared any of the responsibility for the crash of the PT and, if so, her punishment for the crime. She could only hope that whoever sat in judgment of her would have the good sense to see through Bayard's lies, and to realize that a flight instructor was supposed to know more about flying than his student.

Dixie stabbed at the food on her plate. It reacted like rubber, seeming to challenge her fork to a bending match. "I just don't see how they expect a body to eat this stuff," she moaned, "much less to go out and fly on it." She pushed the plate away. "I can tell you one thing. If this is typical army food, we could get the war over with a lot sooner if we'd donate this stuff to the Germans and the Japs. They'd lose the will to fight in a hurry."

Twila put down her knife and fork. "That would be an act of cruelty, even in wartime," she said softly.

Geri, who so far had disagreed with nearly everything, nodded solemnly.

A pimply-faced youngster who'd been sopping empty tables with a dishrag passed by. He was one of several locals Sally had seen around the base doing menial jobs. Dixie grabbed his arm. "Hey, what do ya call this, anyway?" She indicated her yellow lumps.

"Them's eggs, ma'am. Or at least they used to be before the army got ahold of 'em."

Dixie nudged the agglomeration. "Yeah? Well, if you ask me, this chicken's boyfriend was a tire!"

The youngster, clearly taken by Dixie's beauty and obviously in no hurry to continue the business of sanitation, pointed to her plate with his filthy, dripping rag. "What happens is, the army turns the eggs into a powder. Then the cooks add water to 'em and turn 'em back into eggs. It's a thang the army come up with ta keep 'em from spoilin'. I heard one o' the cooks talkin' 'bout it. He said a can o' processed, powdered eggs'd probably last till hell freezes over—and then some, if you don't open the can all the way." He grinned, revealing a mouthful of gray, uneven teeth. But Dixie had turned away and no longer was listening. Realizing that no further conversation would be forthcoming, he drifted away despondently, a soapy trail dripping behind him.

Sally felt Dixie's elbow in her ribs. "Hey, hon, cheer up. That idiot instructor's the one who crashed, not you. When you get in that meeting, you just remember what I told you. Look 'em right in the eye with your big browns and kind of hunch your shoulders up and forward a little bit like you're real helpless. To a man, that's the same as a big juicy worm is to a fish; they go for it every time. But if there're any women on the board, sit up straight and act like yourself when you talk. That way, they'll know you're telling the truth."

Geri snorted. "If you two think that's going to impress Ira Waterman, then you really are hicks."

"Who're you calling a hick?" Dixie's eyes blazed.

Geri smirked. She was learning how to get under Dixie's skin. "Ira Waterman has argued cases in front of the Supreme Court, and he's counsel to some of the most powerful corporations in America. He brags that the greatest compliment anyone's ever paid him is that his heart pumps ice water. What's more, he's got some of the most powerful friends in the world, including J. Edgar Hoover of the FBI. They're regular pals." She paused for effect. "You start imitating a worm and he'll eat you alive!"

Twila, seated on the other side of the table next to Geri, turned to her bay mate. "In my experience, deciding that you're going to lose a fight guarantees you will. Do it often enough and it becomes a habit—and eventually, you also lose respect for yourself."

A metal fork collided with a metal tray and Geri spun around. "Don't tell me what to do! And don't ever tell me what to think!"

"I was telling you my experience, Geri," Twila answered. "You don't need anyone to tell you what to do or think. You're already perfectly equipped with your own good brain."

Geri returned to glaring at her browns and her yellows. As silence settled over the table, she seemed to uncoil.

Sally broke the stillness. "Well, Waterman's not going to stop me. I've spent my whole life around people who spent their whole lives trying to keep me from doing what I wanted to do. I beat them. And I'll beat Ira Waterman." She wondered if her words sounded as hollow to everyone else at the table as they did to her.

. . .

The air in the hallway was hot and still, the bench she was waiting on hard and uncomfortable. Sally wondered if they were that way by order of the board to soften up its victims. Certainly she felt like a prisoner waiting to be thrown into a ring full of lions. Her only hope was that Geri was wrong about Ira Waterman being present and that Beau Bayard would provide whoever was inside the room with their fill of meat before she was thrust into the ring.

She knew that Bayard was inside because she'd caught a glimpse of him entering as she came down the hallway. He'd looked haggard, as if he had gotten little or no sleep. That made her feel better. If he was worried, that probably meant he had little or no influence with the board. The faster he was fired, the better, so far as she was concerned. In addition to his other faults, he was a hazard to himself and his students, and to everyone on the ground and in the air, and she had every intention of letting anyone who would listen know it.

More out of a need for comfort than for information, she automatically retrieved Tex's big gold pocket watch. The watch, which somehow had been thrown free of the fire, was the only thing of his that had survived. It was the closest she would ever come to looking at him again; it was the only physical memory of him that she would ever have.

Like so much about Tex, the watch was a mystery. It was beautifully made and obviously very expensive. Its cover was boldly engraved in flowing English script with the initial C, which Tex had never explained and which she had concluded was a holdover from a prior owner. This had caused her to decide that the watch probably came from a pawnshop. How Tex had afforded such an extravagant timepiece, he'd refused to say. But he'd certainly doted over it. He'd carried the watch with him everywhere, and for some reason had made a point of winding it at exactly six o'clock each evening.

She pressed the stem. The cover sprang open, revealing a quality mirror in the back of the cover that surely was put there to stoke the vanity of the watch's owner. But that hadn't been Tex. He'd been humble and as down-to-earth as the day was long, which was another reason why she was sure he hadn't been the original owner.

She held the piece away from herself to see the girl of slender build looking right back at her. The girl's face was tired, her reddish-brown hair kept short out of habit to more easily fit beneath a flight helmet. Though only twenty-one, she obviously had lived a hard life. Even so, her chiseled features hinted at her determination. Tex had once told her that her willpower was like a steel plow—except that steel plows sometimes break, and so far as anyone knew, she never had. He'd laughed and kissed her gently, and she'd fallen so deeply in love with him that the rest of the world had vanished.

Sally was sure they would have been married by now if he'd lived, maybe even have had a child, though she wasn't as certain about that. They'd talked about the possibility but had decided that life together had become too much fun to immediately share it with anyone else. The way they had thought so much alike was eerie. Every day of her life had been a misery until she set eyes on Tex, and he'd said that his life had been the same until he met her.

The hallway was still as a tomb. The windows were closed, in spite of the heat. Somewhere in a far-off office she could hear the faint, rhythmic clicking of a typewriter, and out on the flight line aircraft engines being run up.

The opening of the door took her by surprise, and she jumped. Her nerves, already tight and raw, catapulted her to her feet.

"Ketchum?" The corporal wore an expressionless expression. "Five minutes."

He moved back into the room, and Beau Bayard stepped into the hallway and the door closed.

"Good morning." Bayard tried to smile but the effort was plainly painful. She could see bags under his eyes. "Did you sleep well?" His voice told her that he hadn't.

Without consciously doing so, they began circling each other, their steps narrow and stiff, like two boxers waiting to throw the first punch.

"Like a rock," she said. "You?"

"Yeah, like a rock. Me, too."

The air was lead. They seemed to be the only ones in the world. Even the sounds of the engines out on the flight line no longer ventured into the hallway.

"What's it like in there?" She indicated the room beyond the closed door.

"Scary."

She was surprised that he wasn't trying to act tough or brave or any of the other ways she would expect a man to act who naturally would want to hide his cowardice and ulterior motives.

"What do you mean, 'scary'?" she demanded.

"I mean, *scary!* Skinner wants my head. And there's a major in there, a Hicks, who represents the army. If you learn nothing else in this life, learn that the army does not take kindly to crashing its airplanes."

"What about Waterman?" she asked. "Is he in there?"

"No, for which we both can be thankful."

She was relieved. She wouldn't have to worry about him, at least. And while Skinner was hard, at least he was a pilot, and she suspected, a decent one. Bad pilots had a way of dying before they reached his age. She didn't know anything about Hicks, but if he represented the army she figured there was at least a fifty-fifty chance he would be fair with her.

"Are they going to fire you?" She didn't try to hide the hope in her voice.

He looked at her, and his eyes locked with hers. "I think that depends on what you tell them."

"What did *you* tell them?"

"That the engine quit and a downdraft forced us into the lake."

"Are they buying that?" Sally pressed.

Bayard didn't hesitate. "I told you. It depends on what you tell them."

She laughed in his face. "I've already told you what I'm going to tell them. I'm going to do everything in my power to get you fired. And then I hope you do get sent overseas and you do have to fly combat. And if you get killed, so be it."

She instantly felt cheap and mean. She was about to apologize when he exploded.

"That's the coldest thing that I've ever heard anyone say! What kind of person *are* you?" He moved away as if she had a disease.

"I didn't—"

"I know what you meant!"

She looked around uneasily. His voice could easily carry into the nearby offices. She could imagine what those inside would think, an instructor yelling at a student for wishing him dead. The members of the board were sure to hear him, too. The fool was going to get her thrown out yet. She tried desperately to think of something to say to calm him down. But just then the door opened again.

"Ketchum." The corporal motioned her inside.

She realized that she hadn't asked Bayard who he'd said was flying when they hit the water. But the corporal demanded, "Now, Ketchum!"

She stumbled forward. Out of the corner of her eye, she caught a glimpse of Bayard. He clearly was enraged. But she saw something else, something that made no sense, considering how they felt about each other. He looked strangely vulnerable—childlike, even—as if his feelings were hurt.

The room was small and empty, except for a few airplane pictures on the walls and a dozen or so straight-backed chairs and a sturdy looking rectangular table about five feet long near the far wall. Two chairs next to each other on the other side of the table faced all the rest. She guessed that was where Skinner and Hicks would sit. Like practically everything at Avenger, the room looked hastily built to some rigid specification, its sole purpose to train pilots.

The corporal indicated that she was to sit, adding, "No smoking. No gum chewing." He closed the door and took up a position against the wall.

She settled into the lone chair that obviously had been purposely placed an equal distance from each end of the table; about five feet separated it from the table. She wished she could sit in the back of the room, but she suspected she would only be ordered to move forward. She also wished she'd taken advantage of the water fountain that she'd seen in the hall. More important, she wished she'd visited the latrine.

An inner door opened.

The corporal barked, "Attention!"

Sally jumped to her feet.

Skinner and an officer, who she guessed was Hicks, entered the room. Hicks was the younger, though his hair, cut savagely short per military custom, was starting to gray. He had a squat build and his face had a thick growth that must have required him to shave several times a day, with heavy jowls that reminded her of a bulldog. Neither man smiled as they took the seats on the other side of the table. The room had no window, and the stagnant air had soaked their clothes with perspiration. Her nose detected several odors, all unpleasant. Mostly they were the smells of sweat and tension.

"That's all, Corporal." Hicks's voice was low and powerful, like distant rumbling thunder. Under other circumstances, she would have enjoyed the sound.

She heard the door behind her open and close. The corporal had left the room.

Hicks motioned to her. "At ease. You may be seated."

She dropped heavily, causing the chair to scrape loudly against the wooden floor.

Hicks ruffled through a stack of papers that Sally assumed included notes from Bayard's testimony and the testimony of those who'd investigated the crash. She wanted to sneak a peek, but the chair was too far from the table. Skinner busied himself by scowling at her. The senior flight instructor wore the same wrinkled and soiled flight suit that he'd had on the day before; she recognized the oil stain over his chest. The rest of him needed a trim and comb and probably a good wash down. He had all the makings of an old codger. She'd known plenty of those in East Texas, cranky old farmers who'd grown stubborn as mules as they became elderly and set in their ways. She'd learned that the best way to deal with them was to be just as stubborn. Of course, her opinion of the weather had been the only thing at stake then, while the outcome this morning would affect the rest of her life.

Hicks looked up from his papers. "Miss Ketchum, you are here because yesterday you were involved in the destruction of an aircraft belonging to the Army Air Corps. The purpose of this meeting is to ascertain the cause of that destruction and what, if any, part your actions played in the event. I am Major Hicks. I represent the interests of the army. You've already met Mr. Skinner."

She noted that Hicks wore the wings of an Army Air Corps pilot. That was good; at least he was a flier. His face revealed nothing beyond a sort of gloom, which she suspected was his normal expression. Skinner's intent, on the other hand, was plain as a newspaper headline. He wanted to eat her.

Hicks continued, "We have statements from your instructor, Mr. Bayard, who has given us his side of the story. Now we want to hear what you have to say."

Hicks had honest, soft eyes that reminded her of a puppy. Skinner's eyes were runny and beady. She realized that she'd never seen him blink. Maybe that was the reason why his eyes always looked so watery. Maybe if he'd blink once in a while, he wouldn't look like he was springing a leak.

"Well?" Skinner had a way of shouting even when he wasn't.

"What would you like to know, sir?" Her heart was pounding. She tried to keep her voice from shaking.

"What I want to know is, how two yo-yos, who are supposed to have at least a little experience as pilots, managed to miss ten thousand square miles of perfectly flat, bone-dry ground and crash a nearly brand-new airplane into the only hole with any water in it in all of West Texas. And don't give me that crap about downdrafts, because there weren't any. That air was so still yesterday morning, I could have heard an ant fart." His voice cracked from the strain of trying to keep from screaming.

Sally glanced at Hicks. He looked uneasy, as if he weren't used to so much crust.

Suddenly her plan to expose Bayard seemed fuzzy and confused. She had no reason to believe that either of these men would take a student's word over an instructor's. In fact, for all she knew, Skinner had hired Bayard. Pointing out that blunder almost surely would be like holding a lighted match to a powder keg. She pressed Tex's watch to squeeze some of his strength into herself.

Skinner boomed, "Hey! I didn't call you in here to take the load off. I asked you a question, and I'm getting goddamn tired of waiting for an answer." His face was an angry, purple red.

Hicks made a sour expression. Skinner obviously made him uncomfortable.

"Why don't you just tell us in your own words what happened yesterday," the major said.

"Yes, sir." Sally squared her shoulders. She had already decided to forget Dixie's advice to act coy. Something told her that Hicks wouldn't understand; and as far as Skinner was concerned, if he still appreciated feminine wiles, he kept the fact hidden in the same dark place where he stored his warmth and his charm.

She took a deep breath. "Mr. Bayard had just finished demonstrating a spin when the engine quit. We were at a very low altitude. To keep from turning and risking a stall, he chose to land straight ahead, and that's where the lake was." She almost could hear the watch ticking, the room was so quiet. She felt like she'd fallen into a pit of something disgusting. She was no better than Bayard, worse, maybe, for she had covered up for him. She had just proved that she lacked the personal courage to risk the consequences of telling the truth and that she was a coward.

"Bullshit!" Skinner sprayed the air with spit. "You're lying to me, honey. You do that one more time, and I'll ship your ass out of here so fast you'll think you're a goddamn bullet!"

The explosion caused Hicks to knock his papers all over the table. He scrambled to put them back in place.

"Well!" Skinner's fist crashed into the table, sending a ripple through Hicks's papers.

"Sir?" Sally was trying her best to keep from crying. She wondered if she would at least get to say good-bye to Dixie before they shipped her out. Everything had gone so wrong so fast.

Skinner's eyes bulged, squirting little jets of liquid. "Don't pull that innocent crap on me. I'm giving you one more chance to tell me the truth. You pass it up, and you'll be on the next train out of here!"

Hicks interrupted, "Miss Ketchum, just tell us the truth. It says here you have three hundred flight hours as a barnstormer. Is that correct?"

She nodded. She didn't trust herself to speak.

"That's considerably more hours than anyone in your class. That's more than a lot of military pilots have. Barnstorming is hard, dangerous work, isn't it? You must be a pretty good pilot."

Skinner looked like smoke was about to curl out of his nose. He clearly was fed up with this namby-pamby questioning.

Hicks continued, "Couldn't you have helped Mr. Bayard avoid landing in the water?"

"I tried to, sir!" The words spilled from her mouth. She might as well have tried holding back boiling water. "Mr. Bayard wasn't doing anything to pull us out of the spin, so I had to at the last moment. But he took the controls away from me and put us down in the water."

Skinner's voice lifted him off his chair. "Are you telling me that one of my instructors didn't know how to pull out of a spin, so you had to save his ass? And then he took the controls away from you and made you crash?" She was sure he was going to have a stroke.

"Yes, sir." She barely recognized her voice.

"Well, let's just say for a moment that's true," Skinner demanded. "What do you think I oughta do about it?"

"Fire them both, obviously."

Sally spun around.

Ira Waterman stood in the doorway. Glimpsing him in the car, she hadn't seen how tall and gaunt he really was. He wore a sharply pressed, white, three-piece suit that made him seem even taller. But the thing that pulled at her was his face. It was chiseled like marble and seemed just as hard. She felt a chill when he looked at her.

Waterman stepped into the room. He carried a cane, a beautiful thing carved from some wood she didn't recognize, which was affixed to an elegant handle that looked like ivory. The illusion of age came from the stiff, mechanical way he carried himself, she realized. She tried to visualize him smiling and decided she didn't have that much imagination.

"Something I can help you with, Mr. Waterman?" Skinner obviously didn't like Waterman, but he clearly was trying hard to hide the fact.

That the normally blusterous chief instructor would defer to anyone came as a shock. Until now, Sally hadn't fully appreciated Waterman's power, or how much he apparently was feared. Suddenly she had the sensation of standing at the end of a long plank protruding over the side of a very tall building.

Waterman moved across the room and settled atop the end of the table nearest Hicks. Hicks tried to reposition his chair, but Skinner refused to budge and the major was left sandwiched tightly between the two men.

"This is a closed meeting, Mr. Waterman." Skinner somehow managed to both growl and maintain the pretext of civility.

Waterman's manner spoke of his absolute certainty of power. "You know you can't do that, Bob. Congress has given me liberty to go where I please and to ask what I choose. Or should I have Colonel Bowen remind you? I don't need your cooperation, Bob. Though I, of course, welcome it."

The revelation that Skinner had a first name came as a surprise. Sally had grown so used to thinking of him as just Skinner. Bob Skinner, she decided, sounded entirely too human.

Skinner grunted something unintelligible and slid his chair over noisily, finally allowing Hicks some much-needed breathing room.

"Thank you, Bob."

But the chief instructor had already busied himself with some papers.

Waterman looked at her. "You are Sally Ketchum?"

She recoiled. She could sense no warmth, no compassion nor understanding behind those black eyes, but only intelligence. "Yes, sir."

"You crashed and destroyed an Army Air Corps aircraft yesterday morning."

Sally swallowed. "I've explained to Mr. Skinner and Major Hicks—"

"Explain to me, please."

She began haltingly, "I didn't crash. Mr. Bayard, my instructor—"

"Are we keeping you from some more important business, Miss Ketchum?" he asked suddenly.

"Sir?"

Waterman's eyes dipped to her lap where part of Tex's watch peeked from her fist. "I am under the impression that the sole reason for your presence here is to discover the facts behind your actions, regardless of how uncomfortable or repugnant those might be to the army or to your-self. I am not aware of any military or civilian regulation that affords you the luxury of timing the process of that discovery. May I have the time-piece, please." He held out his hand. His fingers were long and bony, and though expensively manicured, reminded her of claws, and she instinc-tively shrank back. He added sharply, "I will not ask you again." The claws remained extended, the palm belly up and waiting.

"Ketchum!" A vein on Skinner's forehead bulged. His face was the color of fire. "Put that goddamned watch away and stop wasting . . . Mr. Waterman's time!"

She plunged her hand and its precious cargo into her pocket.

Waterman inspected the razor crease of his pants leg. "You are quite right, of course, Bob. My only concern was that Miss Ketchum affords me her undivided attention. Thank you."

Skinner didn't respond.

The instructor was all bluster and bluff. Sally realized that now. He and Hicks would get on with their lives, regardless of what happened at Avenger. Skinner could always go back to running a flight school or being retired or whatever it was that he'd done before the war. Hicks obviously had a cushy job with the army, plus whatever was waiting for him after the war. She was the only one whose life was being destroyed.

Waterman turned his attention back to her. "Do you know who I am, Miss Ketchum?"

She could see why big companies wanted Waterman to do their busi-ness for them. She imagined him scaring a courtroom to death. "Yes, sir, I do."

"Who am I?"

"You're the big Washington lawyer who's trying to shut down the WASP."

He didn't raise so much as an eyebrow. He stood up. "Miss Ketchum, I'm curious to know what it is you think you did wrong that caused you to destroy that aircraft yesterday."

"I've never hurt an airplane in my life, Mr. Waterman!" The words rushed from her mouth. "Mr. Bayard took the controls away from me and—"

"Please." He held up his hand. "You'll do your case no good by blaming your own ineptitude on someone else, especially your instructor. Now please tell us in your own words what happened yesterday. I warn you that it is very important that you tell the truth, the whole truth, and nothing but the truth. Your future may well depend on that. Do you understand?"

"Yes, sir."

"Proceed, then."

Sally took a deep breath. "Mr. Bayard took me up for my introductory flight. He asked me to do a few turns and to show him a stall, which I did. After I recovered from the stall, he grabbed the stick for some reason and put us into a secondary stall, which developed into a spin. It looked to me like he wasn't going to pull out before we crashed, so I took the controls away from him and put us back into level flight. Then the engine quit, and I set us up to land. But he grabbed the controls again, and the next thing I knew, he was putting us down in the middle of the pond." She felt a sense of relief. She had left out nothing of great importance and had put in nothing that wasn't exactly the truth and had avoided saying anything directly bad about Bayard. She had done exactly what Waterman had asked.

Waterman leaned forward from his perch atop the table. "Let me make sure that I understand you correctly. You say you took the controls away from Mr. Bayard?"

She nodded.

"Isn't that highly unusual, for a student to take the controls from an instructor? I am under the impression that the purpose of an instructor is to instruct, i.e., to teach the student what he or she doesn't know. And that, by its very nature, implies that the instructor knows more than the student. Or am I incorrect, Miss Ketchum?"

Something cold and hard smacked her in the pit of her stomach. She'd told the truth, just like he'd warned her to, and he was twisting everything around and making her dig her own grave. She looked hopefully at Skinner, but the old man avoided her eyes. Hicks looked like he wanted to crawl under the table.

She answered as clearly as she could manage, "Yes, sir, I guess it's unusual. But if I hadn't taken the controls, we'd both be dead right now, and staying alive was more important to me at the time than standing on principle."

He struck the cane against the floor so sharply that even Skinner jumped. "Don't you dare get flippant with me, young woman!" He stood and moved slowly to the end of the table, then turned and retraced his path, his cane tapping the floor precisely.

"I may as well warn you. I do not approve of women flying airplanes. Nor do I approve of women inside the military, nor in the workplace. Women belong in the home. I know that's become a hackneyed phrase, but the formula—man in the workplace and woman in the home raising children—is as old as mankind itself. The Bible itself makes reference to it. Change that formula and we risk irreparable change to life as Americans know it. It is, it always has been, the women who raise a society's young. That is the most important task that a society knows. Diminish it and the whole of society is itself diminished, with inevitable chaos."

He would have made a good tent preacher, Sally thought. He would have scared the drinkers onto the straight and the true.

"Many in Congress are convinced, as I am, that the time has come to finally put a stop to this criminality of thrusting young women into the toils of war making," Waterman went on. "The end of this conflict is in sight. Veteran combat pilots are being brought home, each already possessing the skills necessary to ferry aircraft. There is no need to continue risking American women in flying jobs for which they are not suited. Women have neither the physical strength to handle powerful aircraft nor the innate mental acumen to behave appropriately in an emergency. Tests by respected researchers have proved that beyond any shadow of a doubt." His voice was hard and unwavering as bits of steel, the staccato tapping of his cane nerve-racking.

"Compounding this needlessness is the unquestionable truth that every woman who graduates from this base does so at a cost to the American taxpayer that is fifty percent greater than the cost to train a man to perform identically. Yet the attrition rate among WASP is many, many times that of men. Training women to fly for the military is an economic boondoggle. Men are manifestly more stable emotionally. And they don't get pregnant." He looked at her accusingly, as if she were the one responsible for the differences in the engineering of the sexes.

He stepped closer. His aftershave surrounded her with a sense of doom. "Miss Ketchum, my job is to gather information at the behest of Congress so that informed decisions can be made about the future of the WASP. My questioning of you, especially in the context of your actions yesterday, is germane to that task. Hence you will answer my questions promptly and succinctly and with all candor."

She wanted to bolt from the room.

He leaned suddenly into her face. "Miss Ketchum, did your instructor chastise you prior to taking off yesterday?"

"No, sir." Some power that she didn't understand sucked the answer out of her.

"I understand that you have some experience barnstorming. Do you think that you know more than Mr. Bayard?"

"No, sir." The lie, thankfully, came easily.

"Did you attempt to tell him how to do his job?"

"No, sir."

"Did you argue with him?"

"No, sir."

"Were you disrespectful?"

"No, sir."

There was an aura of rot about Waterman that had nothing to do with his flesh. It came from his soul. Sally desperately wanted to wash herself.

He straightened. She sucked in a lungful of sweet air.

"I believe, Miss Ketchum, that you are not being truthful with me." He moved back to better study her. "I believe that you crawled into the cockpit of that airplane yesterday convinced that you didn't have to listen to Mr. Bayard's instructions. I believe that your attitude was one of hostility and superiority."

She tried to block the sound of his voice. She might as well have tried halting an artillery shell.

"I believe the outcome of that fateful flight was sealed from the moment you touched the controls. You admitted in this very room that you fought your instructor. I believe, Miss Ketchum, that the cause of that crash yesterday lies utterly and completely with you."

"No!" The sound was almost a shriek, the voice nearly unrecognizable as her own.

Suddenly Waterman placed his cane across the arms of her chair. His bony fingers pressed the wood, trapping her. "Do not feel that you are being singled out for persecution, Miss Ketchum. The similarities between your unfortunate accident yesterday and that of your fellows who have found themselves similarly compromised are both telling and startling. So much so that a reasonable person would wonder whether there is free will, or if the traits with which we are born truly do ordain us to lives of ineptitude, weakness, and mistake making."

She could only stare back at him helplessly.

"Yes, I have seen it before. The giddy excitement of flight but without the commitment to thoroughly learn the principles of science which allow flight and which allow a pilot to maintain control in the face of the unexpected. The childish attitude that flying is mere fun, without the deeper understanding of its dangers. The haughty attitude of privilege, and the ignorance of its repercussions when given over to the hands of irresponsibility."

He straightened and looked at Skinner and Hicks. Neither looked back. "I have witnessed each during my investigations of the aerial mishaps of the WASP, and I have placed each in my reports to Washington, though they are not my primary concern. I am foremost charged with reporting how well the WASP are trained and how much they actually contribute to the transport of military aircraft. But the crashes do make an interesting, if morbid, addendum. Hence, my visit to your inquiry this morning is, admittedly, a journey more of curiosity than necessity."

His face dipped again. His eyes were inches from hers. "Were you experiencing your time of the month when you crashed yesterday, Miss Ketchum?"

"*What?*" Only shock and the cane above her arms kept her from slapping him.

"Were you in the midst of your time of the month when you crashed?

Was that why you lashed out irrationally toward your instructor? Are you now experiencing your period, Miss Ketchum? Are you bleeding? Is there blood on your inner thighs?"

"Waterman!" Skinner knocked over the table as he jumped to his feet. Waterman straightened but remained expressionless.

Hicks, suddenly deprived of the table, seemed naked and vulnerable.

Skinner reached the lawyer in four steps. His big feet twisted the piles of paper on the floor into waste. "Waterman, I'm unhappy to say that for once the rumors are right." His voice had the texture of a cactus. "You really are an ass—and so full of shit, a corpse six feet under would turn up its nose and roll over in disgust! I've got orders from the army to put up with you. But it's been my experience that the army doesn't know its left hand from its right, so your being here is perfectly understand-able. You don't know your butt from a hole in the ground about flying, but you're spouting off about accidents and the reasons for them. Hell, you don't know enough about airplanes for me to trust you to put air in one's tires, but you're telling this girl that she's responsible for what happened yesterday."

He reduced the distance between them to a nose. "Well, let me tell you something, bub. I *do* know about airplanes, and about pilots and acci-dents, and so here's the way we're gonna work this thing."

He stepped closer somehow. "You're gonna leave the business of train-ing the pilots and the kicking of their asses to me—or you're gonna find out just how good an ass-kicker I am! Understand me? And I don't care who you know or what instructions Congress sent you down here with or what Bowen told you. He can do what he wants with his soldier boys, but I'm a civilian and I'm old enough so I don't give a damn. He can fire me, but he'll find it easier to win a spittin' contest with an elephant than to come up with another civilian who's qualified to do this job. He and I know that. You, like we've already established, don't know your ass from a hole in the ground and so your opinion don't mean shit! Now get the hell out of my meeting!"

Waterman moved for the door. His pace was neither hurried nor halting, but as natural as if he were crossing a room in his own home. If emotions boiled inside him, they remained as safely hidden away as the contents of a bank vault. Sally wondered that anyone's hide could be so thick. In East Texas, any man who'd suffered such an insult would likely have gone for his gun.

He paused in the doorway and turned. "Miss Ketchum . . . Bob . . . Major."

Waterman stepped into the hall and disappeared. The mood inside the room immediately lifted.

Skinner announced, "Hicks, I wanna talk to Ketchum, here. You wanna give us a moment?"

The major got up without looking at either of them and hurriedly left the room, choosing the door opposite the one that Waterman had used.

Sally wanted to kiss Skinner—to hug him and to shout to the heavens that he was a real man. Instead, she held her breath, and kept absolutely still—and waited for what was going to happen next.

Skinner reached into his flight suit and produced a leather bag of chewing tobacco. He stuffed several fingers-full into the side of his mouth. "OK, here's the way it is . . . All I care about is whether we can make you into a WASP. If we can't, you're out of here. If we can, and you keep your nose clean, I'll do everything I can to help you get your wings. It's simple as that. Understand me?"

Sally was too filled with joy to speak.

"I"—he produced a coffee cup from somewhere and spit expertly into its innards—"don't give a crap about that lawyer, and I don't want you to, either. Because I know that Bayard was doing the flying when you hit the water. I saw the whole thing, including your engine quit. It was me that buzzed you in the pond." He almost looked pleased by her surprise.

"I saw how you handled that airplane before Bayard took it away from you. An engine-out over flat terrain is a Sunday walk in the park for a barnstormer. You would have landed OK. But Bayard started trying to do what we pay him to do, panicked, and came up not being worth squat because he doesn't have the training or the experience. But he will, because I'm gonna ride his butt 'til he thinks his arms are wings and his nose is a propeller. I can't get anybody to replace him. That's why I haven't fired his ass, though that's strictly between you and me. He's an instructor and you're just a wet-eared trainee, even if you can fly circles around him and maybe everybody else here except me—so don't let me catch you blabbing about anything I'm telling ya. The only reason I'm saying anything is because I don't want that lawyer messing up your confidence. But talk about this, and I'll stick my foot so far up your butt you'll feel my toes around your tonsils. Understand me?"

She nodded numbly.

"You're off the hook. You did everything right yesterday, in spite of the meathead flying with you. Your record stays clean. OK?"

She nodded again.

"OK." Another dark brown missile exploded into the cup. "You've got a lot to learn, and we've only got a few months to teach it to you. Get out of here and go join your class."

She had barely made it outside when Bayard cut her off.

"Well?" He'd been waiting and didn't try to pretend otherwise. He made a grab for her arm, but she jerked free.

She gave him a look of pure maliciousness.

"Sally, I didn't blame you in there for anything! I swear!"

She stopped suddenly. "Is Skinner going to fire you? Is that what you want to know?"

He inhaled sharply.

She continued, "Firing you would be the sensible, ordinary thing to do. But Skinner's going to do an extraordinary thing. He's going to turn your arms into wings and your nose into a propeller. Now leave me alone!"

She moved away as quickly as her legs would take her, leaving him confused and standing all alone.

# SEVEN

Sally made a slight correction of stick and rudder to keep the PT-19 pointed arrow-straight toward the runway that waited approximately a mile ahead. This was her make-it or break-it moment at Avenger. Instructor Battles could advance her to larger, faster, and more sophisticated basic trainers, or he could send her packing.

She forced herself to loosen her grip on the PT's stick. All she had to do was plant what surely was the world's friendliest airplane onto the same big runway that she'd lifted off of less than an hour earlier. She instinctively advanced the throttle a smidgen to keep up her airspeed and the engine's oil temperature. Only moments separated her from what surely would be a perfect landing. Nothing could go wrong now.

But a blast of air, supercharged to cataclysmic speed by unseasonable moisture and a sun that was said to fry rattlers in their own skin, snatched the PT-19 suddenly and shook it like a mouse trapped in the maw of a gigantic monster. Sally counterattacked using throttle and stick and rudder, weapons that pilots too often found inadequate to stop nature from snapping a nose down, a wingtip up, and flipping and weathervaning a fuselage while hurtling it toward the ground. But as unexpectedly as it appeared, the assault ended and the little airplane once again settled meekly onto its path toward the earth. In the earphones that connected her via the gosport to the front cockpit, Sally heard Instructor Battles make an unintelligible sound.

The tinny quality of the speaking tube was the only thing that her new instructor shared with Bayard. Battles was an ex-airline pilot who'd retired but found he couldn't stay on the ground. He was too old for the military, so he'd come to Avenger. The rumor was that he'd cut his teeth on wire-and-cloth aviation, that he'd known the Wrights and had flown with Lindbergh. This was her fifth time up with him. She'd found him to be a no-nonsense, but steady and fair, instructor who believed in giving his students as much latitude as was safely possible, in order to maximize what they learned. Just now, at the height of the turbulence, she had felt him position his feet and hands on the controls. But he hadn't interfered. He'd sensed that she was controlling the emergency, and he hadn't taken the airplane away from her.

The tires met the runway with a chirp and a rumble, and the PT slowed. Minutes later, she pulled into their assigned parking space and switched off the fuel. The propeller snapped to a stop. She quickly completed the short list of tasks inside and outside of the cockpit that were necessary to securing a PT and joined Battles at the tail of the aircraft. She knew she had performed well, but she still had butterflies in her stomach.

Sally hadn't been impressed when they first met. He was a bald, slightly stooped figure in his middle-to-late sixties, whose expressionless, round, pink face and pudgy middle instantly reminded her of a potato stuffed into a zoot suit. He'd introduced himself, and told her where they would be flying that day and what he expected of her. Then, after showing the scantest interest in watching her preflight the PT, he had crawled into the front seat where—except for an occasional instruction to perform a maneuver—he hadn't uttered a sound until they landed and she'd finished tying down the airplane. Then he'd told her every mistake and near-mistake she'd made from the instant she'd approached the airplane. He never lifted his voice. In fact, he barely moved his mouth, or for that matter, any other part of his body. But his observations had been as precise as a surgeon wielding a scalpel. She realized then that she was in the presence of greatness, and from that moment had hung on any utterance that he cared to share.

He looked at her solemnly. She'd never seen him show the slightest emotion. In fact, other than for his critiques, she'd barely heard him speak. She suspected that Battles was one of those men who needed little more than a sandwich and an airplane to be happy. She had met others like him when she and Tex were flying together. For them, four words were a conversation.

He signed her logbook. Then, suddenly, he stuck out his hand. She was so surprised that for a moment she wasn't sure what he was doing.

"Fine flying. Congratulations, Ketchum."

She was holding the book in her right hand. She quickly shifted it to her left and awkwardly clasped his fingers. The contact lasted only moments before he broke it off and turned and walked away.

She stood there for several minutes, too happy to move. She had passed Primary Trainers; she had wiped away the stain of her crash with Bayard. And John Battles respected her enough to have a conversation, if only one of four words.

She headed for class. She felt like skipping. Today was wonderful, no matter what else happened.

Mr. Alexander, a tiny balding man with a parrot nose, whose thin black suspenders and bow tie gave him the appearance of dressing for a funeral, tapped the blackboard with his pointer. "So you see, because the wing's upper surface is curved, air is forced to move faster across the top of the wing than across the bottom. Since air pressure decreases as its velocity increases, there is less pressure on the top of the wing than on the bottom. So in reality, what an airplane does as it moves through the air is create a failure to maintain equilibrium in pressure above and below its wings, with the result that the top of the wing is literally sucked upward, i.e., lift. And that's why an airplane flies."

The crude airplane that he had drawn an hour earlier was littered now with arrows and numbers and graphs. Each had been put there to illustrate some fact of lift and the apparently endless forms of drag. On an easel to his right, a four-color poster showed the same information plus a multitude more in exploded view. Sitting here and there on the various surfaces of the easel-aircraft were an army of good and bad gremlins who were engaged in either helping the craft stay in the air or working to plunge it to a fiery destruction. They did this through a variety of means, some blowing hurricane winds against the tail to help the plane along, while others used their Herculean strength to try to rip off wings or disconnect control cables or vent hydraulic fluids. Someone in the Pentagon had apparently decided that the little cartoons were a good way to illustrate difficult-to-understand principles, and so they appeared now in practically every piece of technical literature issued by the Army Air Corps.

Sally found this new world intriguing. Her training under Tex had been pretty much limited to the common-sense skills of keeping an airplane from killing her. Now to also learn the science of flight was to peek into a dimension that was as new as it was exciting.

Her first weeks at Avenger had been a roller coaster ride of excitement and frustration. Every moment spent in the air had been better than the one before. But much of her classroom work, and the homework that kept her busy until the barracks lights were turned out, was frustrating. The list of subjects that the army expected her to master was daunting: Military Law; Weather Flying, Clouds & Fog; Plotting & Shooting Bearings; Antenna Use, Tuning; First Aid; Survival, Arctic; Survival, Desert; Survival, Tropic; Camp Sanitation; Pyrotechnics. The list went on and on, and the instructors made it clear that each must be mastered before graduating. There would be no exceptions. A girl could be the finest pilot in the world, but if she couldn't plot a course or perform any of the myriads of other tasks that went into flying the Army Way, she would be sent packing.

Sally now realized how poorly her country education had prepared her for some of the skills that she would need as a WASP. She had already embarrassed herself in front of her navigation class when she forgot how to perform what turned out to be a simple calculation. A handful of girls had already been sent home. Her nightmare was that she would join them.

Mr. Alexander put down his pointer. "That will be all for today. You may take your break."

The big room, the same one they'd assembled in on the first morning, suddenly filled with noisy chatter as the class moved outside to the Coke machines. Sally drifted with them, her mind still afire from her flight with Battles.

The Coke machines were located inside a little open-air shelter. The temperature under the crude pine roof quickly skyrocketed with the rush of bodies eager for a cold drink. Finally with Coke in hand, she pushed her way free of the crowd and walked toward Dixie, who'd found a spot under a tree. Twila and Geri were behind her. The two had begun to spend virtually all of their time together. What Twila saw in Geri, Sally couldn't imagine.

Dixie wrapped an arm around her. "Congratulations on passin' Battles, hon. Everybody with any sense pretty much knew you'd ace him."

"Thanks." She grinned. She was still reliving her performance.

Dixie pointed her Coke at the near-brawl taking place around the machines. "Do you believe that crowd? The government's missin' out on a great way to pay for this war. All they'd have to do is put out more Coke machines." She swabbed at the sweat running down her neck. "I bet I pay for a whole bomber all by myself by the time we get out of here."

Sally nodded. "Mark me down for an entire bomber group." She leaned against the tree and rotated the heavy green glass Coke bottle across her forehead, letting its coolness soak into her skin.

Dixie drained her bottle. "Naw, on second thought, it'd never work. The politicians wouldn't be happy until they'd slapped another tax on the taxes they've already got—until they taxed themselves right out of the Coca-Cola business."

Cathy Lee Smith, one of the girls from their barracks, joined them. Short and chunky, she'd already gotten a reputation for being too loud, too clumsy, and too dense. "I bet I buy a whole air force." She laughed shrilly before tilting her bottle. She remained oblivious to a sizeable dribble on her chin.

Most of the people who'd met Cathy Lee were betting that she would be among those shipped home soon. Sally wondered why Cathy Lee had even volunteered for the WASP. All she ever talked about was how much she missed her extended family back in Colorado and how much they loved cooking for her. She obviously didn't enjoy flying and had little talent for it. She complained constantly about how unfair the instructors were and how hard the PT-19's were to fly. Her insistence at laughing at what wasn't funny and restating what needed no explanation had distanced her from even the friendliest members of the class. So far as Sally could tell, the only thing that Cathy Lee excelled at was eating. For some reason, she loved the food at Avenger and often went back for second and even third helpings.

"Look!" Twila yelled suddenly. She pointed to the sky.

Low on the horizon, coming in almost wingtip-to-wingtip, were two silver specks. At first Sally thought they were trainers, but then she saw that they had twin tails and were moving too fast.

"Those are P-38 Lightnings!" Dixie hollered.

"He's on fire!" Cathy Lee shrieked.

The right engine on the nearest speck had begun to trail smoke. At first, only a puff could be seen. But that quickly turned into a solid black trail.

The normal sounds of the base were broken suddenly by the shrill wail of emergency sirens as fire engines and ambulances raced for the runway.

Everyone got a better look as the specks banked toward the runway. The P-38's fuselage was a delicate, slender pod suspended between its wings. A streamlined nacelle protected the powerful engine in each wing, trailing back into a graceful tail. In the European and Pacific theaters, the plane had gained a reputation as one to be feared, not only by the enemy but by the men who flew it, for it was a fast, agile fighter that demanded much of its pilot. Allies and enemies alike called the P-38 "The Forked-Tail Devil." Sally pictured herself at the controls of this one, which soon would either be safely on the ground or broken into a thousand burning pieces. Mentally, like a doctor watching an operation from the sidelines, she began to work its controls. The pilot had shut down the stricken engine and the propeller hung lifelessly. The second P-38 moved into a hovering spot slightly above and to his right, as if trying to help.

A gasp of fear came from Cathy Lee's throat.

"I'm prayin' for him, too." Dixie whispered.

Suddenly out of the pencil-thin belly and wings of the stricken craft, three dark specks appeared.

"His landing gear's down!" Geri shouted.

"Let's just hope it locks!" Dixie warned.

"I hope he makes the runway," Twila added. "If he lands short, he'll flip for sure!"

Cathy Lee covered her eyes, and then spread her fingers.

Only a few feet of space remained between the burning aircraft and the ground. Smoke from the right engine left a black, boiling scar across the sky. They could see flames around the cowling. Sally imagined the pilot's intense concentration, and wondered if his fear was as great as her own.

The escort P-38 suddenly pulled away. The plane seemed to zoom straight up. At the same moment, the stricken P-38 settled onto the runway with the grace of a ballerina recovering from a high flight of fancy. With one engine burning, fire trucks and ambulances racing and screaming, and now virtually the entire base watching in fascination and frozen horror, the pilot steered the craft to a stop.

People began to move, a great wave of humanity, running wildly toward the burning aluminum silver sculpture that had been saved by superb piloting skill. Sally's feet suddenly seemed to have a mind of their own. They took her with the crowd.

Overhead, the other P-38 stood on its wingtip. Sally heard the bark of the engines as the pilot worked the throttles viciously, causing the engines to load up with fuel and backfire. He was lining up to land and wasting no time.

They were past the hangars now, a giant blur of arms and legs and streaming hair beneath a blistering sun. Ahead was all open fields and runways and the waiting P-38 with its broken, burning engine and the screaming fire trucks and ambulances. Sally vaguely heard the chirp of rubber as the other Lightning touched down.

The pilot of the stricken craft had thrown open his canopy, and some of the firefighters were helping him from the tiny cockpit, while the rest started a flow of water onto the engine. In less than a second, it seemed, huge men in ungainly fire suits had put out the fire, muscled him free, and led him to safety.

Amazed, admiring voices rose from the crowd.

"Did you see that?"

"What a pilot!"

"God!"

The voices were broken exchanges wedged between huffs and puffs of exertion.

The whole great, sweating, panting crowd arrived as one. Like a stampede cornered in a box canyon, they rushed to a dusty, milling halt, most not even noticing the arrival of the second plane, whose pilot had coasted to a stop near the crowd. So intense was the focus on the incredibly skilled hero figure dressed in a flying suit and parachute straps that the world could have stopped and most wouldn't have noticed.

An ambulance driver worked to unsnap the pilot's helmet. The soft leather, attached to headphones and goggles and wires, pulled free easily, setting loose a mane of blonde hair.

"She's a WASP!" Sally's throat clogged with surprise, joy, relief, pride.

"Good god!" Dixie said.

The crowd had fully circled the planes and the women flying them. The crippled ship's pilot waved to her companion, a redheaded girl who shouldered her way through the mob. Sally was startled to see that the two pilots looked her own age.

"Did you see me, Judy? Smooth as silk. Just like the eagles do it." The face of the girl who'd brought in the burning P-38 was pumped red from adrenaline.

The redhead grinned. "Any eagle would be proud, Dotty. Especially if her tail feathers were burning."

They giggled and threw their arms around each other.

Sally didn't know what she had expected P-38 pilots to look like, especially now that she knew they were female; though she imagined they *would* be different. But Dotty, who'd saved her plane with such extraordinary skill, was short and a little dumpy. Judy was neither tall nor short nor chubby nor lean. Neither looked much different from any ordinary American girl in her early twenties, who could be found in any malt shop in any town in America on any Friday night. Except that these two American girls had just landed two of the hottest airplanes in the world under circumstances that could have so easily ended in a deadly fire-ball, killing one or perhaps both of them. She swallowed the lump in her throat and caught her breath. Dotty and Judy essentially looked no different from her. She knew that, given the proper training, she could have done the same thing.

A girl in the crowd hollered, "You *are* WASP, aren't you?" The yearning, worshipful reverence in her voice suggested an eight-year-old meeting Babe Ruth.

"Sure are, honey," Judy answered. "And you must be a newbie."

Startled by the question and flattered by the unexpected attention, the girl said, "How'd you know?"

"Because your zoot suit's still new. The seat and the knees will be worn out by the time you graduate." Judy laughed, and the eager crowd joined her.

Sally looked over her shoulder. She half expected to see a disappointed Waterman, armed with his photographer and a reporter to record the carnage that hadn't happened. But he was nowhere in sight. Nor was Bayard. She had seen him only once since their hearing before the board, and that had been from a distance. The rumor was that, true to his word, Skinner was keeping him busy day and night practicing his flying skills—or more accurately, developing some. For the moment, the magic that these two WASP had performed belonged entirely to them and to their rescuers and to the throng of adoring, worshipful trainees.

Everyone started asking questions at once.

"What happened?"

"Weren't you scared?"

"How many hours do you have?"

"Are pursuits hard to fly?"

"What else have you flown?"

"Where did you take off?"

Grinning, Dotty held up her hands. "One at a time. We picked up these P-38's at Lockheed in Burbank, out in California. We're taking 'em to New

York. They'll probably be shipped by boat to Europe."

"Why don't you just fly 'em over?" someone yelled. "They'd have the range, wouldn't they, with extra gas tanks?"

"Because we're women and the army won't let us," Judy answered. "I think the Allies could be out of planes entirely, and they wouldn't let us fly to Europe." She smiled hollowly. "I think they'd really rather lose the war than let us do the same thing that men are doing every day. The Russians are our allies and we ship P-39 Airacobras to 'em all the time, but they have to meet us in Alaska. That's as far as we're allowed to go. By the way, the Russians have women flying for their army, too, and I don't mean just ferrying. They're flying combat! I handed off a P-39 to a Russian gal last week. She told me her best friend had just shot down a German Messerschmitt while she was six months pregnant."

The crowd gasped.

Sally was shocked. She had never seriously thought about flying combat, nor, she suspected, had the other trainees, and certainly not while pregnant. She hadn't even known that the Russians had a program like the WASP. The knowledge that their women were fighting the German Air Force in air-to-air combat, virtually with a gun in one hand and a baby in the other, gave her a new respect for them.

Cathy Lee asked, "What's a P-39?"

Judy laughed. "One hell of a ride!" The crowd laughed, too. The two WASP could have told their audience the sky was green and every head probably would have obediently nodded in agreement. "It's a little fighter made by Bell Aircraft," Judy said. "The engine's in the rear, behind the pilot. The cockpit's got doors, like a car. The problem is that in an emergency, the pilot has a tough time getting out, because the top of the cockpit doesn't open. More than one pilot's gone home in a box because those doors got in the way."

Cathy Lee stared at her in disbelief.

Judy chuckled. "But you'll get used to that. Pretty soon, you won't even think about it. American pilots don't fly the '39 much because they don't perform very well at high altitude. So we give 'em to the Russians, and they love 'em. They use 'em to blow up German tanks!"

"They sound dangerous." Cathy Lee wrapped herself in her arms.

Judy's grin became wolfish. "They are! And fast and fun! Anything that flies and is fast is fun, so far as I'm concerned."

Two dozen throats roared their approval.

A girl yelled, "If these two '38's are new, how come yours caught fire?"

"Just because they're new doesn't mean they're any good," Judy said. "A lot of times we get planes that've barely been test hopped, and sometimes not flown at all, though we're not supposed to. When that happens, we just hope for the best."

The trainee looked puzzled but didn't ask anything more.

"I've heard that WASP are delivering bombers. Is it true?" Sally almost didn't recognize Geri's voice. It literally dripped adoration.

"That's right," Judy said. "We've both flown B-26's and B-25's, but no one's gotten their hands on a B-24 yet. The army thinks women won't be strong enough to handle the '24 if an engine quits."

A voice called, "How many hours do you have?"

Judy looked at Dotty. "Oh, about five hundred now, I guess. How about you?"

Dotty nodded. "Yeah, I guess about the same."

A hundred-plus voices cried, "Wow!"

As the two talked, Sally noticed things that she'd missed at first. While both women were still young and pretty, deep crow's feet already sprouted from around their eyes, and their faces and arms and hands were red and dry, testament to many hours spent inside hot cockpits exposed to the sun. But she was struck the most by how tired they looked. She wondered if she would come to look like that, too—old before her time; and if so, how soon.

Twila asked, "Everyone says we're going to be militarized. Do you think we will be?"

Dotty shrugged. "Who knows? I've been hearing that ever since I joined."

Judy nodded. "Yeah, me, too. But I'm not holding my breath."

Someone hollered, "Don't you think we should be?"

"We're doing the same work as the men," Judy replied, "plus sometimes more. But they're getting more money and benefits. Damn right, I think we should be militarized! If we were part of the army, the army would have to treat us like everyone else."

A chorus of voices cheered their approval.

"Of course, it may soon be a moot point," Dotty added. "I guess you've all heard that Congress is trying to decide whether to disband the WASP."

A near-desperate voice asked, "You don't think they will, do you?"

Dotty shrugged. "I don't know. They just might. The army and the navy still need planes, for sure. But an awful lot of good combat pilots are being rotated home. And an awful lot of men in high places don't like the idea of women in cockpits."

"Ira Waterman, for one." Sally bit her tongue. She'd promised to put what had gone on inside the review board behind her. She hadn't even told Dixie everything.

"Especially him," Dotty agreed. "He's on a crusade to single-handedly ground us all. He shows up everywhere I fly, it seems like."

"What about the rumor that it costs a lot more to train a WASP than a male pilot?" Sally asked.

"Yeah, right." Dotty laughed thinly. "I read that in the Washington papers. The washout rate for WASP is exactly the same as for men. And they pay us less, so it actually costs less to make a WASP than some hotshot headed for fighter school."

A middle-aged mechanic dressed in greasy coveralls wedged his way through the crowd. His work shoes and pants legs were wet from crawling on the damaged P-38's wing. He tipped his cap to Dotty. "Happy to see you're OK, ma'am. We won't know for sure until we finish the teardown, but my guess is we've found the problem. Come over here." He motioned for her to follow him to the stricken aircraft's right engine. The cowling had been lifted, and the scorched and blackened metal underneath was exposed. He pointed a work-hardened finger to a broken fixture. "Lookee here. There's your problem, right there. Someone cut into your fuel line."

"Sabotage?" Dotty didn't sound surprised.

"Oh, yes, ma'am, for sure. But they didn't cut deep enough. 'Course, all it takes is a little cut and the line'll rupture eventually. It's under pressure. And when it goes, fuel hits that hot engine, and *whoosh*." He used his hands to illustrate burning gasoline. "I guess they never expected you to get this far. I'll betcha that if we check the other engine, we'll see it's been monkeyed with, too. And maybe that one over there as well." He motioned to the other Lightning.

"You mean, someone tried to make you crash?" Disbelief and alarm covered Cathy Lee's face.

Dotty didn't bother to look up from her inspection of the fried goo on the engine. "Yeah, it happens a lot. Someone found a bottle of acid in a parachute a couple of weeks ago. It'd almost eaten through the top of the container. Lucky we found it in time; it would've gotten the silk. We've got orders now to check our chutes regularly. We're not supposed to let 'em out of our sight while we're on duty, not even when we're in the latrine. No one seems to know for sure who's responsible. Probably it's enemy agents, but it could also be workers with a grudge."

"It's not just airplanes, either," Judy chimed in. "We've heard stories about all kinds of things that've been sabotaged, including trucks and tanks."

Cathy Lee was so taken aback by the revelation that she might get killed in this war that her mouth fell open.

"Hey, Ed. Look at this." A mechanic standing on the wing of Judy's plane pointed to its exposed engine. "This one's cut, too. Probably wouldn't have lasted another hour."

The elder mechanic pulled a piece of greasy waste from a rear pocket of his coveralls and wiped his hands. "Well, that's it, then, miss. I'm afraid you're stuck here. It'll take some time to get a replacement for that engine. It may or may not be all burnt up inside; we can't tell without pulling it apart. But sure as hell, I wouldn't fly behind it. And somebody's gonna have to replace these lines and check everything out. The army'll have to send its own people to do that. We don't have the parts."

"Or the time," the other mechanic added sullenly.

Dotty made a face. "Oh, no! I remember the food here. It's just terrible!"

A sudden handclap cut through the conversation. "Alright, girls, time to go back to work." Mrs. Teetle, though tiny, had somehow moved through the throng like a soldier atop a charging warhorse. Four steps behind her, and nearly running to keep up, was Sergeant Crawford. The sergeant was sweating heavily and looked badly in need of rest.

"Hello, Mrs. Teetle." The two WASP came more or less to attention. Neither looked happy to see their former supervisor.

The little woman studied them, obviously trying to remember their names. Up close, she looked even more like a bulldog than she had in the auditorium on their first day at Avenger, Sally thought. Apparently her natural expression was anger, a condition that was exaggerated by the thrust of her chin, which seemed to be challenging the world to a fight. Her hair was prematurely streaked with gray and she looked tired and haggard. But whatever her failings, she was certainly hard-working.

"Judy Peveto and Dotty Leguenec." Mrs. Teetle allowed herself no con-gratulatory joy for resurrecting their names from her obviously harried mind.

"Yes, ma'am." They answered as one.

"How are you girls?"

"Fine, ma'am."

"Where are you stationed?" Mrs. Teetle obviously was in a hurry and maneuvering toward an end to these pleasantries.

"Palm Springs," Judy answered.

"How do you like it?"

"We don't!" Dotty said. "It's hotter'n Hades down there."

Mrs. Teetle, her foot already engaged in a hard right turn, her body screaming of the importance of more pressing matters, snapped, "There is a war on and we all must do our part. Both of you had better come with me. You need to report, and the army'll want to get someone out here to fix those planes. I'm sure our own people are too busy to be of much help. We'll find room for you until you're on your way."

The two WASP grabbed their chutes and followed, first at a walk and then at a trot.

Obviously relieved to be left behind, Sergeant Crawford fell into the fa-miliar role of herding. "Back to class. Back to class. Back to class." His weary voice carried across the flight line and the featureless plateau beyond. He waved his arm over his head as if spreading a lasso to snap back any strays.

The mob of chattering young women fell obediently into step.

"Well, I can tell you one thing right now," Dixie said to Sally. "Rationin' or no rationin', I'm not goin' up in another one of these damn airplanes without drenchin' myself first in some kind of lotion. Did you see their skin? I've seen overcooked chickens that looked better!" Dixie's mouth was set, her brow worried.

"I'll trade dry skin and a few crow's feet any day of the week for the chance to fly a P-38," Sally said.

Twila intervened. "Oh, they've probably been flying a lot and just ran out of lotion. I'm sure being a WASP doesn't mean we'll wind up looking like scarecrows."

Dixie's jaw jutted. "Well, it had better not. Because this war can't last forever. And when it's over I expect to get back to doin' what I was doin' before it came along. And I can tell you right now that there's damn little call in the modelin' business for women who look like overcooked chickens!"

Sergeant Crawford barked, "Hey, you! Get to class!"

They looked behind and saw that Cathy Lee was the straggler. She hadn't moved from the damaged P-38.

"What's wrong with her now, do you think?" Twila asked.

"What's not?" Dixie said. She had taken to calling Cathy Lee "The Little Blonde That Couldn't." More than once, she had suggested that Cathy Lee was really a German agent sent to break or eat everything in sight.

Cathy Lee wasn't moving, in spite of the sergeant's shouts.

"I'll get her." Sally started back. "I'll catch up to you, Dixie."

Dixie growled, "You sure you don't want to take along half a steer and a sack of potatoes for protection?"

As she approached Cathy Lee, Sally could see that something, indeed, was wrong. She touched the girl's shoulder. Her muscles were hard as rocks. A wind had come out of the north and was kicking up little tornadoes of grit that stung the nose and ground the eyes. The heat and dirt were evaporating Cathy Lee's tears almost as fast as they slid down her cheeks, leaving behind jagged little trails of mud.

"What's wrong, Cathy Lee?"

"I can't."

Sally looked around, but no one was in earshot. They were completely alone, except for the two P-38's and a handful of mechanics who were too busy with the planes to notice them.

"What can't you do?"

Cathy Lee stared at the burnt airplane. "I couldn't do what Dotty did," she whispered. "I'd have crashed. I'd be dead." Her tears were outrunning even the dirt and the heat. They dripped off her cheeks and disappeared into her zoot suit. "I'm not like you and the rest. You can do anything you put your mind to. You don't let anything or anyone stop you." She cried harder.

"I'm sorry, Daddy." She sank to the ground. "I'm sorry, Daddy." She closed her eyes.

Sally put an arm around her. Cathy Lee finally had come clean with herself. She would never fly a P-38. Sally suspected she hardly had ever flown a Piper Cub. She was the last to recognize the truth about herself that the rest of the barracks had known all along. Today, tomorrow, sometime soon, the army would have sent her home, anyway. At least now she wouldn't have to face that embarrassment. By this time tomorrow, Cathy Lee would be back in Colorado, where she could eat all that she wanted of whatever she wanted, and her family would love her and protect her from the world.

Sally felt a pang of jealousy. Cathy Lee would never fail at anything again because she probably would never again risk anything. Her family, extended to numerous aunts and uncles and nieces and nephews, would shield her for as long as she lived. A bile taste crept into her mouth. Cathy Lee had everything. Luck had handed her the sweet life on a platter. She could even have been a WASP. But she was too much of a child to appreciate it.

# EIGHT

"One! Two!

"One! Two!

"One! Two!

"Come on, girls!

"One! Two!

"One! Two!

"Snap it up!"

Lieutenant Olson was so fixated on his band of bouncing, sweating trainees that Sally was sure she could have shot him dead and he wouldn't have noticed.

"Get those arms in the air!

"Spread those legs, girls! Spread 'em wide! Show me your enthusiasm!

"One! Two!

"One! Two!"

"If . . . that jackass . . . don't find somethin' . . . pretty soon . . . to look at . . . besides my chest . . . I'm gonna use . . . my knee . . . to show him . . . my enthusiasm!"

Sally normally would have warned Dixie to shut up. But she was too winded and too tired from doing push-ups and sit-ups and knee-bends and now jumping jacks. Besides, Lieutenant Olson never ogled her chest during these daily calisthenics sessions. But his obsession with jumping jacks, and desire to pursue that exercise longer than any other, certainly was both exhausting and irritating.

"Wider, girls! Wider!

"Now get those arms up!

"Stick them way up!

"Jump, girls!

"Jump!"

The lieutenant reminded her of the tent preachers that her daddy dragged her to when she was a child. Their wild-eyed behavior had repulsed and embarrassed her at first, until the novelty wore off and she became bored. Now she just wanted Lieutenant Olson to get his fill of whomever he was gawking at, so he would end physical training for today, and she could get a Coke and relax in the rec room until chowtime. Annoying as the lieutenant was, she understood why the army had chosen him to lead calisthenics instead of Sergeant Crawford. The sergeant wouldn't have lasted three minutes, while Olson, short and wiry and, she guessed, no more than twenty years of age, seemed eager to jump with his charges for as long as there was light.

"One! Two!

"One! Two!

"Stop!"

He landed lightly on his feet. He rested his hands on his hips in a gesture that not so subtly thrust his pelvis forward. The absolute joy on his face suggested he couldn't have been happier if he were dating Betty Grable.

"You are dismissed!"

"I hope I meet that guy in a dark alley sometime when I have my skinning knife with me," said Sandy Friggins. Sandy told entertaining stories of growing up hunting and fishing and racing her coon dog through the hills of Kentucky, and she was one of the best athletes in the class. But right now she looked like she'd fallen into a lake. Her workout shorts and blouse were soaked through. Her dark hair was plastered to her neck and forehead. And her normally pleasant expression was angry.

"I'll settle for a baseball bat." Dixie was bent over, panting. To Sally, she sounded like an old steam locomotive struggling up a hill. Dixie wasn't out of shape; but she wasn't athletic and she made no bones about it.

Her most hated subject was calisthenics. As she was only too eager to explain to anyone who would listen, "The opportunities are mighty slim for sweaty models, and for dirty ones, too; but if you happen to be both, they're none at all!" Whether that was true, Sally didn't know. But she did know that Lieutenant Olson was out of line and taking advantage of his power, and he deserved to get his butt kicked. And she would have been happy to do the job, if she wasn't sure that would be the last thing she ever did as a WASP-trainee.

The class scattered. Where scores of girls had occupied a large bare spot between buildings moments before, now less than a half-dozen remained. Summer had given way to fall, but the Texas sun still packed a terrific wallop. A strong wind blew, and the gritty dirt blasted Avenger's wooden buildings and all those foolish enough to remain outside them. The buildings were painted white, except for some that also had a band of blue extending upward from the foundation for several feet. Thanks to the constant assault of sand and light and heat and winter cold, keeping the paint looking fresh was an impossible task.

"Come on, Dixie; let's get a Coke." Sally took Dixie's arm. Her eyes stung and her mouth was full of sand, and they still had to change into their zoot suits before going to chow. "I want to clean up."

Dixie fell into step. "I'm real interested in seein' how ya gonna do that, honey," she moaned. "Seein' as how this is the one place in the whole world where takin' a shower just makes ya dirtier!"

The rec room was probably like every rec room on every United States military base in the world, Sally thought. Its builders' mission had been frugality and speed of construction, while its decorators had been constrained to military-issue couches and chairs. Obligatory photographs of airplanes, suitable for framing, were tacked to the bare walls, and a cheap Ping-Pong table and surfaces adequate for playing checkers and chess were wedged wherever they fit. In a nod to homesickness, a hodgepodge of well-thumbed magazines lay here and there.

She tossed hers onto the other end of the couch. She'd already looked at that issue of the *Saturday Evening Post* twice. Why the army could develop ever-faster and higher-flying aircraft but couldn't supply the magazines that graced the tables of practically every household in America was a mystery.

She drained the last of her Coke. All the windows were closed, but she could still taste the wind. Despite the heat and the dust, a ball was already in perpetual motion above the Ping-Pong table, and girls were hunched at the chess and checkers boards. The rest of the class either hadn't arrived yet from their bays, or was clustered into chattering groups or milling about without apparent purpose. She looked at her watch. Dixie was late. She'd promised to take a quick shower, then collect her mail at the base post office, before meeting up for chow. Mrs. Teetle took a dim view of tardiness, be it for class or for chow.

Twila dropped onto the couch. "Where's Dixie?"

"Late. As always." Sally didn't get to spend a lot of free time with Twila, though their quarters were only feet apart, and she cherished the moments. Twila's knowledge of science and math and of most things aviation-related seemed endless, and despite the unyielding workload, she never hesitated to help anyone who needed tutoring, even though she had little time for herself.

Twila laughed. "Dixie will never get into B-17 training if she keeps that up."

Sally snapped to attention. The B-17 was the big four-engine bomber that the newspapers had nicknamed the "Flying Fortress." Hundreds and hundreds of them made raids daily across German-occupied Europe and suffered horribly at the hands of anti-aircraft gunners and the Luftwaffe's fighter pilots. She hadn't known that WASP would be allowed to fly the giant machines.

"Are we being trained on B-17's?"

Twila grinned knowingly. "A few WASP are. The army's sending them through the same combat flight training that the men get. Bombers have to be ferried, just like everything else, and there aren't enough men Stateside to fly them. That's why I started carrying this." She produced a tennis ball from one of the cavernous pockets in her zoot suit. She tightly squeezed and then released the thing several times in rapid succession.

"What's that for?" Sally asked. Twila wasn't known for making jokes, or for playing jokes. If she said there was some connection between the B-17 and a tennis ball, then there undoubtedly was. Though for the life of her, she couldn't imagine what it could be.

"It builds my upper-body strength. See." Twila clenched her fist until her arm muscles became taut. "I've got a friend who's going through training now. She said this is just one of the tricks they teach you. The 17's so much airplane that it'll eat you real fast if you don't know what you're doing."

"What does she say it's like to fly?" Sally asked eagerly. Despite all the chatter in the rec room, she was aware only of Twila.

"It's a pussycat! Almost a Piper Cub—until something goes wrong! She said the first time her instructor chopped the power on an engine, her leg muscles really yelped. Then when he killed a second engine, she thought her arms and leg were on fire from straining to hold it level. I just got a letter from her yesterday, and she said on her last flight he cut three engines at once. She was sure they were going to stall and spin in. But she retained control of the airplane."

Sally could imagine the terror—and excitement—of flying a huge airplane on only one of its three engines. Pilots she'd spoken to who flew them explained in graphic detail what happens when an engine dies. In the case of a B-17 with only a working engine on its right wing, the plane would swing violently to the left. Its pilots would have to instantly push down on the right rudder pedal and sling the stick over in the same direction to keep the wings from stalling, and pull back on the stick to keep the nose up. It was a lot to do almost instantly and it all had to be done correctly, especially on a huge, complex machine like the 17—or the plane would tumble past the point at which recovery would have been possible, and men and machine would fall to Earth and die in a terrible, fiery crash. That's why multi-engine pilots were drilled over and over and over again in engine-out emergency procedures.

"I can't believe the instructor cut three engines at once!" Sally said. She was perched on the edge of the couch.

"Her instructor taught her a trick," Twila said. "She pushed as hard as she could on the rudder pedal on the side of the good engine. And she hooked her foot under the pedal on the dead side and pulled like hell!"

"Ha!" Sally smacked her hands together. She wasn't particularly strong. Certainly she wasn't as strong as even the average man. But she was sure that with the proper training, she could recover a B-17 from a power-out emergency. She vowed to grab some tennis balls the next time she went to Sweetwater, if in fact a store could be found that stocked such an un-Texas-like commodity. But if not, she would improvise somehow.

"What's up?" Geri plopped down between them, and Twila quickly moved farther down the couch to give her some room.

"I was just telling Sally about the letter I got from Rosalie," Twila said. "You know, the one about flying the 17."

Sally felt Geri's eyes upon her.

"Something you plan on doing?" The sneer in Geri's voice was unmistakable.

"Yes," Sally said defensively. The joy that she and Twila had shared vanished.

Geri produced an apple from her zoot suit and took a bite. "Well, that will be a miracle." She made a show of taking another bite. "Because I was under the impression that all of your schooling happened right here in Texas." She looked at Twila to see if she understood the joke. Twila seemed slightly uneasy but also mildly annoyed. Plainly, she didn't approve of what Geri was doing, but not enough to stop her.

"So?" Sally felt a twinge of anger. She considered Twila her friend. She didn't appreciate her violating that bond.

Geri flipped her head to one side, causing her beautiful red hair to rise and fall. "So I guess you don't know that they won't let you into B-17 school if you can't read and write!"

"Geri!"

Geri ignored Twila and stood up. She took a final bite of her apple before tossing it into a nearby trash can; her face showed her satisfaction. As she sauntered toward the door, she retrieved a white tennis ball from one of her pockets and began to squeeze and release it with exaggerated energy.

"I guess she's had a bad day." Twila meant it as an apology.

"I'd say, every day." Sally's face was burning. She thought of all the things she wished she'd said to Geri. "She's a bitch!"

"She has her problems," Twila said.

"She's a bitch!" Sally repeated. She was fed up with Twila's defense of Geri.

"OK, yes," Twila admitted. "She is."

"No one likes her," Sally persisted. "I don't see how you live with her. How can you stand her?"

Twila turned so they faced each other. Her flushed cheeks were the only outward sign that she wasn't her normal, relaxed self. "I understand her anger and I understand why she's the way she is. We have more in common than you can imagine.

"But I haven't answered your question." She rose and smiled sincerely. Despite whatever emotions she felt, it was plain to Sally that Twila wanted to continue their friendship. "I like her."

She moved across the room and followed her roommate through the door.

"You'd get into B-17 school," said a man's voice.

Sally looked up to find Beau Bayard. A wave of irritation washed over her. She wanted to be left alone to digest what had just happened between herself and Twila.

"How have you been, Sally?" He was trying hard to sound upbeat, but he looked uneasy.

She'd seen him around, but they hadn't spoken since the crash. After working him almost day and night to teach him some flying skills, Skinner had recently been sending him up with students in the advanced classes as an observer. The word was that Bayard had finally become more than just ballast. In fact, he was supposed to be a decent pilot now.

"Fine!" First Olson. Then Geri. Now this one. She'd had enough aggravation for one day. She looked at her watch. If Bayard wouldn't leave her alone, then she just wanted Dixie to show up so she could get some chow, hit the books, and go to bed.

She stood up, forcing him to move back a foot. He was almost standing on her toes.

"I hear good things about you, Sally. They say you're a regular virtuoso with a stick and a rudder."

She didn't know what that meant and she didn't care, since he'd said it—though she reminded herself to keep a civil tongue. Jerk or not, he *was* an instructor.

"Excuse me. I don't want to be late for chow." She stepped around him.

He still appeared disappointed several minutes later, when she looked in the window on her way to find Dixie.

The wind had died down and the sun was low in the sky. The day's last gasp was a brilliant spectacle of reds and oranges. It was going to be a beautiful Texas night, lit by more stars than a person could count in a lifetime.

Dixie popped out of nowhere. "Hey! I got a letter for ya!" she said. She was freshly scrubbed and wearing a clean zoot suit. They fell into step together.

"Where have you been?" Sally asked. "You almost made us late for chow!"

"I told ya! Tryin' to scrape off the mud—and Olson's eyeballs—and runnin' to grab the mail! Why? Did I miss somethin'?"

"Yeah! A nut and a rat and my everlasting surprise at people!"

"What?" Dixie stopped.

"Never mind." She stuck out her hand. "I have a letter?"

In the whole time they'd been at Avenger, she'd never gotten a piece of mail. She examined the thing. It was a homemade contraption of folded paper that had been glued together. It was addressed simply to "Sally Ketchum, Avenger Field." The author hadn't seen fit to advise as to town, and there was no return address. The handwriting was large and awkward and done in pencil, as if by the hand of a child.

"That's a mighty thrifty friend you've got there, hon." Dixie had begun to tear into the topmost of her apparently endless supply of packages, cards, and letters that arrived almost daily, mostly from men. Who these correspondents were and what was on their minds, Dixie never shared, though she took great delight in the opening and reading of each, and often responded with chuckles of satisfaction or occasionally with harrumphs of displeasure. Sally caught the scent of men's cologne. It smelled expensive.

Her own poorly glued piece parted easily. The lone paper inside proved a twin of its envelope, as did the barely legible pencil scrawl. As she started to read its contents, she came to a stop.

> *Sumthin bads happpuund that u need to no bout.*
>
> *See me.*
>
> *B.D. Horne.*

"Who's B.D. Horne, hon?" Dixie had been reading over her shoulder. She took the papers, her frown deepening.

"I don't know."

Dixie looked at her quizzically. "This B.D. Horne doesn't ring any kind of a bell?"

"No, I've never heard the name."

Dixie turned the paper over, but the reverse side proved blank. "Then it's gotta be a joke." She handed back the pieces.

"A joke? What's funny about this?"

"Nothin'. That's the whole point. The army's got no sense of humor and it's rubbin' off. Some of the knuckleheads in our class, like that jerk, Geri—she wouldn't recognize a joke if it walked up and kicked her. That's what this is. Somebody's jealous of your flyin', so they thought they'd have a little fun with you. I'd just throw it away, if I were you."

The mention of Geri's name soured Sally's curiosity. She was sure that she had never known a B.D. Horne. Dixie had to be right. Her country background was no secret, nor was her flying skill and reputation as the best pilot on the base. She wouldn't put it past Geri to play a stupid joke. She wadded up the papers and hurried to a trash barrel on the other side of the street and tossed the mess inside.

"That'll show 'em, hon." Dixie had resumed walking and examining her booty.

Sally hurried to catch up before she was left behind. And within a few moments, she had nearly put the note out of her mind.

# NINE

"They're gonna hit!" Dixie's shout from the rear cockpit rattled the headphones.

Sally gave the throttle a hopeful shove, but their engine was already screaming for all it was worth. She scanned the cockpit. The ship was properly trimmed. There was simply nothing more that she could do to keep up with the two airplanes passing her left wingtip.

She pressed the intercom button. "I know!" Her urgency matched Dixie's.

At first Sally had thought the pilots of the two airplanes were playing a friendly game of cat-and-mouse. Now she saw that she couldn't have been more wrong. The lead plane, with markings that plainly showed it was from Avenger, was flying too desperately. The other one, with markings she didn't recognize, was flying too closely, its propeller at times mere feet from a collision. She'd gotten a good look at the Avenger pilot and knew she was frightened. The girl kept looking over her shoulder. The other pilot, whose face she hadn't been able to see, was hunched down like an animal on the scent of blood. Both planes were AT-6's, the most advanced trainer at Avenger. Sleek and powerful, with a tandem cockpit covered by a clear, narrow canopy like the BT-13 that she and Dixie were flying, the AT-6 was said to be the sweetest trainer in the military; whoever was flying this one from Avenger would be nearing graduation. Certainly she knew what she was doing. She was twisting and turning the big machine like an ace.

Dixie demanded, "Can't you make this piece of junk go any faster?"

Dixie knew as well as she did that they were powerless. Their BT-13 was a big step up from the little PT that Bayard had crashed on Sally's first day at Avenger months earlier. But no Basic Trainer was a match for an AT-6.

They couldn't even alert the outside world. Their radio seemed to be working, but atmospherics were keeping it from reaching Avenger, or for that matter anywhere but across the one hundred or so feet that separated their right wingtip from the BT-13 being flown by Geri and copiloted by Twila. This was an all-too-common occurrence with aircraft radios. The things seemed to always work the least when they were needed the most. They couldn't even talk to or hear the AT-6's, which apparently were either having their own radio problems or were using some frequency that she and Dixie hadn't identified. Without the radio, they could only watch and guess at what was going through the minds of the pilots.

One thing was certain. The pursuing pilot was in the wrong. Almost from the moment they'd arrived at Avenger, they'd been lectured that dogfighting was forbidden, the penalty an immediate one-way ticket home, whether the offender was a trainee or a graduate—no exceptions. The same held true for men, who faced court-martial. Sally assumed this pilot was a man, though she couldn't be certain. It could be a WASP out to harass a trainee for sport. But whoever it was, flying so dangerously close to another airplane labeled him, or her, a fool.

Suddenly the girl from Avenger dropped her plane's nose. She apparently intended to escape by diving.

But the trailing aircraft also nosed over, and at the same time lowered a wing. With a start, Sally realized its pilot was going to attempt a barrel roll around her.

The pursuer's wing sliced into the Avenger pilot's cockpit like a hot knife cutting butter. The two continued as one for an instant. Then the wing jerked free, and the craft from Avenger began a sickening plunge toward Earth.

The surviving AT, built as tough as a safe and as powerful as a fleet of automobiles, staggered on the verge of a snap roll in the direction of its wound. Several feet were missing from the wingtip; wires protruded from the stump like ligaments from a severed hand. But the pilot somehow regained enough control to return to more or less level flight.

Sally jerked the BT's throttle back, stomped the right rudder, and adjusted the stick. The wing dipped and the nose swung around, allowing her to follow the lead AT's death plunge.

Suddenly a figure struggled from the mangled cockpit, and a plume of white billowed from her parachute pack. The silk briefly snagged the stricken craft's tail before slipping free. And the figure continued her earthward tumble beneath the fluttering wing of worthless, collapsed parachute. The tangle of wrecked and twisted metal fell with her, until finally a dirty black ball of smoke appeared on the ground.

"Damn." Dixie drew the sound out softly.

The BT began to vibrate. The clear Plexiglas canopy above their heads rattled as if about to explode. Sally had let her airspeed decay; the wings were on the edge of a stall. She was going to fall out of the sky, too, if she didn't start paying attention to what she was doing. She applied power and eased up on the controls.

The other AT-6 was already moving away. Even with a destroyed wing, the big trainer was faster. Sally noted that the pilot was choosing to fly straight ahead instead of turning back to Avenger.

"Did you get any tail numbers?" she asked.

"No." Dixie's voice was almost unrecognizable.

She hadn't, either, and both planes had flown right by them. She felt like a fool. The numbers would have let the authorities quickly identify the pilots.

"Did you get numbers?"

Sally recognized Twila's voice. As Geri's copilot, she was seated in the rear of the other BT's cockpit. They were flying a cross-country exercise. Midway through, they all were supposed to land and refuel. Then each crew would switch duties, with copilots becoming pilots and moving to the front seat and pilots taking the rear responsibilities.

She thumbed the mike button. "I didn't see the numbers. How about you?"

"No."

She looked around. Avenger was some distance away. No other airplane was in sight. No houses were nearby. Summer was gone now, and fall had nearly finished sucking away the modest green that had come to West Texas. The area below was all mean wilderness and brown ranch land, for as far as the eye could see. For the moment, the four of them—and the pilot of the quickly disappearing AT-6—were the only ones in the world who knew what had happened.

"Watch your right!"

Dixie's warning snapped her back to the business of flying. Geri was also piloting a circling pattern above the ugly black column below, and the two planes were getting dangerously close. Midair collisions were a constant danger wherever airplanes congregated. More students seemed to die in the closely packed traffic pattern above Avenger than in bad weather or because of mechanical problems. Sally quickly reduced power and lifted the nose until the other BT was opposite them in the circle.

Twila's voice came over the radio again. "What do you think we should do?"

"What the hell? Tell her we're goin' back to Avenger!" Dixie almost didn't need to use the intercom, Sally thought.

She looked down. A crude trail ran near the spot where the wreckage lay, put there by decades of passing cattle. There was no wind; smoke from the crash rose straight up. Her idea was crazy, but not impossible. She would have to be careful, though. A radio could be as ineffective as a noodle hammer one minute, and then for no apparent reason blast out everything you said to everyone and his brother.

She pulled the throttle back and pushed the stick forward. The nose instantly dropped, and the BT fell smartly out of the circle.

She keyed the mike button. "Understand?"

A moment passed. Then Twila's disembodied voice returned. "Roger."

Dixie yelled, "Hey! You wanna let me in on what we're doin'?"

The sound of air rushing past the long, clear canopy became louder. Sally alternated between scanning the world outside and the instruments inside. The BT was a stout bird, but like all airplanes, it had its limits. One of those was a maximum dive speed of 230 miles per hour.

She doubted the wings would come off if she went a little faster, but she didn't plan to find out.

"Hey! I said, what are you doin'?"

She gritted her teeth. Dixie knew very well what she was doing.

She pulled on the stick. The BT flattened its descent and leveled off. The centerline of the engine cowling was lined up with the trail now.

The ground appeared flat. No machine or anything created by man was visible in any direction. Except for the cow trail, the area looked exactly as it had for probably two thousand years.

She completed the landing checks. Her eyes told her that they still were going too fast. She pulled the throttle farther back and lifted the nose slightly.

"Hey!"

"I'm landing, Dixie! She may still be alive!"

"Like hell! We were at three thousand feet when that chute collapsed! Nobody falls three thousand feet and lives!"

Common sense told Sally that Dixie was right. But her brain refused to believe that the girl was dead. Maybe her chute caught some air at the last moment. Maybe she had been saved by a miracle. "We have to find out," she insisted.

The throttle, duplicated in the rear cockpit like every other control and instrument in the trainer, suddenly jerked forward. The big Pratt & Whitney R-985 radial engine snorted and roared. The BT instantly picked up speed and altitude.

"Dixie, stop it!" She snapped the engine back to near-idle. The plane immediately slowed.

"Sally, she's dead!" Dixie jerked the throttle to the wide-open position. "You can't make an off-field landin'! They'll wash us out!"

The engine roared and then fell nearly silent and roared again. The BT's nose rose and fell and rose crazily. She was using all of her strength, but Dixie was stronger. They were only feet above the ground. A crash was certain. She made a final desperate plea.

"Dixie! I'm flying the plane! Let go!"

The engine fell to an idle, and the BT's tires brushed skinny grass and then hard soil and they rolled to a stop.

Neither spoke. They both knew how close they'd come to killing each other.

Sally set the brake and slid back the forward part of the canopy. The nights had become nippy but the temperature during the day hovered in the mid-seventies. The blast of air from the propeller felt good on her face. "You don't have to go. You can stay here and watch the plane." She unsnapped her bulky harness and stood up.

Dixie's part of the canopy slammed forward, and she stepped onto the narrow walkway atop the wing. Her face twisted with rage. "I didn't put my modelin' career on hold and put up with a pile of crap from the army just so you can be a hero!"

"Now, wait!" Dixie's anger enflamed her own.

"You wait, Sally! She's dead! Accept it! There's nothing in the world that you can do for her!"

Self-doubt was trying to grab hold, but she wasn't going to let Dixie know that. She straightened to her full height. "You know me better than that. Landing was the right thing to do. It is the morally right thing to do."

Dixie snorted. "The morally right thing?" She sounded like the idea was new to her. "God save us all from people who want the world to do the morally right thing. More crimes have been committed in the name of doin' the morally right thing than there are Baptists in Texas!" She jumped to the ground.

"Hon, do me a favor the next time you plan on doin' somethin' real stupid. Let me know ahead of time, so I can go find somebody else to fly with. Because I didn't come into this war with any busted bones or gray hairs. And I sure don't plan on takin' any with me when I leave!"

A reflection of light interrupted the argument.

The other BT was on final approach. The trainer seemed to hang in the air for a moment before slipping gracefully to the hard-packed ground.

Sally turned away, her thoughts distracted. She and Dixie had nearly killed each other. She had started a course of action that, if discovered, would wreck all their lives. And Geri, surely one of the most arrogant and nasty and spoiled women in the world, had somehow become a good pilot—or maybe even, a great pilot. It almost was too much to digest.

Dixie studied the slowly approaching BT. "Do you think Geri's flyin' that thing?"

Sally jumped off the wing. She knew that she would make the same decision again about landing, if the situation repeated itself. She answered, "Yes."

Dixie, apparently focused only on Geri, hissed, "Just goes to show that even a jackass can learn to land an airplane . . . if the government's stupid enough to spend enough time and money trainin' it." She crossed her arms. "Monkey see. Monkey do. That's all that was!"

They both knew that Dixie couldn't have made that landing—just as they both knew that even the prospect of dying or being washed out wasn't as threatening to Dixie as Geri outshining her. Sally allowed herself a brief smile. It was comforting to know that if she somehow shot Dixie this afternoon, or set her on fire or caused her to tumble down an abandoned well, it wouldn't make her friend as angry as seeing Geri make a perfect landing on a cow trail.

The BT rocked to a stop. As Sally had done, Geri set the brake and opted to leave the engine idling in case it proved difficult to start later. The front part of the canopy slid back and the rear moved forward. The two pilots emerged and dropped to the ground. They joined Sally and Dixie.

No one spoke as the four women moved, as one, toward the boiling, black smoke rising from behind a hill.

As they approached the wreck, the only sounds were the slow idling of the engines behind them and the soft crackling of the flames in front of them. Everything that wasn't metal had already burned away, except the black ham that had landed within the flames of the wreck. No arms or legs or neck or head were still connected to the ham. They also had burnt away.

They stopped. They could have gone closer, but there seemed no point. A grasshopper fleeing the flames sped by in search of safety.

Sally heard a low moan and turned to find Geri a handful of steps behind. She was throwing up. Her vomit came in hard, gagging explosions that left just enough time for her to gasp a breath of air. This was Geri's introduction to death, she suddenly realized—or at least, to this kind of death, so naked and so violent. No flowers here. No music. No expensive cloth for the cold flesh, or comfort for those death had left. No one here to step forward to assure Geri that all would be alright. This was death. And it was horrible.

Her belly apparently emptied, Geri started to sob. Twila moved to steady her. She placed her arm around Geri's shoulder and drew her head to her chest, and her body began to move ever-so-slightly to the motion of Geri's sobs.

Sally stared at the remains of the girl. "I'm so sorry." Her throat muscles closed. Not that it made any difference. There was nothing more to say.

There was no reason in the world for this to have happened. The day was a good one for flying. The planes were obviously airworthy, the pilots obviously skilled. What had caused the other pilot to do such a thing? And this was the result: the ruined AT-6, the ruined dreams of the ruined girl, the unkindness of a world festering in unkindness. Why?

She felt Dixie's hand on her arm. "You can't do anything for her, hon. Men have been killin' women since day one. Either because we wouldn't give 'em what they wanted or because they got their bow and their arrow pointed in the wrong direction or because, like here, he wanted to show off what's between his legs. Unfortunately for her, it turned out not to be much."

Sally turned away from the ruins. "Are you sure a man was flying the other plane?"

"Yeah!" Dixie said. "I saw him. I got a good look at him."

Twila joined them. "I saw him, too. It was a man."

"There are four of us! How could we all have missed their numbers? It just doesn't make sense!" Sally shook her head.

"We weren't expecting this to happen," Twila said. "When it did, it happened so quickly that we couldn't react. Don't beat yourself up, Sally. This isn't your fault, or the fault of any of us. They'll find him—and he'll be punished, unless he crashes and dies first. Which wouldn't surprise me, since part of his wing is missing. But she won't go unavenged. You can be sure of that. He'll either go to the morgue or the stockade."

Dixie spun around. Her eyes were wet. "A hell of a lot of good that'll do her! She's dead!"

"Justice is for the living," Twila said.

Dixie exploded. "Bullshit! That's just a lot of bullshit . . . just like everything else you learned in that college you're so proud of going to! It was a waste of time! And everything you're sayin' now is a waste of time! She's dead! That's all that matters. She's dead and that's the end of it! Anything else is just a bunch of highfalutin crap they taught you that won't put a morsel in your mouth or the first thread of a shirt on your back or so much as a penny in your pocket. And if you can't see that, you're not nearly as smart as you like to think you are."

"Maybe you're right, Dixie," Twila answered kindly. "But the only way to judge a philosophy is to examine the lives of those who live it. So in the end, we won't know if you're right about the beliefs I lived my life by until I'm dead."

Dixie looked like she was searching for more to say. But she apparently was unable to settle on anything, and she angrily turned away.

A breeze was coming up. The flames licked in their direction. But Sally wasn't ready to abandon this girl, whoever she had been, so immediately after dying. Suddenly she didn't care if she had broken a dozen regulations. Landing had been the right thing to do. If it had been her lying in those flames, and if her spirit somehow managed to survive and she was aware of what was going on, she would have dearly appreciated someone caring enough to stay with her a moment to share her sorrow and perhaps her fear. It was the right thing to do. It was the human thing.

"Why?" She asked the question aloud.

Dixie didn't hesitate. "Same reason it nearly always is. He's an asshole!" She wiped her eyes. "I betcha he's part of that bunch that keeps gettin' just lost enough to find Avenger. The word's out to every air force on earth, ya know: Women are flyin' out of Avenger Field in West Texas. There's even a rumor we're flyin' around topless! I'm just surprised the Germans and Japs haven't shown up yet with their cameras."

Twila stared at the flames. Her face was wet. She whispered, "Good-bye, sweetie. It wasn't your fault. You gave everything you had . . . and he still killed you. I wonder sometimes if I'm not locked up on a planet for the insane." She looked so sad, Sally thought. No—it was more than that. In that moment, Twila had become old.

Geri moved close to Twila but avoided looking into the wreck. "We should pray for her."

Sally had considered the idea but decided it would be hypocritical. Her father had beaten her to make her pray. She still remembered those lashings as if they were yesterday. Geri could pray if she wanted, and she would bow her head respectfully, but nothing more.

Geri clasped her hands and closed her eyes and lowered her head. "Oh, Father, show justice to this poor innocent girl. Take her into your all-powerful arms and protect her from further tragedy. Be merciful to her soul, Father. And allow her to live with you and Jesus and Mary and the apostles and the angels and all those who are pure of heart that are in heaven with you right now. Amen."

"Amen," Twila echoed, as did Dixie, though beneath her breath.

Geri dried her eyes. "She's in heaven! I'm sure she made it to heaven! God wouldn't keep her out of heaven after this!"

Dixie's mouth tightened. "How would you know?"

Geri's vulnerability vanished. "She'll go to heaven! She was murdered!"

"What are you, five years old?" Dixie growled. "Is that what they taught you in that big church your daddy gives lots and lots of money to? If you get murdered, or you pay off the preacher enough, you'll get to heaven?"

"That's blasphemy!"

"No, stupid! It's horse sense! I don't know where she's goin', or where she is right now, any more than you do. But I do know that if buyin' your way into heaven is possible, then bein' there's no more of a good deal than bein' on a used car lot!"

Geri pointed her finger. "You're going to hell!"

Dixie smiled grimly. "Maybe. But I'll show up with a clear conscience!"

"Stop it." Twila stepped between them. "It's not important! Whatever is, is! Praying or hoping or wishing or arguing isn't going to change that for her. All any of us can change is what we do and how we act while we're alive. To argue over what happens after is idiotic! There's no way to know until you're dead! Can't you see that? Can't you see how stupid you sound? Can't you understand how it must confuse her—maybe even hurt her, if she can hear you?" Her voice was broken off by tears.

Dixie and Geri looked away from each other.

Sally wiped her face on her sleeve. She would never be as smart as Twila. She learned something every time Twila spoke, though she often didn't fully understand everything she said. Twila seemed bigger than life, a sculpture on the side of a mountain. She would never have imagined Twila losing control.

She pointed to their footprints. "We have to get out of here."

Twila was still having difficulty, but she nodded.

Dixie and Geri also nodded, while ignoring each other.

"One thing . . ." Sally added. "We are all in this together. And we were never here! If any of us says otherwise, we'll pay the price equally. Does everyone understand? And do we all agree?"

Everyone nodded. Twila took a deep breath and added, "Yes."

Sally turned to the thing in the flames. "I'm so, so, so sorry." There was nothing more to be said and nothing more to do. They moved toward the planes.

The BTs waited just as they had left them. Except for the heat on their backs and the smell and sound of burning gasoline and grass, there wasn't a clue that death had come here.

They wordlessly climbed into the cockpits and got out of there as quickly as the propellers would take them.

No one was waiting when they taxied to a stop on Avenger's flight line. Sally cut off fuel to the engine and watched the big propeller snap awkwardly to a stop. The radio had remained quiet during the ride back to the base, and she and Dixie had barely spoken over the intercom.

Dixie finally broke the silence. "What's your idea?" She made no move to unbuckle herself.

"I'm going to report." Sally gathered her things and stood up.

"Report what? What are you gonna tell 'em?"

She moved onto the wing. "The truth. Or at least, the most important part of it."

# Ten

Colonel Bowen listened intently. Mrs. Teetle followed every word grimly. Ira Waterman, who seemed to have appeared out of thin air upon hearing of the crash, left the impression that he was permanently recording every sound and expression and gesture within his brain.

Only the four Avenger trainees remained standing. They had not been offered chairs, despite four comfortable looking ones that faced Bowen, Teetle, and Waterman. Colonel Bowen's office, while not luxurious, was far plusher than any other Sally had seen at Avenger. In addition to the standard airplane photos that apparently came pre-attached to every wall owned by the Army Air Corps, the desk and chairs and the long table that Bowen and Teetle and Waterman were seated behind were of fine, sturdy oak construction.

The inquiry was winding down, but tension in the room remained high. Colonel Bowen's questions had been lengthy and direct, and each of them had told him what they'd seen. Mrs. Teetle had asked a few curt questions about the dead girl's appearance, which none of them could answer because they hadn't gotten a good look at her. Now she had grown quiet, though she continued to look shaken, Sally thought. Waterman had mostly spent his time studying them. Sally noted that he was wearing the same white suit that he'd worn the day of her crash inquiry, and that the creases in his trousers still looked like the business end of razor blades. So far as she could tell, no one suspected they had broken any regulations.

Waterman suddenly piped up. "Miss Delaney, I would like to hear what else you have to say about today's unfortunate events."

Sally's heart sank. Geri was the weakest, the most immature, the most vulnerable. She hadn't known that before the crash. But Waterman had the instincts of a wolf; she was sure he'd sensed Geri's weaknesses the moment they walked into the room. If he started badgering Geri, and she broke down or had one of her tantrums, today would be the last for all of them at Avenger.

Geri had come awkwardly to attention, though no one had ordered her to. Her lips were tight as a string. She was just one big coiled spring, Sally thought. A blind man could see it.

"Well, Miss Delaney?" Waterman's voice had the dangerous edge of a knife.

Out of the corner of her eye, Sally saw Dixie stiffen. If Geri said the wrong thing, she worried what the big model might do.

"Excuse me, Mr. Waterman." Impossibly, Twila managed to be both commanding and unthreatening.

Waterman looked at her.

"Geri never saw anyone die before," Twila said. "It's been very traumatic for her; she cried all morning. She's afraid she'll start crying again now and embarrass herself in front of you."

Waterman glared at all of them at once. "You're women! Crying is what you do! I'm very much aware of that, but my only concern is getting to the truth."

"Sir, the truth is that an accident occurred because of the stupidity, arrogance, and incompetence of a male pilot," Twila said, "resulting in the death of a student. If he's still alive, he should be court-martialed on a charge of murder."

"Nobody asked you what should or shouldn't happen!" Waterman snarled. "I only want to know what you saw; I couldn't care less what you think!"

"Yes, sir," Twila responded easily. She seemed unfazed.

Bowen shifted uncomfortably in his seat. But Teetle straightened almost imperceptibly. She actually looked *proud* of Twila, Sally thought.

Suddenly she understood what Twila was doing. Maybe by working together, they could keep steering Waterman away from Geri.

"Well?" Waterman glared at Geri. "I'm waiting! What can you add?"

"I was nearest to the AT-6's, Mr. Waterman," Sally said. Now that she had a plan—or an idea for a plan—she wasn't quite as afraid. "Geri and Twila were some distance off my right wingtip. I got a better look at what happened than either of them."

Waterman's eyes snapped to her. She could *feel* them lock on her.

"Your morass of bad luck continues, doesn't it, Miss Ketchum?" Those eyes were penetrating.

"Sir?" Her heart was racing. She had diverted Waterman, but at what cost?

He leaned forward ominously. "Aircraft seem to fall in your wake— and now a death. Are you sure you've left out nothing? Was there nothing you could have done to help this unfortunate girl? Are you in no way at fault? Are you saying that this was entirely out of your hands—an act of God, so to speak?"

Sally was afraid of Waterman. But he was wrong. Everything about him was wrong. He didn't care about the girl who'd died. His only concern was destroying the WASP. Her anger was uncontrollable. She blurted, "God wasn't there today, Mr. Waterman. I've been in a fatal crash. I know! Tex Jones, my boyfriend, died in Oklahoma in 1941, and fault had nothing to do with it. We ran into a couple of turkey buzzards while we were landing, and we crashed and Tex died. God himself couldn't have saved us that day, Mr. Waterman. Tex tried to, but there was nothing he could do, either. But as to your question, I couldn't help that girl this morning. No one could. So she died! So instead of trying to crucify her or the WASP, why don't you go after the man who killed her? He's the one who could have done something. He could have minded his own business and left her alone, instead of trying to mount her like an animal!" She was breathing hard. But Waterman's face remained cold as ice, and as unreadable.

Somewhere in the back of her mind, she expected Colonel Bowen or Mrs. Teetle to reprimand her, but she was beyond caring.

Skinner suddenly jerked open the door. He didn't bother to knock. His sunburned face was even redder than usual, and grimmer. "It was one of ours, alright. Midair. The other plane landed in El Paso. The base over there just called me. Some damn fool from Houston, a lieutenant on a training mission. He was showing off and admits it. He'd been drinking. They found beer in his plane. He tried to do a barrel roll around her and put a wingtip through her cockpit. Wasn't even supposed to be this far west; he was supposed to be in Oklahoma. Claims he just wanted to see some WASP and got carried away. He's OK, but she's dead. A rancher came across the crash right after it happened. The boy turned himself in as soon as he landed."

Sally held her breath. Had the rancher seen them land? But Skinner had said all he had to say, it seemed. He was waiting for Bowen's response.

Bowen slapped the desktop. "As of right now, Avenger's off-limits to anyone and everything not having official business here." His voice rose. "And that includes those horny bastards at the bomber school over in Big Spring! I'm tired of them landing here on the pretext of an emergency. The next one that tries it had better be on fire *and* have a flock of Messerschmitts on his tail! And that lieutenant's gonna spend the rest of this war in the stockade! I'm personally going to see to that! Read me?"

"Sure do, Colonel." Skinner had a cup in his hand. He spat a brown bullet into it.

Bowen stood up. He was red with rage. "You four are dismissed!"

They lunged for the door.

Sally couldn't believe it. Bowen intended to overlook her outburst! Probably, he agreed with her, but didn't have the guts to say so—nor did Teetle, nor did anyone else. That's why Waterman and those like him would win. She could see that now.

She moved quickly down the hallway. Dixie and Twila tried to follow but she waved them away. Geri charged off in her own direction. Sally guessed she was running so no one would see her when she broke down; she was trying to save face. Frankly, she didn't care. The inquiry was behind them. They had all survived. They were one step closer to becoming WASP.

She rushed into the clean air. She desperately needed to be alone.

But she'd only taken a few steps when a voice ordered her to a halt. She turned. Waterman stood in the doorway of the headquarters building.

She had always assumed he needed the cane. Now she realized he carried it for effect. He moved toward her purposefully, his back erect, his gait smooth. He stopped in front of her, his eyes locked with hers. Anyone else that she had ever met would have smiled or frowned or coughed or looked away or tried to stare her down. Those would have been human things to do. But he would have none of it. He remained purely himself, his body stiff, and his eyes as cold and black and dangerous as a wintry lake at midnight. She wanted to spit in those eyes.

"Miss Ketchum, my apologies."

Sally marveled that he could speak and still move so little of his face.

"You obviously think me a monster. I assure you that I am not." He anchored the tip of the cane into the ground with the weight of his hands. There was so little distance between them that he could whisper and no one would overhear. "I merely am doing a job which members of the United States Congress feel is important. Please do not take it personally."

She looked at him disbelievingly. "Don't take it personally! I think I'd be crazy to take it any other way. If you destroy the WASP, you'll be destroying everything I want in life. I love flying, Mr. Waterman. The WASP are my chance to have everything I've ever dreamed of. Or are you so different from the rest of us that you don't have any dreams? Have you never loved anything?"

A flicker crossed his face. It came and went so quickly that she almost missed it. But she could have sworn it was an emotion trying to get loose.

Suddenly he patted his vest pockets. Clearly, whatever he had just felt was so well hidden that it might as well never have existed. "May I trouble you for the time, Miss Ketchum? I'm afraid I don't have my watch with me."

She'd started carrying Tex's watch with her when she flew in the hope that it would bring her luck. She automatically retrieved the gold case from deep in her pocket and flipped open the cover with a push of her thumb. "Eleven-hundred hours. Eleven o'clock." She extended her hand so he could see the dial for himself.

He moved so quickly that she didn't have time to react. She tried to draw back but he already held her prize. He was holding Tex's watch! Suddenly she couldn't breathe.

"A beautiful piece." He turned the case over, studying the gold work.

She tried to tell herself she should be complimented that such a powerful and rich man would find Tex's watch so interesting. But she knew that the watch, though wonderful, was nothing that should interest anyone but herself. Waterman surely had a finer watch, and if not, he certainly could afford to buy one. The watch was important only to her. Waterman was simply showing off his power over her by denying her something that he had sensed was dear to her. She fought the instinct to claw out his eyes.

He snapped the cover shut and extended his palm. She snatched Tex's watch back to where it belonged, buried deep in her pocket. And she kept her hand around it, just in case.

He returned his attention to her. "Miss Ketchum. I want you to listen to me very carefully. I will win. You will lose. I will disband the WASP; all that remains undecided is when the final act will close. That's God's decision—and Congress's. Though I assure you I pray for a speedy termination with each communiqué that I send to Washington."

She tried to turn away, but his presence held her as surely as rivets.

"I want you to understand something. I don't care what happens to your classmates or to the people on this base or to the WASP as a whole. That's what I meant by 'don't take it personally.' It's not personal, not with me. It's a job." He paused for her reaction. She proudly gave him none.

"But sometimes my work becomes my pleasure. That has happened now. I have started to take pleasure in my work—real pleasure—not just professional satisfaction, but real, personal pleasure. Do you know why?"

She shook her head. She had no choice in the matter.

"Because I don't like you, Miss Ketchum. And because of that, it's going to give me the most extraordinary pleasure to destroy you." He turned and began retracing his steps.

She also turned. She ran in the opposite direction. She ran until she was completely alone. Then she threw up. She retched until nothing was left in her stomach. She retched to clean away the poisons that killed the girl in the plane, and the poisons of unfairness and bad luck in her own life. And then she collapsed to the ground and sobbed until she could cry no more.

# ELEVEN

A solemn porter slowly wheeled the cart with its pine box across the platform to the waiting train's baggage car door. The sun had disappeared from the sky and a universe of cold stars stared down from the darkness, broken only by the station lights and a weak glow from inside the car. A shiver ran down Sally's back and she turned up her coat collar. The air was brisk, but not cold enough to account for the chill she felt.

The whole base had turned out for the memorial service. Now a few close classmates had also come to the station to say their final good-bye to the remains inside the sealed casket. She hadn't known Emma Kelley. But because she and Dixie and Geri and Twila had witnessed her death, Mrs. Teetle had allowed them to miss evening studies to join those who counted her as a friend. Only Geri had declined, Sally suspected because it would have made her face up to her own mortality. The death had affected Geri deeply. She had become angrier but also had thrown herself into her studies with a new intensity.

The platform was made of large, roughly hewn planks, and the cart's steel wheels exaggerated their unevenness, jostling the casket unmercifully. No flag adorned the box, nor would one be given to Emma Kelley's family, as was customary had she been a member of the military. No insurance benefits would arrive for her family or dependents, a right of the lowliest private. Her family would be denied the privilege of even hanging a gold star in their window to announce her death. In fact, because she was a WASP-trainee, and therefore a civil servant without benefits, no money had been provided for the cheap casket that now held her remains. In a storm of protest, her classmates had threatened to smash open every Coke machine on the base to collect enough money to ship her home. Upon hearing of this all the way back in Washington, WASP Director Jackie Cochran had dipped into her own pocket to pay for both the box and the train ticket that would return what was left of Emma Kelley to her grieving parents. Sally knew all of this because disgraceful news is the most difficult news to hush, and within hours of the crash, everyone on the base knew about the army's disgrace.

A needle of steam rose from a coupling beneath the railcar and briefly enveloped the porter and cart and their sad cargo. A moment later, he stepped away, and the heavy door slammed shut. Suddenly he placed his cap over his heart and closed his eyes and bowed his head in prayer. Then he turned and moved away into the night.

There was nothing left to do. The wind was threatening to make icicles of Sally's tears. She joined Dixie and Twila. They turned toward the parking lot where the converted cattle trailer waited, and Sally tried to forget that a porter had shown Emma Kelley more respect than the entire army and government of the United States of America.

# TWELVE

Sally put down the astronomy book. She'd studied the thing until her head ached. But looking at constellations in a book and finding them in the night sky were two entirely different things. No matter how well she memorized the pages, with their outlines of the mythical men and animals that the ancients had imagined navigating the heavens, she knew that once beneath the real night sky, she likely would see just stars.

She scooted her chair back and turned off her desk light. The doors to the adjoining latrine were open, and she could hear Twila and Geri in their bay on the other side, going over some homework problem.

Dixie, as usual, was nowhere in sight. She had vanished right after making a brief appearance in the library after evening chow. Dixie was a decent pilot but a mediocre student, yet somehow she got by. Sally had tried several times to find out where Dixie went on her evening missions, but her vague answers only deepened the mystery. Knowing her, Sally suspected a man was involved. How Dixie managed to slip past the MPs, she could only guess and hope that her friend didn't get caught.

One person who *never* seemed to disappear was Waterman. Just prior to Emma Kelley's death, the rumor mill had him away inspecting other airfields. But in the month since the memorial, he'd popped up often at Avenger. He'd taken no notice of Sally before the midair. But now, whenever their paths crossed, he looked at her hatefully. Graduation was near. She intended to stay out of his sight as much as possible and keep her nose to the grindstone.

Thinking about Waterman made her headache worse. She returned to the star charts and the instructions for the use of the bulky sextant through which she was expected to sight in order to navigate the sky at night. The sextant was a precision handheld instrument, but that did nothing to lessen the difficulty of its use. How she would ever manage to squeeze the thing and herself into the tiny observation bubble atop some bouncing airplane's fuselage, then find one particular star through the sextant's stubby telescope, knowing all the while that the safety of her plane and crew depended upon the absolute accuracy of her readings, she couldn't imagine. But that's what the army demanded she learn to do, and so somehow she would.

She took the tool and her leather flight jacket and headed outside with the intention of practicing one last time on the deep Texas sky, before falling into bed. It was November now, and the night brought cold that chilled the bones.

Her intent was to reach the darkness beyond the runways, but she'd taken less than two dozen steps when a familiar voice stopped her in her tracks.

"Out to battle the evil night vapors?" Bayard stepped into the diluted light from a bulb high atop the barracks. He grinned and raised his hands above his head. He wiggled his fingers to imitate something scary.

She knew he'd been drinking even before she spotted the bottle. The stench was overpowering. Ever since her father took up the habit, she'd been unable to stomach the smell of liquor. Drinking was a weakness. She'd seen the proof of that firsthand, and she'd promised herself she would never have anything to do with a man who drank. Now Bayard had given her a new reason to despise him.

She tried to move away, but he matched her steps. "Or maybe you're rushing off to meet the boyfriend." He snickered. "That's a laugh, isn't it? You having a boyfriend."

Seeing him threw the switch to a thousand memories of her father. "I have a boyfriend!" she snapped. "Tex!" She immediately regretted the admission. Her private life was her own. But from experience, she knew he would forget what had been said once he was sober.

"You! A boyfriend?" He laughed loudly. "And I've got a hippopotamus in the hangar!" He was so amused with himself, she wanted to smack him.

"No way have you got a boyfriend," he cackled. "Not unless he's made out of steel."

"What's that crack supposed to mean?" She looked around. At any other time, a male voice would have brought a squad of MPs running.

Standing was becoming difficult for him. But his mouth still worked fine. "No man's gonna have anything to do with you. He'd never survive. You'd skin him alive and boil his carcass. You'd pop him between two buns and slather him with mustard. You'd laugh every time you took a bite, too." He made a hideous show of chomping air. "Lady, you'd scare cannibals!"

"Shut up!" She balled her fist.

Bayard wobbled closer. "If you've got a boyfriend, where's he at?"

"He's dead." Sally wanted to kick herself the moment the words left her mouth.

"Ah, hah!" His legs gave way, sending him crashing onto his butt.

He looked at her blearily. "They rejected my novel again. I am a failure!" He waved a finger. "But you wouldn't know anything about that. Because you don't need anybody and nobody needs you!"

He reached into his shirt pocket and clumsily pulled out a picture of a child. Even in the dim light, Sally could make out enough detail to see that she was a beautiful thing, with curly blonde hair and a devilishly happy face. Except for the color of her hair, the resemblance to Bayard was striking. "This is my Rose." He held the picture higher to give her a better view. "Skinner got me a pass to see her. I'm the only parent she's got."

Bitterness crept into his voice. "Natalie—that was my wife—died having Rose. Rose is only four, and she's already lost her mother. If she loses me, she'll only have my parents. No draft board is going to leave my Rose shipwrecked in this world!"

Sally wondered if she was becoming hard-boiled. Maybe she had buried her feelings for so long and had become so focused that she couldn't feel pity even for a little girl without a mother. But the fact was that little Rose would have to face up to her own problems in her own way, if and

when the time came, just as she had. And that had nothing to do with being hard-boiled. That simply was the way of life. She started to turn away.

"You think I'm just looking for a free ride, don't you?" He pointed a
wobbly finger. His voice rose. "My father wanted to be a writer but my
mother wanted security. For forty years, he taught college literature and
died a little every time someone published a book that he wished he'd
had the courage to write. If I'd followed him like they wanted me to, the
army might have given me a cushy office job. But I learned to fly, and
here I am."

He grabbed her hand. "You're lucky nobody needs you, Sally. You're
even luckier that *you* don't need anybody." She wrenched free just as he
passed out.

Dixie stepped from the deep shadows between the buildings, a trick
of the unevenly spaced overhead lights. "I don't wanna try to tell ya how
to run your love life, honey. But if you're gonna be sneakin' men into
the barracks, next time ya might try pickin' one that's still got some life
in him. This one's pretty well used up." Her hair was in disarray and her
lipstick smudged.

Sally felt a grim vindication. She had been right. Dixie *was* seeing a
man! She reached for Dixie's arm. "Where have you been? They're gonna
catch you one of these nights, sneaking around. And then where do you
think you'll be?"

Dixie jerked free. She stooped down and pried the nearly empty bottle
from Bayard's fingers. She examined the label contemptuously. "While
you're out man shoppin', try to find one with better taste in hooch. This
stuff's barely a step up from shoe polish, in my opinion. But like I always
say, any port in a storm." She tilted the bottle and emptied the liquid in
one gulp and made a hideous face.

Sally snatched the bottle away and tossed it onto Bayard's sleeping
form. "You know that I did no such thing! He's drunk, as you plainly
could see if you weren't drunk yourself. I'm waiting for the MPs so they
can arrest him."

Dixie looked at her woozily. "Arrest him! For what? For bein' drunk?"
She snorted. "Hell, you can't arrest somebody for that. I'd get drunk, too,

if Skinner was ridin' me the way he's been ridin' *him*. He gets all the crap details. He flies his butt off from mornin' to night. Hell, I'd be drunk, too." She steadied herself against Sally's shoulder.

"You *are* drunk! Come inside before the MPs find you." Sally tried to start her for the barracks, but Dixie stood her ground. "No! I'm not gonna let you get him arrested. 'Cause everybody needs to get drunk once in a while. It's a right, like votin'."

Sally was becoming more frustrated and angry. She expected to hear the sound of running boots at any minute. She was trying to keep her voice down. "No, it's not, and that's a stupid thing to say! I've never touched liquor in my life, so I sure have never been drunk. And he has no right to be, either. He misses his daughter and somebody rejected his book and he doesn't want to fly, and he's using that as an excuse to crawl into a bottle. Instead of setting a good example for his daughter, he gave up and turned to alcohol. He's a drunk! And he's lazy! And he's a quitter! And he deserves what he gets! Now come on before you get us both arrested!"

Dixie suddenly seemed to sober up. "I call that pretty hard-hearted, hon. Not everybody has your backbone, nor your armor-plated skin. Some of us need a little help gettin' through life."

"Don't make fun of me, Dixie. I'm not in the mood."

Dixie straightened to her full height. "I'm not. There's usually a reason why people get drunk. His sounds like a pretty good one."

Sally's head truly felt like it was splitting, and she had no intention of listening to a lecture about alcohol from Dixie, who obviously had sampled more than her share. She gave her a shove. "There are no good reasons! Come on. Let's go!"

"What about him?" Dixie indicated the snoring figure lying in the dirt.

"Leave him! Let the MPs haul him off."

Dixie stopped. "Like I was sayin' before, that's pretty short on the milk of human kindness, don't ya think?"

Sally snorted. "Look who's talking. Remember those soldiers on the train? You're the one who stole their money."

Dixie didn't blink an eye. "They were out to do the same to me—that Milton, anyways. He was cheatin'. Though not very well, as I showed him." She indulged in a smile and nudged Bayard with her toe. "But this fella's tryin' to make somethin' of himself, as well as be a father to a young'un, if I overheard right, and the world's holdin' him back. You can understand that, hon. We both can. So he did what normal people do when they're frustrated and angry and feel helpless about their lives. Notice I said 'normal people,' which excludes you. He got to feelin' sorry for himself and blew off a little steam in a bottle."

Sally had had enough of this. Turning for the barracks, she said, "That's pretty funny, coming from you . . . talking about the milk of human kindness and understanding and all. I've never known anyone in my life who looks out for herself as well as you. You'd stab a blind man for a pencil!"

Dixie responded indignantly, "There's a difference between steppin' on a bug that's mindin' its own business and just tryin' to get along, and one that's tryin' to stick a stinger into ya. You oughta have learned that by now, hon."

Sally didn't want to hear any more. Nor was she comfortable with the rising tension between them. Suddenly nothing seemed right. She hurriedly crossed the short distance to the barracks door.

"Hey, hon . . ." Dixie's voice cut the night air. "If you're not careful, you're gonna wind up bein' just as narrow-minded and ornery as those relatives and neighbors of yours that you're runnin' so hard to get away from."

Someone had parked a truck in the shadows of a nearby building. The last thing Sally saw as she angrily jerked her barracks door open was Dixie jockeying Bayard into its canopied cargo compartment to sleep it off.

# THIRTEEN

"Alright, listen up. This is Link training, and I'm Corporal Zimmer."

He was short and skinny, his voice high-pitched—cruelty enough in a man's army. But fate had dealt him two further misfortunes: a nose that more resembled the colossal beak of a gigantic bird than the snout of a human, and sinuses that kept the thing perpetually wet.

"The Link Trainer was developed by Mr. Edwin Link to give pilots instrument training without leaving the ground." He fished a handkerchief from a pocket. He'd barely succeeded when an explosion rocked his body, turning his face crimson. None of the dozen or so other soldiers in the room bothered to look up from their work.

Dixie whispered, "He could blow somebody's brains out with that thing."

Sally jabbed her to keep quiet. Neither had mentioned Bayard this morning nor the words that had been exchanged the night before.

She was nervous enough already. The Link training building was void of everything but the little machines that were its namesake. Even the walls were bare, save for the occasional window, all of which were closed at the moment because of a sandstorm that suddenly had kicked up outside. The big room felt hot and dirty, and thick with tension.

The Link itself looked like a carnival ride from the outside, but its interior was a close replica of a real airplane cockpit. Once the opaque canopy was closed, the student wouldn't be able to see outside, simulating flying at night or through clouds. Scuttlebutt had it that the Link was a real little monster, with little or no likeness to the feel of flying a real airplane, and so was almost impossible to control. She and the nine others who had been summoned to begin Link training this morning had heard plenty of horror stories about perfectly good pilots who'd emerged from the contraption only to resign on the spot.

The nearest Link was empty, its canopy propped open like the waiting mouth of a lion, though the others were in use. She watched the little squadron of wooden boxes, with their stocky miniature wings and tails, dip and sway and jerk in response to the control inputs of the hapless student hidden inside and the soldier-instructor stationed at the control console beside each. By manipulating knobs and levers, the instructor could feed the student all sorts of situations that were supposed to mimic flying a real airplane on instruments. As she watched, an instructor turned a knob on his console and the Link in front of him began to act erratically as the student attempted to recover from whatever problem he'd thrown at her. Affixed to each console was a map onto which a mechanical arm drew a continuous line. This line represented the flight path being "flown" by the student.

Corporal Zimmer, his handkerchief at the ready and his feet parked solidly on solid ground, resumed his lecture. "The Link is a simulated airplane that provides movement through the various axes of flight. This movement can be controlled by the instructor, who is able to induce a variety of flight conditions by manipulating switches from his console. You, the student, will be expected to deal with these, just as you would in a real airplane. The difference, of course, is that when you crash a Link, you don't die."

He paused for a response. Sally noted that her classmates had the good sense to look stoic. Getting no reaction from his little audience, Corporal Zimmer continued. "We're not able to completely simulate a real airplane, of course, but we come close. For this reason, you will each be provided with one of these." He held up a brown air sickness bag. "Should the need arise, you will use it. Anyone not doing so will clean up her own mess, no exceptions. Everybody got that?" He waited for all ten heads to nod.

Dixie murmured, "If he gets any fuller of himself, he's gonna bust wide open."

"Question?" Corporal Zimmer's eyes became dagger points, fixed on Dixie.

"No, Corporal."

The points gleamed dangerously. "Then shut up!"

"Yes, sir." Dixie flushed.

Geri and Twila stood nearby. Geri smiled viciously.

Corporal Zimmer scanned the faces of his little audience. "Alright. Who wants to go first?"

His eyes stopped on Sally. "You. What's your name?"

"Sally Ketchum."

He consulted a clipboard. "Alright, Ketchum, you're first. Climb aboard." He motioned to the waiting Link.

Her heart was pounding as she stepped onto the stool at the base of the trainer and squirmed into the little cockpit. The thing felt cramped, even though she was, by military standards, small. She wondered how men, especially those who were tall, managed to fit.

As promised, everything more or less resembled a real airplane. A small fan mounted near the top of the instrument column blew a narrow stream of air onto her face, but even with the canopy open, the Link felt hot and confining. She could sense the ghosts of frustration and anxiety of the countless students who had sat in the seat before her.

"Alright, here's what I want you to do." Corporal Zimmer leaned one arm against the lip of the cockpit. "See these numbers?" He pointed to a collection of figures penciled onto a narrow piece of paper, which was clipped to the instrument column. Sally recognized them as course headings, altitudes, and air speeds. "This is the heading from Dallas to Harlingen. I want you to fly it as if you were flying a real airplane. We'll take it easy on you at first. But once you get the hang of it, don't be surprised to see some weather. And if you're a real good girl, maybe you'll find yourself with a little engine problem." He smiled threateningly. "Questions?"

She shook her head.

"Good. Put it on." He indicated the radio headphones in the leather flight helmet hanging from the rim of what should have been a windshield. Then he turned to a bored private seated at the Link's console. "You ready?"

The young man nodded.

Corporal Zimmer turned back to her. "OK, there's just one more thing. Don't worry if you crash. Everybody does their first time out. Ready?" He didn't wait for her answer. His hand was already on the canopy. He brought it down quickly. The cockpit suddenly pitched into darkness. The only source of light was a dim red glow on the instrument faces and a white circle projected onto the strip of paper by a penlight. She cautiously moved the rudders and the stick, and felt the cockpit lurch downward and to one side. The controls had an odd mechanical sensation to them that was unlike a real airplane.

A voice interrupted the soft hiss inside the headphones. "Pilot, take up your heading."

The altimeter in the center of the instrument column showed that she already had five hundred feet of altitude. She moved the throttle forward to climb and eased the stick to the right to pick up the prescribed heading. The instruments came to life. The magnetic compass moved, and the little airplane in the gyro horizon tipped its wing, and finally the altimeter and the air speed indicator came unstuck and began to creep along. The gyro horizon consisted of the outline of a pair of airplane wings that rode up and down and tipped in relation to a stationary horizontal line that represented the meeting of the sky and the ground. The thing was powered by a gyroscope. Whatever the real airplane did, fly straight-and-level or turn, its miniature twin would do likewise. Thus, a pilot could see the attitude of her airplane in relation to the ground by looking at the gyro horizon. When used in conjunction with compass, altimeter, air speed indicator, directional gyro, turn-and-bank indicator, and a good timepiece, experienced pilots could fly to just about anywhere without seeing the ground.

But even experienced pilots sometimes failed to find their way in the dark, and crashed and killed themselves. In an attempt to solve this problem, the government had installed, at great expense to taxpayers, a network of radio transmitters that spanned the country's air routes. This newest navigational aid, called a radio range, continuously spewed forth Morse code in two-letter combinations. All a pilot had to do was pick up the desired beam in her earphones and follow it to her destination. The combinations acted as shoulders on a highway. When an aircraft was exactly on course inside the beam, the letters meshed together to form a solid hum. This was called flying the beam and was a good thing. When the letters disappeared suddenly without reason or became indecipherable from crescendos of static, this was called losing the beam and was a bad thing. The beam could be infuriatingly difficult to pick up, especially in snowstorms, which reduced all radio signals to static. Scuttlebutt had it that when a pilot was most frightened and disoriented, and her plane desperately low on fuel, was when the beam would become its most elusive.

The instruments showed that Sally was at the correct altitude and heading. She pulled back on the throttle. Ever so faintly, she heard the repetitive *dot-dash* of a Morse code A and then the *dash-dot* of an N through the earphones. She had found the radio range and was drifting from one shoulder to the other. Now all she had to do was stabilize her airplane, listen for the comforting hum and follow it. Everyone who had flown the Link told her this was one of the hardest parts of instrument flying.

Attitude. Altitude. Airspeed. Heading. Engine temperature. Oil temperature. Fuel remaining. Radio beam. Again and again, her eyes scanned the instruments as her ears strained to detect any change in the range, and each time both affirmed what her instincts already knew: every needle and every knob was positioned exactly where they should be. Slowly, she began to relax. For the life of her, she couldn't understand why anyone would think the Link was difficult to fly. Except for its stuffy cockpit and uncomfortable seat and lack of a real airplane feel, the thing was a piece of cake.

Suddenly the beam's familiar repetition died. One moment it was there, the next there was only static. Frantically, she pushed the earphones closer to her head, but all she heard was the soft crackle of background static. Her fingers worked the little knobs on the radio, but no amount of twisting helped. Then, for no apparent reason and as quickly as it had disappeared, the headphones again filled with the steady, repetitive pulse of Morse code. Just as she was about to shout for joy, she realized that something was wrong. She was hearing *dash-dot*, not *dot-dash*. Somehow, she had crossed over the beam. Her eyes jumped to the artificial horizon. Sure enough, she had drifted off course, though she could have sworn she hadn't deviated by as much as an inch. She nudged the stick until the little airplane regained its proper place in relation to the horizon painted on the instrument face, and once again the reassuring hum appeared in her earphones. She allowed herself a tense smile. She had done it! She was truly flying the beam!

Suddenly the Link began to bounce as if caught in a tremendous thunderstorm. The instruments became blurs. She reached for the throttle. She had to reduce power to keep the ship from breaking up. All sense of the Link's artificiality was gone. Her only thought was to keep the wings attached until she could fly out of the grip of this storm. A sixth sense told her she was turning and diving. The sensation screamed for her attention, blocking all other thought and reason. She instinctively tried to see the ground, but the canopy was all darkness. Sweat dripped maddeningly into her eyes. She tried not to panic. Frantically, she pulled back on the stick, at the same time kicking in the rudder to counteract the turn.

Bright, blinding light exploded into the cockpit, causing her to jump.

"You're dead!" Corporal Zimmer's face gloated grimly. "We didn't even last long enough to have our little engine problem, did we?"

Sally was shaking, her brain still caught up in the illusion. Never in her life had she felt so helpless. The back and armpits of her zoot suit were soaked. She took a deep breath, but the shaking continued. Her hands hurt. She was still strangling the stick and throttle. Zimmer was right. If the Link had been a real airplane, she would be dead now.

He turned to his little audience. All looked somber. Most looked scared. She could imagine what they were thinking: she'd gone into the Link a pilot, and had come out a crash victim. "Now you know why pilots who aren't instrument rated, who keep flying when the weather turns lousy, are stupid." He examined each face until he was sure his message was getting through. "You can't trust your senses. You can only trust your instruments. Ketchum, here, just found that out. If she had been in a real airplane, she—and a very expensive piece of Army Air Corps equipment—would be at the bottom of a smoking hole right now because she followed her senses instead of her instruments. I hope every one of you is listening. Because if you can't fly instruments, you can't fly weather. And if you can't fly weather, you're no good to the army. Do you all understand that?"

All heads nodded.

"Good. Ketchum, get outta there." He glanced at his clipboard. "Delaney."

"Here." Geri stepped forward. The class's most obnoxious member had suddenly turned meek as a mouse.

"OK, Delaney, in the box.

"You." He pointed to Dixie. "Take Ketchum outside so she can get some air. Then come right back. You're gonna be next."

"Yes, sir." Dixie hurried to obey. She whispered, "Come on, honey . . . before you waste that government breakfast."

Sally felt her hands on her arms. But suddenly she didn't want to go outside with Dixie. She wanted to crawl back into the Link and lock herself into its cocoon cockpit until she knew every trick of the hellacious little box. She would train until she could fly any plane through any weather. Fear was the enemy, not the Link nor the weather nor even Corporal Zimmer. Skill was her best weapon against fear. If she could conquer the Link, she was certain she could conquer any assignment the Army Air Corps could throw at her. But Geri had already settled into the seat, and Dixie was shepherding her outside. Her feet followed along obediently. She felt too woozy to protest.

The fresh air felt good. The dust storm had disappeared, leaving fine flying weather for two enormous turkey buzzards that were amusing themselves with lazy circles overhead. Dixie found a nearby bench that someone had placed in the shade of one of the base's few trees.

"You look terrible, honey. You just wait right here. I'm gonna get you a Coke." She headed for the cluster of soft drink machines.

Sally concentrated on trying to make the Link building stop turning. Most pilots experienced vertigo at some point. But in all her hours in the air, this was her first brush with the experience.

"Tough day in the box?"

She looked up. She recognized him instantly. He was the most hand-some instructor on the base. Her stomach did a flip-flop.

"Buddy Gregg." His smile was warm sunshine. He stuck out his hand.

She recoiled from the unfamiliar attention, mentally slapped herself for being rude to an instructor, and grasped his flesh with hers. She'd not paid attention to a man since Tex. She still had sexual urges, but they'd proved no match for the exhaustion that went with farming, and more recently the weariness of flying and studying from dawn until late at night. Her thoughts suddenly traveled to places she hadn't visited in a long time, and hadn't planned on visiting again anytime soon. She yanked her hand from his.

His self-confidence remained unruffled. "You're Sally Ketchum, aren't you?"

That smile could have coaxed lilies to spring up in the middle of the desert, she decided. He stood about six-foot-two. He had thick black wavy hair, and a jaw that was square as a snow shovel, and lips that were full and soft. And he had dimples, one right in the center of each of his tanned cheeks. Smiling down at her, his zoot suit small at his waist and bulging at his chest, he looked like a Greek god. And he knew her name! But how? They'd never flown together, nor even spoken. The instructors were under strict orders to avoid fraternization except at officially sanc-tioned events. Not that the sexes didn't manage to get together: there were stories of off-base drinking and parties and secret rendezvous. But the instructors who were lecherous had never so much as given her the time of day . . . until now.

"Yes, sir, I'm Sally Ketchum." Her tongue felt like fourteen pounds of cotton balls.

"Oh, you don't have to both'r with that 'sir' stuff. Just call me Buddy."

She couldn't think of what to do with her hands, so she squeezed the edge of the bench.

"Was this your first time in the box? What did you think of the Link?"

"I killed myself," she blurted.

He laughed. His teeth turned out to be perfectly white and straight and as strong-looking as steel. He propped a boot on the edge of the bench. He could have propped his big boot anywhere, but he chose a spot that was nearly in contact with her thigh.

She wanted desperately to move away and as desperately to stay put.

He hung a masculine thumb on one of the belt loops on his zoot suit. "Sally, the word's out on you."

Her stomach suddenly felt like a basketball.

"Everybody who flies with you says you're the best pilot they've ever seen. I'm sorry I haven't had that pleasure yet, but I'm sure looking forward to the experience." He paused, but when she didn't speak, he just kept right on going as if her participation in their conversation wasn't even necessary. "They tell me you were a barnstormer. You must be quite a woman. I've never met a woman barnstormer before. I'd sure like to hear all about what it was like. Say, I've got an idea."

He paused again, apparently struck dumb by the sheer magnitude of the thing. "You know, don't you, that one of the churches is throwing a military dance this Saturday night? The boys from the bomber school over in Big Spring will be there, as well as lots of folks from Avenger. Why don't we meet there? I bet you're a great dancer, and I'd sure like to hear all about barnstorming. What do you say? Unless of course, you already have a date?" The sudden, terrible possibility of the instructors from Avenger and the boys over at the Big Spring bomber school having already asked her for a date made his gorgeous face frown.

Sally knew about the dance. Churches regularly hosted such events for personnel at military bases. She'd gone to several and had decided against repeating the experience. The churches meant well, but the affairs were dreary and over-chaperoned, the music provided by scratchy records that mostly were dated. There'd been twenty restless, chain-smoking soldiers for every WASP and the occasional local female. Avenger's stubborn reputation for wickedness had kept away Sweetwater's respectable women. The elderly church ladies who hosted the events were the exception because they no longer worried about wickedness, except as it concerned others. Worse, a zillion MPs and all of Sweetwater's little police force had been there. In fact, so many pious eyes had been watching the goings-on, ensuring that none led to too good a time, that what little party there had been soon fizzled. Long before ten o'clock curfew, all pretense of dancing had been pretty much extinguished. The men and women had broken up into separate frustrated groups, talking mostly of loved ones back home and of flying. The only good part had been the food. Those church women had cooked up a storm.

She couldn't imagine Buddy Gregg, who was supposed to be a carouser and the biggest wolf on the base, going to such an event. There were stories about Buddy's temper, too; he was said to fight at the drop of a hat. That kind of man didn't appeal to her normally. But that kind of man generally didn't look like Buddy Gregg. More incredibly, she couldn't imagine him wanting to dance with her. Buddy Gregg was the handsomest man she'd ever seen in her life, and one of the most charming, and every time he smiled at her she wilted. But she had enough sense to know that princes don't go around begging poor farm girls to go dancing, except in the movies. Something was fishy. A blind man could have spotted it from a mile away.

"Do you already have a date?" His worry lines deepened.

She swallowed. "No, I don't have a date." The scuttlebutt was that his fingers had a way of moving so no girl with any sense would trust him. He wasn't supposed to be the brightest bulb, either. But he was so good-looking that the temptation to ignore her common sense was overpowering. She heard someone who sounded exactly like herself ask, "Are you asking me for a date?"

He smiled. "I sure am."

"You want me to be your date at the dance; you want to dance with me?" If that smile had broadened a fraction, if he had shown a smidgeon more teeth, if those dimples had winked at her an instant longer, she knew that she would have accepted. "I'm sorry, but . . ."

"Mr. Buddy Gregg!" Dixie returned, a Coke in each hand and a grin as big as Texas all over her beautiful face.

"Hello, Dixie!"

The loss of his attention was as jolting as a dive into ice water.

He said to Dixie, "Long time no see. They been keeping you busy?" The smile, which had merely beamed for her, radiated for Dixie. If a bag of marshmallows had been handy, Sally was sure they would have roasted.

Dixie swelled up. "Busy? Sure have been, honey . . . they've been keepin' me busy as a beaver in a logjam. How 'bout you? What've you been busy at?"

His big boot slid from its spot on the bench and planted itself heavily in the dirt a good two feet from its twin. He parked his hands on his hips, which caused his pelvis to thrust forward. His smile turned impossibly wicked. "Oh, same old same old . . . you know."

"Oh, I know, alright." Dixie met his wickedness and raised him a face-full of her own.

Suddenly Sally knew the purpose of Dixie's mysterious night missions. She felt a rush of surprise and anger and jealousy. Dixie, who could have any man on Earth, had obviously already had this one, and now, incredibly, was acting like she was going to take him again right here in front of the Link building. She pranced around like a princess on a big white horse, as if Sally weren't even present. Humiliation and jealousy overcame Sally's common sense. She was sick and tired of being run over. She heard herself announce, "I'm going to be Buddy's date for the dance this Saturday night."

"Really!" The Princess nearly dropped her Cokes. The sight was so delicious that Sally decided she could have lived for a week on bread and water and not minded one bit.

"Uh, huh," Sally cooed. "Buddy just asked me."

Dixie shot him a look that was three-quarters razor blades and one-quarter lightning. "Well, that's great, honey." She stiffly handed over one of the Cokes.

But Buddy remained the picture of confidence. His thumbs relocated to his belt loops. "Yeah, I thought I'd catch up on the barnstorming news."

"And what's Sally likely to catch?" Dixie snapped. The air between them crackled.

Dixie was jealous . . . of her . . . Sally Ketchum! It was impossible! Dixie was master of her own destiny. She was invincible and beautiful. Men were gaga over her. The world was her oyster. Yet standing there, her face ugly with rage and hurt, she was like any ordinary girl who'd ever reached for a prince and gotten run over and left in the dirt. Buddy Gregg had run her over. Maybe there was a Buddy Gregg for everyone, even princes and princesses. A moment ago, Sally wouldn't have thought so. Now, she wasn't sure. The possibility put a whole new spin on life. It meant the misery was being spread around.

Buddy produced a toothpick. Plainly, he was toying with Dixie. Sally could see now what they had in common. They both were alley cats.

Buddy worked the toothpick with his tongue so the stem moved in and out obscenely. "What's she likely to catch? Why, nothing but a real good time, Dixie. Nothing but a real good time."

The Coke exploded from Dixie's hand. The bottle headed straight for his head, but he ducked easily and it flew harmlessly an impossibly long distance before shattering against the Link building.

"Careful. You'll make her mad."

Sally would have recognized Beau Bayard's voice in the dark of a coal mine. A parachute pack hung rakishly from his shoulder.

Buddy spat out the toothpick. The thing traveled furiously for a few inches before falling at Bayard's feet. His mouth twisted. "I was just asking Sally to the dance, Bayard. Too bad you'll miss it. I hear Skinner's got you flying nearly around the clock to try to turn you into a pilot. Personally, I don't see the point. My guess is you'll drown first."

Bayard's face blushed flame-red. But Sally sensed something beyond the men merely disliking each other. She'd heard that Buddy was a natural pilot, with no tolerance for anyone of lesser talent, especially another instructor. The word was that he never passed up an opportunity to let Bayard know what he thought of him. Was that why Bayard seemed so agitated? Or had he been turned down for a date to the dance by one of the other trainees, and Buddy knew it? Whatever the reason, she was sure it had nothing to do with her. In her world of uncertainty, *that* was the one thing she was certain of.

"You watch your mouth, Gregg!" Bayard suddenly squared-off against the towering instructor.

Buddy scowled and stepped forward. "You watch yours, Bayard, or you're gonna get a mouthful of busted teeth."

Bayard planted his feet firmly. "That's 'broken,' Gregg. If you'd spend a little of your time improving your mind and less than all of your time fighting and trying to fly the trainees, you might put a stop to those rumors about having a pea for a brain."

Buddy swung. A fist the size of a meatloaf barreled through the air with the speed of an artillery shell. But Bayard had moved out of the way, and the meatloaf fizzled to a humiliating stop.

Buddy's fist exploded again, this time with such force that his knuckles whistled. And again, the only connection he made was with thin air.

Sally watched in horror and fascination. Bayard might be a a no-good and a coward, but he had guts, standing up to a man twice his size. The thought didn't make a bit of sense, she realized. But then neither did Bayard. One strike from either of those ham-sized fists could kill him. He must know that. So why was he picking a fight with the biggest and toughest man on the base? He might know a lot of big words, but he certainly wasn't very smart. She was watching the proof of that.

Buddy loosed a terrific punch.

Bayard ducked and dodged. But instead of landing on his feet again, he stumbled and fell.

Buddy drew back his boot.

She gasped. Buddy clearly intended to kick him.

A voice boomed, "Get your asses out of the dirt! What do you think this is, the infantry?"

Bayard scrambled to his feet just in time for Skinner to grab his collar. "Listen to me, the both of you." He glared at Bayard and then Buddy, whom he had similarly grasped. "If you wanna fight, I can arrange for a little chat with a draft board. The marines would be real happy to have two such big brave fighting men." He pulled each closer with a twist. "And that, gentlemen, is exactly where you're going unless you knock off this crap right now and get your asses in gear and start acting like instructors. Do we understand each other?"

They nodded.

"Good! That's real good, Instructor Gregg and Instructor Bayard. I'm so happy that you see things my way." He turned them loose with a shove and turned to Dixie and Sally. "And you two . . . I'm assuming there's a couple of empty seats somewhere with your names on 'em?"

"Yes, sir," they answered as one.

"Then why the hell aren't your butts parked on 'em?" His face was apple colored.

"We were in Link class, Mr. Skinner," Dixie said. "The instructor sent us outside for some air."

"Did you find any?"

"Yes, sir, we did."

"Then why the hell aren't you back in class?"

Sally nudged Dixie to start walking. "We were just about to go back, sir," Sally said.

Buddy, still dark with rage, bent toward Sally and whispered, "Saturday night!" He hurried away.

Sally watched him tromp toward the hangars. She'd only agreed to dance with Buddy because she wanted to get back at Dixie for always having everything her own way. The truth hit her. She had a date: the prince and the farm girl!

"Now you've gone and done it!" Dixie hissed. "That guy's twice as dangerous as a loaded cannon, and four times as dumb, even if he is gorgeous. And he's got ten pairs of hands! He's nothin' for an amateur to fool with. And you've gone and got a date with him!" She seemed far more upset by Buddy's infidelity than by her betrayal of their friendship. Sally guessed that Dixie also suspected Buddy's motives.

Sally pulled Dixie to a stop. "All I said was that I'd dance a dance with him." She kept her voice low. Skinner and Bayard were talking nearby. Actually, Skinner was doing the talking and Bayard was doing the listening.

Dixie snorted. "You said you'd be Buddy's date!"

The idea of Buddy Gregg touching her, even if only on a dance floor while surrounded by MPs and little old ladies, terrified Sally. Her imagination couldn't even hint at the things he might do, which made them all the more dark and frightening.

"Whatever you think you said," Dixie persisted, "*he* thinks you agreed to be his date. And what *he* thinks goes, because *he's* a flight instructor."

Dixie was right. Buddy had the power to foul her up. A black mark from him could keep her from a choice assignment after graduation. He might even get her bounced out of the program. That made her all the angrier and she snapped, "Well, you didn't seem too worried!"

The idea that she had snatched away one of Dixie's men, regardless of the reason, was obviously still sinking in for Dixie. Sally wondered if the situation was a new one for her, or if Dixie had held onto every man she'd ever known until she decided to dispose of him.

"I'm not afraid of Buddy," Dixie snipped. "It's the other way around. He just doesn't always remember it. See this pinkie?" She held up her hand. She gloated with the satisfaction of someone who's eaten a whole chocolate cake after months of deprivation. "Buddy's spent more time wrapped right here in the last week than he's spent in a cockpit. And he's had more fun, too!" She smiled wickedly.

"I'm still the one he wants to dance with," Sally said with more confidence than she felt.

"Don't let it go to your head, hon!" Dixie growled. "He wants somethin', all right. But I wouldn't be too sure it's dancin'. And I don't mean the obvious, either, though he'd take some of that, too, if you let him have it. No, he's after somethin' else." She didn't explain.

"Hey!" Skinner yelled. "You two get a move on!"

Sally grabbed Dixie's arm again. "Yes, sir!" she said. They started again for the Link building.

"I'll see you this afternoon," Bayard suddenly yelled. He was walking in the opposite direction.

Sally was still fuming over Dixie's none-too-gentle reminder that they weren't in the same league. And now Bayard was annoying her, too. She turned to look at him. "No, you won't!" she snarled. "I'm flying with my instructor this afternoon!"

He beamed over his shoulder.

"No!" The cry erupted from the center of her being.

"Barnes crashed his car last night," Bayard hollered. "He's laid up in the hospital with a broken leg. I'm taking his place."

"No!"

"See you on the flight line." He kept walking.

A violent sneeze came from the Link building. "Beaumont! Ketchum! What do ya think this is, teatime? Get your butts in here!"

Corporal Zimmer stood in the doorway. He held a soggy handkerchief to his snout; the thing looked exactly like a diaper. At any other time, Sally would have laughed, but just then she was too worn down and discouraged.

Dixie took her hand. "Come on, honey. Maybe you can catch yourself some germs and go to sick bay . . . and stay there right through Saturday night."

# Fourteen

A blob of rain splattered the windscreen and a fist of violent air slammed the underside of the wings. Sally instinctively tightened her grip on the AT-6's control stick and tugged at the straps that crossed her lap and shoulders. The weather forecast that she and Bayard had gotten at Love Field in Dallas an hour earlier had called for sporadic showers to the east with clearing. That prediction had obviously been for some other part of the east. The part they were in was socked solid with great black columns that reached from the ground apparently to heaven itself. Fantastic fingers of lightning danced between the boiling cauldrons, making her wish she could hide, or at least slink farther down into her seat.

The storm had sprung out of nowhere. Only a short time earlier the sky ahead and to the sides had been a muddled white, the path behind still sprinkled with blue. Now the only spot not swallowed up by the black giants was the ever-narrowing trough of roughening air that they were flying through, and she knew that, too, soon would disappear.

She closed the throttle a crack. The powerful, six-hundred-horsepower Pratt & Whitney engine instantly dropped from a throaty roar that tingled every muscle in her body to an almost-roar that merely tickled the bottoms of her feet atop the rudder pedals. The AT-6, identical to the one that she and Dixie had watched crash, was as rugged as any airplane in the sky, but that was no reason to beat the poor thing to death. "Take care of your airplane and your airplane will take care of you," Tex often had said. As with everything he had taught her, she had found his wisdom to be true. But it was another of his teachings that circled in her head as she watched the closing darkness ahead: "Always leave yourself a way out."

She scanned the ground again. She'd already brought the big trainer down to considerably less than a thousand feet, but the railroad tracks, which had disappeared beneath a cloud minutes earlier, were still nowhere to be found. Either the tracks had turned sharply or a crosswind was blowing her off course. The tracks had been her ace in the hole. Railroad tracks inevitably led to towns, and towns inevitably had their names painted on their water towers. Finding one's way via "the iron compass" was as old as the airplane. But the trick required the pilot to first find the tracks.

"Love Field, this is Army 36. Do you read me, over?" She pressed the headphone inside her helmet closer to her ear, but as had been the case for fifteen minutes, all she heard was static. Either the storm was interfering with reception or the antenna had come loose or the radio itself was on the blink—or maybe all three. The AT-6, equipped with numerous aids, was suddenly no more capable of helping her find her way than the old Jenny had been.

Bayard's voice rattled her headphones. "I put us near Longview. How about you?"

This was supposed to be a cross-country navigational exercise. The instructor's job was to merely sit in the seat behind her with a map in his lap and watch how well she navigated along a predetermined course, while keeping his mouth shut. Bayard had done all three exceptionally well until this weather blew up. Now he was pestering her. This was the third time in as many minutes that he'd spoken.

She pressed her throat microphone; conversation over the racket of the engine was impossible without the intercom. "I put us in an airplane somewhere over Texas." He'd flown with her twice in her short army career, and both times she'd wound up in trouble. He was jinxed; or maybe he jinxed her. Whichever, her anger toward him continued to grow. He already owed her for one airplane. She wasn't going to let him make it two.

He ordered, "You wanna try it again—this time without the sarcasm?"

A terrific bump shook the plane. The intercom sputtered and temporarily died. She glanced into the mirror over the windscreen, half-expecting to find his seat empty, and was annoyed that he was still there. He was doing his best to look calm, though he had a death grip on the aluminum sides of the cockpit. She just hoped he wasn't bending anything important.

He pressed the button again. "Don't get me wrong. I'm happy that you're doing the flying."

She keyed her own microphone. "What's that supposed to mean?"

"You're the best pilot in the army. You're not gonna crash."

She reminded herself that a fool falls for flattery and flatterers fool fools.

He persisted, "I ask again: Where do you think we are?"

"You've got a map and you're supposed to be an instructor," she snapped. "Don't you know?" The canopy was in two separate parts. She angrily released the locks on her front half and slid the clear Plexiglas back on its rails. Cold, wet air, full of the moist aromas of earth and the exhaust gases of Pratt & Whitney, hit her full in the face. Droplets of condensation blown back by the big propeller pummeled her face and goggles.

A lightning bolt flashed up the spine of one of the miles-high black giants. One . . . two . . . three . . . four . . . five more bursts quickly followed in the space of a heartbeat. With each explosion, the roiling monsters grew blacker and angrier. From such Texas storms came tornados, and hail that could drive through a man's skull like a nail, and rain that could drown cattle by the herd. Even the best instrument pilot wouldn't try to fly through this hell. Nor could she fly over it. The trainer carried no oxygen. But even if it had, Sally was sure the storm reached higher than the AT-6 could fly.

A vicious rocket of air grabbed the wings. The plane shuddered. Then before she could react, the express elevator ride reversed itself, and they dropped like an anvil. Her earphones picked up a groan. She looked in the mirror and saw that Bayard was pale. She wondered if he'd brought along an airsickness bag.

The clouds were giving her a little sample of what they could do, and she didn't like the taste. The trough that they'd been flying through was shrinking. In a matter of moments, the alley that had been four or five miles wide had shrunk in half. She had to land.

Off to the right was a clearing in a rich green carpet of trees. She banked toward the spot, at the same time pulling back on the throttle and cranking down the flaps. She watched part of the rear edge of the wings obediently angle down into the slipstream. The flaps slowed the plane and provided lift that warded off a stall. The effect was similar to a child changing the angle of his hand as he sped down the road in a car with his arm extended through the open window.

A farmhouse slipped under the left wing, and a small lake and a road. She could see cows standing among the trees. They knew that a storm was coming. A dog was standing in the yard barking. But no people were in sight.

The clearing was nearly even with the left wing. They'd be on the ground in a minute. She ran through the landing checklist: gear down, full flaps, fuel mixture . . . A burst of rain closed around them. The downpour came and went quickly but left her soaked from the shoulders up.

"Hey! Close that canopy! I'm getting wet back here!"

"Would you rather burn?" she asked.

"What do you mean?" He had stopped trying to sound unconcerned.

"If the ground's wet and the tires sink in when we touch down and we flip and your canopy jams, you're gonna burn to death."

His part of the canopy slammed open with such force she was sure he'd bent the rail stops. She smiled. She didn't expect the ground to be mushy. It looked firm enough.

They were parallel to the clearing. She looked for anything that might get in her way: farm equipment, ditches, telephone lines, wandering cows. She was alert and tense but not scared. The AT was many, many times more sophisticated than the Jenny and so placed far greater demands upon her, but it was, after all, just an airplane. If there was one thing she was certain she knew how to do now, it was fly an airplane, even one that was about to be wedged into the corner of a cow pasture, instead of slipped onto the long, smooth runway that its designers had intended.

She dropped the left wing hard. Moments later, she had completed a turn that brought the clearing into the center of the windshield. The field was narrow and short, its parameters defined by fences. She created a mental picture of the distance between those wires. Stay between them and everything probably would be OK. Stray, and there was a very good chance that she and Bayard would get wrapped up in one mess of a wreck.

He made some sort of noise. She couldn't tell whether he was throwing up or praying.

She closed the throttle as they flashed over the fence. They floated briefly. Then the main tires kissed the grass and the uneven ground shook everything for a moment and the small wheel beneath the tail settled firmly and they rolled to a perfect stop.

Someone had built a crude shelter at the end of the field. Little more than a wooden lean-to, the thing was obviously intended for cows, or maybe horses or mules. She gave the engine some gas and applied first the left rudder pedal and then the right to swivel the tail back and forth. Visibility over the nose of a tail-dragger like the AT-6 was always a concern, especially for a pilot who was short. The only way to see what was ahead while taxiing was to swing the nose back and forth by fishing the tail. On a smooth runway, that wasn't a problem. But in a pasture that was full of dips and rises, the ride quickly became uncomfortable. Sally looked in the rearview mirror above her head. The rough pasture was jarring the fillings out of Bayard's teeth, but he didn't complain.

The shed was only a few yards away. With a little luck, she'd be able to get the plane tied down before the bottom fell out of the clouds. A storm could do more damage to a plane on the ground than to one in the air. She locked the right brake and gunned the engine. The AT swung around in a tight one-hundred-and-eighty-degree arc that pointed its nose back in the direction they had come. She turned off the fuel, and the big engine clattered to a stop.

"Help me get us tied down," she ordered. "I don't want this thing blowing to Kansas."

She threw off her lap and shoulder belts and stood up. The sky blinked white light, and thunder shook the ground. The sound sucked at her breath. The air tingled with electricity. She swung her leg over the side of the cockpit just as a handful of raindrops hit her in the face. They would have to work fast. The temperature was dropping. The storm would arrive at any moment. She grabbed a handful of stakes and a hatchet and rope from the emergency kit and jumped to the ground.

A hard gust of cold wind shook the plane.

The stake went into the ground with several easy whacks of the hatchet. But her fingers were cold and the rope was stiff, and again and again as she tried to make a knot, the rope slipped free. Finally with a hard tug, she managed to shore rope and stake together and saw to her relief that the wing was tightly tethered.

The sky blinked white again. She held her breath for the coming explosion. This time, the sound was like a whole dynamite truck going up. The concussion pressed against her and threatened to make her cry.

"Give them to me." Bayard held out his hand.

She shoved the equipment at him.

He brought stake and rope and ground and plane together in what seemed like two snaps of his fingers, and he grinned at her.

"Stop patting yourself on the butt," she snarled, "and help me get the rest!"

Together, they set to work securing the AT.

Bullets of hail suddenly appeared beyond the end of the field. The tall grass shuddered and bent and dropped from sight as if chopped by a giant invisible lawnmower.

"Run!" he warned from atop the wing. "Get in the shed!" He stood next to the fuselage, her parachute slung over his shoulder. He quickly dipped into the rear cockpit and retrieved his own chute and a canvas bag before slamming the canopy shut. "Run!" He jumped to the ground.

An unreasonable fear gripped her. She had lived in Texas all her life and had never seen anything like what was coming toward her. This was white death, its sound like the thud of a million hardballs. Any living thing caught by this monster would be cut to shreds.

The shed was a few-dozen steps away. Her feet flew. But when she looked over her shoulder, she saw that the bulky chutes were slowing him, and she turned and raced back. He was out of breath and sweating, despite the blast of cold air racing ahead of the storm. She jerked her chute from his arms. She swung the heavy thing over her head for protection and ran for her life.

The shed was nothing more than a crudely fitted collection of weather-roughened boards crowned with some rusty tin. They got inside just as the sky opened up with a million rounds of buckshot.

"The plane!" She looked outside. The AT-6 and most of the field had disappeared behind a wall of white. Something hit her shoe. Hailstones—some the size of golf balls—were driving themselves into the ground.

"Better move over here where there's more roof." Bayard motioned to his corner.

She remained frozen in the doorway. To leave would somehow be like abandoning the plane. At least the AT-6 was mostly metal. But she had seen the kind of damage that hail could do to even a modern airplane. She had the sickening feeling that once again, she would be logging one fewer landing than takeoff at Avenger Field.

"Ouch!" She rubbed her head. Her leather flight helmet offered little protection from the ice balls.

"Over here!" He motioned to her.

"I'm not taking orders from you!" she yelled. She felt something gooey. She looked down and saw she'd stepped in a cow pie. The mess covered her shoe.

He pointed. "Watch out for those."

"Damn you! Damn, damn, damn, damn, damn you!" She threw the parachute at him. The heavy pack traveled about a foot before burrowing itself in the filthy ground. She quickly snatched it up before it could settle in the muck. She had enough explaining to do to the army. No need to add cow droppings to the list.

The storm, the forced landing, Bayard's mere presence . . . they all were conspiring to make her hysterical. She lunged forward and pinned him against the wall with the parachute. "Every time you come around, you wreck my life!"

His eyes flashed fire. "You're the most disagreeable woman I've ever met. Every time I see you, you're either yelling or pushing or threatening. Is it just me, or are you at war with the rest of the world, too?" He shoved her away.

She held her ground. "Oh, it's you!"

"What's that supposed to mean?" He looked like he was going to hit her. She promised herself she'd hit right back.

"You're supposed to be smart. You figure it out!"

He glared.

"I don't like you!" she added. "Is that clear enough for you?"

His jaw muscles tightened dangerously.

"Why don't I like you? Because you're incompetent and arrogant and bossy. And you're dumb!"

"Dumb?" he exploded.

"That's right!" She stabbed him with her finger. If his chest had been a tire, he'd have had a blowout. "You're just a little bigger than me, but you pick a fight with a guy who could roll you like a cigarette. If that's not dumb, I don't know what is!"

His face became the same blaze-red that she'd seen when Buddy Gregg humiliated him. He quickly turned away. "I had my reasons."

She was getting to him. The knowledge was inspiring. "You had your reasons for trying to get yourself stomped into the ground like a bug? They must have been awfully good reasons . . . the best reasons that anyone's ever had for doing anything. Because picking a fight with Buddy Gregg was just plain dumb!"

She could see he knew she was right, and they both knew anything he had to say from this point on would just be baloney. In a strange kind of way, she almost felt sorry that she'd won. In her whole life, she'd never known anyone who was so plainly wrong, while she was so plainly right. It felt so good.

CRASH! The ground shook. The air shuddered. The walls and roof of the shed bulged under the force of the thunder. She flew forward, and her arms found his neck, and she held onto him as if he were a windowsill and she was slipping off a sliver of ledge a hundred stories high. Another crash followed, and another and another and another. Stabs of lightning burnt the ground seemingly only inches away. The air smelled of fried electricity. She shook uncontrollably. Fears that hadn't visited since she was a child came alive, and she knew she was very near to wetting her pants. She held onto him unashamedly, as if he were the last toehold between her and the fangs of every nightmare she'd ever had. She was so scared that she barely felt the warmth of his arms around her and the comforting pat of his hands on her back. She closed her eyes and held onto him with all her might.

Slowly she became aware that the shed had stopped shaking and the thunder had rolled into the distance and the heavens had stopped blasting the tin roof with buckshot and she was wrapped around him like an octopus. She jumped back. No man had gotten so close to her since Tex. She quickly moved until there was plenty of room for daylight to pass between them. Her heel sank into another cow pie, but she no longer cared. She hated this man. But some part of her brain screamed that his only guilt was giving her the comfort she'd demanded.

He looked so surprised by her behavior that she was compelled to explain: "Lightning scares me."

"I'd say you're scared of a lot more than that." He started for the door. His canvas bag was in his left hand and his parachute in his right; he adjusted their weight as if preparing for a long trip. He clearly was disgusted. He brushed past her, his boots making sucking sounds in the filthy, waterlogged ground. "I'd say you're afraid of men!"

The accusation was so harsh, so unlike the way she viewed herself that she immediately wanted to blurt out a denial. But nothing would come, and she watched helplessly as he disappeared through the door. She remained where she was for what seemed like a long time, the drip of rainwater through the roof into the manure her only companion, until finally she managed to regain her composure and trudge outside after him.

The sky was a patchwork of gray and black wedges that still oozed drizzle. The plane, to her relief, remained where they had tied it. Bayard stood beside the tail, his back toward her. She worked her way across the soggy ground. Pockmarks of ice were everywhere, some big as softballs. She noted with a growing feeling of unease that many were deeply buried, proof of the terrible fury that had flung them from the sky.

She was halfway to the plane before she saw the real extent of the damage. The Plexiglas canopy was shot full of holes. The aluminum fuselage and wings were dinged beyond repair and looked as if they had been attacked by an army of angry ball-peen hammers. The few places that had been covered with fabric were so shredded that there wasn't enough material left to make a decent handkerchief. She felt sick. In addition to everything else, the ground under the wings had turned to mud, and the tires had sunk up to their hubs. Avenger would have to send a crew of mechanics to take off the wings and truck the AT-6 home, or make repairs here in the field and wait until the ground dried. Either way, she knew the effort required would be enormous. She felt a pang of guilt. Had she done the right thing by landing? Or should she have tried to make it back to Dallas, where the AT might now be safely parked on a nice dry perch of concrete? She knew the answer. The storm had been too powerful. If she had turned around, the plane would be splattered across some hillside, and she and Bayard would be dead. Even if they had bailed out, the chances of making it down alive would have been zero.

"Skinner's not gonna like this! Skinner's not gonna like this one bit!" He shook his head.

Memories of his arms and how readily he'd comforted her when she had been so terrified vanished. "I suppose you're going to tell Skinner that I was wrong to land and that everything was my fault," she said. "Because if that's what you're thinking—"

He spun around. "I'm mighty tired of you getting mad at me every time you feel a little frustrated, just because you hate men. You sure wouldn't be the only one at Avenger who prefers women. I have nothing against lesbians. I like to think of myself as more sophisticated than that."

She stopped dead in her tracks. "A little frustrated? Hate men? Prefer . . ." Words abandoned her. "How dare you . . . after all the things you've done to me! And I sure never said I don't like men. Whatever gave you that idea? All I said was that I don't like *you!*"

He stepped toward her, his expression a grim sandwich of anger and exasperation. "I know what you said. I know what you are, too."

She took a step backward, then another and another, carefully pacing her retreat to his advance. "What?" She immediately regretted letting her fear of what he would say show in her voice. Why should she care what he thought of her?

"You're rude. You're angry. You're disagreeable." He marched with her. "A mad dog would make better company."

She considered dropping her parachute to free up her hands for when he hit her, but she was afraid the wet ground would ruin the chute. She decided to use the thing as a shield.

His march was unrelenting as a bullet.

"Sally, you're brave. You're honest. You're smart. You have the tenacity of steel. And remarkably, you not only know what you want to do with your life, but you're extraordinarily good at it. I admire you tremendously."

She stopped. He wasn't acting like he was going to hit her. She was confused.

He freed up a hand by shifting his knapsack to the same shoulder that held his parachute. "But you're not honest with yourself, Sally." He reached for her arm. She started to pull away, but his gentle fingers held her. That surprised her, until she remembered that he'd been gentle with her back in the shed, too. His gentle fingers held her as surely as iron bands. "There's not a girl at Avenger who works half as hard as you, Sally. Yet I think if it were humanly possible, you'd work even harder. I've never seen a pretty woman who has less of a good time than you. No one's ever seen you laugh. They've barely seen you smile; I asked around. You try so hard at succeeding at life that you fail at living."

Tex had been the only one who'd ever called her pretty, except for less than a handful of awkward farm boys and lowlifes on the air show circuit who wanted something. Her anger started to die. But then her experiences jumped up in her face again like a jack-in-the-box, and her defenses sprang into action and she jerked free. "Just who do you think you are, anyway? Just because I don't have much of an education, don't you think for a minute that I'm some dumb country girl who'll fall for some slick talk and a few cheap compliments. You got that?"

She freed one hand to stab at Bayard, which left only the other hand to hold the parachute. But that was OK, because the big pack suddenly no longer felt heavy. "I've been all over Texas and Louisiana and Arkansas and Oklahoma, and probably heard every line there is. So don't think you can pull anything over on me. You hear me? Because it won't work!" He had allowed her to pull free, Sally realized, through her anger and fear. If he'd wanted to, he could still have her arm locked in his hand.

He looked at her carefully. "I know who I am, Sally; that's not the problem. The problem is you." He reached for her hand. "You don't think much of yourself, so you think any man who's attracted to you must be rotten. Well, that's simply not the case. In addition to everything I've already said about you being good-looking and hard-working and a tremendously talented pilot, you're also a good person. The only person who doesn't know that is you. Most any man who knows you is going to be attracted to you. I know I am. I've been attracted to you ever since I first saw you." He squeezed her fingers. He was as gentle with her hand as he had been with her arm.

Tex had held her exactly the same way. Thoughts of him washed over her. Normally when that happened, she immediately felt better, no matter how bad things were. But this time she only felt more confused. The vilest creature in the world was holding her hand like Tex used to, and telling her how attracted he was to her, like Tex used to, and she was letting him. Everything had turned upside down. If her hands hadn't been so occupied, she knew that she would have pinched herself, just to see if she were dreaming.

"Hey, thar! Hey, thar, you two men! What do you men thank you're adoin' in broad daylight in my field?"

Sally turned.

An old man was watching them from the fence. He wore faded overalls and worn work boots and a giant old black hat. With him was a big yellow mongrel dog, the same one, she guessed, that she'd seen in the yard before landing.

She pulled free of Bayard and turned to face him.

The old man took a step forward, favoring his left leg as he did. His face had the hollows of a washboard, testament to a hard lifetime of hard-dirt farming. He moved warily, as if he were confronting the Devil himself—but determinedly, the Devil having made a big mistake by messing around on his property.

"I said, what do y'all men thank your adoin' out here in the broad open daylight on my land?" His voice was scratchy and high-pitched, like something nearly worn-out. "And where'd that aeroplane come from?" He pointed with his stick, causing him to pause. Either age or some accident had left his leg lame, so he was careful about giving it his full weight. . The dog paced him step-by-step, its eyes darting from master to strangers. "Who are you-all, anyhow?"

Sally removed her leather flight helmet. "We're with the Women Airforce Service Pilots training base, sir, at Sweetwater in West Texas. I'm the pilot of this aircraft. Weather forced me down." She started forward to meet him.

He froze. "God Almighty! You're a woman!"

"Yes, sir."

"You was the one that put that thang in my field?" He had great bushy eyebrows that reminded her of janitors' brooms. They swept up and down when he talked.

"Yes, sir."

He pointed to Bayard. "And what about that over thar? Is that a gal, too?"

Bayard yanked off his helmet. "Certainly not!"

She almost laughed, he looked so offended.

The old man took a deep breath, apparently relieved that they weren't two men, or two women, who'd come to his farm on Devil's work.

He shouted, "You're on my land, young woman—uninvited, I might add." He worked up a scowl. "That gives me the right to a truthful answer to a civil question, which I'll ask again. What are you two up to and what are you adoin' on my land? And answer me true this time, or I'm a-callin' the sheriff."

"I am telling you the truth, sir. My name is Sally Ketchum. This is Beau Bayard, my flying instructor."

Bayard had slung his parachute over his shoulder in a masculine pose that was right out of a recruitment poster.

She continued, "I'm sure you've read about us, sir. We're called the WASP."

The janitor's brooms rose sharply. "WASP, you say. What the hell's a WASP?"

"We're a group of civilian female pilots who get special training from the army to deliver airplanes to wherever the military needs 'em."

"Well, the military don't need no aeroplanes here on my land. And sure as hell, I don't, neither." His brushes moved tirelessly as car wipers in a downpour.

"Papa, what's happened? Did somebody crash? Is somebody hurt?"

A heavyset woman came from the direction of the house. She moved quickly, despite her size. She wore a large apron, which she twisted in her hands as if it were the neck of a chicken. Her kindly face was taut with concern.

"No, Mama. Nobody's crashed. Nobody's hurt." His roughness disappeared. Even the dog sat down, its fangs politely covered from view. Sally grinned to herself. She had thought she would have to go head-to-head with the old codger. Now she knew that wasn't going to be necessary.

The woman arrived in a clatter of huffs and puffs. Her long gray hair had come loose in the rush of her exertion, and she pushed back the strands with her fingers. Sally could see flour on her hands. She had been cooking. Her eyes darted from face to face and to the AT and then finally over the land and the shed. Seeing no carnage or concern on the faces of those who'd gotten there before her, her distress melted and she stuck out her hand, being mindful to give her fingers a final wipe first. "I'm Mrs. Black. I guess Papa's already introduced himself. He's my husband, but I call him Papa. We've never had flyers come to visit before. Did you set down to ride out the storm?"

Sally took her hand and Bayard followed. Bayard tried to get the old man to shake, but his hand remained firmly inside the pocket of his overalls.

"Yes, ma'am, we did. My name's Sally Ketchum, and this is my flying instructor, Beau Bayard. We're from the Women Airforce Service Pilots school in Sweetwater, over in West Texas." She suspected that Mrs. Black was nearly as old as her husband, a churchgoing woman whose heart was good as sunshine. "I was just explaining our predicament to your husband. I'm afraid the storm tore up our plane pretty badly. If you've got a phone, I'd sure like to call our base and let 'em know where we are and that we're alright."

"You mean, all the way to West Texas?" Mr. Black's eyebrows nearly jumped off his head.

"Yes, sir, if you don't mind. I'll reverse the charges, of course."

· "You're damn right, you will!"

"Papa!"

Mr. Black became quiet, but the tightness of his mouth and downward set of his brows left no doubt that he wasn't happy about his phone being used to make any long distance calls, even if the charges were reversed.

Mrs. Black touched her shoulder. "Of course, you can use our phone to call whoever you need to, dear. Don't pay any attention to Papa. He's just feelin' a mite grumpy today. This weather makes his leg act up, you know." The old man avoided her eyes. "Where did you say you and your young man are from, dear?"

Hearing Bayard referred to as her young man sounded so strange. She was about to set her straight when he interrupted.

"Sweetwater, Mrs. Black. Our base is about two hundred miles west of Fort Worth. It's called Avenger Field."

"And you've flown all that way by yourself with your young lady. My goodness! You must be an awfully good pilot!" She looked at him with wonder. He beamed back.

Sally stifled a laugh. "The storm threw us off course, Mrs. Black. Exactly where are we?" She retrieved the map from her zoot suit and spread it open.

"Crawfish," Mr. Black snorted. "That's the nearest town. But you ain't gonna find it on that thang." He extended a gnarled forefinger to the paper. "Lookee here: Over here's Turtle. And over here's Gator." He stabbed downward, almost knocking the map from her hands. "Now right here, that's where we're at, which ain't on that paper of yours, neither. If you're awantin' to go to Crawfish, go down that road over thar." He pointed to a slit of raw dirt that had been sliced from the hillside beyond the fence. "Just keep a-goin' about a half mile, and you'll wind up smack-dab in the middle."

She stared at the map. Its maker hadn't seen fit to give so much as an ink dot to any of the places he'd mentioned. But that wasn't what worried her. She said, "Mr. Black, you're pointing to Louisiana, not Texas."

His brows jumped. "Of course, Louisiana! I wouldn't give ya spit for Texas!"

They were hundreds of miles off course. She'd even followed the wrong railroad track.

She folded the map. She wondered what kind of explanation she would give Skinner. Not that she thought for a minute that Skinner or anyone else at Avenger could have done a better job of surviving the storm. Without a working radio, the only way a pilot could navigate was to use experience and whatever landmarks he could find on the ground. As glimpses of the ground had been in short supply, her experience had been her only tool; luckily, she and Tex had found their way through many a storm. But for that, she and Bayard would be dead.

Mrs. Black only seemed concerned with the comfort of her guests. "Y'all come on up to the house," she said. "Papa can make your call for ya from there. I expect you're hungry. I'm sure I can dig up somethin' for ya to eat. We still got biscuits and gravy from breakfast, though we're plum out of coffee 'cause of this rationin', but we got all the buttermilk you can hold. You might as well feed your faces till somebody comes to fetch ya, since I don't see how starvin' to death is gonna serve the national cause."

The dog stood up. A big pink tongue sprang from its mouth and made a licking movement across its fangs. The animal started eagerly for the house but paused and looked back at Mr. Black. The old man finally moved forward, and everyone fell into step together.

The farmhouse kitchen proved to be a simple affair, but with more than enough room for Mrs. Black to fawn over her guests.

"I must say, y'all sure make a handsome couple." She worked her way around the table. "I think you're just the luckiest thing, Miss Ketchum, to have a boyfriend who's a flyer. When I was young, I thought flyers were the most exciting men in the world. Here, dear, have another egg and some more steak. Would you like more buttermilk? How about you, Mr. Bayard? More biscuits? More gravy? More butter and honey for anyone? More potatoes?" She ladled and carved and poured like an artist spreading colors.

Bayard made a slurping sound. A dribble of buttermilk hung to his chin but he didn't slow to wipe away the spot.

Normally a slow and meticulous eater, Sally understood. Everything was so good that she was sure a bowl of gravy could turn upside down in her lap and she wouldn't have stopped to clean up the mess unless she had a handful of biscuits. The food was so good, in fact, that she had let Mrs. Black rave on and on about her and Bayard. She had tried to correct her several times in the beginning, but the good-hearted, simple farm woman just hadn't grasped the idea that women were flying for the army, and after a while she had decided that it made no difference anyway. Mr. Black, who had been in the hallway for what seemed like forever trying to place a call to Avenger, would return shortly with word from the army. Soon they would leave and never see this kind woman and her grumpy husband again.

Mrs. Black moved toward the icebox, where Sally had spotted a reserve pitcher of buttermilk. "I think it's wonderful that the Air Corps lets you take Miss Ketchum flying with you, Mr. Bayard. I bet the navy boys would be mighty jealous if they knew that army pilots get to take their sweethearts around with them. Please have some more buttermilk. I churned it just this mornin'."

"No, thank you, Mrs. Black. I couldn't eat another bite." His plate, which had been heaped with enough food for two men, now lay naked.

"Oh, my. I hope you're not quittin'. I was thinkin' you might like to try some ribbon cane syrup with hot cornbread and butter. The ribbon cane's especially good this year. Papa picked up this can just last week from over in Turtle."

"I couldn't, Mrs. Black. I couldn't." He shook his head.

She looked disappointed. "How 'bout you, dear? You gotta keep up your strength if you're gonna go flyin' with your boyfriend all over the country."

"It's the other way around, Mrs. Black." The sharpness of Bayard's voice took them both by surprise.

The old woman put the buttermilk pitcher down slowly on the table.

"Sally's the one who picked your field to land in, Mrs. Black . . . not me. She flew the plane. She made the decision to land. She brought us down by herself; she needed no help from me. I'm her instructor in name only. She's a far better pilot than I, or anyone I've ever met, could ever hope to be. Sally can make an airplane dance with the clouds, Mrs. Black. I don't fly her anywhere. It's the other way around." He looked so serious—so protective, even. Sally wondered if this same Beau Bayard had been right in front of her all along.

She'd never had anyone pay her such a compliment. Her back straightened and her shoulders squared and she sat up tall. But the thing that caused her to blush, caused the blood to race to her face, was what he hadn't said. Bayard had told Mrs. Black in no uncertain terms that she was the best pilot he'd ever seen, but he hadn't done a thing to change her idea about their relationship. The meaning of that hit Sally like a punch in the stomach. Bayard was more than just casually attracted to her. That's what he'd been trying to tell her in the shed, but she'd kept missing the point because she'd been so angry at him and scared from the storm and worried about protecting her future in the WASP. Now she knew why he'd looked so hurt when he'd said she didn't like men. Suddenly she also knew why he'd picked a fight with Buddy Gregg. The reason was the oldest one in the world: he'd been trying to impress her. She grabbed the edge of the table. Thankfully, it still looked and felt the way a table should look and feel, even as the rest of the world changed right in front of her eyes.

Oddly, she realized that she'd never even thought about finding another boyfriend after Tex. Bayard had accused her of working so hard at life that she never got around to living. Dixie had said something similar on the train way back on that first day when they headed to Sweetwater. Was it possible they were right? Had she become so single-minded that everything had been squeezed out of her life but the dream of bettering herself, of earning WASP wings and a cozy job in aviation?

She looked at the young man sitting across from her. His hair was still disheveled from his flying helmet and his zoot suit soiled with who-knew-what and he certainly was no Clark Gable. What's more, he was still just as arrogant and full of himself as ever. But maybe he had a right to be. For all she knew, he was another Shakespeare. To his credit, she'd never heard him promote himself as anything but a writer. In fact, he seemed to go out of his way to avoid taking credit for anything else. He'd just proved that in front of Mrs. Black.

More important, his eyes were clear and unblinking, with no apparent regret over what he'd said. Folks in East Texas were fond of saying a man's eyes were the windows to his soul. If that were true, something told her that Bayard's soul, if not squeaky clean, at least was no worse off than the majority she'd met. In fact, maybe his was a little better. That conclusion, brought on by his eagerness to stand up for her and the new way she looked at him, made her squeeze the table until she nearly hurt herself.

He smiled at her, though not so broadly as to make her feel threatened or put upon. Almost against her will, she returned the gesture and he immediately brightened, and she felt herself drawn into his dimples.

"You mean, you fly an airplane all by yourself, without a man showing you how? And the army lets you?" Mrs. Black had settled onto one of the chairs that stood like sentries around the big table. Her look of astonishment would have done justice to the sight of cows flying.

Sally edged her plate toward the old woman. "Yes, ma'am. We fly all by ourselves. That's the whole point. The army and navy need us to deliver planes and cargo. We fly just about any kind of mission you can imagine, in all kinds of weather, except for combat. It doesn't make any difference what kind of airplane it is—bomber, fighter, cargo, trainer—we're expected to do the job the same as any man. A plane doesn't care whether there's a skirt at the controls or a pair of pants. You know, I think I will have a little bit of that syrup, if you don't mind. I haven't had ribbon cane since I don't know when."

A wedge of cornbread appeared on the plate. A platter of fresh butter slid across the table, followed by a half-gallon jug. Mrs. Black waited for her to finish slathering the cornbread with butter. Then she dipped a ladle the size of a gourd into the jug. Dark, rich syrup flowed downward and mushroomed across the cornbread.

"But aren't you afraid?" Mrs. Black looked at her in amazement.

Sally postponed her attack on the bread. "No. America's got the best airplanes in the world. I think I will have some more of that buttermilk, if you don't mind." She pushed her glass forward. Mrs. Black retrieved the spare pitcher from the icebox and began to pour automatically.

"But . . ." The old woman's voice trailed off.

Sally was tired of these questions. Mrs. Black was just like the people she'd known back in East Texas. Her world barely extended beyond the fences that marked her family's farm. She probably had been born near here. She would die here. Explaining anything to her about why she was driven to make her mark in the world was pointless.

Mrs. Black returned the pitcher to the icebox. "How do the men feel about women flying aeroplanes?" she asked.

The cornbread was still steamy hot, the butter fresh as any she'd ever tasted, the syrup gloriously rich and sweet. She couldn't remember ever tasting anything so delicious, and she had to make herself hold her fork back to answer. "Most are helpful. A few don't like the idea of a skirt in a cockpit." The fork completed its journey, and she sighed with happiness.

Mrs. Black occupied herself with washing glasses beneath a giant old hand pump on the sink. Her voice grew so soft Sally could barely hear her over the falling water. "When I was young, girls didn't do such things. Pity."

Mr. Black appeared from the hallway and settled onto one of the chairs. Without a word spoken between them, Mrs. Black placed a glass of buttermilk before him. The old man kept everyone waiting while he took a long swig, more to annoy than to quench a thirst, Sally suspected. Finally he put the glass down and wiped his mouth on his sleeve.

Bayard prodded, "What did Avenger have to say?" His boldness surprised Sally. Old codgers like Mr. Black as a rule just needed a little coddling. Bayard surely knew that. She wondered if he were still annoyed at being mistaken for a girl.

Mr. Black gave him a hard look. He clearly didn't like being rushed, and to drive that home, he ignored the question while he studied the thick milk mark on the side of his glass.

"My hair could be on fire and you wouldn't tell me, would you?" A crooked smile pulled at Bayard's lips.

Mr. Black took another long drink before answering. "I wouldn't know, sonny, not having met anybody before now who's dumb enough to get himself inta that fix."

Sally grinned. Bayard had met his match. She touched the old man's arm. "What did you find out, Mr. Black?"

He let her hand stay, though he avoided acknowledging it. "Couldn't get through. The storm took down the lines somewhere between here and the other side of Texarkana."

Mrs. Black turned from the sink and gave her apron a terrible twist of worry over the storm and the wires and the life that took place beyond the boundaries of her fences, and so beyond her ability to understand and to control. The anguished look of helplessness that came over her could as easily have wracked the face of a savage following a sign of displeasure from the gods.

Mr. Black pushed away his depleted glass. "I called up Camp Fenton. That's the army base down the road a ways." His eyebrows worked up and down with a fury. "Talked to some feller who said he was in charge of thangs. Told him you was here and that he had better come ta git ya. Said he'd git right to it. I told him he'd better, 'cause army business ain't got no business on my land."

Telling the army what's what had brought him considerable pleasure, Sally could see. She suspected that in coming years, the retelling of this story would become even more satisfying.

Mrs. Black placed a wedge of buttered and syruped cornbread on the table next to her husband's glass. He pulled out an old red bandana from his pocket and polished a fork. Then he cut off a goodly sized chunk of the bread and proceeded to chew in silence, while Mrs. Black returned to her washing.

With nothing left to do but wait for the army, Sally settled back and examined the room, which was typical of farm kitchens. Thick bowls

were stacked on the shelves, and great iron skillets burnt black by countless meals hung on pegs. But the centerpiece of the room was the stove,
a giant green thing, thick with ornamentation, that included an array of
doors. A box of wood sat on the floor.

Mrs. Black interrupted her work at the sink. "Papa's kin brought that
stove with them all the way from Germany."

"Germany?" Bayard's voice went off like a gunshot in the quiet room.

The hard stare Mr. Black gave him made the old man's earlier looks
seem like putty. He put down his fork. "We're Americans." His voice had
a quality of Abraham Lincoln speaking.

He pointed with his fork to three large pictures atop the mantel in the
next room. One was navy. One was a marine. One was army. The resemblance to their father was striking. All looked old for soldiers, Sally thought.

He used the fork to indicate the nearest photo. "Roy's in a hospital in
Hawaii. His ship was torpedoed."

Mrs. Black made a sound that was sudden and sharp, as if she couldn't
breathe. She turned away to the window over the sink.

"He lost an arm and a leg, but they say he'll be OK," Mr. Black went
on. "We think Jobe—that's the one in the middle, the marine—was
taken prisoner by the Japanese in the Philippines. We don't have word of
whether he's alive or dead. We pray for him every night.

"The third one—Rudy, that's our baby—is somewhere in Europe. He
joined the paratroopers—jumps out of aeroplanes. We haven't gotten a
letter from him in a couple o' weeks but I guess he's pretty busy, with all
the fightin' goin' on. We listen to the news of it every night on the radio."

He put down his fork to give them his full attention. His voice was as
steady as the massive green stove behind him. "My people and mama's
people come over from Germany a long time ago, but we're as American
as Eisenhower." He solemnly shoved another forkful of cornbread into his
mouth and returned to his eating.

Bayard shifted uncomfortably in his chair. Sally didn't know what to
say, either.

Silence settled over the room.

Mrs. Black returned to the table. She was doing her best to maintain her composure. "Would anyone like more of anything?"

They shook their heads.

Mr. Black ignored her. He seemed lost in his plate, which was empty.

The dog began to bark.

They heard the sound of engines in the yard.

Mr. Black stood up. "That's the army, I guess, come ta get ya."

Sure enough, Sally could see through the window that a Jeep and an army truck had pulled to a stop in the yard. A squad of armed men sat in the rear of the truck.

A young lieutenant climbed out of the Jeep. His driver, a sergeant, remained where he was. She noted that each wore a .45 pistol strapped to his leg.

Mr. Black stepped onto the porch, and they followed him. He nodded to the lieutenant. "Afternoon, Lieutenant. How're ya today?"

The young man—built like a reed and filled with the seriousness of one charged with an errand of grave importance—gave Sally a sweeping glance and then concerned himself with the men. He consulted a slip of paper. "Are you Mr. Orlo Black?"

"Yessir."

He looked at Bayard. "Would you be Ketchum or Bayard?"

Sally felt a stab of annoyance. "I'm Ketchum, Lieutenant."

He reconsulted his slip. "I'm looking for a student pilot and his instructor who made a forced landing. My orders say they'll be at this house."

She persisted, "That's us, Lieutenant. I'm the student. He's the instructor." She pointed to Bayard, who smiled innocently.

The lieutenant showed his surprise. "You're Ketchum, the student pilot?" His eyes widened. "But you're—"

"That's right, I'm a woman." She'd had enough for one day. First Bayard and his pack of surprises, which she still didn't know what to make of, then Mr. Black and his wife, and now this lieutenant. "I knew that already, Lieutenant."

His face, which no longer belonged to a boy but wasn't yet mature enough for a man, showed his frustration. "My orders don't say anything about you being a woman."

She stepped off the porch. Bayard followed. They'd already grabbed their parachutes. "Can't help that, Lieutenant. I'm afraid I was already the way I am before your orders were cut. So I don't suppose that oversight is my fault or yours, but the army's."

He stared at her until he finally regained the presence of mind to hold out his hand and to ask with exaggerated stiffness, "May I see your orders, please."

She reached into her pocket for her identification card and flight plan. Bayard also handed him his card. He studied them carefully. She was sure he didn't understand a word of their flight plan, but he tried to hide the fact.

He handed back the papers. "Alright. I guess you are who you say you are. I'm Lieutenant Elwood Mitchell. I have orders to place a guard around your aircraft and to transport both of you to Camp Fenton." He looked around. "Where is the aircraft?"

Mr. Black pointed. "Out thar in the clearin', beyond them trees."

"Very well. If you would join me in the Jeep, we'll secure the aircraft." He turned to the sergeant. "Sergeant, get the vehicles turned around. We'll be heading out to the clearing beyond those trees."

The driver of the Jeep, who looked no more than eighteen, acknowledged with a nod and motioned to the driver of the truck to follow. As the two vehicles began to move, one of the soldiers in the rear of the truck turned toward the porch and stuck out his tongue. The pink organ extended and extended, until it became an impossible length that hung down to his chin. Suddenly the thing began to flip up and down. The other soldiers hooted and hollered, and a few made crude remarks and gestures.

Sensing that something was going on behind his back, the lieutenant spun around just in time to catch the perpetrator, who quickly retracted his instrument. Sally couldn't see the lieutenant's face, but she heard him mumble something that sounded like an apology.

"No harm done, Lieutenant," she said. "He was just trying to be friendly, I'm sure."

But Lieutenant Mitchell had already stalked off in the direction of his Jeep.

# FIFTEEN

The ride proved anticlimactic. Sally decided that either Lieutenant Mitchell wasn't comfortable with his role as their chaperone, or by nature he was quiet. He hadn't said another word, nor in fact so much as acknowledged their presence, since leaving his men behind to guard the plane. Not until they reached the waiting room outside the office of Camp Fenton's Commanding Officer, Colonel Kaskall, had he even looked at her again, and that had been only to point to the hard chairs that she and Bayard had occupied since he disappeared into the colonel's office ten minutes earlier.

For the fourth time since that had occurred, a powerful voice inside the office rattled the door. "Goddamn it, Lieutenant!"

The voice lowered, and so she couldn't hear the rest of what the shouter said.

They weren't welcome at Camp Fenton; that was obvious. Someone, she assumed the colonel, had started yelling soon after the lieutenant closed the door. She wondered what kind of report this Colonel Kaskall would send back to Sweetwater. Almost half of the eager trainees who had crowded into the lecture hall with her and Dixie on that first day at Avenger were already gone. The reason was often lack of flying skill, but almost as many wash-outs had occurred over some petty regulation. She had started to question whether the army's real goal wasn't so much to train WASP as to send them home in disgrace. If this colonel caused her to be sent before another review board, she feared this time Waterman would get his way.

A new blast of curses rocked the door. She wasn't able to understand much that was being said, but one word, repeated often, stood out: "Women!" The voice erupted fire. "I don't give a goddamn! I want that . . ."

A sergeant at a nearby desk looked up, his face uneasy.

The door burst open. Lieutenant Mitchell was the color of chalk. "Ketchum! Bayard! Get in here!"

She snapped upright. The seat of her zoot suit was glossy from hours of sitting, the knees thin from inspecting nuts and bolts in remote corners of airplanes. She could count a dozen wash-stubborn stains that had come from living with engines that literally oozed oil and squirted gas. Bayard looked even worse. They were in no condition to meet a commanding officer. She tried to put that out of her mind as they marched forward.

Lieutenant Mitchell closed the door behind them and came awkwardly to attention. Sally noticed that his underarms were soaked with half-moons of dampness.

The room was large and plain, its furniture arranged with the precision of a military regulation. A major was seated off to one side. He peered at them with unblinking eyes through a haze of smoke that curled from an enormous pipe. His hawkish nose and gaunt, unsmiling face reminded Sally of an undertaker. Colonel Kaskall sat behind a huge desk that had been swept clean of everything but their papers. A cold grayness clung to him. He was about sixty years old, and his face was hard, as if rigor mortis had set in, probably from years of not smiling, she decided. She and Bayard stopped in the center of the room and came to attention. Two empty chairs waited, but no one invited them to sit.

She recognized the colonel's voice the instant he spoke. "This is an army base." He could have nicked steel with that voice. "The only women allowed here are in photographs of mothers, wives, and fiancées." His knuckles squeezed white.

"We train men for combat here. That's our mission. The trip into combat will be one-way for some. But many will live because of the skills they learn here." His tone strayed neither up nor down, but marched each word along with biting sameness. If the army awarded medals for barking, he surely would have one, she thought.

"A woman on this base distracts from that mission," he went on. "I will not tolerate that. Do you understand me? I will not tolerate anything that distracts from the mission. Anyone or anything that tries will be removed or arrested. Or if necessary, shot!" His knuckles looked ready to burst through his skin. "Major Stewart tells me you're part of some sort of half-assed program the Air Corps dreamed up to train women to fly."

The major stared at them, his smoking pipe the only proof that he, indeed, was alive.

"As I understand it, you were on an exercise and were forced down by weather." Kaskall scowled. "For the life of me, I can't understand what sane person would allow women to go flying around in aircraft, especially army aircraft, every one of which we presumably need to fight this war." He leaned forward. "That's the dumbest idea I've ever heard. And believe me, after forty years in the army, I've heard plenty!" His long-suffering knuckles turned ivory.

"I don't care if Eisenhower himself sent you. You would not have been allowed on this base if I'd known what you are. The only reason you're standing here now is because my chain of command slipped up. And I can assure you that won't happen again!" He shot Lieutenant Mitchell a look, causing the lieutenant to blanch to a near-albino state.

"Women have no business on an army base. We don't have the special"—his scowl deepened while he searched for the right word— "things that women require; to say nothing of the fact that it's against army regulations." He glared at Lieutenant Mitchell, but the lieutenant was already so stiff and so pale that becoming more so was impossible.

Murderousness crept into the colonel's voice. "Women in factories. Women driving trucks. Women joining the army . . . wearing uniforms!" He looked ill from the thought. "The next thing we know, you'll be wanting to crawl into foxholes with us. The army needs that like it needs another front to fight in this war."

Sally felt numb. He was going to throw them off the base. It would be dark soon, and probably raining again. What would they do? Where would they go? God only knew where the nearest hotel was. They hadn't even passed a village on the way here. She fought a growing feeling of panic.

The colonel was still talking. He seemed to have been talking forever. Being a woman was obviously a crime in the colonel's army, his authority to lecture offenders boundless.

"Sally had to land, Colonel. We would have crashed, otherwise. She saved our lives."

Bayard's unexpected interruption affected Kaskall like a bolt of electricity. He jumped to his feet. The act was so violent that he knocked his desk out of plumb. "I am your superior officer!" he shouted. "You will not interrupt me! Learn that and learn it quickly or you'll find yourself in the stockade!"

Lieutenant Mitchell looked like he might faint.

The major's pipe glowed.

Sally had two simultaneous thoughts: She was going to be thrown out of the WASP because of Bayard. She was going to spend the rest of the war in jail because of Bayard.

But he continued as if Kaskall hadn't said a word. "We're civilians, Colonel."

"Civilians!" Kaskall spewed flame. "In an army aircraft? What's wrong with those idiots in Texas! Have they lost their minds?"

Bayard showed no sign of quitting. "Women aren't the enemy, Colonel. Putting them in airplanes is one of the smartest things the army could do. They free men for combat, and the army paves the way for peacetime. A lot of women are going to want to keep their wartime jobs after this conflict's over."

A rock-hard fist rattled what must have been five hundred pounds of solid American oak. "This is your last warning! No more!"

The major puffed his pipe rabidly.

Lieutenant Mitchell wetted the underarms of his shirt thoroughly.

Bayard looked confused. He'd told Kaskall something the colonel hadn't wanted to hear, and he had actually expected to be patted on the back for pointing out the old man's blindness and stupidity, Sally realized. Beau Bayard didn't understand the way the real world worked. And he had all but come out and told her that he wanted to be a part of her world! Perhaps he wasn't the cad and good-for-nothing she had thought;

and there was always the possibility he would earn a living from his writing, which she had to admit appealed to her enormously. He was smart, too, and not bad to look at. But she could already see where anything serious would lead. She would have to protect him from himself. And she'd never be able to lean on him the way she had on Tex. If she let Bayard into her life, the rules would be flip-flopped. The irony was so deep that she would have laughed until she cried, if she hadn't been so sure that Colonel Kaskall was about to give the order to have them dragged away in chains.

The colonel's cadaver-gray cheeks flushed. "I've never heard of such a thing . . . civilians lecturing a senior officer and flying military aircraft . . . and a woman, at that! If this is the future army, the army better look out, or it won't have a future. Once this war's over, no man worth his salt will want to serve. The next thing you know, we'll be fighting our tank battles with steel that's been painted pink!"

He moved around to the front of the desk. He snorted. "Young lady, I'm no flyer, so I can't judge whether your decision to land was right or wrong. I do, however, believe you are here through no fault of your own." His face wrinkled, and she realized he was trying to smile at her. The act was like cardboard bending.

He draped a leg over the edge of the desk. The attempt at casualness only made him look more like a tyrant. "Miss Ketchum, you want to help the war effort; I understand that. But surely you understand the army is no place for a woman, especially a pretty young woman. The place for you to do your fighting is at home."

Sally could almost hear his cheeks crinkle.

"Let me ask you something," Colonel Kaskall said. "You have a boyfriend in the military, I imagine. How do you think these shenanigans of yours—running around wild all over the sky and almost getting yourself killed—how do you think they make him feel? A soldier needs to know that someone back home cares about him and is keeping the fires burning. That's the greatest morale builder we have. It's what keeps men going in combat."

He folded his arms over his chest while he considered whether to spill the rest of what was on his mind. After a moment, his face turned to hard sincerity. "It might interest you to know that in Germany, young women such as yourself are taken to breed with Hitler's soldiers. They're recruited to special homes, where their sole duty is to birth future Nazi armies. That's the kind of enemy we're fighting!" He let that sink in. "Instead of running around almost getting yourself killed, you should be at home, young lady, doing what women do best." He crinkled.

She throttled her revulsion. She no longer feared this old man, or what he might report to Colonel Bowen or to Mrs. Teetle or to Skinner or even to Waterman, because she'd done nothing wrong. She'd saved herself. She'd saved Bayard. She'd saved her airplane. No man, not even a starchy old colonel, could ask more. The world was already paying the price for appeasing Hitler, Mussolini, the Japs, and all the two-bitters who worked for them. Another bootlick wasn't going to do anyone any good. Kaskall needed to be set straight.

She felt a rush of guilt for condemning Bayard for trying to do just that. She'd kept her mouth shut while he'd done the right thing. She felt ashamed. At the same time, suddenly she felt proud of Bayard. He had the tact of a claw hammer, but he was no coward. He'd proved that just now. He'd proved that with Buddy Gregg. He'd proved that in the pond. She had been wrong about him; maybe not completely, but enough so that she was looking at him in a new light. She was the one who was the coward for not backing him up.

She imagined Dixie coaching her as she looked Kaskall in the eye. "If you're suggesting, Colonel, that I could better serve my country by whoring, let me assure you that airplanes are the only things I ride."

Lieutenant Mitchell turned whiter-than-white.

The major's pipe looked dangerously close to exploding.

Colonel Kaskall's neck bulged over his collar, and a palette of red rushed to his stunned face. "How dare you speak to me that way!" He turned on the major. "Get them out of here! You have two minutes! If they're not off this base in two minutes, you and everyone in this whole goddamned command is going on report!"

The major leapt into the air.

Colonel Kaskall bellowed, "Get me Avenger's CO on the phone! I mean, right now!"

The sergeant appeared in the doorway. "Yes, sir!" He disappeared as quickly as he had come.

Major Stewart shepherded them across the room. They passed Lieutenant Mitchell. The lieutenant was frozen in place. He had the look of a condemned man.

"Off this base, Major! Do you hear me? I want them off right now! Or I'll have those gold leaves and your ass!"

The major pushed them out the door. Sally's parachute pack caught on something, but he gave a mighty shove and the canvas broke free, and she lurched forward.

They blew past the sergeant. He was dialing furiously.

"Where's that call, Sergeant?" The walls shook with the fury of Kaskall's voice.

They picked up speed in the hallway. They had to make a ninety-degree turn, but the reward was a slingshot effect. Suddenly the main door was behind them and they were outside and the darkening sky was misting and Kaskall's screams were lost.

"Quickly! Quickly!" Major Stewart shoved them into a Jeep. Bayard clamored into the front after Sally took the rear. A canvas top and side curtains had been rigged, but the seats were still wet and cold. The dampness quickly seeped into her skin. The major sprinted into the driver's seat. The engine started with a roar, and he ground the gears savagely before remembering to push in the clutch. They lurched backward and stalled. Finally he found the right combination of clutch, gear, and gas, and they careened forward.

The mist turned to rain. The single wiper blade left long blurry streaks across the windshield. They barreled through a muddy puddle. The Jeep's hard suspension bucked them skyward, and the world briefly turned liquid brown as the tires threw muddy water everywhere.

A wooden traffic arm blocked their exit at the main gate. The major skidded to a stop beside the guard shack. He twisted around. "Don't move! Or so help me, I'll personally see to it that you're both put on bread and water for the rest of your lives!" He kicked the door open and jumped outside, leaving the Jeep to fill with water.

They sat in silence. The rain pattered on the canvas top. The world might have been void of everything but the sound of rain on canvas.

"Thank you for sticking up for me." Sally found her own voice so strange, so soft and vulnerable. She couldn't remember ever speaking to him when she wasn't angry.

"You're welcome." He stared through the windshield.

A glow surrounded her. She had never felt so deliciously vulnerable. Hopes that she'd kept buried since Tex's death suddenly were exhumed.

The rain came down harder. The red-and-white warning stripes on the traffic arm blurred.

"I was wrong . . ." She hesitated only for an instant before plunging ahead with the rest of it. "I was wrong about you. You're no coward."

He studied the world outside the windshield before answering. "If Skinner gives you any trouble about the plane, you can count on me to back you up one hundred percent."

The rain grew louder and the silence deeper. The canvas became a snare drum.

She felt young again, the way she'd felt after meeting Tex. She made a sound that was part giggle and part self-conscious embarrassment, and explained, "This is new to me. I'm not used to not being angry at you."

He turned around. He was grinning. He gave her a whole face-full of dimples. "I bet that won't last."

"What do you mean?" She hadn't meant to sound so sharp.

But then he added, "You're so used to the wrong kind of men, you don't know what to do when you meet the right kind. So you get scared, and to protect yourself, you get angry. That's the real reason you have so much trouble talking to me." He might have just sold a book, he looked so pleased with himself.

"I have trouble talking to you?" She choked. Her wonderful warmth, her wonderful hopes . . . she could feel them slipping from her grasp; her regular anger was coming back with the ferocity of a bear. She locked her arms over her chest. "And to think that I almost—" She stopped in time to challenge, "You don't know any more about me than you know about airplanes!"

His dimples stayed in place. "'And to think that you almost,' what?"

He was no different from any other man, except Tex. He was using her to make himself important—to hide his ignorance, his fears, his failures, and whatever the other demons were that drove him. And though he hadn't hit her yet, he might as well have; the hurt was already almost as bad. That would come soon enough, anyway, if she were stupid enough to let him get close.

He repeated, "'To think that you almost,' what?"

She was so nearly certain that he was mocking her, she was so almost positive that he knew exactly what she almost had said, that she was practically convinced he wanted to complete her humiliation by forcing her to admit her stupidity. Her hand found her parachute straps. The heavy bag flew through the air and made a smacking sound against his upraised arms before falling harmlessly back into her lap. But no anger, no triumph, no smirk of the conqueror marked his face.

A wave of panic grabbed her. Suddenly she didn't know what to do; the realization hit hard. She no longer could tell if he was sincere or if he was making fun of her or if she was going crazy.

"'To think that you almost,' what?" His persistence was as gentle as a spring rose.

"You go to hell." She whispered the command softly, hiding the choking in her voice. She was one breath away from crying.

The door burst wide open. The major clamored inside, bringing a shower of water with him. The guard gate lifted, and he gnashed the transmission into first and slammed the accelerator to the floor, and they leapt forward, the engine screaming like a banshee. The MP who'd followed him out of the guard shack had to jump for his life.

The major found second gear without bothering to lift his foot off the gas. The rear tires skidded on the wet ground. "Listen very carefully." He ground his way into third. "I've found a place for you to stay tonight, but it's strictly off the record." He turned to glare at them and then barely avoided clobbering a tree. "If either of you ever tells anyone about where we're going or that it was me who took you there or anything about any of this, I'll call you liars and file charges against you! Do you both understand?" He spat the words out like poison.

"Yes, sir!" they answered as one.

He hunched forward and whipped the poor little four-cylinder engine into an even higher state of frenzy. "You better!"

Daylight's haze had settled into twilight, and the rain had once again become a mist. The Jeep's headlights were so feeble that the major twice ran off the road and once almost rear-ended a truck. Sally's fingers hurt from clutching the edge of her seat.

After what seemed like forever, he swerved onto a dirt road that cut through a thick forest. The Jeep bucked and swayed, and its tires churned up geysers of mud from the deep ruts left by earlier travelers, but he pushed the hapless little vehicle for all that it was worth, twice sliding sideways so violently that they almost overturned. Too scared to protest, she hung on for dear life.

The road ended suddenly. He locked the brakes, and Sally was flung forward so quickly that she nearly hit her face on the back of the major's seat. Through the streaks in the windshield, she could see a large old two-story house. A collection of vehicles stood nearly bumper to bumper in the yard, many of them military.

He twisted around. "Listen to me very, very carefully." His voice filled with promises too terrible to say. "Say nothing! Do nothing! Don't look around once we're inside. Don't so much as breathe! After tomorrow morning, I don't want you to remember any of this. I don't want you to remember me, or how you came here. Forget everything! Do you understand?"

They nodded.

"Someone's going to show you where to stay. You go there, and you stay there until I come for you in the morning."

They nodded.

"Once you're inside your room, lock the door from the inside. Until you hear my voice, and my voice only, tomorrow morning telling you it's

OK to come out, you're not to unlock the door again for anyone or for any reason. If this place burns to the ground tonight, I'd better find your ashes inside that room tomorrow morning. Or so help me God, I'll go down to hell itself to bring you back, just for the satisfaction of seeing you shot! Do you understand?"

They nodded.

Her heart was beating like a tom-tom.

He flung open his door, and a cold mist hit her face. "Let's go! Stick close!"

They grabbed their things and scrambled outside.

The house was far larger than Sally had first thought. There was no particular architecture to it other than bigness. But unlike so many homes that had fallen on hard times because of the war, the siding glistened with fresh white paint, the eaves and windowsills with bright green. Whoever lived here obviously not only had plenty of money, but connections. There were more vehicles in the yard than she had originally thought, too. Many were Jeeps, but she spotted army trucks and a half-dozen or so cars.

Instead of approaching the front porch, Major Stewart led them to a path that ran along the side of the house. The ground was wet and slippery, but a finely crafted walkway of rock made the going easy. The walk was perfectly level and its pieces fitted together flawlessly. An eave projected over a small service porch at the rear of the house.

The major tapped twice on the door. A woman's face appeared from behind a window curtain. They heard a heavy lock turn, and the door opened. He pushed them inside. Sally found herself in a dark hallway. She could hear loud music and laughter coming from other parts of the house. Some of the voices were male and some female. She wanted to ask what this place was, but decided not to risk inciting the major's hysteria.

The woman motioned them farther into the gloom, while she lingered at the door with the major. They spoke for several minutes in hushed tones that made overhearing impossible. Suddenly, without another look in their direction, the major bolted into the night, and the woman closed the door quickly, taking care to secure the lock.

There must have been a light switch beside the door, for a dim bulb clicked on midway down the hall, which was about fifty feet long and otherwise barren. As her eyes grew accustomed to the light, Sally was able to get a good look at the woman. She had beautiful shoulder-length red hair, and she was middle-aged and large, though exceptionally pretty. She reminded her of a future Dixie, though Dixie would never have used so much makeup. But her most memorable feature was her dress, a red affair that was cut shockingly low to expose a scandalous amount of her generous bosom.

"This way." She pressed them toward the light. She had a pleasing Cajun accent. Her perfume, a heady blend, was intoxicating in the close hallway. The air otherwise was dank. The ceiling and walls were peeling and in great need of repair, as if this part of the house was seldom visited.

Bayard was trying his best to walk and at the same time look back at her ample features. He grinned mightily. "Is this place what I think it is?"

She seemed perfectly at ease having her chest ogled, as if that were an everyday occurrence. She made a chuckling sound that was soft and sultry. "I guess that depends on what you think it is, honey."

"I think it's a whorehouse." He sounded tickled as a four-year-old on Christmas morning.

"We prefer house o' joy, honey," she corrected gently. "But you call it anything you want, seein' as how you're our guests tonight, courtesy of the United States Army."

Sally stopped, causing Bayard to crash into her, and the woman's breasts into him. Sally noted with irritation that he made no effort to extract his arm from her cleavage. "I'm not spending the night in a whorehouse!"

The woman smiled. She was so well tended that her skin might have been ivory. "Oh, but little pilot honey, you are! Of that, you can be sure as the sun risin' tomorrow." She nudged Bayard forward before Sally could object again. In the narrow hallway, she had no choice but to continue walking. They finally stopped at a door beneath the light.

Sally spun around. "I'm tired of being pushed around like secondhand furniture! What's your name? And what do you mean, 'courtesy of the army'?"

"Cherry LaRue." She remained unruffled. "And I don't see anybody pushin' anybody around, little pilot honey. The major asked me to do the army a favor by puttin' the both of you up for the night. Bein' a friend of the army and always willin' to lend its members my hand for any cause, that's what I'm doin'. Now you can stay right here in this cozy little room, where you'll be safe and dry and snug as a bug in a rug, or you can stay out in the swamp with the gators." She smiled sweetly. "Your choice, honey."

"What a name! Cherry LaRue!" Bayard was apparently already working her into his novel. If he'd had a pen and paper, Sally was sure he'd have started writing right there. She tried to control her rage. She nearly expected him to start howling at the moon.

Tex was the only man she'd ever slept with, yet her daddy's neighbors had called her a whore for running off with him. Then she and Dixie had nearly been arrested on the train on suspicion of being prostitutes. Finally she had learned that half of Sweetwater thought WASP were whores because they couldn't imagine them being pilots. And now—through no fault of her own—she actually was in a whorehouse. The indignity and unfairness were so overwhelming that she wanted to ball up her fists and start swinging.

"I am not spending the night in a whorehouse!" The musty plaster and ancient wood soaked up her voice, and the music and laughter masked whatever was left over. She might as well have yelled at herself. The realization caused her to sink backward against the wall.

Cherry turned the doorknob, revealing the pitch-blackness of a room without access to the world. A bulb on a ceiling cord came alive to show a tiny storeroom furnished with a dusty old cot and some bare shelves.

"Cot or gators, honey. But make up your mind quick, 'cause I gotta get back. The army showed up in force tonight. I could use twice as many girls and four times as much booze. When it gets busy like this, I'm just a bear about lookin' after my troops. I don't want anybody gettin' battle fatigue, if you catch my drift." She winked.

Bayard grinned back at her stupidly. He looked like he might drown on his own drool, Sally decided. She wondered if he would have shot himself if Cherry had told him to. She was sure she knew the answer.

She angrily threw her parachute into the room. The pack hit the wall with a thud and bounced onto the cot, lifting a cloud of dust from the ancient canvas. The whole room wasn't more than four steps wide. Sleep wouldn't come easily, especially for whoever drew the floor. The thought of spending the night alone with Bayard only inflamed her anger. She was so confused . . . about her feelings toward him . . . about her feelings toward herself and toward men in general . . . about her feelings toward the army and what it was putting her through. More than anything in the world, she just wanted to crawl into her bunk at Avenger and sleep for about a million years. But because that wasn't likely to happen, she had already decided that sharing a room with Bayard would be better than taking her chances with the wildlife and the rain.

She headed into the room and Bayard started to follow, but Cherry grabbed his arm. "Oh, no, instructor honey, you're comin' with me. The major was real plain about that. The army isn't toleratin' any hanky-panky between you two, and I'm not, either. I run a real moral house. Almost half my girls go to church regular—those that aren't too wore out on Saturday night, that is." She tugged his arm to her chest, causing his grin to expand. "Now you just tag along with me, honey. I know some real nice people who'll just be tickled to death to make your acquaintance." She moved him forward.

"Hey!" Sally grabbed his other arm, jerking him to a stop. "He's staying here with me!"

Bayard looked at her and at Cherry and back at her. She wanted more than anything in the world to kick him in the butt, just for the pleasure of knocking that obscene grin off his face.

Cherry gave a mighty jerk that nearly lifted him off his feet; he offered no more resistance than a rag doll. Her voice turned icy. "Now you listen here, little pilot honey. Don't you make me make you get into that room. 'Cause if you do, you're gonna regret it. I've thrown out drunks four times your size. They didn't know what hit 'em, and I guarantee you won't, either. Two got turned into gator bait, and the rest got used for pincushions by the snakes." She used her arm that wasn't wrapped around Bayard to point to the door. "Now all I need to know is which it's gonna be. Combat? Are you goin' peacefully?"

They eyed each other. Sally was sure the ground near the back door was no more crawling with vipers than it was with alligators. But she also was sure that at least one of each was likely to be nearby, and that was too close for her. She spun on her heel and charged into the room, slamming the door behind her. It immediately opened again, and Bayard's parachute and knapsack sailed inside. They landed on the cot, and the door closed with a bang.

"You have yourself a real nice rest now, you hear, honey? We'll be seein' you in the mornin'." Cherry's voice easily penetrated the door.

She—and presumably Bayard—moved down the hallway, and Sally heard the back door open and close.

She gave the cot a vicious kick. The thing lifted into the air and came down on its side, tumbling the parachutes and Bayard's bag onto the floor. She angrily righted the cot and plopped down in its center. The wooden frame creaked, and the ancient canvas groaned as if about to split wide open. She hurriedly got up. After an examination, she determined that the contraption would support her if she was careful how she lay down and didn't put too much of her weight in one place. This time, she gently lowered herself into a prone position.

She no longer felt tired. She was too angry. The vision of Cherry tugging at Bayard, and of him grinning like an idiot, replayed over and over in her mind, as did fantasies of bursting upstairs and dragging him away. But she knew those were fool's dreams. Besides, just when she thought she was getting to know Bayard, he had completely confused her by going with Cherry all too willingly. His tongue had nearly been hanging out of his mouth. This was the same man who earlier had told her how attracted he was to her! How could the sight of a mere pair of breasts change a man so quickly, and what did that say about the man?

She tried to imagine Tex acting the same way as Bayard had, and couldn't. She was sure he hadn't even looked at another girl while they were together. Bayard was smart and he was cute and he could be charming, but he was no Tex. Trying to convince herself otherwise was just plain stupid.

She ignored the cot's warning sounds and rolled onto her side. She considered getting up and turning off the light, but she knew she wouldn't be able to sleep. The walls amplified everything that was going on in the house. A radio was as clear as if it were only feet away. She could hear women squealing and men laughing, as well as snippets of embarrassing conversation. But the worst sounds by far came from the beds. The springs were in constant motion: either fast or slow, or sometimes steady for what seemed like an eternity. Despite her anger at Bayard, the knowledge that he was somewhere among those sounds, and perhaps contributing to them, made sleep impossible.

She put her hand under her head to cushion the cot's hard frame but found the effort useless. She considered using one of the parachutes for a pillow, but feared its weight plus her own would be too much for the cot. Her eyes fell on Bayard's knapsack.

It was heavier than it looked. She unbuckled the flap and was surprised to find nearly half a ream of paper inside. Curious, she pulled out the whole handful. It was his novel. She hadn't actually believed he had written a novel. Novelists were magicians. They had made her life on the farm bearable. She couldn't imagine Bayard having that kind of power over her, especially not now, when he was upstairs doing who knew what.

She stared at the first page, reading and rereading the neatly typed words.

OUR WARRIORS WORE LIPSTICK

*By Beau Bayard*

She turned the page over, intending to stop after a few sentences. But then she saw the book was about the WASP.

Minutes had flown into an hour by the time weariness finally forced her to stop reading. The work obviously wasn't the one that had driven him to drunkenness the night that Dixie lifted him into a truck to sleep it off. This book wasn't even finished yet. Still, it had been years since she'd read anything that so grabbed her. Bayard was a writer, after all. He was a damn good writer. His story had made her laugh and cry and had held her attention as surely as a good movie. But what had pulled at her heart most was his obvious love for the female main character. Beau Bayard had put onto paper a love that was as deep and real as the love she and Tex had shared. She thought about that for a long time as she lay on the cot, and she closed her eyes, remembering how his arms had protected her in the shed as she drifted off to sleep.

Sally awoke with a start, her neck stiff and sore. She pulled Tex's watch from her pocket and was shocked to see that it was well past midnight.

The pages of Bayard's novel were still all over the cot. She carefully shifted her feet to the floor and rose to a sitting position. She had started stuffing the papers back into his knapsack when she spotted an unsealed envelope at the bottom of the bag. She pulled it into the light and saw that it was addressed to "Miss Rose Bayard" in New Orleans. That was the name of his little girl. She gently pulled free the lone sheet of paper containing Bayard's neat handwriting. Like his novel, it was marked up in places where he'd changed his mind, showing that he hadn't yet finished what he wanted to say.

> *My sweet, dearest Rose,*
>
> *You'll be able to read this for yourself soon, so I've asked Monna to keep it safe for you until then.*
>
> *I miss you so much, My Little Rose, and I worry about you. But then I come to my senses and I remember what a big, smart girl you are, just like your mother. She talked about you so often, and about all of the things she planned for us to do together.*
>
> *This war will be over soon. Then I'll come back to you, and we'll make up for all the time I've been away. I promise.*
>
> *Rose, I love you so much. Remember that always.*
>
> *Daddy*

Sally lowered the sheet to her lap. This was still another side to Bayard that was new to her. Rose Bayard was a lucky little girl, as had been her mother.

She stopped herself. Bayard had many sides, and not all of them so noble. He'd proved that this evening with Cherry . . . and who knew how many times more with her whores? She'd be a fool to get mixed up with him. She promised herself to remember that the next time she started getting soggy.

She hadn't visited a bathroom since the Black's farm. She looked around hopefully, but the room was bare of everything but their belongings and the cot. Once again, the humiliation of being shut away like a leper sank in, and her anger returned. Even prisoners got a bucket to pee into.

She stood up. At first she was afraid Cherry might have locked her in, but she found, to her relief, that the door opened when she turned the knob. The hallway light was off. She worked her way along the wall using the glare from the storeroom to pick her path.

The air outside felt good after spending so long in the stuffy room. She lifted her face to the sky. The rain had stopped, and a partial moon hung in the sky. She wrapped her arms around herself. She had foolishly left her flight jacket in the plane. Nighttime in a Louisiana swamp was cold this late in the year.

Sally gingerly found her way across the soggy ground. Any snake foolish enough to be out and about on a cold night like this was likely to be sluggish as an old woman, and the same for alligators. But that was no reason to step without looking first.

She headed for a clump of bushes on the other side of the drive. She wasn't particularly worried about anyone seeing her. The party inside was raucous, so she was fairly sure no one would be outside. No wonder Cherry had chosen this out-of-the-way location for her business. She could entertain an entire army division, and her nearest neighbor wouldn't hear a thing.

The ground was gooey and uneven, but a blaze of light from a dozen windows made the going fairly easy. The wet branches quickly soaked her zoot suit as she moved into the shrubbery. As with everything in the army, the suit's designers had apparently been unaware of any sex but male. After opening the thing up from neck to crotch, she slipped the upper part off her shoulders, causing the cold air to hit her chest and back like so many ice cubes. She quickly wrapped as much of the cloth as she could around herself while she squatted, at the same time trying to keep the baggy lower portion of the suit out of the mud. She had just settled into this position when she heard a rustle. Her first thought was of some wild animal, perhaps even an alligator, moving through the brush toward her. But that idea instantly vanished when she spotted someone in the darkness ahead. She froze, hoping against hope that she hadn't been seen. But like something in a nightmare, the figure turned in her direction and stopped as if sniffing the air. Then he came for her.

She fought back. But he was stronger. They tumbled backward—his weight pinned her to the ground. The air turned heavy with the stench of liquor. She groaned, and gasped for breath.

His hands found her breasts. Fingers pinched and pulled her flesh. Her chest felt as though it were being ripped from her body. She screamed. The sound cut the night like a knife. She screamed again—and again and again.

Running feet crashed through the underbrush. New arms reached out of the darkness. Hands with the strength of steel groped for the flesh of the thing atop her and jerked it away, as other hands lifted her upward and landed her on her wobbly feet. The stench of liquor breath was replaced by cold night air on her naked flesh and strange faces staring at her in the thin moonlight. A powerful flashlight blinded her. A man's voice demanded, "Who are you? What are you doing out here?"

The zoot suit was a tangle of cloth. She turned away as best she could from the eyes and, working as quickly as she could, began unwinding the mess. After what seemed like forever, she was able to slip her arms and torso back inside the cloth and fasten the front.

"I said, who are you and what are you doing out here?" The voice was hard and unsympathetic.

She angrily pushed the light away from her face. The beam came to rest on the face of a soldier lying on the ground. He couldn't have been more than eighteen. His eyes were closed and his shirt was partially dislodged from his pants, the buttons manhandled mostly into the wrong holes. He was mumbling incoherently, and he obviously was drunk out of his mind.

Her foot lashed out with so much force that she partially lifted him off the ground. He groaned and tried to roll away, at the same time bringing his arm tight against his body to protect his ribs. She lifted her foot again, this time intending to kick his face, but the same strong arms that had rescued her lifted her as though she were a feather and carried her out of striking distance.

"Can't let you do that, lady," the holder of the flashlight said. "But if it makes you feel any better, him and his pals are shipping out. Chances are, he'll be dead in two months, anyway. Now I'm asking you for the last time. Who are you and what are you doing out here?" He tried to turn the light back to her face. This time, she knocked it from his hand.

"I'm trying to pee!"

He retrieved the light. As he bent over, she saw that he was an MP, and senior only slightly to the boy on the ground, who now was crying. He put the light on her again, this time being careful to aim the beam low. To her horror, she saw that her zoot suit was covered in mud and that the entire front was soaked, she suspected not only with water from the bushes, but with urine. She looked at the faces in the circle. They all were MPs.

Knots of people were running from the house. They arrived in a huff and a puff.

"What's goin' on here, James honey?" Cherry stopped in front of the big MP who held the light. His manner instantly turned submissive.

"I'm sorry, Cherry." He played his light across the boy on the ground, who moaned. "This one got outside somehow without us seeing him. He's pretty well liquored up. I'm just now finding out what she's doing out here." He flashed the light across Sally's face.

Cherry grabbed the thing away from him and played the beam over Sally. "You OK, honey? You hurt? *Did anything get busted?*"

Sally shook her head. She was still too shaken and too cold and too angry to speak.

Cherry examined her carefully. "Oooooweee, but you are a mess, honey. We gonna have to get you inside and get you cleaned up. We'll get that thing you're wearin' washed out, and I'll find you somethin' to put on tonight while it's dryin'." She turned on the MP. "James honey, you boys aren't doin' your jobs. You're not out here to keep each other company in the moonlight. You're here to keep these soldier boys in line. I can see right now I'm gonna have to kick me some MP butt!"

"I'm sorry, Cherry." He lowered his head. He sounded sincerely hang-dogged. But she'd already turned to other matters.

"You and you!" She stabbed a finger at two MPs. "Get this little fella inta a truck and get him back to the base. He's actin' like he's got a couple of broke ribs, so stop off at the doc and get him patched up. I'd hate to think I was in any way responsible for makin' him late for the war."

She turned back to the waiting MP. "Now James honey, here's what you're gonna do." The big man bent down to catch every word. "You and your men are gonna search every inch of these grounds to make sure no-body else got loose. I have a hard enough time keepin' these boys under control when they're inside. Let 'em get a little booze in 'em and get out-side without anybody watchin' 'em, and no tellin' what they'll try to get into. I wouldn't be a bit surprised if come mornin', we don't find one or two who've tried to hump the gators. And I wouldn't know who I'd feel sorrier for, them or the gators." She handed back his light. "You under-stand me now, James?"

"Yes, ma'am."

"Then I suggest instead of standing there like some kind of big dumb lump, you get your tight little ass in motion. You hear me?"

He barked orders. Silhouettes scurried off in all directions.

"Little pilot honey . . ." She turned to Sally. "I'm real sorry about this. But if you'd stayed in your room like I told you to, you'd have been safe as a bug in a rug, just like I promised." She reached for her shoulder.

Sally knocked her hand away. "And do what—pee in my pants? I will *not* be treated like a prisoner! Do you hear me? I'm a *licensed pilot,* train-ing under the auspices of the United States Army; and by God, I expect to be treated accordingly!"

Cherry eyed her. "I'm sorry, honey. I'm real sorry; I really am. But I can't treat you like any pilot because you're *not* any pilot. You're a woman, which means you're different; and neither you nor I nor anybody can change that. The army gave me orders to keep you out of sight because—frankly, honey—they're scared to death you're gonna embarrass 'em. That's why I hid you away. It wasn't anything personal. I was just doin' what I was told. Personally, I think it stinks, but the army's actin' like you got 'em by the short hairs, and they're not takin' any chances."

"Sally, are you OK? What happened?" Bayard puffed to a stop. He was still zipping up his zoot suit.

"Bastard!" She bent double from the effort of screaming. "I needed you and you were screwing a whore! Bastard! Liar! Liar! You're a liar!"

Cherry grabbed her by the arm. "You got it all wrong, little pilot honey. He was sleepin' by himself. He did a heap of lookin', but he didn't put so much as a fingernail on the inventory. He could have, too—and purely free. Every one of my girls thinks he's so cute, they just want to eat him whole!

"Little pilot honey, I think the army's wastin' you by puttin' you in an airplane. If they had any brains, they'd give you a gun and turn you loose with the infantry. You wouldn't even have to shoot anybody. You'd scare 'em to death! Honey, I do believe you are about the meanest little thing I've ever seen."

Sally threw her arms around Beau, and his arms enveloped her in return.

"Don't leave me again!"

She whispered the command again and again and again.

# Sixteen

The train, probably like every train in the world, was packed to bursting with soldiers and civilians and their belongings. The frigid Texas night air made opening a window unthinkable, despite the smoke from the cigarette or cigar or pipe that seemed to smolder in every hand. And so while all living things trapped outside shivered and sought shelter from the night, those trapped inside the dark, swaying coaches alternately sweated or froze—depending on their nearness to the fickle steam heaters—and slowly suffocated.

Sally giggled as she again pushed Beau's fingers away from her breast. She'd stopped being self-conscious about someone seeing them. The lateness of the hour had sent almost everyone to attempt sleep or to converse in hushed tones that mostly were drowned out by the squeaks and rattles of the car. The train that was returning them to Sweetwater was almost as tired as the one that had brought her and Dixie there more than six months earlier. She wondered if any first-class trains were left in America, or if, like the country itself, they all were worn out by the war.

She was exhausted but couldn't sleep. Too many things had happened in the blur of the past twenty-four hours. Major Stewart had arrived as promised just before daybreak. But instead of spiriting them away, he'd forced Sally to remain out of sight until late evening when, now literally hysterical with anxiety, he'd pushed her and Beau onto the first available westbound train.

She wasn't still worrying about whether she'd done the right thing by landing the AT-6. Beau had used Cherry's telephone to report to Skinner, while managing to sidestep questions about where he was calling from. Two aircraft from other bases had been lost in the storm, along with their all-male crews. The storm had been one of the most violent on record; the weather people had completely misjudged its path and strength. Skinner had wholeheartedly approved Sally's decision to land. Even Waterman wasn't going to be able to come after her this time.

She snuggled deeper against Beau's shoulder. Her breasts, which some-how had moved into a position of greater convenience for him, were like magnets for his fingers. She allowed him to play with her for a few delicious moments before pushing him away. He immediately returned to nibbling her ear. She sighed. She couldn't help herself. Hiding out at Cherry's, and now being together on the train, had given them time to get to know each other, and to her astonishment, she liked what she'd learned.

She whispered, "How come we didn't get around to doing this sooner?"

He interrupted his work on her ear. "Couldn't."

She giggled. "Why?"

He kissed her softly. "Because you are the world's greatest pilot, and I am the world's greatest writer, but even two such geniuses couldn't crash airplanes *and* fight with each other *and* do this, too! Personally, I don't care much for the first. But I like this part a lot!" He offered her a deep, lingering kiss.

When finally they broke it off, she'd barely gotten settled in her seat before he whispered, "Did you hear what the German general said to the Japanese general in charge of training kamikaze pilots?"

She shook her head.

"Now that's a crash course!"

She punched him gently in the ribs. Beau's jokes were only slightly worse than his flying, but she didn't mind. She couldn't remember when she had been so content. Her anger and distrust had disappeared, and she felt an unbridled attraction for this man, whom she had so loathed. She realized, quite happily, that she was falling head-over-heels for him.

They clasped their hands together and rode in silence for some time.

"Sally." He somehow made her name sound exciting.

She automatically lifted her face to his, knowing from experience that his lips and tongue would be waiting for hers. She wasn't disappointed. The kiss lasted a long time.

He was the one who finally broke free. "Sally, I want to tell you something. Something very important."

She straightened.

"Sally, you read my new novel and you do like it?"

"Yes, of course. It's wonderful." She wondered where this was going. Did he need her reassurance? In the movies, writers seemed to always be troubled. Did he need someone to lean on? If so, she was prepared.

"You think it will sell? That's what you told me."

She nodded. She wanted to offer her help in any way she could.

His voice lifted with excitement. "I do, too! I'm sure that it will provide a good living for many years to come. I have plenty of ideas for other books, too. If I live to be a hundred, I'm sure that I'll be able to keep churning out books. Don't you?"

She'd loved his manuscript, and she assumed it would bring him money. But that wasn't what he was asking. He was going the long way around to get to something. Her every instinct, honed by twenty-one years of survival in a sea of hardship, warned that it was going to be something she wasn't going to like.

He continued guardedly. "You know, Sally, my mother would love nothing more than for me to stop running around having adventures, as she calls them, and settle down and teach English at the college, or some other god-awful thing, and get married. And in spite of his unhappiness with his career, my father feels, for some reason, that I should suffer the same fate, as he reminds me in every letter. So if the book doesn't sell, he can get me a position at the college."

He paused.

She waited.

His hand found hers. He squeezed her fingers. "What I'm trying to say is, one way or the other, I'll be able to provide for a wife . . . if I can survive the war. Sally, will you marry me?"

His touch, so welcome moments earlier, suddenly felt foreign. She resisted the urge to remove her hand from his.

"Why?" She had some trouble making her mouth form the word.

"Why? Because I love you."

Love. Hearing the word was like the shock of cold water. Tex was the only one who'd ever told her he loved her. She'd never heard her father or relatives even use the word. Growing up, it had become her own secret, sacred oath, something to be repeated only in her dreams, and to be uttered aloud in adulthood only for her best friend and true love. In truth, she'd never expected to find that man. But then she'd met Tex.

An invisible force pried her fingers from his. The lovely pink cloud that had covered her world since he'd taken her in his arms at Cherry's blew away.

"Why?" she asked.

"Why, what?" He reached for her, but she pushed him away.

"Why do you say you love me?"

"Because I do!"

She studied him. "What's happened?"

"What do you mean?" He met her eyes. She wanted to tell herself otherwise, but she could see his near-panic.

She kept her voice low so no one else in the car would hear. "We kissed for the first time less than eight hours ago. We barely know each other. Your reason for wanting to marry me has nothing to do with loving me. Something's happened. What is it?"

He didn't try to conjure up a dimple. He didn't try to soften the blow. "Married instructors are going to be exempt from overseas duty if and when Waterman shuts down Avenger," he said. "If you marry me, I might be able to get a classroom assignment in ground school and not have to fly anymore."

He'd put it right on the line. She had to give him that. He wanted to marry her because he wanted to use her. Having him confirm the crime made the hurt no less painful.

She remembered the time when she was young when some larger children gave her a doll, supposedly for her own, and then snatched it back and laughed at her when she cried. She'd promised herself on that awful afternoon that she would never cry again. She'd kept the promise all these years, except during the most terrible tragedies. She reminded herself that this wasn't one of them. She jumped to her feet and bolted for the aisle.

The door at the end of the car was stiff and difficult to open. She finally managed the mechanism and found herself on the cramped platform between the cars. The flexible curtains that enclosed the space gave little protection from the cold, nor from the smoke that drifted back from the engine.

She'd barely closed the door when he jerked it open. He tried to take her in his arms, but she shoved him away. Something wet was on her cheeks. Some part of her over which she had no control was making her cry. That was OK. That was within the bounds of the promise that she'd made to herself.

"Sally! Please!" He tried again to take her in his arms.

"You go to hell!" She pushed him away.

The wind's roar and the clamor of wheels beneath their feet forced him to shout. "Sally, listen to me." He snaked his arms around her. She struggled to break free, but he held her tight. "You're poor and you're alone in the world. I'm neither. I have everything you so desperately want, and I want to give them to you. A comfortable life. Security. Love. Social standing. A guaranteed future. You can even have an airplane! I'll buy it for you. You can fly anytime you want, to anywhere you want. I know you don't believe that I love you, but I do. I think I've loved you from the first moment I saw you. But you can't have any of those things—and I can't have them with you—unless you marry me."

She stopped struggling.

He loosened his grip.

"Sally, I'm not asking you to kill yourself for me. I'm asking you to marry me so you can have everything you've ever wanted, and so I can live to have *you*."

She broke free. "What you really mean is, so you can avoid fighting! Thanks, but no thanks! I'm not going to be your free ticket. I'm not going to marry you for your money, either! I know what love is. I had it once. I'm holding out for it again. And I *am* going to have my career in aviation . . . no matter what anybody thinks. I'll get along just fine on my own without your help!"

He gave her a plaintive look. "I told you that I love you."

She sneered. "Yeah, I've seen how much you love me. I saw how you acted around those whores. You were slipping on your own spit!"

He had stopped trying to touch her. He glared. "I just looked, for Christ's sake. They were nearly naked. In fact, some of them *were* naked! That's what women do. You use your bodies to get us interested. We don't have any control over it!"

She tried to turn away in disgust, but he stopped her. "I'm only a man, Sally. I can't compete with a god, especially one that you've drawn to perfection in your own mind. I'm not going to try. I have my faults. I admit it. But at least I'm honest with myself. I don't close my heart to the future so I can wallow in the past. And I don't go through life making love to the dead. Or weren't you and that Christ-like boyfriend of yours like that? I suppose all you ever did was fly around in his raggedy old airplane, giving rides to pious farmers with twenty kids, and admiring sunsets and discussing Nietzsche."

"What do you mean by that?" She didn't know anything about Nietzsche—she'd never heard of him. But Tex was out of bounds. She wasn't going to allow him to bring up Tex. She'd been as honest as she could be about her feelings for Tex. She wasn't going to let Beau use him against her.

He leaned forward. His voice rose. "I guess you two didn't fuck!"

She slapped him. The sound was louder even than the scream of the wind and the whine of steel rolling over steel. It might have been the loudest sound ever heard.

She found the handle on the door to the next car. She jerked and the door opened, and she ran inside, slamming the door behind her. She ran through that car and the next one and the next, until no cars were left to run to and she was exhausted from crying. She found a seat that was empty and collapsed into its padding. She couldn't run any more, even if there had been more cars. The world was too much against her, and she was too worn out. She couldn't take another step. She was beaten.

Sometime much later, she was awakened by someone slipping his arms around her and drawing her head to his shoulder. The someone whispered, "My God, but you are the most hardheaded woman to ever walk the face of the planet. Cherry LaRue was right: you could win this war single-handed. The Japs and the Germans wouldn't know what had hold of them. You'd scare 'em to death. I know, because you keep me scared to death about half the time." Some trick of her ear erased everything but his voice, even the rumble of the wheels and the creaks and groans of the old car.

"Yet I admire you more than any person I've ever known," he went on. "For your strength. For your determination. For knowing exactly what you want and how you're going to get it. And even for your fears when you're on the ground—and certainly for your courage and skill in the air. In the air, Sally, you're a goddess—an artist! My God, I think sometimes that you can *see* air! I can't help myself. I do love you so."

His warmth felt so good, after so long without the touch of another human being. She'd been starving and hadn't even known it. She smiled sleepily. "I'm mad at you," she murmured. But she snuggled deeper into Beau's arms, and allowed herself to postpone their differences and inevitable arguments for another day.

# SEVENTEEN

Dixie examined herself in the bathroom mirror. She'd already run a brush through her hair so many times her mane shone like the new hood on a black car, but she still eyed herself critically. "Hey, Sally, the next time you make one of those emergency landin's you're always havin' to make, how about doin' me a favor and make it next to a place that's got some real good shampoo. I swear this army soap is turnin' me into an old woman before my time. If I don't get my hands on some real good shampoo soon, I'm afraid I just might go bald!" She brought the brush downward, causing the bristles to make a silky, whispering sound through her thick strands.

Sally finished tucking her blouse into her slacks. The tension between them over Buddy Gregg had disappeared in her absence. Since her return, Dixie had been treating her like a long-lost sister, thanks in no small part, she suspected, to her confidential confession that she and Beau had become a couple. Dixie, unable to believe that she'd truly been thrown over, and more convinced than ever that Buddy had some ulterior motive for inviting Sally to the party, had urged Sally to limit the evening to one dance. Then Dixie would step in, and Sally would duck out with Beau. That was OK with Sally. The sooner she parted company with Buddy Gregg, the better. She'd told Dixie as much, and her admission had brought the big brunette considerable pleasure.

She and Beau had made up early that morning before rolling into Sweetwater. She knew that she didn't love him . . . not yet, anyway. But having a man again, someone to touch, someone to talk to and to laugh with, had made her happier than she'd been in years, even if he did have ulterior motives for wanting to marry her. The idea still galled her. But after examining her own feelings, she had decided to put that aside and to enjoy Beau's company for what it was. If her feelings for him grew, she would face the consequences when the time came. If they didn't, so be it.

Skinner had questioned them at length about their landing and the storm damage to the AT-6, and then had produced a mountain of paperwork. Since Beau was the instructor, his was twice as high as Sally's, which was why she was free to go to town this Saturday afternoon and he wasn't.

Dixie demanded, "Say, are you listenin' to me, or has that instructor still got your brain stuck on a busy signal?" She walked into the bay, her appearance apparently good enough to pass her own inspection, and that of every fashion magazine on the planet, Sally thought.

"Sorry, I guess I was thinking about Beau," she said.

Dixie snorted happily. "Congratulations! I'm happy to see you've finally developed a lastin' interest in somethin' besides carburetors and wing flaps. I've always said if you resemble a girl in your birthday suit, you're probably a girl, even if nobody's ever seen you lookin' like one or smellin' like one." She produced one of her lipsticks. Rationing made makeup hard to come by, and Dixie guarded hers jealously. "Here. As long as we're goin' to town, you might as well start practicin' what the rest of us have been doin' all our lives. By the way, I can't wait to see how you're gonna juggle a date at the dance tonight and a new boyfriend, too, seein' as how you haven't handled either in years."

Sally took the lipstick. Dixie was right. Why could nothing ever be cut-and-dried? Let her win a thousand dollars, and she was sure that she'd come down with rabies the same day. She finally had a boyfriend—after three years of loneliness—and also Buddy Gregg. Her life had been mostly beans for so long, and now that she was getting a little taste of steak, a whole stupid steer wanted to land in her lap.

Twila came into the room. She looked worried. "Sally, someone named B.D. Horne just called the base switchboard, wanting to talk to you. A friend of mine took the call, which is why I know about it. He said if he can't get on the base to see you, he wants you to come to his room in the Blackstone Hotel in Sweetwater." She lowered her voice. "Waterman's sure to hear about this, Sally. He's gone through your personnel files. He's written to Washington about you, too. My friend told me. She works part-time in the secretarial pool and got a glance at the letter. Sally, I really think he's trying to get you for standing up to him."

Dixie interrupted. "B.D. Horne. That's the name that was on that envelope we thought was a joke."

Sally sat down. A knot was balling up in her stomach. Men calling to make dates with WASP in hotels was no joke. Waterman was behind this. He had to be. She hadn't really thought he would come after her. Certainly she had never imagined he would rifle her personnel file, or write to Washington about her. She wondered whom he had written to and what he had said.

"I don't know a B.D. Horne, Twila," she said. "But if I did, I wouldn't go to his hotel room."

Twila started for the door. "I didn't think you would, Sally," she replied. "No one who knows you would think that. But if Waterman is out to get you, he'll make it look like you did."

Out in the street, Sergeant Crawford honked the truck horn. Anyone wanting a ride to town would have to hurry. "Better get a move on with that lipstick, hon," Dixie urged Sally. "But remember, this is Sweetwater we're goin' to, not Dallas. You don't wanna look so good that you start a gunfight." She added gently, "Cheer up, hon. Anybody as mean as Waterman is bound to get bit in the butt eventually."

"Yes," Sally mumbled. But she knew she sounded even less convinced than Dixie.

The Lone Star drugstore was bustling with a cross-section of wartime West Texas: lonely servicemen, fidgety bobby-soxers, married women towing squirmy children, and old men with nothing better to do on a Saturday afternoon than gossip and play checkers. A cold wind had come down out of the north during the night, and the loafers and stragglers who normally would be outside were firmly inside where there was heat.

Dixie motioned to the waitress. "Coffee, please."

A tired-looking, heavyset woman with run-over shoes that had been cut open to let her bunions breathe responded by shoving an empty cup across the counter.

"Two, please." Sally tried to offer a sympathetic smile. But she was too worried about Waterman to care about a watered-down cup of coffee. With graduation only weeks away, her future suddenly had been thrown deeper into doubt. She had dreamed of becoming one of the WASP who were testing aircraft for the manufacturers. The job was dangerous but also rewarding and exciting, and that kind of experience would be worth gold after the war. Everyone was predicting that aviation would really take off once peacetime returned. There was talk of airplanes with folding wings in every household. With luck, she might even get a permanent job flight-testing for one of the big plane builders. But if Waterman somehow got her grounded, she wouldn't be able to give away rides in a Piper Cub.

A second cup slid over. The waitress poured mechanically and shuffled along sourly to the next customer. Sally took a sip and grimaced at the taste of the stuff.

Whatever the shortcomings of its soda fountain, the Lone Star at least was lively. A jukebox alternately blared Frank Sinatra, Benny Goodman, Artie Shaw, and Glenn Miller. Advertisements for soft drinks and virtually every patent medicine ever invented clogged the walls and shelf tops. An ancient pharmacist worked ceaselessly behind a cluttered counter. Still, Sally already regretted letting Dixie talk her into this trip. She'd long since discovered everything in Sweetwater worth discovering. She wished now that she'd stayed back in the barracks.

An infantryman who'd been eying Dixie worked his way through the crowd.

"Hey, good-lookin', what's cookin'?" He leaned over her shoulder. He was tall and hard with muscles, and almost surely home on leave. He reminded Sally of a hungry man who's discovered a plate of roast beef.

Dixie didn't bother turning. "Nothin' you're gonna get."

He put his hand on her shoulder. "Aw, now honey . . ."

She flung him off with a shrug. "You do that again, soldier, and you'll be usin' a hook to pull your trigger. Now, git!"

He moved back into the crowd, muttering an angry curse.

Sally looked at Dixie in awe. "Has there ever been a time in your life when men weren't swarming all over you?"

Dixie stopped her cup in midair. "No."

The Lone Star was full of familiar faces. Sergeant Crawford was reading and re-reading labels on the boxes of foot remedies. Dixie, never wasting an opportunity to belittle the sergeant, observed, "You can't hardly blame his feet for actin' up. I don't like him, either, and he only gets on me a couple of times a day."

Twila and Geri had crowded shoulder-to-shoulder into a booth and seemed unaware of the commotion going on around them. Coke glasses in hand and a heaping plate of French fries before them, they were deep in conversation. Suddenly Geri threw back her head and laughed loudly, and Twila beamed and slid a ketchupy fry into her own mouth. They spent an awful lot of their free time together, Sally thought.

"Ma'am?"

A bony finger touched Sally's shoulder. She turned to find a face of leathery wrinkles burnt deep brown by a lifetime of sunshine.

He smiled uncertainly, exposing a yellow tooth that leaned at a crazy angle as if trying to take a nap. He was at least seventy and thin as barbed wire. Something about him was vaguely familiar, though she couldn't place her finger on it.

He removed his hat, a great gray Stetson, to reveal a head of thinning black hair. He had arthritic fingers stained chocolate brown by a million cigarettes.

He sort of bowed. "I don't mean to be no trouble, ma'am."

Sally's first thought, thanks to Dixie's influence, was that he was trying to pick her up, and she recoiled. Men would still be chasing Dixie on her one-hundredth birthday, while she—currently young and in the bloom of health—could only attract the old and wrinkled! Only the slimmest thread of courtesy kept her from turning back to her coffee.

"Yes."

He shuffled self-consciously. "I come originally from a little ol' dust ball of a town not far from here that nobody's ever heard of, 'cept them that's lived 'round here for a while. I worked cattle on one ranch or 'nother all my life till I retired. Now I'm just 'nother old wore-out geezer, come to town to sleep on soft sheets and bathe in runnin' water and live out my days in the lap of luxury." He grinned nervously, revealing that his tooth had a twin.

He seemed too shy to step on a bug, much less to be a masher. Sally's annoyance was turning to cautious curiosity.

Dixie had put down her coffee cup, too, and was studying him intently.

Sally would have expected her friend, who could sense a man a mile away and tell what was on his mind to boot, to have jabbed her good naturedly in the ribs by now. She heard herself ask, "What can I do for you?"

His hand moved beneath his coat to his denim shirt pocket and emerged with rolling papers and a drawstring pouch of tobacco for a roll-your-own. "I hate to bother ya, but"—he sprinkled and his tongue added a dab of moisture to the edge of the paper, which he rolled; his fingers slid quickly over the tube to even out the stuffing, and he lifted the smoke to his lips and brought it to fire with a match that came out of nowhere and flamed against the edge of his thumbnail; the whole trick was done in the blink of an eye—"ain't you part o' them gals from up on the hill?" He exhaled. The smoke flowed gently from his nostrils, probably as it had done every day of his life since he was ten or twelve.

"Yes." She suddenly had a thought that made no sense at all.

He studied the tips of his cowboy boots. Though veterans of much use like him, they were clean and well-shined. "I almost went up in one o' them aeroplanes once." He removed his cigarette and used his little finger to flick the ash onto the wooden floor. "It was back in what they called The War To End All Wars . . . that was the first big World War, though I never did see none of it—never left Texas, in fact. I was part o' the cavalry. I helped 'em train the horses. Guess the army figured since that's what I'd been doin' all my life, they might as well put what

I knowed to good use." He coughed. The sound was soft and sickly and came from deep down in his throat. "That was a terrible thang, that war. Terrible for the horses and for the men who were in the war with 'em. Almost none came back, and them that did weren't never the same again." He took a final drag off what had become a stub and dropped it to the ground, crushing it beneath his boot.

He fixed her with his eyes. "Ma'am . . . if it ain't gettin' too personal, would your name be Sally?"

Dixie grabbed her arm. Dixie had had the same thought.

He waited, a tall drink of water in simple cowboy come-to-town clothes, his face sincere and honest as the day is long.

"Yes, that's my name," she said.

He buried his hands deep in his pockets as if he were fourteen again and the conversation had turned from horses and cows to something that was purely thin ice, like girls. It took him a moment to screw up the rest of his courage. "Sally Ketchum?"

She recognized him now. He'd been in the crowd on the sidewalk outside Solomon's on her first day at Avenger, when they'd been trying on clothes. He'd stood out, because unlike the others, he'd looked embarrassed to be there.

"You're B.D. Horne, aren't you?" she asked.

He removed his Stetson again and began rolling up the brim. "I was hopin' we'd meet up. I've been on the lookout for ya. I've been lookin' for ya just 'bout every Saturday since the army set up up thar on the hill. I was about ta give up, what with all the talk 'bout the army closin' it down, so I'm real glad I finally come across ya." The Stetson was taking a terrible toll. Arthritis had crippled his hands, but they still held considerable strength, probably thanks to years of stringing fences and roping.

"What do you want with Sally?"

Horne hadn't looked at Dixie until now. He froze like a deer caught in a headlamp.

"What can I do for you, Mr. Horne?" Sally demanded. She was damn tired of watching men go to jelly over Dixie, even old ones who might die at any moment from the strain.

He pulled his eyes back into their sockets. The Stetson was nearly wrenched in two. "I have somethin' for ya, Miss Ketchum. Somethin' that's more rightfully yours than mine, even if it was originally given to me."

Sally glanced around the room, but no one else was paying attention. Sergeant Crawford still studied the foot remedies. Twila and Geri huddled over their booth table: Geri giggled uncharacteristically and Twila reached up to push a lock of hair out of Geri's eyes. The old woman behind the counter had taken to leaning hard against the wall to make the building take up some of her weight.

"What do you have for me?" Sally asked.

"I'd rather show ya than tell ya, if ya don't mind comin' with me for a bit."

"Come with you where?"

"Over thar, ma'am." He pointed a blunted finger to the window.

She didn't have to look. She knew he was pointing to the Blackstone Hotel.

"To your hotel room?" She barely stifled her anger. If Waterman was behind this, he almost surely would have a photographer waiting in a closet, and maybe a newspaper reporter, too!

"Yessum. That's right." He fell silent and stood a little taller, as if wounded.

Dixie smiled at him. "You know, Mr. Horne, we're not in the habit of goin' to men's hotel rooms," she chided playfully, "especially those of men we don't know."

Sally looked at her friend. Had Dixie sensed something about B.D. Horne that she hadn't?

He blushed all over. "Oh, yessum, I know that. I'm sure that's the truth, too, ma'am, and I'm real sorry I didn't brang it with me. But to tell ya the truth, I'd pretty much give up on thankin' I'd ever find Miss Ketchum, and I was afraid it'd get wore out if I kept carryin' it around with me."

Dixie continued, "That's not to say we don't ever make an exception for a good cause, so long as we have assurances that we'll be safe." She eyed him teasingly. "Do we have your word of honor, Mr. Horne, that we'll be safe in your company and that you'll conduct yourself in a gentlemanly manner once we're out of the pryin' eyes of the public?"

He wilted. Sally was certain his knees were buckling and shaking inside his pants. He held up his right hand solemnly. "Oh, yes, ma'am! You won't have nothin' to worry about on that account from me, ma'am!"

Dixie scooted to the floor. They were nearly the same height. She plopped her arm around his shoulder. His eyes bugged, and he looked like he might faint. "Well, Mr. Horne, that bein' the case, I think we better go see this thing that you've got of Sally's." She steered him purposefully toward the door, her arm firmly around his body.

Sally got up irritably. Thanks to Dixie, she once again was bringing up the rear. She dug into her pocket and dropped three nickels onto the counter, two for the coffees and one for the long-suffering waitress.

As they reached the door, she spotted the soldier who Dixie had reproached; he was following Dixie and B.D. Horne with his eyes. His jaw had dropped impossibly, and she decided he looked exactly like someone who'd seen cows fly.

A sign hung from a rusted pole that jutted from the ancient brick above the front door. The faded wording announced, BLACKSTONE HOTEL.

The building was too narrow for its two stories, creating the impression that its sides had been squashed in. The place hadn't been painted in years, and its wood was cracked and buckled, making it look even older than it probably was. The lobby was empty. Tattered green wallpaper, an old potbellied stove, and a few ancient rocking chairs illuminated by a single bare ceiling bulb were the only amenities. Planking creaked beneath their feet as they neared the open stairwell.

"Up here, ma'am." He used his Stetson to point to the upper landing, at the same time stepping aside so they could go first.

His room proved no less gloomy than the lobby. An overstuffed bed, a dresser and mirror, a small nightstand and a straight-backed chair left little room to move around. A big porcelain bowl sat atop the dresser, apparently for washing hands, since there was no bathroom. Nor was there a closet, Sally noted with relief. A few wall pegs provided the only place to hang clothes.

He closed the door. "I'm real sorry I can't offer you nothin', not even a glass o' water. I don't get many visitors." He hung the critically injured Stetson on a peg on the backside of the door.

"That's OK," Dixie said. "We're not thirsty."

Sally was sure he'd never had a woman in this room before, much less two. In fact, she wondered if a woman had ever been part of his life. So she was surprised to spot a small picture of a smiling young woman in a simple frame atop his dresser. Her right shoulder and face were turned toward the camera, and her thick black hair partially covered her forehead in a pose that obviously had been arranged by the photographer to capture her exotic Mexican beauty. But her most sensational feature was her eyes, which were filled with dark, liquid life.

"That's Sofia." He indicated the picture. "She didn't have any folks left when that was took. I was her only kin."

With some effort, he lowered himself to his knees and groped around under the bed. His slowness suggested that his arthritis was more serious than Sally had suspected. Finally he pulled out a large box, which he plopped onto the bed. Then he slowly climbed to his feet, putting out his hand to the headboard to steady himself. He stood for a moment to catch his breath.

"I bought this for her to go adancin' in when they graduated her from high school. It come all the way from a big store in Fort Worth."

A pink ribbon and bow held the box together. He carefully slipped the ribbon aside and ever so gently lifted the top, exposing a sea of tissue paper tainted pink by the object underneath. He pulled the paper aside and his hands dipped deep down into the pink and lifted the object free.

"Oh, my!" Sally stepped forward for a better look.

Dixie whispered, "God a'mighty!"

He hoisted the dress tenderly into the air so that it became a great pale-pink waterfall of rayon taffeta, cut low in a sweetheart neck and puffed where the arms met the shoulders. It was the stuff of dreams . . . a full-skirted prom dress with flared petticoat, and inside the box even snow-white sandals. He held the dress high, not quite against himself but not at arm's length, either.

Sally touched the material cautiously. She'd never seen such a beautiful dress.

Dixie whispered, "How in the world did you ever come by such a thing?"

"Mr. Horne," Sally added, "it's the most beautiful dress I've ever seen in my life. Doesn't Sofia want it? Why in the world did she leave it here?"

The dress made a silky sound as he returned it to its box.

His hand reached for the package of roll-your-own, and he took a little step backward as if to distance him from the object on the bed. "She's dead."

He began the process of making the smoke. He worked slowly, as if not really interested. "It ain't much of a story. She joined up with the army, and they sent her and a bunch o' other nurses over to that place the Japs attacked, that Pearl Harbor. She'd been there 'bout a week when her and some others went for a swim. She drowned."

He finished stuffing, rolling, wetting, and lighting. He inhaled deeply and coughed. "The army sent me a letter expressin' their regrets. Had a bunch o' big words in it. They said she was honorable and a person for her country to be proud of, which was real nice." He took another drag. "But that weren't worth a damn for bringin' her back."

Sally lifted the dress. The material felt nearly alive, almost as if the dress were begging her to liberate it from its box beneath the bed in this sad little room so it once again could hear laughter. Its rustle wasn't really the sound of a dress at all, but the faraway voice of a young woman who once had laughed for a camera and probably had driven young men crazy with ideas, before dying beneath the waters of a far-off land, in a war she'd never had a part in.

She returned the dress to its resting place.

She'd somehow known all along that Horne didn't have anything of hers. The old fox. He'd probably asked one of the trainees for her name, though why he'd chosen her was a complete mystery. She wasn't angry with B.D. Horne. She was too sad to be angry.

He'd backed up to the bed. The way he let himself plop down should have caused the springs to protest, but his weight barely made a sound. His cigarette had shrunk into a stump that was ready to burn the chocolate brown parts of his fingers. He punched the embers out in a small metal ashtray beside the bed. As he did, he had a coughing spell. The sound wasn't loud. It was shallow and sickly.

On an impulse, Sally leaned down and kissed his cheek. His skin was hard and leathery and smelled of cigarette smoke, but for that second she wouldn't have cared if it'd been alligator hide. He stayed still as a sponge and soaked up every morsel that she gave him. When she pulled away, he prolonged the moment by trying to rise with her.

"Good-bye, Mr. Horne. Good luck to you." She turned to join Dixie at the door.

"That's not why I brought ya up here." He spoke softly; he was having trouble gathering the air to talk normally. "I didn't bring you up here to show you Sofia's dress."

"What then?" She wanted desperately to get as far away as possible from this tiny room and its dying man.

He pulled open a drawer in the nightstand with some difficulty and fumbled for a moment before producing a picture. "Here. This is why I brung ya up here." He thrust the paper at her.

Puzzled, she turned it over.

She gasped.

Dixie hurried to her side. "What is it, honey?"

She knew the picture as well as she knew the cockpit of every plane she'd ever flown. She could repeat every detail from memory, had repeated them a thousand times—a million times—in her dreams and in her nightmares. A young man and a young woman stood beside an airplane in an open field. He was tall as a tree and handsome as a movie star, and he was smiling at the camera. The smile was as dazzling as the headlamp on a new locomotive. The woman stood next to him. She was slender and three-quarters his height. She wore her hair cut short to fit easily inside a flight helmet, and she was dressed in pants and boots to accommodate a cockpit. Her face was turned up to him, her expression so bursting with love that the angels surely had been jealous. The airplane was of ancient design, worn and greatly patched. The picture was of herself and Tex and the Jenny, snapped by a grateful customer following a

ride at an air show. It was the only picture ever taken of them. Her copy
had burned in the wreck. So far as she had known, no other existed.

"Where did you get this?" Sally knew she sounded crazed, but she
didn't care. Dixie was staring at the picture, too. She reached out as she
might to touch a precious piece of art, but Sally quickly pulled the photo
away, and almost reluctantly Dixie allowed her hand to drop.

He lay down. "Tex . . . he mailed it to me."

"You knew Tex?"

He nodded.

"How? Where?" It was all she could do to keep from shaking the
words out of him. She was dying for water and he was torturing her
with trickles.

"We rode together. Before he met you. He'd come through looking
for work. They put him on doin' brandin'. That was before I retired. We
got along fine; I think he kinda looked on me as his daddy." He smiled,
revealing both teeth. "Tex was the smartest fella I ever knowed, and the
kindest. I sure did hate to see him go. Funny, I never did learn anythang
about whar he come from. He was just driftin', like he was lookin' for
somethin'. So I was real happy to learn he'd found it." He coughed.

"What do you mean? Found what?" She sat down, pushing him over
with her hip. Dixie hovered overhead. The thought occurred to her that
they probably looked like a couple of vultures on a carcass.

"He found what he was lookin' for. He found you. Tex was more in
love with you than any man I've ever knowed. He thought you raised the
sun in the mornin' and took up the moon at night. He was talkin' 'bout
marryin' ya."

She felt like she was burning and freezing at the same time. She nearly
shook him to make him talk faster. "How do you know all this? Tex and I
were never apart, except for when one of us was giving rides."

She had to wait until another spat of coughing spent its course.

"His letter."

"*What letter?*"

He moved for the drawer again but found reaching it impossible. She
dipped inside and grabbed the meager collection of paper. Finding Tex's

precise handwriting took only a moment. She didn't wait for Horne's permission. She tore into the envelope.

*Dear B.D.,*

*I hope this letter finds you well. I told you you'd hear from me again and here I am.*

*I found her, B.D. I found the woman I've been looking for all my life. Her name's Sally Ketchum. She's smart as a whip and honest and pretty. She loves to fly. I helped her get her pilot's license (you didn't believe me when I told you I'm a pilot, did you). I used the money I made on the ranch to buy an old World War One airplane called a Jenny. It's not much of an airplane, but then cowboying doesn't pay much of a wage, as I guess you know. We're barnstorming and having a swell time.*

*I'm going to marry her, B.D. I haven't asked her yet, but I'm sure she loves me. I've been looking all my life for a woman with whom I really have something in common and whom I can trust. I hit the jackpot. We don't ever seem to run out of things to talk about. She's my best friend. I'd trust her with my life. Here's what she looks like. Isn't she beautiful? This picture was shot at an air show.*

*I've got to go now. Sally's checking the oil right now, and then she's going to help me fill up with gas. We've got to be in Oklahoma before sundown.*

*I was a dead man before I met her, B.D. Now I'm as alive as a man can be. I want to spend every minute with her. Wish good thoughts for me. I'm the happiest man on this earth.*

*Take care.*
*Tex Jones*

Sally let the paper slip from her fingers. The date on the page was the same as their crash. The letter was the last thing he'd ever written. She remembered he'd asked a stranger to mail it for him. She'd been curious at the time, but hadn't pried. Tex had his secrets. She'd figured he'd fill in the blank spots in his own good time.

She was crying. The tears were running down her cheeks in sheets, the sounds coming from her throat wet and tragic. Everything had come back, everything that she'd thought she'd buried. The clock had jumped back. The dust from the field lifted into her nose again. Tex's hand touched her shoulder. He kissed her gently on the cheek before pulling the prop. The engine burst to life. The Jenny lifted, and they winged through fields of puffy white hung under a blue ceiling. She fought away the rest. The rest was even worse. It was killing her all over again. She lifted her hands to her face, but nothing helped: the tears burned her eyes; she bent over double with pain.

"Do you have other letters, Mr. Horne?" Dixie asked. She sounded helpless.

He apparently shook his head. Sally didn't look at him. She wasn't sure she could ever look at anything again.

"But you knew that Tex was dead." Dixie was on the verge of crying, too. "How? And how did you know to look for Sally in Sweetwater?"

He was worn-out. His voice was a whisper. "The FBI man told me."

The answer was so unbelievable that it took a moment to sink in.

"What do you mean?" Dixie demanded. "What FBI man?"

The bed was too narrow for the two of them. Sally got to her feet.

Dixie produced a handkerchief from her endless supply. Sally swabbed her eyes. "What FBI man, Mr. Horne? What are you talking about?"

He sat up a little. He pulled a bandana from his pocket and wiped his mouth where his coughing had brought up a little spittle. "He come around three times. The first time was right after Tex left the ranch. He asked a lot of questions, especially to me, since Tex and me was pals. Wanted to know how Tex had acted and what I thought he was up to . . . things like that."

"And what did you tell him?" Sally leaned close to catch every word.

"I told him Tex acted like everybody else, except a lot smarter and nicer. As to the rest of it, I told him I thought he was lookin' for somethin'. Tex was one of them dreamers, for sure. But I didn't know what he was lookin' for at the time. Course, I do now." His teeth peeked at her.

"You said there were three times," Sally interrupted. "What was the second?" Her eyes were drying as fast as hot rocks. She didn't believe for a second that Tex had been mixed up in anything illegal. Someone was trying to frame him. She was sure.

The old cowboy straightened. His strength was coming back. "The second time was more'n a year ago. The same FBI fella come around. He sat down in that chair over there." He made a motion. "We talked for a long time. Wanted to know if I'd heard from Tex again, and like that. Anyhow, that's how I learned Tex was dead. He told me."

"Did you ask him why he was interested in Tex?" Sally asked.

He hesitated. He obviously had been hoping the conversation wouldn't get around to that part.

"Well?" she demanded.

"He wouldn't come right out and say it, but it sounded like they thought Tex was either murdered or mixed up in a murder somehow, or in somethin' else that was real bad. I wasn't able exactly to get it straight in my mind."

"That's a lie!" she shouted, and Dixie jumped. "Tex wouldn't have hurt a flea!"

She wanted to get her hands around that FBI man's neck to choke the truth out of him. Tex hadn't been murdered. He'd died in an accident. And how dare anyone think of him as a murderer, or anything else that wasn't honest and good and kind-to-the-bone! She had a mission. She somehow would set things straight for Tex.

"That's what I told him," Horne said. "I used those exact words. 'Tex wouldn't hurt a flea.' That's why I didn't say anythang about that letter or the picture. He left not knowin' I had 'em."

"How did you know to look for Sally?" Dixie asked.

"I figured that part out for myself." He looked pleased with himself. "If Tex taught you to fly, I figured you might wind up here."

He was avoiding their eyes. Sally could see that there was something else. She persisted. "Yes? What?"

He looked pained. "He was hintin' that you was mixed up in whatever Tex was mixed up in. He said a girl was flyin' with Tex, but they didn't know her name. He asked if I knew anything about it and I told him no."

"Me?" Her anger turned to fear. Why would the FBI be investigating her? A thousand imagined crimes raced through her mind. She had to think. It did make sense that no one would have known her name. She and Tex had kept to themselves. Few people knew anything about their lives together. And what little identification she had carried had burnt up. The day after the crash, some hick sheriff had shown up at the farmhouse where she'd been taken to recover from her injuries—sprains and bruises and some minor burns and cuts—but he hadn't asked her much and she'd had no reason to volunteer her real name nor that she was a pilot, since Tex had been doing the flying when they actually hit the ground. She'd figured Tex's death was his and her business alone. So far as she knew, what details she had given him were buried in a file somewhere, unseen and forgotten. She'd made a point of moving on as quickly as she was able, leaving no forwarding address or details about who she was.

"You ever kill anybody, honey?" Dixie examined her critically.

"Not that I know of." She shook her head in disbelief. "This is a mistake. This is a terrible mistake."

She examined the figure on the bed. "What was the third time, Mr. Horne? When did you last see the FBI man?"

He was having a hard time breathing. He pressed his hand to his chest. "About fifteen minutes ago. I saw him when we come up. He's havin' lunch across the street."

She all but leaped across the room. She beat Dixie to the door, even though Dixie had the head start. Tex's letter and picture were firmly in her hand. The last thing she saw as she closed the door behind her was a frail old man lying on a bed, coughing quietly.

She spotted him in a blink. The only other person in Sweetwater to wear a three-piece suit was Waterman. This man's was dark blue and fitted him poorly, as there was a bit less of him than there was of it.

"You're the FBI man, aren't you?"

She didn't wait for him to answer. She jerked one of the chairs back from the table and sat down. Dixie, perhaps reluctantly, took the other.

"I *said*, you're the FBI man, aren't you? You're the one who's been sniffing around about Tex Jones and me. I'm Sally Ketchum."

He looked to be in his mid-thirties. He had a boyish, no-nonsense face and brown hair, and he wore wire-rimmed glasses and he was sunburned. She knew somehow that the burn stopped at his cuffs and collar. She didn't know much about men, and nothing at all about FBI men, but she knew a suit that got used every waking minute when she saw one.

He finished the drink of coffee he'd already started. A plate sat before him, empty but for crumbs. "I know who you are, Miss Ketchum." He put the cup back on its saucer.

If she'd been an FBI man, and a stranger had come storming up to her table, she wondered if she'd be as cool—or if she'd have reached for her gun. But his blank wall expression hadn't changed one iota. In fact, she wondered if he had any other expressions, or if FBI men came with just that one.

"Well, if you know who I am, then you should know that Tex Jones wasn't any murderer. He wouldn't have killed a flea. And he wasn't mixed up in anything that he shouldn't have been, either! Now I've told you that, and B.D. Horne over at the hotel across the street's told you that. Tex wasn't murdered, either. He died in a plane crash. I know because I almost died with him." She added, "And I didn't kill anybody, either; and if you or anybody else in the FBI thinks any differently, you're wrong; and if anybody tells ya any differently, they're lying. Do you understand?"

He rested his arms on the table edge. His eyes were the shade of cold gray that went on bank vault doors. He stared silently. Next to Sally, Dixie clearly was uncomfortable with the way the conversation was starting. She shifted in her seat like there was a tack under her butt.

The rest of the tables were empty. Only two other customers were in the place, local businessmen taking a late lunch at the counter. The diner was small, the fare typical Texas, which meant mostly barbecue and beans, eggs and steak, and the like. The businessmen had stopped eating and were watching with unconcealed interest.

"Have you heard that someone has accused you or Mr. Jones of a crime, Miss Ketchum?" the FBI agent asked finally. The bank vaults looked right through her.

"Well . . ." She had been so angry that she hadn't thought through what she would say to him, so the idea of stumbling had never entered her head. But she recovered in a heartbeat. "You know I have. B.D. Horne told me that's what you told him."

"And have you heard anyone *else* say it?"

"No! I just told you that!"

"Then you have nothing to worry about." He leaned back and folded his fingers over what there was of his stomach. His coat had slipped back a little, and she could see his gun. It wasn't big by Texas standards, but she had no doubt it would get the job done.

"I want to know why you are investigating me and why you are investigating Tex."

"I can't tell you that." His tone was the same one that bankers used when they turned down loans to poor dirt farmers. She knew what that meant. Hell would freeze and the fountains in heaven would squirt sinners before she'd get him to change his mind.

She stood up. Dixie, she noticed, beat her there. "What do you want me to do to convince you that Tex and I didn't kill anybody? That all we did was mind our own business?"

"Nothing." His face might have been coated with cement, for all the emotion he showed.

"What do you mean, nothing?" Sally shrugged off Dixie, who was trying to tug her toward the door. She had no intention of going anywhere until she got some answers, even if the place burned down while she waited.

"Just that. I don't think, and I don't think anyone in the Bureau thinks, that you did anything wrong—besides fall for your fella."

"What do you mean by that? I never did anything wrong in my whole life!" She took a step toward the table. She could still see the gun butt.

She promised herself she'd cool down if things got to the point where she saw all of it.

"I didn't say you did. My job's to follow up on what other people say. And if what they say is the truth, I arrest somebody."

"Are you gonna arrest me?" Dixie was still jerking on her arm as if it were a pair of reins. Sally pushed her away.

"No, I'm not going to arrest you."

"Well, what *are* you going to do?"

"I'm going to finish my coffee and catch the next train to El Paso, and hopefully get a good night's sleep in my own bed for a change." He lifted the cup again. When he put it down, they were still staring at each other.

Dixie gave a mighty tug. She hissed, "Come on, honey, while the gettin's good! Trust me, you do not want to be messin' with the FBI!"

Sally felt herself being dragged backward toward the door.

He stood up. She tensed when she saw his hand move, but his fingers only disappeared into his pocket and emerged with a handful of coins, which he tossed onto the table.

"Miss Ketchum, wait."

They froze.

"Perhaps I shouldn't tell you this, but I think you should know, now that the WASP have been disbanded."

Sally's fingers found Dixie's arm. She had a vision of a dam bursting, sweeping her away, of holding onto a tree limb, and drowning anyway.

Uneasiness crossed his face. "I'm sorry. I thought you knew. Congress disbanded the WASP as of noontime today." He checked his watch. "Three hours ago. I'm truly sorry. The WASP performed brilliantly. America owes every one of you a great debt of gratitude. You deserved better."

Her feet were barely supporting her. If Dixie hadn't been there, she would have fallen.

His unease was replaced by real concern. "Miss Ketchum, I'm going to finish what I started to say: Ira Waterman has got a hate for you that's unlike any I've ever seen. You watch yourself, Miss Ketchum."

# Eighteen

A strong wind blew down the center of the runway at Avenger Field. "There's only two places in all of America where the tower's obliged to issue a 'flying gravel' advisory," trainees were told. "El Paso's one, and you're hanging on to the other." Sally knew that to be true. But this wind was different. The chill of death rode this wind: the death of her dreams, the death of her future.

She rested her hand on the wingtip of a parked AT-6. She had stopped crying. That had happened when her body ran out of tears. Dixie had comforted her for a while and then had gone off to phone Pierre Valois, the fashion photographer in New Orleans. Everyone, it seemed, had someone to call to help start the next part of their lives. The phones were jammed.

Sally finally had wandered outside to the flight line where there were no phones to remind her that she was utterly alone and therefore different. Even Beau wasn't there to comfort her. She had desperately wanted to fall into his arms, but Skinner had sent him up earlier with a student. He didn't even know yet that he was unemployed, and therefore draftable. The thought of him going into combat, perhaps never to see Rose or her again, was unbearable.

The one person she had seen plenty of was Waterman. The big Packard had cruised Avenger, sometimes lollygagging along its dusty streets and at other times parking, the figure in its back seat smoking, sitting perfectly still and erect like a conquering general overseeing the destruction of a defeated army. She had even wondered if he were stalking her. But with the end of the WASP, Waterman couldn't possibly still have an interest in her. The warning from the FBI man rang hollow. The WASP were finished, and Waterman no longer had any reason to care about her destiny. That problem was hers and hers alone.

Nighttime was falling. She turned up the collar on her leather flight jacket. Texas got cold in the wintertime. The winter cold atop a Texas mesa could freeze a jackrabbit in full flight. The dark planes, parked wingtip-to-wingtip along the length of the flight line, rocked and groaned against their tie-downs. They would be dispersed to other bases, she supposed, never to be flown again by women.

The base was in chaos. Hysteria, disbelief, anger, vengefulness . . . every emotion had been on parade when she and the other Avenger students crowded into the old trailer and hurried back from Sweetwater. Avenger was a madhouse. Even Mrs. Teetle and the sergeant had looked shocked.

The decision to disband had been a tightly kept secret until the announcement came from Jackie Cochran's office in Washington. The official explanation cited the great number of experienced pilots returning from combat, which made the WASP unnecessary, but a dozen other causes were also making the rounds. The most popular was that Waterman and Congress had gotten rid of the WASP simply because men couldn't stand seeing women in cockpits. Another was that the army had been ready to militarize the WASP, but under the command of someone other than Jackie—something the headstrong leader violently opposed—and so she had shut down the outfit herself.

Whatever the truth, Avenger was finished. The last class would assemble a final time to march in formation and to hear a few speeches and to have their pictures taken, and then everyone would scatter to the winds. A new trickle of tears squeezed out of her eyes. The wind whipped the little streams away before she could even lift her fingers. She stiffened her grip on the AT-6's wing.

The sound of an airplane drew her attention to the sky. A twin-engine C-47, the military version of the DC-3 flown by almost every airline in the world, had entered the pattern to land. The C-47 was no trainer, but a big cargo transport. What one would be doing landing at Avenger on a

Saturday night, she couldn't imagine.

The pilot had turned onto final approach. His landing gear was down and lights on. Because of the stiff headwind, the plane seemed to creep forward. In her mind's eye, she saw exactly what the pilot saw. When one wing dipped, she corrected automatically as the real pilot would do. Finally the plane crossed the end of the runway and settled to earth with several chirps of rubber.

She looked around, expecting a Jeep or perhaps even a staff car to come out to meet the visitor, but no headlights approached. So far as she could tell, she was the only person at Avenger with the least bit of interest in this stranger who'd dropped from the night.

The C-47 had turned off the runway and was trundling toward where she was standing. She squinted against the glare of its landing lights. The pilot was having a hard time controlling the plane in the strong wind. He was working the brakes hard, making them heat up and squeal. The C-47 was a tail-dragger like the trainers at Avenger, which meant that when on the ground it rested on its two main wheels and a smaller one beneath the tail. Such an arrangement tested the skill of a taxiing pilot, for the un-naturally angled wings acted like a weathervane. A strong wind blowing in just the right direction would catch the underside of a wing and spin the plane around, an embarrassing situation for a pilot who was accom-plished enough to be flying sophisticated machinery like a C-47.

The landing lights were blinding. Sally looked away, at the same time shifting uneasily. Common sense told her that the pilot would turn be-fore he ran over her and a half-dozen parked AT-6's. Still, the deadly arc of the approaching propeller tips, caught in the powerful beams, was too real to ignore.

The pilot suddenly stabbed hard on the right brake pedal and the C-47 swiveled safely around and came to a halt. A large clamshell cargo door in the side of the fuselage swung open, and she saw two figures standing in the dimly lit bare metal interior. One jumped to the ground, and the other tossed out a duffel bag and then quickly pulled the door closed. The figure on the ground barely managed to grab the bag and jump clear of the tail before the pilot gunned the engines and the plane started rolling again.

The new arrival squinted against the blast of dirt and exhaust fumes, in an effort to see through the gloom, and hefted the bag wearily and walked in Sally's direction.

"Hey! I need a ride!" the stranger yelled. "Has that bastard Waterman already gotten rid of everybody, or is there still somebody around here who can give me one?" She was loud and angry and sounded like she was spoiling for a fight and didn't care with whom.

Sally hadn't been able to tell at first whether the C-47's passenger was a man or a woman, until she spoke. Now it was obvious the newcomer was older than herself by several years, and taller and more slender, and that she wore a regulation Army Air Corps leather jacket and flight suit. The woman stepped into the glare of the flight line lights. In addition to her face being hard with anger, she looked exhausted.

"I'm sure someone can take you to town," Sally said, "if you have orders."

The stranger dropped the duffel bag. "Screw orders! I'll walk home before I'll put up with any more orders!"

The C-47 had barely reached the runway and turned into the wind when the pilot opened the throttles. The tail rose immediately. After rolling for what seemed like only a few feet, the main wheels lifted from the ground, and the plane climbed into the night.

"He's sure in a hurry." Sally looked around uneasily. Except for the two of them, the flight line was deserted.

"Yeah, they're in almost as big a hurry to get away from me, as I am to get as far away as I can from everything that has 'army' painted on the side of it." The woman angrily zipped up her flight jacket. "There's four feet of snow on top of Detroit right now, and enough ice to cover up Alaska. I had orders to deliver a P-51 to New York, even though there was a real chance of sliding off the runway and burning. That happened to a friend of mine; there was barely enough left of her to bury. I taxied that beast out and when I stood on the brakes to run up the engine, there was so much ice on the runway it was like having no brakes at all. I think I could have taken off with both wheels locked. That's when they told me over the radio that I was out of a job. Just like that. All of us. Every WASP. I thought about that for a long time, sitting out there, and about the way that '51 was scooting around on that ice, and finally I decided that if the army was through with me, then I was through risking my neck for the army. I turned that Mustang around and went back to the operations shack and handed in my paperwork."

Sally examined her closely. She had a no-nonsense air that extended even to the way she stood: straight as a board, and, Sally suspected, she was just as tough. Like the rest of her, her face was long and lean, her chin and nose pointed. She wasn't attractive. But there was an aura of solidness to her—of competence. Sally suspected this woman could tame even the most belligerent airplane.

"There were about forty army pilots sitting in that shack," the stranger continued. "The army wasn't gonna make any of them go up in that weather. I was the only one the army had ordered out to fly. Some major started giving me a lot of lip for not going. He chewed me out royally in front of everybody because I wouldn't fly an airplane that doesn't like ice, into an ice storm that no man was flying into, even though the army had just tossed me out like a bunch of dirty water. What's more, I found out it was gonna be up to me to figure out how to get home once I got to New York—if I got to New York—and to pay for it myself; because once they had their airplane, the army wanted nothing more to do with me. I just turned around and walked away. There was nothing they could do to me."

Her voice turned bitter as the first bite of a lemon. "I did my best. I did everything I was told to do. I flew airplanes that weren't safe to fly—that no man would fly. We all did, every one of us; and we all got kicked in the ass like stray cats. And that's why if I never have anything to do with the army again, it can't happen too soon. The damn army didn't even want to give me a lift out of Detroit. Some jerk in Operations said if I was in such a hurry to get to Texas, I should hitchhike." She indicated the fast-disappearing plane. "I almost had to throw the crew off that C-47 and fly the damn thing here myself; and I would have, too, if they hadn't finally seen things my way."

"You flew the P-51?" The question was so childish and dripped with such envy, but Sally couldn't stop herself. The barracks were teeming with stories similar to this woman's, including some about WASP being marooned in the middle of nowhere, making desperate phone calls to relatives or friends for money to get home. With everything that had happened, she almost *expected* that of the army. But the Mustang fighter was the fastest plane in the world, the most beautiful and sexiest airplane in the world, and the most fun to fly. Men were said to stab each other through the heart for a chance at its controls. Sally couldn't let this stranger get away without asking her what it was like to fly that airplane.

"Yeah." The woman answered absently. She was busy gathering herself before either finding a ride home or striking out into the night on her own. But suddenly she looked at Sally with a new flash of understanding. "Oh, honey, you're not a WASP, are you? You're in the last class." She softened like pudding. "You never even got the chance to know what it was like, did you?" She stepped forward and put out her arms. "Oh, honey."

Sally didn't know what to say. She wasn't looking for sympathy. On the other hand, she was as angry and bitter as a person could be, as well as jealous of this woman. She awkwardly hugged her back and said lamely, "I guess you're glad it's over."

The woman pulled back. Her face was as serious as death. "I've never been as sorry about anything in my life. I don't know a single WASP who's glad. Some of us—me included—are gonna write letters to Cochran offering to fly for free, not that it'll do any good. I think everybody knows that, deep down. They don't want us. They need us, but they don't want us, even though the army's still screaming for airplanes."

"But you just said—"

"I know what I said, and every bit of it's true. Still, I wouldn't trade a moment for anything. To be part of the war, and to be around those wonderful planes. To fly 'em. And the adventure . . . and the wonderful people, both men and women. There're an awful lot of men who're sick to death over what's happened to us." Her voice grew thin. "I'm going to miss it all so." She looked out into the night. "There'll never be another time like it. We were so lucky. So lucky. Of all the women in America, only a little more than a thousand of us got to be WASP. My God, but we did fly the wings off those airplanes. We did it as well as any man!" She picked up the duffel bag. "You take care, honey." She moved toward a clump of buildings and within moments became part of the shadows.

Sally slumped against the AT-6's wing. She hadn't thought it possible, but she felt even worse than she had before coming out to the flight line to be alone.

She stared into the pitch-blackness beyond the runway for a long time, her brain incapable of absorbing any more bad news, until the steadily dropping temperature finally pulled her out of her stupor and she realized she was freezing. She was about to turn back to the barracks when she sensed a presence.

Lighting on the flight line was sparse. The poles were spaced too far apart, which sent deep wedges of darkness creeping into the gaps. She looked up and down the line, but so far as she could tell, she was completely alone. Still, the feeling of being watched persisted, and she quickly stepped away from the AT-6, at the same time pulling her hands from her jacket pockets.

She tried to keep her head. A flight line at night was a spooky place. Airplanes had a way of making noises. Their odd shapes, designed to slip so smoothly through the air in flight, made strange sounds when parked on the ground in the wind. A good breeze could make a flight line whistle and bang and creak. A stiff wind blowing across the line on a dark night could start the imagination down roads better left traveled in the daylight. But she was used to all that, and to the dark, and to being out here alone. There was no reason in the world to be afraid. Yet she was, and becoming more so by the moment; a deep, unreasonable fear that dried her mouth and made her dread closing her eyes even for a moment, even against the blowing sand.

She realized suddenly that she had stupidly been edging toward the runway and the darkness beyond. She immediately turned back in the direction of the base proper, and instantly sensed something moving with her. She whirled and came face to face with Waterman.

"Mr. Waterman!" She struggled to catch her breath. She almost would have preferred any of the ordinary monsters that lurk in nightmares. "You scared me."

The lights of the base suddenly seemed a million miles away. She backed up in their direction. He moved with her.

"What are you doing out here, Mr. Waterman?"

Something hit her in the back. She gasped and spun around and found that she had backed into a wing. She quickly navigated around it and continued in the direction of the lights. She desperately wanted to turn and run, as hard and as fast as she could, but some primordial instinct made her keep her eyes on him.

"I said, what are you doing out here, Mr. Waterman?" Perhaps he really did have ice water for blood, she thought. He wasn't even wearing a real coat, but just the one that came with that white three-piece suit. The wind whipped and snapped the lapels, and lifted and blew his white hair in every direction, though he seemed not to notice.

"Waiting for you, Miss Ketchum."

She shuddered. The uneven light played mean tricks on his face.

"Why?" She tripped and almost fell. The soft dirt and deep shadows made walking backward difficult.

"I have come to view my reward."

"Reward?"

The wind had picked up. The sharp edges of airplanes whistled. A million tiny spaces between aluminum pieces howled.

He stepped toward her. "I assured you I would win. And I have." He paused.

She wondered if he was waiting for her to rip out her entire bleeding soul and chuck it over for him to feast on. She promised herself that she'd burn at the stake first.

"But I'm not through yet, Miss Ketchum. I want you to know that I've set into motion steps to revoke your pilot's license. You will never fly again. You will never earn so much as a penny doing the thing you love most."

She tried to hide her surprise and her fear. Her failure nourished him.

"I'm sending you back to where you belong, Miss Ketchum. I'm tossing you back into the filth and squalor and stupidity from whence you came, never to rise again. You will spend the rest of your life pondering why, of all the women in the world, I chose you to destroy. That question will become torture. It will fester and eat at you. I have doomed you, and you will never know why. That is my reward."

He was crazy. But he wasn't so crazy that he'd picked her at random. She didn't believe that for a moment. Nor did she believe that he would go to so much trouble just because she'd stood up to him. He was a lawyer. People stood up to him every day. Besides, why would he care what a poor farm girl from East Texas had to say?

Suddenly she had a thought. It was a crazy thought, hatched from a dozen seemingly unconnected events. But in a crazy way, it made perfect sense.

"This has nothing to do with Avenger, does it," she asked, "or even the WASP? This has to do with Tex. You knew Tex, didn't you?"

A flicker of emotion crossed his face. She almost missed it, but this time she was watching for it because she'd seen it before. After Emma Kelley's death, standing outside the operations building, when he'd snatched Tex's watch . . . he'd had the same reaction when she'd asked if he'd ever loved anyone. That's why he'd been so interested in Tex's watch. He had known Tex! She was sure now.

"Tell me how you knew him, Mr. Waterman. Please!"

He'd been waiting for that. He'd been waiting for her to beg. Pleasure spread across his face. He was feeding off her agony.

She no longer could control herself. She turned and she ran. She looked over her shoulder only once.

Waterman stood tall and straight, the frigid wind whipping his clothes and hair. He was watching her run. And he was smiling.

# Nineteen

Avenger's streets were deserted. Everyone and everything with any sense was inside, where it was warm. Sally jerked open the door to the bay and found Dixie sitting on the floor of the shower. Keeping her company was a partially empty bottle of bourbon.

"Damn, honey . . . you look like you just saw the Devil himself!" Dixie held out the container. "Come join the party. I'm gettin' drunk, and I suggest you do, too. Because I can tell ya right now that everything looks a whole lot rosier from this side of the bottle."

Sally discarded her heavy leather jacket. Despite the cold outside, the bay was like a broiler. She stuck her head into the room shared by Geri and Twila, but neither was there.

"Where's Geri? I have to talk to her."

Dixie made a face. "Why? Ain't your life screwed up enough, already?" She chuckled. She was having trouble controlling her head, which was trying to flop to one side. Sally resisted the urge to turn the cold water on her.

"Dixie, didn't Geri once tell us that Waterman didn't have any friends or family?"

"Yeah-I-guess-why?" She slurred the words into one.

"Because Waterman knew Tex! He all but admitted it just now out on the flight line."

Dixie cackled heartily. "Honey, you're the only person I know who can get drunk without drinkin'. I just pray that never happens to me."

Sally looked at her hatefully. "You're too happy, Dixie, even for a drunk. That photographer in New Orleans gave you a job, didn't he? You're gonna step right back into the life that you had before Avenger." She didn't care if she was being spiteful. Dixie had everything. Dixie survived everything. Dixie could fall into an outhouse and come out smelling like a rose. Dixie lived the good life, seemingly without even trying—while she had tried with all her might for all of her life, and her life never seemed to smell like anything but an outhouse.

Dixie grinned massively. The act so unbalanced her that she nearly toppled over. "I sure am, honey! Pierre told me, 'Get your pretty pink butt back to New Orleans just as fast as your pretty little feet can get you here.' He's got contracts comin' out his ears. He wants to take pictures of me wearin' my WASP blues for a spread in *LIFE* magazine that they're gonna call 'Women Who Wear The Uniform.' Isn't that somethin'? Everybody in the whole United States and everybody overseas is gonna see me!"

Sally thought about her own beautiful blue dress uniform, which had been specially designed for the WASP under the personal direction of Jackie Cochran, and how proud she'd been when she'd put it on and looked at herself in the mirror for the first time. She'd only worn the uniform a couple of times. It wasn't even paid off yet. But unlike Dixie, no one would be paying her to wear it again, much less to model for any pictures.

Her bitterness was unbearable. She snarled, "I'm real happy for you, Dixie! I'm sure you'll take him for every penny he's got!"

Dixie's head rolled uncontrollably. She beamed. "Damn right, I will, honey. I don't care what anybody tells ya. There's nothing warmer on a cold winter's night than knowin' you've got cold cash in the bank . . . or in my case, Pierre's cash in my bank!" She lifted her bottle in salute and brought the rim to her mouth. She sipped hungrily.

Sally turned away in disgust. She was tired of Dixie, and she still had to find Geri.

But before she could take a step, Dixie added, "Take some advice from me, honey, which I'm gonna give to ya absolutely free. Stop beatin' your head against the world and find yourself a man. Find yourself one that you can count on, one with a job and a steady paycheck. If you have to, marry that little instructor. But get yourself some insurance against the future. That's what I'm gonna do. Pierre's got a nice little modelin' agency that needs a Mrs. Pierre to run it for him. That's gonna be me. He just doesn't know it yet."

She laughed lustily. "You can't do it alone forever, you know. You can't be the only ant that's fightin' its way upstream through a planet of ants. Because someday you're gonna get old or hurt or whatever it is that's gonna mess you up. And on that day you better have your ducks lined up. Otherwise, the world's gonna trample you right down into the dirt. Because unless you've got somethin' stashed away, or somebody who'll at least go through the motions of lovin' ya, you're gonna get screwed. If you can't come up with money or somebody when your luck runs out, nobody is gonna care. Nobody is gonna care what happens to ya."

Sally stared at her friend, dumbfounded. Deep, deep down, Dixie was scared, too! Dixie was no different from her! Maybe no one was, except those who were too rich or too stupid not to know any better. The idea nearly buckled her knees. She'd worried all her life about a future that trapped her on the farm or in some other hellhole. She'd promised herself that she'd move heaven and earth to keep that from happening. But maybe the truth was that she was different only because she didn't hide her fear behind a bottle or religion or anger or lies or any of the other things that seemed to infect most everyone.

Dixie thrust the bottle skyward. "Relax and stop takin' everything so seriously, honey. The whole rest of your life's out there somewhere waitin' for ya. Stop bein' in such a rush to smack head-on into it."

Sally took a deep breath. Dixie was Dixie, and nothing was going to change her. But at least she could do something about the stench of Dixie's bourbon, before life returned her to the gutter. She stepped into the shower. Dixie must have read her intentions, for she tried to hide the bottle behind her back as she struggled to her feet. But Dixie wasn't quick enough, and the glass burst against the hard concrete floor.

Sally felt a bolt of pain. The big model had her by the hair. She grabbed her hands, but Dixie's fingers were like rivets. She and Dixie were locked in a slowly revolving circle. "You dog!" Dixie wailed. "You broke my bottle!"

Sally tried to keep Dixie from ripping her hair out by the roots *and* to hold her up. The floor was littered with glass shards. If either of them tripped and fell, the result would be catastrophic.

"A cat fight! How perfect for you both!" Geri stood in the doorway, a gloating look on her face. Twila stood behind her. Her expression revealed dismay and confusion.

"The army kicks us out before we get to prove ourselves, and the whole base wallows in a giant tear fest," Geri crowed, "but you two decide to duke it out like a couple of common longshoremen! Did you get tattoos, too, while you were in town?"

Sally finally wiggled free of Dixie, who quickly lost interest in fighting and remorsefully started trying to reassemble her broken bottle.

"I've been looking for you, Geri," Sally said. As she stepped from the shower, she saw that Geri's eyes were red and swollen. She was almost sure that coming to Sweetwater was the first big decision Geri had made in her whole life. She was taking Avenger's closing hard. "You once said the only people in Waterman's life are business acquaintances. No family. No friends. But I think he knew Tex. He all but told me so out on the flight line."

"You mean that dead boyfriend you're always bragging about? You think Waterman knew him?" Geri laughed. The sound was cold and cruel.

Dixie struggled to her feet. "You're a bitch! You know that, Geri?"

Geri rolled her eyes. "Jesus Christ, I'll be glad to get back to civilization . . . so I'll never have to see another cow or cow pie or Texan again for as long as I live!"

Dixie straightened to her full height. She nearly filled the shower opening. "And do what? Huh, Geri? What are you gonna do in 'civilization'? Run back to your daddy so you can crawl into your cradle for the rest of your life? You Yankee rich bitches make me sick! You think you're so superior because you've got money. But your money didn't do you any good here, did it? It didn't keep you in the WASP. You finally found somethin' you really wanted that you couldn't buy, didn't you? You finally found somethin' Daddy's money couldn't get you. And you wanted it so badly you could taste it!"

Dixie stepped from the stall. "You wanted out from under your daddy's thumb, is what you wanted. But you didn't make it, did you? The WASP are finished and you don't have any place to go but right back home, where everybody's just waitin' to tell you what you can and can't do. Waitin' to make all the decisions for you. And you don't have the guts to tell 'em to go to hell, because all you know how to do is be rich. You can't cut the purse strings because you know you don't have a chance of survivin' without Daddy and his money."

She moved forward. "And what are you gonna do with your girlfriend?" She indicated Twila, who remained strangely quiet. "How are you gonna explain her? Huh? What's Daddy gonna say when ya try takin' her into the crib with you?"

Geri's hand lashed out. But Twila's was faster, and she grabbed Geri's arm and held her fast. As if an unspoken command passed between them, Geri instantly stopped struggling.

Sally stared at them. Suddenly everything about Geri and Twila made sense: their peculiar friendship, all the time they spent together. Her experience with people who preferred their own kind was nonexistent, so it hadn't dawned on her to question their relationship, though she had known it was odd. No one in East Texas that she'd grown up with was like that. Certainly they wouldn't approve of Geri and Twila. And she supposed she didn't approve, either; but she still liked and respected Twila, who no more seemed like the Devil now than she had a moment earlier, and she still disliked Geri as much as ever. Though standing there in the latrine they all had shared so often—knowing what she knew now—did give her an uneasy feeling, and she almost wished Dixie hadn't exposed their secret.

"You're jealous!" Geri lunged at Dixie, but Twila locked Geri's arms behind her back.

Dixie's face twisted with exaggerated glee. "Of what? Of you? Of sleepin' with girls? Why would I go lookin' for somethin' I've already got, when half the world's got what I don't have, which I like just fine?

Hell, you can sleep with an elephant, for all I care, so long as the elephant don't come whinin' to me about it."

Geri struggled to break free, but Twila tightened her grip. If Twila was hurting her, she didn't protest. Geri snarled, "I'll tell you of what. You're on the outside looking in, and there's nothing you can do about it and it eats you up. You're nobody! You never have been anybody, and you never will be. Nobody who's anybody would give you the time of day. Because you're nothing but a cheap country hick!" She broke free of Twila, who this time made no effort to restrain her.

Sally jumped between Dixie and Geri.

But the fight had left Dixie. The bourbon had caught up with her, and she didn't look well.

Geri started for her bay but stopped and turned, and Sally felt her eyes. There was the familiar coldness and hardness; but something else was there, too, something that Geri had kept hidden all these months. There was desperation, palpable and tragic—and terrible, terrible loneliness. Suddenly Geri pulled it back inside and once again she became the rich, spoiled brat. "The rumor is that Waterman's queer as a three-dollar bill. If he knew your boyfriend, you can bet it wasn't because they were arguing together in front of the Supreme Court." She smiled wickedly. "Which says plenty about you, and gives new meaning to the phrase, 'driving your lover into the arms of another man.'" She turned and disappeared, slamming the door to her bay behind her.

Sally was stunned. Tex hadn't been a homosexual. He couldn't have been. He'd been a wonderful, caring, passionate lover to her. Geri was wrong. She had to be.

Something on the other side of the door crashed against a wall, presumably after being thrown by Geri.

Twila spoke softly. "This"—she indicated herself, then pointed toward the bay she shared with Geri—"was an experiment for her. Now she'll go back to her world, and I'll return to mine. Someday she'll marry a rich businessman, and our time together will be forgotten."

She hesitated before continuing. "I, on the other hand, won't forget. Because I know exactly who I am and what I am, and long ago I stopped being angry because others were angry at me. I don't care what they think. I like me. I like my life. I'm happy most of the time."

Her voice cracked and for a moment Sally glimpsed a stranger. "I did so want to fly for America. I was ready to give my life, if necessary, for freedom. Because I understand what it's like to not be free."

Sally could only stare at her.

Suddenly, as if reading her mind, Twila tossed her head proudly. "I chose her because she was vulnerable and naïve and desperate to become her own person. I understood all of that completely, because I have lived it thoroughly; and I saw all of it in Geri, almost from the instant I first laid eyes on her." She paused before continuing. "I saw another thing, too." She chuckled lustily. "I saw us having sex! And God, it's good! Every time is like riding an earthquake!"

She moved into the bay she shared with Geri, and she closed the door quietly behind her.

Sally remained still for what seemed like a long time. The world had fallen apart and nothing was like it had seemed and nothing was still the same, and if she wasn't careful, she was going to be left behind with nothing to hold onto for the rest of her life but some memories and almost as many questions.

She rushed into the night in search of Beau, leaving Dixie to heave her guts into the commode.

She found him pacing the barracks' outside perimeter. She threw her arms around him and was relieved to receive a hug in return.

"I'm fired and you're going to be drafted and Waterman ruined my life on purpose and everybody's out of a job!" The words poured from her like water from a broken pitcher. Somehow, someway, he would make life better. He had to. She couldn't go back to her old life. She just couldn't. Surely fate wasn't written in stone. What was the point of living if everything was already decided before you even started the journey? He was going to be a successful writer. He was going to have a wonderful life. She would be a part of that life. They would marry. He would protect her and take care of her, and together, they would raise Rose. He would save her.

They would have a life together, the three of them.

Her mouth found his. But he didn't meet her hunger. Instead, something wet and cold touched her cheek, and she realized he was crying. He was crying because he thought she wasn't going to marry him, and without a wife, he would be drafted. The old doubts came rushing back, and a wave of disgust rolled over her. She couldn't ignore her feelings, nor could she change herself. She couldn't respect a man who loved himself more than his country, when his country was at war for the survival of the world.

"I received a telegram." He stopped. His tears left crooked streaks on his cheeks.

An iron claw raked the pit of her stomach. She so desperately wanted to love this man and yet . . . He wasn't the first person to receive a telegram from the War Department, nor would he be the last. She wondered how many others had sobbed upon learning that Uncle Sam was putting their lives on hold until the world was free of Nazis and Japs. An invisible force edged her away from him.

"My father's dead," he said. "He put a shotgun in his mouth and pulled the trigger. He left a note, but all it said was that he'd failed at life and his life had become too painful to go on. I'm flying home tomorrow night. I've got a seat on an army transport."

Even in the poor light, she could see the terrible pain in Beau's eyes. She rushed back to him. She threw her arms around him and she cradled his head, and she stroked and soothed him as she would a baby while he cried and cried, unashamedly. And all of her awful doubts washed away, until she once again was sure that marrying him was the right thing to do.

Sometime later, when there was nothing left for him to cry out, they walked and they held each other tight against the bitter night and they talked, and she told him all about Waterman. Beau was furious. He raged against the lawyer and the army and the system that allowed a monster to destroy her life. And she felt herself being drawn even closer to him.

Eventually they found themselves beside a convoy of army trucks that had been parked in an out-of-the-way spot where they wouldn't interfere with the base's daytime traffic. The army was wasting no time. The trucks had been dispatched from all over Texas and Louisiana to whisk away everything of value. The sight of the sleeping hulks was somehow menacing in the gloom. Beau sat heavily on a step beneath one of the cabs. Most of the base was safely out of sight on the other side. The cold had driven everyone inside, anyway. There was no danger of a passerby seeing them. "Sally, I can't offer you everything that I offered you before." He sounded so tired.

She placed her hand on his shoulder, encouraging him to move closer. His muscles felt like steel knots, even through the heavy coat. "What do you mean?" she asked.

He drew her tight, and she pressed his face to her breasts. The act was more maternal than sexual, and it freed a protectiveness within her that was unfamiliar, causing her to stroke his head. Finally he broke free. "Sally, English professors are a dime a dozen. I probably have no more chance of getting on a faculty now than I do of going to the moon." He stood up. "All I can offer you is the uncertainty that comes with being a writer's wife. If you'll take the job."

His face was an honest, caring face. He would never hit her. He would never carouse, nor do anything that required sneaking around behind her back. She was sure. He was a good man, perhaps the best man that she would find for the rest of her life. More important, in some ways he needed her even more than she needed him, for she could keep his feet on the ground. They would be a team, fitting together as naturally as shoes and socks.

She put her lips against his, and this time she felt the passion that had been missing earlier. Her desperation disappeared. She no longer was alone in the world. She was safe and incredibly happy. She was in control of her life. That's the way it would be from now on.

They moved together to the rear of the truck, and he lifted her up into the dark bed and they fell together onto a pile of cushions that had been intended to protect the army's furniture. A canvas top stretched overhead, keeping away prying eyes.

The cold was forgotten as they ripped at their clothes and he entered her. She gasped, then quickly found the rhythm. Raw pleasure enveloped her, and she moaned. She had missed these feelings for so long.

"Tex!" She froze. Had she actually shouted out Tex's name, or was her brain playing a trick on her? Her pleasure disappeared, victim of her panic.

The hardness inside her slipped away. She couldn't see Beau's face, but she didn't have to. She could sense his surprise and confusion and hurt. She tried to hold onto him with her arms, but he pushed away. She heard the rustle of his pants and the sound of his zipper.

She rose onto her elbows. "Beau!" But he had already jumped from the truck.

She wrapped herself in the cushions and she sobbed quietly, and she wished with all her heart that she could be like Dixie and the rest of the world. But deep down, she knew she could never live a lie, any more than she could forsake the only person she had ever loved—even if he was dead.

# TWENTY

Sally found Dixie sitting on the side of her cot, her elbows on her knees and her head in her hands. An empty Coke bottle and an empty water glass and an empty aspirin container were beside her on the table. She was wearing pink silk pajamas.

"Well, are ya gonna marry him?" Dixie's voice was unusually restrained. She didn't bother to look up.

"No." Sally moved into the latrine before Dixie could see her disheveled appearance.

"Why not?"

"Because I don't love him." Sally turned on the hot water in the basin, luxuriating in its warmth.

"Well, did you at least have sex with him?"

Sally finished drying her face and hands and stepped back into the room. She would have punched anyone else for asking that question. But she long ago had realized that lying to Dixie didn't do any good. Her friend seemed to always know the truth anyway, and so she saved them both a lot of trouble by just going ahead and telling Dixie whatever it was that she wanted to know.

"Sort of."

Dixie lifted her head from her hands. Her eyes were red with pain. "How do ya 'sort of' have sex with a man? Tell me, would ya, so I don't ever get myself inta that situation."

"I let him in me, but just for a moment."

Dixie eyed her unsteadily. "Why, did you suddenly think of somethin' you'd rather be doin' instead?"

Sally threw the towel at her. "That's not fair, Dixie!"

Dixie deflected the missile with her hand and rose cautiously. "Fair? You gotta be kiddin' me! What was one of the first things I told you when we were comin' on the train? I told you the world's full of opportunities, and you gotta take a look around to see what's where so you can see how you can put the world to work for you. I told you ya gotta learn to be an Indian fighter, or you're gonna get scalped. Do you remember that?"

She remembered too well, but saw no reason to admit it to Dixie. For the life of her, she couldn't understand why Dixie was getting so worked up, anyway. She wasn't the one who was going to spend the rest of her life in misery.

Dixie steadied herself against the edge of her cot. "I guess you weren't listenin'."

"I listened." She bit her lip.

"Well, if you were listenin', why didn't you get him to ask you to marry him tonight? Or at least get yourself a good screw? You never can tell when that'll come back to do you some good later."

"Dixie!"

"Sally!"

Dixie walked painfully to the table where another Coke waited. She pried off the cap and took a long swallow, closing her eyes as she did. She returned the bottle gently to the table. Coca Cola & Company was obviously failing to wash away the agony inside her head.

"Can you believe that bitch, Geri?" Dixie glared at the door to Twila and Geri's bay. "I'm twice as good lookin' as her, and I work twice as hard. That's what's so unfair. I work my butt off livin' by my wits. And along she comes with all that money, and she just prances right by without havin' to lift so much as a fingernail. Do you think that's fair?"

Sally pretended to consider the question. Dixie was beautiful. Dixie was invincible. Dixie had an answer for everything, an angle for everything, a scheme to out-scheme the schemers: she seemed to pluck them from the air as easily as breathing. She was so damn tired of life's crap never sticking to Dixie. That's what wasn't fair!

"Oh, I don't know, Dixie," she said. "I don't think fair has anything to do with it. I think Geri's worked hard to become a good pilot. She put her heart and soul into being a WASP. I think she has every right to anything she gets—the fact that she has money is just frosting on the cake."

"What?" Dixie's eyes narrowed dangerously. "Just what the hell are you sayin'?"

Sally suppressed a smile. Playing Dixie along was making her feel better. "I said, I think she deserves whatever she wants from life. She's worked hard. She's become one of the best pilots on the base."

"Deserves whatever she wants?" Dixie used the table to steady herself. "She doesn't *deserve* anything! She's had *everything* handed to her on that silver platter her daddy owns, from the day she was born! That's one reason she's a bitch—that and bein' a Yankee! She's spoiled rotten. She's egotistical! Well, I wouldn't give ya two cents for her looks. Besides, anybody can look OK if their daddy's got enough money. Just like anybody can fly an airplane—if the government spends enough tryin' to teach 'em. And that's what we've got here."

She leaned forward. Sally couldn't tell whether she was trying to press home her point, or if the pain in her head was becoming overwhelming. "If she's so good lookin', how come she can't get a man? Huh? Just tell me that, if she's such hot stuff! It's been my observation that most any woman can get some kind of man if she just puts a little work into it. But not Geri! Noooo . . . all she can come up with is another woman! Which in my opinion is a poor substitute for a helluva good thing! So if she's so good lookin' and all, why's she sleepin' with a woman? Huh? Just tell me that, would ya!"

Sally was sorry she had started this. She didn't really care about Geri. A month from now, she was sure she would have forgotten all about her, except when some job at a second-rate diner or a filthy farm turned especially foul, and she needed someone to dislike even more than her own life. Her memories of Twila would be far more pleasant. If Dixie kept this up, Sally knew she eventually would have to defend *Twila*, too. Because Dixie wouldn't stop until she'd proved herself superior.

"Dixie, you're right!" she agreed. "It's certainly not fair!"

Dixie obviously hadn't planned on such a quick surrender. She looked at her hard. Then she took another long swallow of Coke. "Ha! You're damn right, it's not! Anybody with any sense knows that!" She started for her cot but stopped. "What's this problem with this boyfriend of yours, anyway? Why didn't you get him to ask you to marry him?"

Sally was relieved. She'd successfully outmaneuvered Dixie by changing the subject. "He did," she answered. "But I turned him down."

Dixie stared at her. "He asked you and you turned him down? Are you crazy?"

"Absolutely!"

"Well, at least we agree on that! But why? Just tell me that. Why did you turn him down? He's smart, isn't he?"

"Yes."

"And he's got an education? He'll be able to make a livin'?"

"Yes."

"And you like him, don't you? You think he's cute?"

"Yes."

"And he likes you? He can't keep his hands off you. He wants to marry you?"

"Yes."

"Then what the hell's the problem?"

"I don't love him!" She turned her back on Dixie and flung her coat onto her cot.

"Why?" Dixie picked up the Coke bottle, but set it down again with a bang.

"Why, what?"

"Why don't you love him?"

"What kind of stupid question is that?" Sally spun around. Her face was hot with frustration and anger. "Why does anybody love anybody? I don't know. All I know is that I don't love him. I was in love once, and I'm not gonna settle for anything less the second time around."

Suddenly the night, Tex's death, her whole miserable life, were becoming too much for her to stomach. "I can fly an airplane better than practically anybody!" she shouted. "I can do a lot of things. But I can't make a man. I can't make the right man for me to love. And there's nothing I can do about it. I can't take a course. Or read a book. Or talk to an expert. The one thing I want more than anything, I can't have because no matter how hard I try, I simply can't. And lying to myself or to Beau or to you or . . . to the man in the moon, isn't going to change anything. Beau is Beau. I like him, but I don't love him. And I never will. Because he's not the right man. And he never will be." She fell onto her bed. "You're going back to your wonderful life," she sobbed. "And I'm going to go back to manure!"

Dixie said evenly, "That's right. And you have only yourself to blame."

"What do you mean by that!" She gritted her teeth.

Dixie braced her hands on her hips. "What I mean is, you haven't changed one iota since the mornin' I met you. You act like a hard-chargin' bull. You act like you're not scared of anything. But deep down, you're a victim. You work so hard at not bein' one that you are one. Everything you hate about that farm you grew up on is holdin' you a prisoner just as surely as if your mean-ass daddy, and even the plow and the dirt, were holdin' a gun to your head."

Dixie paused to catch her second wind. Sally fantasized about a Dixie powered by batteries. Batteries run down. Batteries could be unplugged. "You can't stand seein' somebody take a drink," Dixie continued. "You won't tolerate weakness, includin' your own. You won't settle for anything less in a boyfriend than Jesus Christ, himself! And in addition to all that, you're convinced that you're no damn good because of your daddy. And to prove that you're no good, you're already plannin' on makin' yourself go back to the same crap you've worked so hard to pull yourself out of, just so you can be right about bein' no good. You're stuck so deep in the part of bein' a victim that it'd take a case of dynamite and the Second Comin' to drag you out." Her chin thrust forward. "Even though you've got more talent and more brains and more natural ability, all wrapped up in one package, than anyone I've ever met!"

Sally swung her feet to the floor and perched on the edge of her cot. Her mind was reeling. Beau had also accused her of turning Tex into a

Christ-like figure. "I don't know what you're talking about," she said. She was so tired. She just wanted to go to sleep. If she were asleep, she wouldn't have to think—and she wouldn't have to listen to Dixie.

But Dixie was just getting started. "Of course, you don't!" she said. Her eyes flashed. "That's the beauty of bein' a victim. You don't have to know anything. You don't have to do anything. All you gotta do is exist. Because the world can smell a victim. It can smell you upwind in the middle of a typhoon. And it'll be only too obliged to run over you and eat you alive and keep you right where you're at until the day you die." Her voice rose. "Well, honey, let me tell you somethin'! I could be just like you if I let myself. We come from almost the same place. I grew up around the same kind of idiots. Mine just had different faces and names. But there's a difference between you and me, and I'm not talkin' about the fact that I'm a hell of a lot prettier. Do you know what that difference is? I've got *balls*. They didn't come with this package"—she indicated her body—"but after watchin' my daddy float in a sea of prosperity while everybody around him drowned, I decided I'd better grow me a pair. And I did. They're the first thing I strap on every mornin' before I go outside to meet the world, and the last thing I unstrap at night before I slip into my frilly little pajamas. I've got balls! You don't! And that's why I'll *never be* a victim—and why you've *always been* a victim!"

They glared at each other. Sally desperately wanted to tell Dixie that she was wrong. But the words wouldn't come.

Dixie plopped onto a chair. "I'm gonna tell you why I'm angry at you, since you don't seem to be able to figure it out," she said. Her eyes softened. "I'm your best friend. Maybe I'm the only friend you have in the whole world. But soon, that's not gonna do you any good. Because in a few hours I'm gonna go back to my life, and if you're not real careful, you're gonna go back to yours. Now if that's what you want, just keep agoin' the way you're goin'. But if it's not, I suggest you do somethin' about it." She held out a tightly closed fist. "I suggest you start takin' responsibility for your life by startin' to kick some butt."

Her fist opened.

Sally reached out just in time to catch the green piece of paper. She stared at the face of Benjamin Franklin. "That's a hundred-dollar bill!" Her voice trembled. She rubbed the paper, fully expecting the green to come off on her fingers.

"That's right." Dixie settled back in the chair.

"Why?" The question stuck in Sally's throat.

"Why am I givin' it to you?"

Sally nodded.

"Because it's rightfully yours. Or at least, it is now that I took it away from Buddy Gregg."

She'd forgotten all about Buddy. So far as she knew, the dance had been canceled. She couldn't imagine anyone being in the mood.

"That hundred dollars is what Waterman paid Buddy Gregg to ask you to the dance," Dixie said. A look of satisfaction crossed her face. Once again, she'd proven that in real life real princesses never got dirty, much less left in the dirt. "Buddy was supposed to get you drunk and take you to a house outside of town. A bunch of MPs were all set to raid the place and take you away. Waterman wasn't just goin' to get you thrown out of the WASP; he was goin' to send you off to jail on a bunch of morals charges, includin' whorin'. Buddy was goin' to testify that you propositioned him. Lucky for you, Cochran's office shut down the WASP first."

"How do you know all this?" Sally felt light-headed. She grabbed the edge of the cot to steady herself.

"Buddy told me. You can thank my daddy for that, too, by the way, as well as for the hundred." Dixie's fingers made a movement, and a quarter appeared out of thin air—the same one, Sally was sure, that she'd used on the train against Milton and Bobby Ray so many months ago. Her hand moved again, and the piece disappeared. "My daddy taught me how to get almost anything out of almost anybody. That was Buddy's bourbon, by the way, that I was drinkin'. Cheap bastard! I haven't had a hangover in years. He won't be missin' it tonight, though. When I left him, he was plum done in. Turns out old Buddy's not half the man he thinks he is in the drinkin' department. But that's the only part of his reputation that he can't live up to." She grinned savagely.

"Why?" Sally felt weak. Her voice was barely a whisper.

"Why does Ira Waterman want to see you chained to an oar down in the bowels of some slave ship, where some sadistic bastard with a whip can make your back look like a chicken carcass after a picnic for a bunch of POWs? I don't know. And you won't either, unless you get off your ass and do somethin'. Because he's takin' one of our planes out of here tomorrow mornin' for Dallas. He's booked on American from Love Field to Washington. I guess they want him back there in a hurry; I hear he mostly travels by train. I would go with you, but the way I feel right now, I may never get in an airplane again for as long as I live." Dixie closed her eyes and rubbed her temples with her fingertips. "Oh, and your boyfriend's gonna fly him to Dallas."

Dixie might have said more but Sally didn't hear. She was already out the door in search of the one person who could save her from spending the rest of her life in hell.

# TWENTY-ONE

Beau turned away from the window on his side of the cockpit. "No, no sign of him." He returned to staring glumly out the windshield.

Things were going badly already, Sally thought. Waterman was late and Beau was barely speaking to her. Not that she blamed him. She wouldn't have blamed him if he never spoke to her again. Even if he'd blown up in a rage, he still would have been the sweetest man she'd ever known, next to Tex.

Beau had still been hurt and angry with her when she found him after leaving Dixie. But he'd listened to what she had to say, and to her reason for wanting to accompany him on this flight this morning. And he'd been a big enough man to control his shattered pride, despite the terrible way that she'd revealed her never-ending love for Tex.

She had to confront Waterman. Thanks to Dixie, the old Sally Ketchum, who had so accepted the lies of others as a child, was dead. This flight was the new Sally Ketchum's coming-out party. And Ira Waterman was the first person she intended to meet. Ira Waterman, who crushed opponents as if they were made of paper and who forced his will on men and women as if they were his servants, was going to get a taste of his own medicine—and New Sally was going to be holding the spoon! Up in the air, *she* would be in control. He wouldn't be able to walk away, or to call upon his powerful connections, or even refuse to listen. Maybe for the first time in his life, *he* would be powerless, and for the first time in hers, *she* would be whole.

This was the most important time of her life. She'd broken her father's hold on her last night. She would break Waterman's this morning. She would fight with every bit of her strength; not for revenge, but to uncover his relationship with Tex and to discover why he had singled her out to hate. She would do this by pitting her will against his and by betting that Waterman's coolness in the air was a pittance of his confidence on the ground. That idea had sprung from a comment Dixie had made about Waterman usually traveling by train. Sally remembered, too, that Geri had said Waterman originally arrived in Sweetwater by rail. If in fact Waterman was afraid of flying, everything was now within her grasp.

Luckily today was a Sunday and her time was her own. There was no official reason in the world why she shouldn't fly copilot on the short hop from Sweetwater to Dallas and back, if the pilot-in-command gave his consent. That Beau had, showed how much he loved her, which proved all over again the depth of hurt she had caused him last night. That guilt gnawed at her. But guilt or no guilt, she intended to go through with this.

She forced herself to stop rehashing what had already been hashed to pieces. Even if she wanted to back out now, it was too late. She was committed. The airplane was topped off with gas and they were strapped into its cockpit, and in a moment Waterman would arrive. The time for second thoughts was long past. She only wished the cockpit had a door. Everything hinged on Waterman not spotting her before they took off. To make herself less noticeable, she'd shoved her copilot's seat as far back as she could and still reach the rudder pedals. She was counting on the partition behind the seat to keep her hidden, and on Waterman's arrogance to keep him from getting inquisitive about the two mere mortals who would be piloting him this morning.

Beau had gotten the assignment to fly the twin-engine C-45 by pure chance. The plane mildly resembled a C-47, like the one that had landed at Avenger last night, but shrunk to accommodate only a handful of passengers. It was such a delight to fly that crews normally jockeyed for the opportunity, but not this time. Beau had agreed to take Waterman to Love Field because the other pilots had refused. If Beau hadn't accepted this assignment, it would have fallen to Skinner, whose contempt for

Waterman fell somewhere between his dislike of Hitler and of hell. Beau readily admitted that he'd learned much from the senior flight instructor and felt he owed him this favor. This would be Sally's last flight with Beau. He would catch a military transport this evening to New Orleans for his father's funeral. After that, the army would decide his destination.

Sally put the plane's manual aside. She had gone through the thing until she'd memorized the facts and procedures that were most important. She reminded herself to check the rubber deicing boots on the edges of the wings and tail as soon as the engines were started. Her eyes scanned the instruments. She never tired of the dials and levers and switches and knobs in airplane cockpits, each arranged in perfectly logical order. Even the smell of the cockpit was satisfying. The odors of leather and hot radio tubes mixed with oil from mechanics' boots, and spilled coffee and snuffed cigarettes from countless hours spent in the air by countless crews. She already had developed an affection for this airplane which she was about to fly, even though she had never flown a C-45, nor in fact had ever been inside any airplane with two engines before this one. No one knew she was copiloting except Beau. Though with all the hostility Avenger personnel felt for Waterman, Sally suspected they would have happily sent him up with a pilot who'd never even *seen* a C-45 before.

The weather was bad. But the military and the airlines were managing to get into Dallas, so she wasn't too worried. She was confident of her own skills. They both were qualified instrument pilots, and Beau was experienced with this plane. Certainly she had no worries about the C-45. The Beech Aircraft Company made its airplanes as stout as safes. All a Beech needed to arrive at its destination were skilled hands on the control wheel and competent feet on the rudders. The craftsmanship of the Wizards of Wichita, home to the company's headquarters, would see to the rest. Or so she had been told by a pilot who'd actually flown the C-45, as opposed to merely occupying its cockpit while parked safely on the ramp.

She cast a look at Beau. Unlike in a trainer, the C-45's pilot and copilot sat next to each other, separated by a narrow aisle. She pulled aside her earphone. "The weather's going down. I'm listening to a B-17 on its way into Love. He's reporting light icing." Normally she would have expected him to roll his eyes at this news, and perhaps to launch into a speech about the unfairness of the weather gods and the stupidity of the army to insist that humans fly into known icing conditions—especially a human who wanted to live to become a famous author. But he continued to stare trance-like out the windshield.

Her guilt was overpowering. And this time it was justified. No matter how she worked it around in her brain, she couldn't escape that, and so finally she had stopped trying. She had betrayed this man's feelings in the most horrible way, on the night that he'd learned of his father's suicide. She had wounded him terribly.

She took his hand and found his fingers unresponsive. "Beau, please forgive me. I didn't mean to hurt you. Please believe that. I wouldn't hurt you on purpose for the world." She faltered. Suddenly the words that she so badly wanted to express were like boulders in her throat. Some moments passed before she was able to continue. "It wasn't meant to be. We're not the right people for each other. I like you so, so much, but I'm not in love with you. It's better that I tell you that right now. I don't want to hurt you even more." She massaged his fingers. She had to get him to talk. Waterman would show up at any moment. Anything might happen then. She had to settle this now. "Beau! Please!"

"I got another rejection from a publisher last night." He shifted in his seat. "It was for my new book. I sent them a synopsis and the pages that you read. I found their reply in an envelope when I got back to the barracks after we left the truck. It wasn't even a real letter, but just a form they print off ahead of time." A look of such overwhelming pain overcame him that she nearly cried out in despair.

He turned to her. "Sally, I'm not particularly smart." He held up his hand to silence her protest. "The world isn't waiting for my books. I finally admitted that to myself last night. The world doesn't care about me or about what I have to say. The world doesn't even know I exist. Now my father's gone and I have to face the truth. I've lived a fantasy all my life. It was my way of escaping the unhappiness in my family; I'm afraid with the result that I sometimes made a fool of myself." He finally returned the pressure on her fingers. "I was doing that on the day we met. It was my first day as an instructor and I wanted you—I wanted everyone—to think I was smart. I'm not stupid. But I'm not unusually smart. My father was brilliant, but not me."

He again motioned for her silence. "Sally, I love you. Last night was terrible for me. I thought everything was as bad as it could get in my life, and then I found that publisher's letter. I thought I was going to die then. I wanted to die. I didn't want to go on, not as a failed writer and certainly not as a soldier. I seriously thought about shooting myself. And then do you know what happened?"

She shook her head. She no longer could breathe.

"You showed up and you told me you wanted to show Waterman that you refuse to be his victim." The numbness dropped suddenly from his face. "Sally, you brought me to my senses. I finally confronted the truth about myself last night. I confronted the truth that if I want the world to know I exist, I must first be honest with myself. Then I mustn't give up trying, ever—just like you. You are completely alone in the world. And you not only are facing the very real possibility of returning to a life you hate, but someone is maliciously driving you there. Yet instead of feeling sorry for yourself or burying your head in some comfortable fantasy, you are confronting the truth and fighting back."

He twisted so he faced her fully. "I am at heart a novelist. There is nothing else I truly want to do. I would rather spend an hour doing that, and then die, than have a lifetime doing what the world or circumstance or a wife would have me do." He gripped her tightly. "My father could have been so much more, but he never learned how to live on his own terms. Thanks to you, I learned it last night. If I survive this war, I'm going to spend the rest of my life doing what makes me happy. I'll write and earn a living, somehow. I'll raise Rose. And I'll do both standing on my own two feet, without looking for an angle or asking anyone for anything. I'm going to be like you, Sally. I'm going to be unbreakable."

She was speechless. Once again, Beau Bayard was surprising her with a heretofore unseen side to his personality.

The sound of men's voices pulled them apart. One was Waterman's. The other belonged to Colonel Bowen. She couldn't understand what they were saying, but there was no mistaking their veiled hostility.

The outside door near the rear of the cabin opened. The plane rocked gently as someone stepped aboard. The C-45, while roomy for an airplane, wasn't tall enough to stand up in; so Waterman, if in fact he had come aboard, would have to stoop to fit inside.

Someone had placed a small mirror on the windshield, probably to keep an eye on the passengers. She adjusted the thing just enough to glimpse a beanpole figure swaddled in an overcoat. As she had hoped, Waterman settled into the chair nearest the tail on her side of the cabin. She had feared he wouldn't be alone. Even one extra passenger would throw a monkey wrench into her plan. Now she realized those fears had been groundless. There probably wasn't a single person on all of Avenger who would share a ride with him.

The door closed.

A mechanic waited on the tarmac. He signaled that all was clear.

"Mixtures rich." She read from the checklist, keeping her voice low. She doubted Waterman would recognize Beau's voice, but she was sure he could identify hers.

"Check," Beau said, moving the levers that controlled the air-to-fuel mixtures inside the carburetors.

"Props, fine pitch."

"Check." He adjusted the angle of the propeller blades.

Beau selected the right engine by turning a switch and then pressed the starter button. The big propeller began to turn. The engines on the C-45 had come from the wonderful Pratt & Whitney. They, in fact, were identical to the one on the BT-13, an airplane she'd now spent many hours piloting. She knew the likes and dislikes of the C-45's engines as well as she knew herself.

They both counted as the starter motor pulled the propeller blades around and around. Because the engines were round, oil from the top cylinders inevitably drained into the lower cylinders after the engine sat for a while, so one of the pilot's tasks was to use the starter to pump oil into the engine's upper regions. Exactly at the top of the eighth rotation, Beau engaged the magnetos, and the engine caught in a blast of black smoke and settled into an uneasy idle. He massaged the levers until the Pratt purred.

Beau moved the selector to the left engine and engaged the starter again. He counted eight, his finger toggled the magnetos switch to "ON," a cloud of black exploded from the exhaust stack, and he quickly cajoled the nine cylinders into happy harmony.

The mechanic motioned that the chocks were free of the wheels. Colonel Bowen had already turned his back and was climbing into the car, his manner suggesting good riddance.

Sally checked the tachometers. Keeping the speed of the engines below 1,000 revolutions per minute until the oil temperature reached at least 50° centigrade was critical. On a cold day like today, reaching that magic mark took a while because the Beech carried a lot of oil. According to the manual, each engine burned a quart per hour. Cold oil meant premature wear, and premature wear meant engine failure. So it was the wise pilot who became occupied with other tasks until the oil heated.

The temps finally came up. She released the brakes and edged the throttles forward. They began to roll. They'd agreed that Beau would handle the radio. A woman's voice in the cockpit of a plane that officially was being crewed by a man might raise the tower's curiosity. She turned her face away as they passed, though she was fairly certain no one could see her.

They reached the runway, and she stood on the brakes and ran up the engines to make sure they were working as they should. The roaring power plants caused the plane to shake, which usually scared the bejesus out of nervous passengers. She hazarded a look into the mirror. The lone figure in the cabin sat still as a statue, his face emotionless as slate. A stab of doubt hit her in the stomach. What if she was wrong about Waterman? What would she do if he turned out to be as invincible in the air as he was on the ground?

The oil temps showed 75°. The other gauges were in the green. They had clearance to take off. She released the brakes and steered the plane onto the runway.

"Tail wheel locked." She returned the checklist to its holder.

"Check." Beau locked the tail wheel. Doing so kept it from castering, which would let the plane waddle all over the runway.

She shoved both throttles to their stops, and the C-45 leapt forward.

They lifted easily, and she retracted the landing gear.

She banked sharply to pick up the heading to Dallas. She'd made this flight in her head dozens of times since last night. Now that she was airborne, she could appreciate the Beech's controls. The thing was a joy to fly. An angry lump formed in her throat. Real WASP had flown this airplane plus everything that was bigger, faster, and more exciting. They'd seen America, met interesting people, and had experiences that rivaled any man's. They'd gotten to do what no other women in history had done. She hadn't, and the blame rested squarely on the arrogant son of a bitch seated mere feet behind her.

The temperature inside the cockpit was so cold that every breath made frost. Aircraft heaters generally weren't too good, even when new, and this airplane had seen a hard life, so Sally held little hope of getting any warmer before she got a lot colder. The air was smooth but she knew that would change soon enough. The B-17 had reported turbulence. The world outside was already solid white. Their plan was to break out of the clouds as quickly as possible. Two P-51's had indicated tops at six thousand.

Right on cue, the nose met brilliant sunshine at sixty-one hundred feet. She allowed the Beech to continue climbing until the altimeter read seven thousand, then she pulled the throttles back to cruise power. The sound of the Dallas radio range was locked firmly in her earphones. She snuck a look at the mirror. Waterman hadn't moved so much as a muscle. He might have been a damn drugstore Indian. She consoled herself with the possibility that he was frozen with fear. But if he wasn't . . .

She wondered what Dixie would do in her place. Would she abandon this whole crazy scheme or would she charge ahead? The answer was as clear as the dials on the instruments in front of her.

She unbuckled her seat belt. "Take over."

Beau placed his hand on the control wheel.

She took a deep breath. Then she rose and stepped from the cockpit.

Waterman came alive the instant he saw her. "What are *you* doing here?"

The passenger cabin wasn't deep. Her legs quickly collided with his knees. She'd replayed this moment a thousand times. Now that it was real, she realized the rehearsals hadn't been necessary. Her contempt flowed effortlessly. "I'm here for *my* reward, Mr. Waterman."

He knew exactly what she meant. She could tell from his eyes. "Who authorized you to board this aircraft?" His voice carried easily over the noisy engines. Ice wasn't as cold as that voice; nothing human was. But something had changed. The same terrible power that she'd seen after Emma Kelley's death and in the dark on the flight line last night was still there. Perhaps it was even stronger. But his characteristically unnatural calm had come ajar, and she was seeing something foreign. It was fear.

She had been right!

She bent forward. Her first demand would be why he was targeting her. But his hand lashed out instead and she found herself flat on her back.

"How *dare* you follow me!" he shouted. "You murdering whore!"

Her back hurt. She had bounced off a seat edge on her way to the floor. She tasted blood. Her teeth had slashed open the inside of her lower lip.

Waterman loomed over her. From where she lay, he seemed a thousand feet tall. She knew that he was going to hit her again, and that she should do something. But the fog inside her brain made coming up with a plan impossible.

Beau seemed to leap from the cockpit in one step. He came to rest beside her. His fist drew back protectively.

"Beau, stop!" The fog lifted enough for her to shriek the command.

His fist halted. Knuckles and muscles wavered. But he stood ready to drive his rage into Waterman's face.

Sally struggled to her feet, and she pushed Beau's arm down and held onto him until she felt him begin to unwind. And just to be sure, she waited until his fingers uncurled. She didn't want him hitting Waterman. She didn't want Waterman to have so much as a scuffed fingernail when he got to Dallas. That was important. That was the most important thing in the world.

She had picked up the habit of carrying a handkerchief from Dixie.

She fished it from her zoot suit and pressed it to her mouth. When she lowered her hand, she discovered a large red spot. She was going to have a badly swollen lip and probably a black eye.

"Sit, Mr. Waterman."

He nearly refused. But then he looked at Beau and he sullenly obeyed.

She leaned into Waterman's face. This time, she made sure she had a tight grip on his hands. "Why did you call me a murderer? How did you know Tex?" She managed to keep anger out of her voice, but just barely. She was more sure than ever now that he knew Tex. Tex had to be the cause of his hatred for her.

A stream of spittle rocketed from Waterman's lips. The stream hit her just above the eyes and fell onto the bridge of her nose.

Beau sprang to life.

"Don't hit him!" She snagged his fist with an instant to spare. "Don't put a mark on him. Understand?"

He nodded reluctantly.

She had already returned the handkerchief to her pocket. She retrieved it and dried her face. Then she stepped back. "Buckle up, Mr. Waterman. You, too, Beau." She added with deliberate grimness, "Mr. Waterman, I have something to show you."

He glared but followed her order. Beau buckled himself into the seat next to him.

She turned for the cockpit. She felt newly inspired.

She settled into the left-hand seat and snugged the belt as tight as it would go. The Beech wasn't equipped with an autopilot, and their moving about had knocked it out of trim. She restored their course and moved the trim tabs until the plane once again was flying hands-free. The layer of white that had been far below when she entered the cabin to speak to Waterman was much closer now, and she could see towers of white directly ahead. The outside temperature was dropping, too. The weather was worsening much faster than forecast. She would have to act quickly. If things got really bad, she and Beau might be too busy saving the airplane to bother with anything else.

She grabbed the control wheel with both hands. And taking a deep breath, she jerked the plane upside down. The maneuver was far more violent than anything she'd ever done. Her head banged the partition behind her seat, and the belt cut into her lap. Dirt and lost pencils and forgotten debris from a hundred hidden corners showered down onto the ceiling. She glanced into the mirror. Waterman's face was blanched white. He had a death grip on his armrests.

She stomped the rudder pedals. The Beech obediently wagged its tail like a giant whale. Inside the cabin, the motion translated into a gut-wrenching dance that was guaranteed to nauseate all but the toughest. Beau's face was also a picture of unhappiness and he, too, was holding on for dear life. He looked only slightly less miserable than Waterman. Suddenly she wondered if there were airsickness bags aboard, or if some poor soul in Dallas was going to have a hell of a mess to clean up.

She slung the control wheel over, sending the Beech into a continuous roll. Moments later, she jerked the wheel into her lap and slung the controls hard over in the opposite direction. The C-45 threw itself into a climbing roll. The wild maneuver put a terrible strain on the wings and tail, but she ignored the danger. The plane would hold together. And one way or the other, Waterman would spill his guts!

Aeronautical drag finally slashed their speed, and she pulled out of the roll an instant before the wings stalled. Then she let the nose snap down and someone in the cabin yelled something unintelligible, and the plane entered a spin. Her stomach was trying to push through her mouth, but she knew Waterman must be suffering even more. She checked the mirror. He looked terrified.

Finally she decided that she had had enough. Her head was throbbing, and her mouth and eyes were full of the junk from the floor. She leveled the Beech and let the landfill on the ceiling rush back to the nooks and the crannies on the floor. Then she carefully trimmed the controls and unbuckled her belt and once again entered the cabin.

"Are you crazy?" Beau was trying to unbuckle himself. But he was having a hard time making his fingers work.

"Are you OK?" she asked, feeling a new guilt.

"No." The belt finally sprang open, and he stumbled past her. He had found an airsickness bag somewhere, and he was holding it to his mouth.

"Are you OK to fly?"

"I doubt it." He disappeared into the cockpit.

She turned to Waterman. His eyes had rolled back into his head, and he was sweating. He still had a claw-like grip on the seat. She wouldn't have to worry about him hitting her again.

Suddenly a volley like gunfire rang out, and the plane began to shake. Another round quickly followed, this time even louder. The plane shuddered as if struck by a giant fist.

She understood immediately. They had flown into ice. The Beech was slinging the accumulation off its propellers into the side of the cabin. That meant the wings and tail were icing up, too. Ice would add weight, and change the shape of the wings until they became no more aerodynamic than a two-by-four.

"Sally!"

She ran to the cockpit. Through the windows, she could see the outside world was solid white.

She'd barely strapped herself in when the left engine coughed. The right quickly followed. The engines were losing power. Ice was choking the carburetors. Without fuel and air, the engines would quit. Without the engines, they hadn't a chance.

She reached for the levers that controlled the engines' carburetor heat, but they were already in the full-heat position.

"Come on!" Beau demanded. "Gimme carb heat!"

"They're already on FULL!"

"That's impossible!" He knocked her hand aside and grabbed the levers himself, but met the same result. He turned to her, his face tight. "I'm taking her down. Maybe we can find warm air there. It's our only chance."

Maybe, Sally thought. But how much altitude would they have to lose? And what about visibility? The terrain was mostly flat. But before they broke out of this soup, there was always the chance of smacking head-first into wherever the one high spot was between Sweetwater and Dallas. They needed a solution now—before squandering their altitude—before the engines quit. They needed something she knew would work.

"No!" she ordered. There was no time to explain. "Pumps on! Full rich!"

He obeyed instinctively. His hand flew to the levers that controlled the fuel pumps and the carburetor fuel mixtures.

"Mags off!" She ignored the shock on his face as she reached across him and her fingers flipped the toggle switches to the magnetos. The engines, starved of electricity for their spark plugs, died instantly.

But as quickly, she reversed the switches and two violent backfires shook the engines, followed by the eruption of a sheet of flame from the carburetor intakes. The engines sputtered with new life.

Beau held the wings level, freeing her to deal with the engines.

Sally repeated the action. Again and again, she toggled the magnetos off and on; and again and again, the Beech shook from the violence on its wings. At some point, she knew the backfires would either clear away the ice—or the engines would blow themselves apart.

Suddenly the right engine regained its familiar howl. Moments later the left one followed.

She scanned the instruments. Oil pressure. Fuel pressure. Oil temperature. Cylinder head temperature. Tachometer. She fixed on each for an instant before moving on to the next. She was searching for the warning that would signal a catastrophic engine failure. But the Pratts continued to purr, and she began to have hope that the Beech and its passengers might yet survive.

To her horror, she could see the wings were covered with ice. She grabbed for the switch to the deicing boots and her hand collided with Beau's. Someone's—she wasn't sure whose—fingers finally completed the task, and a sheaf of white cracked and flew free of the leading edge of the wing. Back in the rear of the airplane, she knew other boots on the horizontal and vertical stabilizers were working identically. The boots were made of rubber and constantly expanded and contracted under the force of compressed air, which was driven by the engines. The boots shattered the ice, and the slipstream whipped it safely away. They were lucky to be flying this C-45. Most weren't so well equipped.

She returned her attention to the windshield. The boots were the

Beech's sole defense against ice. Unless they could get out of this weather, she would have no choice but to find a hatchet or a knife and reach outside and around the edge of the windshield in an attempt to scrape a hole to see through.

"We'll never make Dallas," she said to Beau. "We're going back to Avenger!"

He nodded. He knew as well as she did the danger they were in.

"I don't think we're going to be able to climb out of this stuff," she said. "Let's try your plan, before these engines ice up again. Maybe it'll be warmer on the deck."

He didn't waste time acknowledging, but set the plane into a gentle turn toward Avenger, keeping his eyes on the instruments to avoid stalling and spinning.

"I'll take the controls," she said after they again were flying straight. "See if you can raise Love." The side of her face where Waterman hit her was beginning to hurt like the blazes. The last thing she wanted to do was talk on the radio. "Let 'em know our intentions." She pulled the throttles toward her and began the descent in search of warmer air.

He lifted the microphone. "Love Field, this is Army C-45, flight 25. We're encountering heavy icing and returning to Avenger Field. Repeat, we're returning to Avenger Field. Do you read, over?" He released the transmit button but static was the only reply.

"Keep trying," she said. "This weather is lousy for radios."

His voice remained steady as he pushed the button again. This wasn't the same Beau Bayard whose fear and incompetence nearly killed her on her first day at Avenger, Sally thought. He had learned well from Skinner.

She reached for the switch to the deicing boots. The boots were meant to be worked in short bursts. More than one pilot had met his end after leaving the boots on, only to discover ice had formed a dome above them. She moved it to ON and squinted into the white outside and watched a thin blister break from the wing and disappear.

She concentrated on the unwinding altimeter. They had been in overcast for a long time and now were nearing one thousand feet. Luckily the chances of hitting the ground were slim. But that didn't change the rule about all air and ground meeting somewhere eventually.

Suddenly the whiteness outside changed to wisps. She looked past her shoulder. The boots were flailing against pure, ice-free air.

"Whooh!" Beau murmured softly. He looked at her. "That's about as close to dying as I wanna get for a *long* time!"

She'd been too busy to be afraid until now. She gripped the control wheel.

He reached for her hand, and she quickly squeezed his fingers in return. They remained locked for several moments, until the task of flying demanded their separation.

"Can you take over while I take care of our other problem?" she asked. "Keep pouring on the coal. Maybe we can beat this ice to Avenger." She took a deep breath and stood up.

Sally reminded herself to keep her distance from Waterman this time. If he was still belligerent, she would have to handle him herself. At the altitude they were flying, Beau couldn't be spared from the cockpit.

Waterman had gotten some of his strength back. He proved that the instant she stepped into the cabin. "Attempted murder! Kidnapping! Assault! I can go on and on! You'll never see the light of day after I'm through with you . . . either of you!"

She was prepared for threats. She forced her voice to rise above his. "I can spin this airplane until your insides corkscrew out of every hole in your body, Mr. Waterman. Do you want me to do that?"

His eyes were an angry red. They glared at her with awful hatred.

She continued, "How did you know Tex? Why did you call me a murderer?"

He didn't hold back this time. Words spit from him like bullets. "I was his uncle. His mother was my sister. When his father died in a car crash, my sister committed suicide. I adopted him when he was four. His name was Charles Asbury. I gave him the best schools, the best contacts, breeding. You gave him death!"

To hear that Tex had a different name, an entirely different identity, was almost too much to bear. She desperately wanted Waterman to shut up. Even more desperately, she wanted to hear more. "Go on!" she demanded.

"Charles went on holiday. He intended to see the country . . . to find himself. But he found you! And you learned somehow that he had money and you attached yourself to him!" His voice rose above even the scream of the engines. "You lied to him! You tricked him! And he died because of your filthy barnyard ignorance and incompetence, just as surely as if you'd stuck a gun into his mouth!"

She so badly wanted justice to take this man whose every word was a lie, whose mere presence spoiled the air she breathed. The words leapt from her mouth: "He left you at six o'clock in the evening, didn't he?" His face revealed his surprise. "Do you know how I knew that? Because that's when Tex wound his watch every day. At six o'clock. And do you know why? Because that's when his life began. That's when he escaped from *you!* He celebrated his freedom from *you* at six o'clock every day!"

A look of terrible pain overcame Waterman. "You're lying! He'd still be alive if it weren't for you!"

She grabbed his collar. He fought back, but she was stronger. Suddenly she felt stronger than anyone in the whole world. "I didn't kill anybody. Do you hear me? I want you to hear me. Do you hear me?" She was choking him, and it felt good. "If anybody's a murderer, it's you. You're your own victim. You've been killing yourself for years. You're dying right now. You're drowning in your own hate and poison. You're not even a person. You're cold and pitiful, Mr. Waterman. You drove him away. You made him hate you. You tried to make him think like you and be like you, and to save himself he ran away and had to pretend you didn't even exist. He had to deny his own life to have a real life. You've made yourself into something so rotten and no-good that no decent person will have anything to do with you, and the only ones who can stand you are just like you. How does it feel, Mr. Waterman, to love power so much that you end up alone?" She turned him loose.

Waterman made a noise. It was dry and hard and unnatural sounding, and at first she didn't recognize it. Then she realized he was crying. He had slumped forward in the chair. He was trembling. She wondered how long it had been since he'd cried—or if he ever had.

"You killed Charlie!" he said. His voice choked.

She grabbed him, and this time she used such force that she jerked him hard against the seatbelt. But he no longer resisted. His strength was draining away, right before her eyes. "You say that again and you're gonna go flying without an airplane, Mr. Waterman. Do you hear me? Do you?" She yanked his face close to hers. "Now you stop blaming me. And you stop sicking the law on me. I loved Tex as much as life itself, and he felt the same way about me. I saved him from his hell—the one you created for him—and he saved me from mine. You had your chance to love him, and you ruined it. That's purely your fault. Live with it. Or die with it. I don't care. But you get out of my life, and you stay out!" She pushed him hard.

"Charlie!" he murmured. "Charlie . . . Charlie." He was drifting into his own broken world.

She snarled, "His name was Tex Jones! His own blood hurt him so much that he couldn't even stand his own name. You did that, Mr. Waterman. You did that to your only living relative! And now you're gonna live with it!"

"Sally!"

The sound of her name pulled her to the cockpit.

She'd barely entered when Beau announced, "I never got through to Love, but I reached Avenger. Their ceiling has dropped to five hundred, with the probability of heavy icing."

She groaned. Was there to be no good news today? "How about alternates?"

He shook his head. "This stuff is closing in on every field we can reach. Going somewhere else doesn't make any more sense than just going back to Avenger."

Things weren't desperate yet, Sally told herself. They'd picked up a strong tailwind after they turned around and they had enough fuel, though they were burning it at a ferocious rate. They'd make Avenger soon; probably before the weather completely closed in.

She checked the mirror. Waterman hadn't moved. That was one positive, at least. She wondered if he would make good on his threat to have her arrested. If so, it would be his word against theirs. It must be common knowledge among those who knew him that he was afraid of flying.

She and Beau could claim they'd hit unusually rough air, and Waterman had panicked and started imagining things. There were no marks on him, other than maybe redness where she'd grabbed his collar. What's more, practically everyone at Avenger knew that Waterman was out to get her. There probably would be an investigation, but with no physical evidence, and with the army's desire to avoid bad publicity and to put the whole WASP experiment behind it, she felt pretty confident an investigation would quickly stall.

"Roger, Avenger. Thanks for the advisory."

Beau's radio chatter drew her back to the task at hand. She looked at him questioningly.

"They're starting to get sleet," he said. "The tower says it's gonna be slicker'n a skating rink. They think by the time we get there, they could have ice up to their armpits. What do you want to do?"

"Sit by a fire with a good book and a cup of hot chocolate!"

He pressed grimly, "Yeah. But before that?"

"Exactly what we are doing. And anything more that we can think of to keep us out of an early grave."

"Roger."

She pulled her seat belt tight.

"I'll take the airplane," she said.

His hand lifted from the control wheel.

"How far out are we?" she asked.

"About twenty minutes, I think," he said. "That tailwind's really kicking us along."

"OK," she said. "I'll keep an eye on Waterman. You stay on the radio."

He nodded his agreement, and they settled down to the job of flying.

The minutes crawled. Sally checked the mirror frequently. But Waterman remained motionless. She almost wished he would do something. Wondering when—or if—he was going to strike was nerve-racking.

"Avenger's getting really heavy icing right now!" Beau announced, turning to her. He pulled his right earphone askew so they could talk. Up until now, they'd been flying in silence.

"OK," Sally said. She began the process of wiggling her way out of the copilot's seat. "Nothing we can do about it until we get there. I'm gonna check our friend."

Waterman ignored her as she entered the cabin. He had regained some of his color, she thought.

"We'll be on the ground in a few minutes, Mr. Waterman," she said. "Is your seat belt tight?"

His answer was a hate-filled stare. She gave the belt a healthy tug.

It was fine with her, if he didn't want to talk. She'd gotten what she wanted from him. Now if she never saw him again, or heard from him again, or had to think about him again, it couldn't come too soon. The only reason she'd even bothered to check on him was because she didn't want him claiming she'd not done her job.

She returned to the cockpit. Avenger's runways were still several miles away, but everything for as far as the eye could see was buried under a sheet of white—the runways included.

"Do you want to take it?" Beau asked.

Her hands moved to the controls. From now on, she would fly the airplane and he would continue to handle the radio and checklist.

"It's gonna be slick," he said.

"Roger," she said, and double-checked that the boots were working.

They started running through the checklist.

"Gear down," he finally called. The landing gear was almost the last item on the list.

"Gear down," she echoed, moving the lever.

"Two lights," he said. The lights confirmed the landing gear was down and locked.

"Tail wheel locked," he said.

Sally reached for the control. "Locked."

The runway waited ahead, a ribbon of white.

She reduced power.

Suddenly the outer airport boundary flashed beneath their belly. Sally pulled the throttles all the way back. Out of the corner of her eye, she saw Beau tense.

The air was cold and still. She worked the control wheel, at the same time feeling for sensations through the rudder pedals. The Beech was talking to her. It was whispering secrets about angle of attack and lift and drag and yaw and stall that only real pilots heard. It was a lovely airplane. And in these final moments, the two of them were making love.

The Beech settled with a sigh and the wheels touched the ice and her feet touched the rudders and the brakes ever so gently, and the artwork that had come from the Wizards of Wichita rolled to a stop.

"God, you're good!" He shook his head in wonder.

"At least at one thing," Sally said softly. The truth was sinking in. This was the last time she would ever fly an airplane.

A staff car was edging its way toward their parking spot on the flight line. Apparently that was Waterman's ride. She advanced the throttles carefully. She had quickly learned that the slightest miscue would send the tires sliding in the wrong direction.

She looked in the mirror. Waterman was busy tidying himself up. His sickly pallor was gone. He had transformed, now that he was back on the ground.

"Oh, Christ." Beau was watching, too.

He shut down the engines while she unhooked her belt and stepped quickly into the cabin. Her hand intercepted Waterman's on the handle to the door.

He snarled, "You'll be in jail this time tomorrow. You have my word."

"No, I won't." She felt a presence behind her. It was Beau.

"See this?" She pulled on her lip. The pain nearly made her cry but it was for a worthy cause. "I'm the one who's beaten up! I'll have a shiner the size of a basketball come tomorrow. And I've got a witness. All you've got are enemies. There's not a person on this base who wouldn't love to see you behind bars. Do we understand each other?"

They glared at each other. But suddenly he broke eye contact, and she instinctively looked to see why. She nearly screamed. There on the floor was Tex's watch. It must have fallen from her pocket and rolled into the cabin while the Beech was on its back. They both dived for the piece, but he got there a split second sooner and clamped the prize in his fist. Then he opened the door, and she and Beau somehow became tangled in a pile of arms and legs and before she could do anything about it, Waterman was gone!

She catapulted through the door. She could see Tex's watch . . . a dot of gold glistening from Waterman's fist. But he had already reached the staff car. The most precious thing she had ever owned was disappearing!

Her foot hit ice. She tried for one desperate moment to find something to hold onto. But her slide across the tarmac continued, and she landed hard, breaking her leg.

# TWENTY-TWO

Tex had liked to say that the one consistent thing about Texas weather was its inconsistency. That certainly had proved true since their return to Avenger. The temperature had risen to an almost balmy sixty degrees, changing the ice to rain. Rain had come down in buckets and wheelbarrows and finally in whole dump trucks. So much rain had come down that no airplane dared risk the West Texas sky. Traffic on the ground had stayed put whenever possible, too, and even the trains had crawled. In the days since the ice storm, West Texas had been gripped by the jaws of a monsoon the likes of which only the oldest of old-timers had seen before. Then the sun had finally tried to come out, changing the hard rain to a drizzle, and West Texas once again had started to move.

Sally turned away from the ticket agent. She hadn't completely mastered the art of walking with crutches yet, so she was careful about negotiating the train station's slippery floor. She hobbled away from the long line of other travelers desperate for a ticket out of Sweetwater. The tiny station was a madhouse. Soldiers, girls from her class, and civilians milled about like cattle in a pen, but because of the backlog of travelers caused by the bad weather, she had learned, anyone not already holding a ticket was out of luck. Dixie, anticipating this problem, had finagled her ticket early. Now she and Geri and Twila and so many of the others were gone, and Avenger was as good as closed. The army was through with its experiment with women and aviation. There had been a ceremony, with many brave words delivered by speakers, including Jackie Cochran herself. But now the army wanted nothing more to do with women in cockpits, and that included helping them board trains that already were bursting at the seams.

The spectacle of so many bodies in such a hurry to go someplace was providing fine entertainment for the locals. The geezers, cooped up by the weather for so long, were out in force and having a field day. Sally had to hobble her way through an obstacle course of canes.

The army had accepted her aborting the mission to Dallas. And Waterman apparently had decided to keep his mouth shut. She hadn't seen him or heard from him. She even was all cried out over Tex's watch. Waterman had it, and there was nothing she could do about it. She and Tex hadn't been married. Tex had been his son. The law would see things his way.

But all that was in the past. From now on, she would concentrate on the future. The future stretched ahead like an empty highway, its landscape not yet filled with experiences. She was positive of one thing: she wasn't going back to farming. New Sally was very much in control. Old Sally was buried; the moment she tried to rise again, she would be returned to her resting place.

Sally looked around in hopes of seeing a familiar face. She recognized a number of girls but none she'd been close to. She already missed Beau. He'd gotten a cozy assignment teaching navigation at a ground school in Louisiana. She'd promised to write as soon as she knew where she would be staying. But she had no idea where she wanted to go.

At first she'd considered looking up her mother's relatives, but she didn't know where they lived. All she knew was what her father had told her: he'd met her mother in Indiana. Then he'd changed the subject and refused to talk about it any more. She'd decided to put off that task until later, and so she'd told the ticket agent she'd take any train.

For the first time in her life, she was completely free and unafraid. She no longer wore a hand-me-down dress, but instead her brown slacks and white blouse and brown loafers. The rest of her things were tucked neatly inside her army-issue duffel bag. And best of all, she had three hundred dollars, two hundred of which she'd squirreled away from her pay.

Whatever life brought, she was ready for a head-on meeting.

"Miss Ketchum."

She turned and came face-to-face with Colonel Bowen. Behind him, standing tall and straight as a building, was Waterman. He looked past her as if she weren't there.

The colonel stuck out his hand. "Miss Ketchum, I want you to know how proud I am to have met you. You are an extraordinary young woman, in addition to being the finest pilot I've ever had the privilege to know. I want to say that I feel Congress and the army have made a grave error in what they have done to the WASP." He paused. "If you were anything but a woman, my counterparts in Washington would not only have made you an officer but a fighter pilot with a front-line unit. I'm certain you would have become an ace. But I'm afraid the army, and the civilian corps, is filled with many stupid people." He looked right at Waterman, but the lawyer ignored him. "I can only hope for the day when that changes." He squeezed her hand.

She mumbled, "Thank you, sir." She was so surprised by this outpouring that she was unable to think of anything else to say.

The screech of a steam whistle saved her. She turned and saw the train.

Bowen squeezed her hand a final time. "Good luck to you, my dear. May life be more generous to you than the army has been." He pushed forward, but Waterman lingered. Sally could feel his terrible power, but he had become no more frightening to her than a garden worm.

Waterman lowered his voice so no one else could hear. "All things eventually are insignificant, Miss Ketchum." He retrieved a common envelope from his pocket and tossed it onto her duffel bag. "Sometimes because they die. And sometimes because they never were of value. Charles is dead. And you are trash."

He moved into the crush of bodies, leaving her alone with the rest of her life.

She reached for the envelope. Inside was Tex's watch—she knew the instant her fingers touched the paper. She snatched it up. She held it to her heart and she cried, and she didn't care who saw her or what they thought. She hugged Tex's watch to her soul.

Then she slipped the watch into her pocket. She slipped it deep, where no one could find it, and no one could ever take it from her again. She didn't bother drying her eyes. The tears felt good on her face. Suddenly she was more alive than she'd ever been in her whole life.

One of the geezers had been watching from nearby. He shook his head. "You was one of them gals from up on the hill that was tryin' to learn to fly them aeroplanes, wasn't ya?" he asked. "There's no more trains today, honey. You'll have to wait 'til tomorrow if you're leavin' this town."

She lifted the duffel. Everything was going to be OK. Somehow she would find a job in civilian aviation. Skinner had even offered to help her. She would have a life, after all.

The geezer was still waiting for her to say something. She looked him in the eye. Her tears made doing so difficult, but they didn't stop her.

"I wouldn't bet on that, mister. I'm tired of waiting."

She hobbled outside to the street and extended her thumb to the line of passing cars.

# Epilogue

In November 1977, Congress passed legislation that authorized the Secretary of Defense to make a determination regarding military recognition of the WASP. On March 8, 1979, the Secretary of the Air Force granted that long overdue military recognition, and finally the WASP got their veteran status. On March 10, 2010, the WASP were awarded the Congressional Gold Medal, the highest award Congress can give to a civilian or group of civilians.

# Acknowledgments

Many thanks to Professor Howard Foss, to "Red" and Joanne Redmond, and to George Fischer. Also special thanks to Carys Bowen for her incredible kindness and help, to Sofia and Professor Woody Hain, to Professor John Heilman, to Judi Rollnick for her thoughtfulness and quick thinking, and to my editor, Jackie Swift, for her excellent insights into the crafting of a novel. And finally, thank you to my wife, Rhonda, for her encouragement and courage.